THE LAW

'LEGE OF EDUCATION

THE
LAW

A novel by

ROGER
VAILLAND

Translated from the French by Peter Wiles

WITH A NEW PREFACE BY
JONATHAN KEATES

ELAND BOOKS, LONDON
&
HIPPOCRENE BOOKS INC., NEW YORK

20312.

Published by
ELAND BOOKS
53 Eland Road, London SW11 5JX
&
HIPPOCRENE BOOKS, INC.,
171 Madison Avenue, New York, NY 10016

First published by Librairie Gallimard 1957
© Librairie Gallimard

First English translation © Jonathan Cape 1958

First issued in this paperback edition 1985

British Library Cataloguing in Publication Data

Vailland, Roger

   The law.
   I. Title   II. La Loi English
   843'.914[F]   PQ2682.A3/

   ISBN 0-907871-11-9

Printed and bound in Great Britain
by Redwood Burn Ltd, Trowbridge, Wiltshire

Cover Design © Patrick Frean

NEW PREFACE

A few weeks after reading Roger Vailland's *The Law*, I set off for my first visit to Italy. I was eighteen and as innocent and impressionable as it is possible for anyone of that age to be, but the shocks I encountered that year were those of recognition rather than authentic surprise, as one by one the scenes and characters of Vailland's story sprung to life around me.

Most English people encounter Italy via the great art cities of the north, Florence, Siena, Venice, Urbino, where the Italians themselves invariably take second place in the tourist's consciousness, and the visual memory preserves the bland loveliness of a postcard or a souvenir guide. I was lucky to meet the country on its own terms, without the interpolations of culture, and in a place which most of the Italian friends I have made since regard with amazed horror, as if I had spent a season in South Georgia or Queen Maud Land.

Potenza, where my brother was currently working as an English teacher, was then the regional capital of Basilicata, one of the poorer areas of the Italian south. The town stands on a windy plateau in a landscape of rocky plains and bald, brown hills. Whatever it may once have possessed of artistic merit was destroyed by an earthquake in the last century and more recent tremors, together with some well-meaning attempts at civic improvement during the Fascist era, have robbed it of any distinction. It is more or less what it claims to be, a small, unpretentious provincial city, unvisited either by tourists or, more seriously, by any of the benevolent intentions of successive Italian governments. It is the south in a nutshell.

Living there, I began to absorb, and even finally to enjoy, the forms and rhythms of southern life, that particular day-to-day existence which Italians in opulent Milan, bustling Bologna or self-consequent Florence are so embarrassed by because it constitutes such an insidious reminder of the past. Your Milanese and Florentine acquaintance, prosperous, energetic, bang-up-to-date, hasten to assure you that Calabria, Apulia and Sicily are simply a portion of the Third World, and that Italy is really two nations, with the dividing frontier somewhere on the fringes of the old Papal States. The less palatable truth seems to be that the whole region is simply an unreconstructed version of an Italy which lurks just below the surface of even the most polished sophistications of the north. No wonder, then, that Italians hate their past with such bitterness.

Potenza had it all. There was, for example, the *passeggiata*, the evening stroll along the Via Pretoria, where the unattached of either sex were carefully segregated and a watchful eye was kept from the balconies on who walked with whom. There were the enormous meals, like tribal feasts, designed to show off the wealth and abundance of the household. There was the feast day of the local saint, San Gerardo, who had miraculously arrived in a ship (Potenza is miles from the sea and the rocky river Basento is a trickle for most of the year) to drive off the marauding Saracens, with fire-crackers, penitents and holy water sprinklings.

There were the inevitable dramatis personae: the doctors desperate to persuade their peasant patients that a prayer to the Madonna and a dish of maccheroni were not the only sovran remedies for illness; the *avvocati*, foxy-faced, all-powerful orchestrators of interminable lawsuits; the young men of the town's 'good families', whose hands sported at least one extra long fingernail as a sign of proven idleness; the sad agronomist who had come down from Lombardy on a mission to solve the problems of rural poverty and now sat contemplating them in near-suicidal despair; or the surveyor's blonde wife from Trieste who still thought it rather a jape to have settled à la Lady Hester Stanhope among these swarthy savages.

Much, it was reasoned, might be forgiven her because she came up from 'up there' and knew no better. Nothing was otherwise pardoned a true woman of the south. The unmarried girls went demurely in pairs and lived at home under the grim surveillance of mothers and black-shawled harridan grandmammas. In time would come marriage and childbirth, its rigours offset by a complete Clytemnestra-like domination of the household. Now and then the bolder ones slipped through the net: when, for instance, my landlady went off to spend the afternoon with her sister on the other side of town, her buxom niece used to go upstairs with a boy who came in through the garden, and the chandelier quivered in the dining room below. But the girl who actually went off to America to study was mentioned invariably in a scandalized whisper. Only bad girls did that.

Even if an ignorant contempt and impatience made me despise much of all this, I felt I knew some of it already from the pages of *The Law*. The essential mood of the south, its ruthless lack of sentimentality, its resigned, shrugging acceptance of the sheer vanity of historical experience, its exaggerated sense of hierarchy, all this, I realized, coloured the novel's characters and episodes; but only now, having grown to love Italy, can I begin to appreciate the deftness and lack of condescension with which Vailland evokes the hard, unyielding quality of that world.

The Law (*La Loi*) was born directly from a crisis point in its author's life, and in its very nature marked a significant renunciation of practically everything with which French literary consciousness had hitherto linked him. The reading public knew Vailland as a staunch Communist, wedded to an image of the Bolshevik hero whom nothing could intimidate and, as it then seemed, eternally preoccupied with notions of struggle and triumph centred on the looming figure of Stalin himself. Life was the drama it had been since the days when, a precocious schoolboy in Reims, he thrilled to the tragic sublimities of Corneille as an antidote to the humdrum temper of his bourgeois homelife, and the raw metaphors of protest and revolt made perfect materialfor such early novels as *Drôle de Jeu* and *Les Mauvais Coups*. No wonder he was delighted when *L'Humanité*, serializing *325,000 francs* in 1955, hailed him as 'Roger

Vailland, a writer in the service of the people'.

The volte-face which occurred a year later must therefore have shaken French Communist orthodoxy to its roots, yet in reality it was no worse than the customary process of disillusion which has overtaken so many artists in mid-career. In Moscow for the 20th Communist Congress, Vailland was a horrified witness of the removal of Stalin's statue from the air terminal, a symbol for him, like so much else on that occasion, of the last act of a tragedy. Bolshevism had become the business of bureaucrats and state technicians. When, some months later, he signed a protest against the use of armed force by the Russians in Hungary, the gesture sealed the close of his political career.

It is scarcely accidental that *The Law* should have proved Vailland's finest achievement. Had his disenchantment not come upon him, with its resultant wave of self-analysis, had he remained yet another hero-bedazzled French writer, he might not have uncovered those more enduring, less localized sensibilities which the years of ferocious activism had effectively suppressed. He had gained an acute awareness of things Italian during his visits as a journalist in the early 1950s, and now he was writing in his journal 'I was so battered and broken with fatigue that for some time I thought only of sleeping, covered in oil, naked in the sun, on an Italian beach beside the Adriatic.'

His refuge was in Apulia, that wild, remote heel of the Italian peninsula, with its enduring memories of the mediaeval emperor Frederick II, whose own potency as an image of lost heroic grandeur overshadows the novel. In choosing as his central figure a liberal monarchist, Don Cesare, who has lost faith not only in the victory of his cause but even in the worth of such a victory, Vailland symbolically proclaimed the death of his own Communist hopes and aspirations. 'He gave himself up to what he had been and what he remained at the hour of his death. This acquiescence was of value only for himself, in relation to himself, but in the hour of his death, of his lucid death of an atheist accepting death, this acquiescence acquired an absolute value.' Don Cesare's final act of touching the breast of the young girl who nurses him in his last hours can inevitably be seen as an affirmation of the triumph of humane values over emptier ambitions and expectations.

Don Cesare, however, is even more profoundly representative of the south itself. His creator well understood how southerners, unlike their northern counterparts who sweep it under the carpet, continue to confront their past and try to comprehend it. The waves of successive invasion by Greeks, Saracens, Germans and French, the figures of charismatic impact such as the Napoleonic Joachim Murat or the Emperor Frederick himself, and the occupational layers left by antique civilizations are all used in the region as proofs or pretexts, justifying what the place is or what it might have been.

Out of this intense historical awareness springs that preoccupation with ranks, degrees, titles and hierarchies which marks southern life from Naples to Syracuse. In every tiniest village there is somebody to be deferred to, someone to be addressed as 'Don', and it often seems as if the entire Bourbon aristocracy might overflow a fair-sized telephone directory. The grotesque game of the Law, to whose popularity other writers than Vailland bear witness, is a potent example of this vigorously hierarchical view of existence. He claimed to have played it himself, but its popularity is vouched for elsewhere by writers such as Carlo Levi in his *Christ Stopped At Eboli*, and though currently outlawed, it is surely too vital a reflection of the southern outlook to be suppressed altogether.

As Vailland explains, the object of the game is to produce a 'chief' and a 'deputy' among the players, who then earn the right to humiliate the losers. To anyone with the least notion of primitive societies, the purpose of this is neither more nor less than what was aimed at in the Roman feast of Saturnalia, the antics of the Christmas Lord of Misrule or the creation of a Boy Bishop among mediaeval choirboys. Order and degree will for a moment be up-ended, and a new, topsy-turvy world be set in their place, designed not merely to parody its original but actually to probe its weaknesses.

In the novel itself, the game of the Law is only part of a broader analysis of the way hierarchies are both respected and challenged in Manacore. While the men, for example, play out their rituals of insult and derision, the women of Don Cesare's harem follow similar patterns in their chastisement of Marietta and their dire threats of a Carrara onion, whose juice inflames and swells the mucous membranes, sets the body on fire and leads even to death – '*I'll mate you with a Carrara onion* … it was the punishment inflicted on girls who upset happy homes.'

Yet Marietta, already so far from innocence, emerges ultimately as the winner. Experience has toughened her, substituting for her sentimental outlook on the world a calculating materialism entirely typical both of her background and of her time. This, after all, is the booming Americanophile Italy of the '50s, where Vailland himself had cynically observed the Hollywood razzmatazz of the Via Veneto and Cinecitta, and we need hardly raise an eyebrow when Don Cesare's lordly impedimenta are peddled to a Naples antique dealer for the sake of modern varnished plywood, a Fiat 400 and a television set.

The Law, however, is neither Don Cesare's story, nor Marietta's. Vailland's method is in fact not so very distant from those of Mrs Gaskell in *Cranford* or Miss Mitford in *Our Village*, weird as such parallels may at first seem. He was still sufficiently imbued with Marxist theory as to view his protagonists in terms of the world which produced them. Figures such as the hopelessly amorous Donna Lucrezia or the universal 'controller' Matteo Brigante behave as they do because of Manacore itself, because of the very layers and subtleties of the town's experience as a southern community. We are not asked to pardon or to condemn, merely to observe, and it is in this sense that the book seems more a series of colourfully drawn, shrewdly noted travel sketches than an essay in pure fictional narrative.

When, three years after publishing *The Law*, Vailland noted that 'disgust is as respectable a sentiment as enthusiasm … humankind in general makes my stomach turn over' he was exaggerating, with cynical amusement, that detached quality, neither indulgent nor censorious, which makes him so reliable a witness. Few writers have approached the Italian south without awe, ῾ιorror, maudlin compassion or benign pomposity: Vailland magnificently avoids them all.

On the corner of the main square and the via Garibaldi, the court house of Porto Manacore stood facing the palace of Frederick II of Swabia. It was a bleak, four-storeyed building: on the ground floor the prison, on the first the police station, on the second the court room, on the third the flat of the Chief of Police, on the fourth that of the judge.

At siesta time in the month of August the little town was deserted. Only the idle, the *disoccupati*, the unemployed, were at their posts, all around the square, standing against the walls, arms at their sides, silent and motionless.

Behind the Venetian blinds of the prison, their slats tilted towards the sky, the prisoners sang:

Tourne, ma beauté, tourne ...

The unemployed stood listening to the prisoners, but did not sing themselves.

In her room on the fourth floor of the court house, donna Lucrezia had been awakened by the prisoners' singing.

Donna Lucrezia was superb, lying half-stretched on the bed, propped up on one elbow, her breasts showing in the opening of her wrap, her black unruly mane falling to below the waist. In France she might have been judged too tall and too plump. In this province of southern Italy, where women were never so much in demand as when they were conspicuously pregnant, she was proclaimed the most beautiful of them all. Her eyes were not large; but they were always expressing something, expressing it intensely; at this period of her life it was most often anger, hate or a hostile indifference.

From the moment she had arrived in Porto Manacore ten years ago, the day after her wedding, everyone had called her *donna*, though she was the wife of a magistrate of the lowest rank and nothing was known of her early years, all of which had been spent in the city of Foggia; she was one of the numerous daughters of a chief clerk at the prefecture. In Porto Manacore you are not *donna* unless you are the wife or daughter of a landowner of the old stock. But nobody had ever called her *signora*, madam, or — as people called foreigners they wished to honour — *Signoria*, Your Ladyship. She was quite clearly donna, *domina* like the Empress of the Romans, the mistress, the head.

Her husband, Judge Alessandro, entered the room and approached her. She pushed him away.

'You don't love me any more,' said the judge.

She made no reply, but rose, went to the window and half-opened the shutters. A blast of hot air enveloped her face. The prisoners were now singing a Neapolitan *canzonetta* featured in the last radio concert. Donna Lucrezia leaned forward and saw a pair of hands gripping one of the prison blinds; then, in the darkness beyond the slats, she distinguished two big eyes watching her. The man spoke to his companions, other eyes flashed into life, the song was discontinued, and donna Lucrezia threw back her head.

Now she looked straight ahead, without leaning forward.

On the terrace of the post office the postmen lay sleeping in deck-chairs, in the shadow of the tower of Frederick II of Swabia. Convolvuluses, with giant turquoise blue flowers, climbed from the terrace to the top of the tower. Their petals opened at dawn and would close again at five o'clock, when the sun reached them. The scene had been the same every summer since her husband had brought her from Foggia to Porto Manacore as a young bride.

All around the square, against every wall, the unemployed waited for some tenant farmer or overseer to appear who might need someone for a casual job; but the tenant farmers and overseers rarely had need of the unemployed, their families sufficing for the upkeep of the orange and lemon orchards and the tending of the meagre crops in the dried-up soil of the olive plantations.

To the right of the main square, workmen were hanging electric-light globes from the branches of the giant pine (said to have been planted by Murat, Field-Marshal of France and King of Naples). That evening the town corporation were putting on a ball for the summer visitors.

The square ended in a terrace, overlooking the harbour and the sea. Donna Lucrezia looked at the sea. It had been the same blue since the end of spring. It was as it always was. It had not changed for months.

Judge Alessandro approached from the rear and placed his hand on his wife's hip.

'What are you thinking about?' he asked.

She turned round. He was smaller than she was. He had lost weight in the last few months and his belt was too big for him. She saw that he was trembling and that there were large beads of sweat on his temples.

'You forgot to take your quinine,' she said.

He went to the dressing-table, poured some water out of the jug into the tooth glass and swallowed two pink pills. He suffered from malaria, like most of the inhabitants of the region.

'I never think,' she said.

Judge Alessandro went through to his study and opened a volume which had just been obtained for him and sent to him by his bookseller in Foggia: *Del Vecchio Alberto, La Legislazione di Federico II Imperatore*, Torino, 1874. Its hero was Frederick Hohenstauffen, Emperor of the Romans and King of Naples, Sicily and Apulia in the thirteenth century. But the fever rose and he could not follow the text. He stretched himself out on the narrow divan on which he had spent his nights since donna Lucrezia had insisted on sleeping alone.

In the next room the children were quarrelling. The woman-servant must have been sleeping in the shade somewhere, in the well of the stairs or the outer office of the prison; on summer afternoons she could not breathe in her room under the roof. Donna Lucrezia went through to the children's room and did what had to be done, in silence.

The prisoners were now singing a Charles Trenet song, the words of which they did not understand and which acquired in

7

their mouths the tone of a lament. On summer evenings a loud speaker filled the main square with the entire programme of the Italian Radio's *Secondo* network, and the prisoners' repertoire was endless.

'Let me touch,' begged Tonio.

He stretched his hand towards the breast which swelled the linen frock.

Marietta slapped his hand hard.

'*Please*,' said Tonio.

'I don't want to,' she said.

He had cornered her beneath the steps of the house with the colonnades, in a patch of shade. All around them the August sun, the *solleone*, the sun-lion, scorched the marshland. Inside the house everyone was still sleeping the heavy sleep of the siesta hour.

Tonio grabbed the girl's wrist, pushed her against the wall and pressed himself against her.

'Let me be or I'll call the others ...'

She struggled and succeeded in shaking him off. But he was still very close to her.

'Marietta,' he whispered, 'Marietta, *ti voglio tanto bene*, I love you so much ... let me touch you at least ...'

'Go and play your dirty games with my sister!'

'If you liked ... I'd leave everything ... the kids, the wife, don Cesare ... I'll take you North ...'

Maria, Tonio's wife and Marietta's eldest sister, appeared at the top of the steps. In six years Tonio had given her five children; her stomach sagged on to her thighs and her breasts on to her stomach.

'You're after her again!' she shouted.

'Don't wake don Cesare,' Tonio said.

'And you,' she shouted at Marietta, 'why do you keep leading him on?'

8

'I don't lead him on,' said Marietta. 'He hangs around me all the time.'

'You'll wake don Cesare,' protested Tonio.

Julia, Maria's and Marietta's mother, now made her appearance on the stairs. She was not yet fifty, but she was as deformed, as shapeless, as the roots of prickly pear which the sea washed up on the beach, thin and withered, her skin yellowed and her eyes bloodshot from malaria.

'I don't want your husband,' Marietta shouted to her sister. 'It's him who hangs around me all the time.'

Julia, in her turn, attacked Marietta.

'If you don't like it here,' she shouted at her, 'why don't you get out?'

Marietta lifted her head to face her mother and sister.

'You can shout as much as you like,' she said. 'You won't get me to go and live with the Lombard.'

'You prefer to steal other people's men,' roared old Julia.

A shutter opened among the colonnades on the first floor. Don Cesare came forward on to the balcony. There was immediate silence.

Don Cesare was seventy-two; apart from a little added stoutness he had not changed since the time when he was a captain in the Royal Cavalry, at the end of the First World War; he stood just as erect and he remained the best huntsman in the region.

Behind don Cesare, Elvira stood outlined in the shadow of the room.

Elvira was another of old Julia's daughters. Maria was twenty-eight, Elvira twenty-four, Marietta seventeen. Julia and Maria had in their time been don Cesare's mistresses. Now Elvira shared his bed. Marietta was still a virgin.

'Tonio,' said don Cesare, 'listen.'

'I'm listening, don Cesare,' replied Tonio.

He went and stood directly under the balcony. He walked barefooted, his trousers were patched and he was not wearing a shirt, but his white jacket was freshly starched. Don Cesare had always insisted that his confidential men should wear

9

white and impeccable jackets. From the time that he had married Maria, Tonio had been don Cesare's confidential man.

From his balcony don Cesare could see the whole of the marsh and, beyond, the lake whose outlet ran down to the sea among the reeds and the bamboos and watered the terrace in front of the steps of the house with the colonnades; and farther off he could see the sandbanks of the isthmus and, farther still, the whole bay of Porto Manacore. Don Cesare stared at the sea which had not changed for months.

'I'm listening, don Cesare,' repeated Tonio.

Julia and Maria went back into the house. Marietta disappeared among the bamboos with light, quick steps, heading for one of the reed huts which housed the families of don Cesare's fishermen.

'Well then,' don Cesare said to Tonio, 'you are going in to Porto Manacore.'

'I'm going in to Porto Manacore,' replied Tonio.

'You will call at the post office ... at don Ottavio's ... and at the tobacconist's ...'

Tonio repeated each in turn to show that he understood.

'You won't forget anything?' asked don Cesare.

Tonio again ran through the list of what he had to do.

'How shall I go in to Manacore?' asked Tonio.

'How did you think of going?' asked don Cesare.

'I could perhaps take the Lambretta,' said Tonio.

'If it gives you so much pleasure, then take the Lambretta.'

'Thank you, don Cesare.'

'And now,' said don Cesare, 'I am going to work. Warn them not to make a noise.'

'They'll be quiet,' said Tonio. 'I promise you.'

The siesta was over. Don Cesare watched his fishermen coming out of the reed huts scattered here and there over the marsh and making for the terrace where the nets hung drying. He returned to his bedroom, then went through to the larger room which housed his collection of antiques.

Tonio joined the women in the big ground-floor room.

'Maria,' he said, 'fetch me my shoes.'

'Your shoes?' asked Maria. 'What do you want your shoes for?'

'Don Cesare has given me permission to take the Lambretta!'

'And why has don Cesare given you permission to take the Lambretta?'

'He's sending me in to Manacore.'

'I suppose you couldn't walk to Manacore?'

'He told me to take the Lambretta.'

'The engine disturbs him in his work,' said Maria.

'He never has liked engines,' said old Julia. 'If the government hadn't made such a fuss, don Cesare would never have allowed them to build the road this far.'

'He's in a good mood today,' explained Elvira. 'This morning one of the fishermen brought him an antique.'

Marietta came back into the house, carrying the fish for the evening meal. She placed them in the fireplace in one corner of the big room. Then she stood with her elbows propped on the window sill, turning her back on the others. She was naked beneath the white linen frock, which reached to her knees.

Maria went to fetch Tonio's shoes, which hung from a beam beside her own shoes and those of Elvira and Marietta; the women wore them only on high holidays and when they went to Mass in Porto Manacore.

Tonio looked at Marietta, who kept her back to him, still standing with her elbows propped on the window sill.

Maria returned with his shoes.

'What are you looking at?' she asked.

'Put my shoes on,' said Tonio.

He sat down on the bench facing the seignorial table with the top carved from one single piece of olive wood. Nobody but don Cesare ever sat in the big eighteenth-century Neapolitan armchair with the grotesquely carved gilt elbow-rests.

'Don Cesare must be mad,' said Maria, 'to let you take the Lambretta. God knows where you'll get to or what time you'll be back.'

She knelt down in front of him and helped him on with his shoes.

'If I run into don Ruggero,' said Tonio, 'I'll prove to him that our Lambretta is faster than his Vespa.'

'Is it true,' Marietta asked without turning round, 'is it really true that don Cesare has given you permission to take the Lambretta?'

'Why shouldn't don Cesare give me permission to take the Lambretta? Aren't I his confidential man?'

Tonio looked at Marietta. The light of the declining sun fell on the girl's loins, encircling the shadowy hollow which the linen frock outlined between her thighs.

'I can ride a Lambretta too,' Marietta said.

'Who taught you?' asked Tonio.

'Surely you haven't been crazy enough to let her ride on don Cesare's Lambretta?' Maria asked Tonio.

'That's enough from you, woman,' said Tonio.

He stood up, went down to the stables and got out the Lambretta which he pulled on to its stand, in front of the house, on the terrace. The women followed him. Children seemed to appear from every direction. The fishermen abandoned the nets they were folding and stood round in a circle.

'Fetch me some water,' said Tonio.

Julia and Maria went and drew buckets full of water from the outlet of the lake. Tonio flung the water full at the wheels and mudguards of the Lambretta. Then he dried the machine and polished it with chamois leather.

'Do you mean to say don Cesare's given you permission to take the Lambretta?' said one of the fishermen.

'It's nothing unusual,' said Maria.

Marietta held back beside the steps.

Tonio tinkered with the carburettor to make the petrol rise. He checked that the gear lever was at neutral. Reflectively he adjusted the throttle, opening it a little more, then a little less.

The fishermen came closer, the children standing between their legs.

Tonio depressed the starting pedal. One kick, two kicks: the engine started. He played with the throttle and the noise of the engine increased, decreased, raced madly, died away.

'That's quite a machine!' said one of the fishermen.

'It runs truer than a Vespa,' said another.

'I think,' said a third, 'I'd still rather have a Vespa.'

'If don Cesare bought a Lambretta,' countered the first, 'it was because he had found out it was a better machine.'

Tonio eased it off the stand and sat astride the saddle. He accelerated once more, in neutral.

Marietta ran hurriedly forward.

'Take me along,' she said.

'You see — it's you who lead him on!' Maria shouted.

'I don't give a hang for him,' said Marietta. 'But I want him to take me on the Lambretta.'

Marietta put both hands on the handlebars.

'Tonio,' she asked, 'let me ride behind you.'

Maria had posted herself on the other side of the Lambretta and stood watching both of them.

'You should have asked don Cesare's permission,' said Tonio.

'Don Cesare won't mind,' said Marietta.

'We aren't to know that.'

'I'll go and ask him.'

'Listen to her,' threw in Elvira. 'She thinks she can disturb don Cesare!'

'Hold on,' Tonio said to Marietta. 'Don Cesare doesn't allow people to disturb him while he's working.'

'Are you his confidential man or aren't you?' Marietta asked. 'Take me along!'

'I *am* his confidential man, certainly,' said Tonio. 'But he has given me some very important commissions. That is why he's letting me use the Lambretta. I ask you: does a man take a girl with him when he is charged with an important mission?'

Marietta released the handlebars and stood aside.

'*Femminuccia!*' she cried.

She turned away and walked towards the steps.

Tonio started off, accelerated and disappeared among the bamboos, heading for the bridge.

The fishermen watched Marietta climbing the steps up to the house. They joked very loudly to make quite sure she could hear them.

'That one needs a man,' said one.

'Failing a man,' said another, 'she could have done with the Lambretta between her legs.'

'A machine like that,' said the third, 'it's hard.'

All three of them laughed, without taking their eyes off the girl; her quick steps pulled the frock tight across the thighs.

From the top of the flight of steps she called down to them:

'Go home to your goats, *men*!'

The menfolk of the marsh were reputed to prefer goats to women.

Marietta went into the house. The Lambretta, across the bridge by this time, could be heard racing along the other bank of the outlet, behind the curtain of bamboos.

Chief of Police Attilio had prolonged his siesta. He was awakened by the din Judge Alessandro's and donna Lucrezia's children were making in the upstairs flat.

Stripped to the waist, he crossed to the dressing-table and sprayed lavender water on to his cheeks and under his arms. He was a good-looking man of around forty. He carefully brushed and combed his hair, putting the waves in place with a new, non-greasy American preparation. He had large, dark eyes with rings that devoured half his face. He put on the white shirt which Anna, his wife, had laid out for him on the chest of drawers; in summer he changed his shirt twice a day. He chose a tie to blend with his linen suit. He began to hum the Charles Trenet tune the prisoners had been singing a while ago; but he, unlike they, knew what the words meant. He had studied French at high school — he was a bachelor of laws.

He slipped into his jacket and gave a tug to make it hang straight. In the buttonhole he put a carnation freshly plucked from the window box.

He went through to the living-room, where his wife Anna sat knitting with Giuseppina, whose father ran the hardware store in the via Garibaldi.

Anna was fat, limp and very fair. Her father was a magistrate in Lucera, the juridical centre of the province, near Foggia. Her family had been looked up to locally for generations, their name figured in thirteenth-century archives, and Judge Alessandro maintained that she was descended from one of the Swabians the Emperor Frederick II had imported when he made Lucera the capital of his kingdom of southern Italy.

Giuseppina was thin with black hair and the shining eyes of the malaria victim. The fever had not yet yellowed her cheeks as it had those of the judge and of don Cesare's Julia; she had the lustreless colouring of lands baked by the sun. The judge claimed that she was descended from the Saracens Frederick II armed against the Pope when he lost faith in his German cavalry; a whole company of them had been garrisoned at Porto Manacore.

Giuseppina was knitting herself a halter, a strip wound in a spiral which would double the size of her breasts and accentuate the nipples; this year Lollobrigida and Sophia Loren were setting the pace on the beaches throughout Italy.

'Signor maresciallo,' asked Giuseppina, 'will you do me a favour?'

'Have I ever turned you down?' the Chief asked with a laugh.

'Tell me you'll do it.'

'Promise her you will,' begged Anna.

'I can see you've both made up your minds,' said the Chief. 'Do you want me to send you out for some ice-cream?'

'We can eat ice-cream without coming to you for it,' laughed Giuseppina. 'What I want to ask you is this: let signora Anna come down to the beach with me tomorrow.'

'There,' said Anna.

'Anna goes on the beach with you, and takes the children, whenever she feels like it,' replied the Chief.

'You know perfectly well what I mean,' insisted Giuseppina.

'Say it, then.'

'Let her come bathing with me.'

'So that's what you've hatched together!'

'The answer is yes?'

'The answer is no,' he said drily.

'Nowadays it's only peasant women who don't bathe,' said Giuseppina.

'What on earth do I look like,' Anna protested, 'wearing that old beach dress when all the others are in swimsuits?'

'This season,' Giuseppina pursued, 'even lawyer Salgado's wife has started bathing.'

'And the swimsuit she wears,' added Anna, 'shows every inch of her back.'

'Donna Lucrezia doesn't go bathing,' the Chief said, 'and I'm sure she doesn't grumble about it.'

'That Lucrezia,' cried Anna, 'is too proud to bathe in Manacore. I'm not sure that she'd condescend to show herself in Rimini, even. For her it's Venice or nothing.'

'Are you scared of people seeing your wife in a swimsuit?' asked Giuseppina.

'That's my business.'

Giuseppina fixed her brilliant malarial eyes on those of Chief of Police Attilio.

'We'll talk it over later,' she said.

'You little bitch,' he said.

'What are you two still going on about?' asked Anna.

'Your husband is a reactionary,' said Giuseppina. 'He doesn't want you to keep up with the times. He'd like to be able to shut you away in a convent. You were better off in Lucera.'

'That's true,' Anna said.

'I suppose it would suit you nicely if she went back there,' the Chief said to Giuseppina.

'I'd willingly go with her.'

'I'm not so sure.'

'Calm down, both of you,' Anna said.

The room was furnished in the style of the kingdom of Naples at the end of the last century—shallow, high-backed sofas and chairs, a marble-topped table with Louis XVI legs, enormous red plush curtains. A tapestry peopled one whole wall with lions and tigers. A tall mirror encased in gilt plaster rested against a giant vase full of artificial flowers and draped with red plush. The old oil-lamp beneath the statue of the Madonna had been replaced by a red electric-light bulb, always alight. All these items had been given in dowry by the Lucera family.

'The Madonna's lamp has burned out again,' said the Chief.

He went up to the statue, crossed himself and unscrewed the bulb; then he pushed the shutters open and examined it in the daylight. A blast of hot air and the sound of the prisoners' singing came into the room.

'This is the tenth time,' the Chief said, 'I've had to change this bulb.'

Anna made a pair of horns with her first and fourth fingers — a classic spell to ward off evil.

'There's something odd in this house,' she said.

'Something that's very good business for the electrician,' said Giuseppina.

'You,' said the Chief, 'you don't believe in anything.'

Giuseppina wrapped the halter she was knitting in an old number of *Il Tempo*.

'I believe what one has to believe,' she said.

Chief of Police Attilio put his hand to his groin — another kind of spell.

'Do I scare you, signor maresciallo?' asked Giuseppina.

She laughed. She had the thick lips of a Negress and her teeth were yellow.

'I must get down to the office,' the Chief said.

'They're keeping you busy?' asked Anna.

'There's this affair with the Swiss camper …'

'The one who's gone and got himself robbed of half a million lire?'

'Yes,' said the Chief, 'down by don Cesare's villa.'

'It's a funny idea,' Anna said, 'going off and leaving half a million lire in your car.'

'It's a funny idea spending the night on the marsh,' laughed the Chief. 'He's probably caught malaria.'

'I must be going too,' said Giuseppina.

'You're leaving so soon?' asked Anna.

'I've got to iron my dress for the ball this evening.'

'You're going to the ball this evening?' asked the Chief.

'I haven't a husband to imprison me in my own house.'

'Now you two,' said Anna. 'Don't start arguing again.'

Chief of Police Attilio and Giuseppina left the flat together.

The court house was an ancient palace, built by the Angevin kings to face the palace of Frederick II of Swabia after the latter's son, King Manfred, had been beaten by them. The landings were full of dark nooks.

Chief of Police Attilio pushed Giuseppina into a corner of the old wall and put his arm round her.

'Give me a kiss,' he said.

'No,' she said.

Her arms taut, her hands pressed flat against the man's chest, she held him off. But with the same movement she thrust her stomach against him. She laughed.

'Just a kiss,' he insisted.

'No,' she said.

'Why yes yesterday and no today?'

'That's how it goes.'

She had plenty of stamina and the Chief could not bend the two thin arms which held his shoulders at a distance. She laughed. In the shadows he could distinguish only the two large feverish eyes and the thick lips stressed with rouge.

'I beg you …' said the Chief.

'You can do better than that!'

18

'I implore you.'

'Say "I implore you, my beloved Giuseppina".'

'I implore you, my beloved Giuseppina.'

Back to the wall, belly thrust forward she continued to hold the man's shoulders at a distance.

'You'll let your wife come to the beach with me tomorrow morning?'

'Yes.'

'In a swimsuit?'

'Yes.'

'Swear you will!'

'I swear.'

'Swear it on the Madonna!'

'I swear it on the Madonna.'

Giuseppina relaxed her elbows and let herself be kissed. She was good at kissing. He caressed her and she allowed herself to be caressed.

'I'll be waiting for you,' he said, 'with the car, when you leave the ball.'

'No,' she said. 'People will see us.'

'I'll wait for you near the bridge, at the end of the beach. We'll go into the pine woods.'

'You know I don't want to be the mistress of a married man.'

'I won't do anything you don't want me to do.'

'Perhaps I'm the one,' she said, 'who won't be able to restrain herself.'

'All the better.'

'You know my conditions,' she said.

'But,' he said, 'it's as though you were my mistress already.'

She took advantage of his words to disengage herself.

'No,' she said. 'It's not at all the same thing. Luckily for me.'

She was already on the first step of the staircase. Quietly she sang the old southern proverb:

Baci e pizzichi
Non fanno buchit![1]

— then ran down the stairs.

From the window of his office, Chief of Police Attilio watched Tonio slowly circling the main square on the Lambretta.

His deputy stood waiting, a batch of reports in his hand.

'Where,' the Chief asked him, 'did don Cesare's Tonio get the money to buy a Lambretta?'

'I've already asked myself that question,' replied the deputy. 'Naturally,' he added.

'I have made inquiries,' he continued. 'The Swiss's money has nothing to do with the Lambretta. It was don Cesare who bought it.'

'Just as I thought,' said the Chief. 'Tonio hasn't the brains for a half-million lire job.'

He smiled.

'Don Cesare on a Lambretta. That's something I'd like to see.'

'No one has ever seen don Cesare on his Lambretta.'

'What made him buy it?'

'There must be some girl at the end of it.'

'At the end of what?' asked the Chief.

He laughed. So did the deputy.

'If I were rich like don Cesare,' said the Chief, 'I'd buy myself an Alfa-Romeo.'

'Which model?'

'The Giuletta sports.'

'Me,' said the deputy, 'I think I'd rather have a Lancia: the Aurelia.'

The deputy did not have a car. The Chief of Police had a Fiat Mille Cento, the monthly payments on which absorbed a third of his salary. Judge Alessandro, a man of culture, had an ancient Topolino which he had picked up second-hand.

[1] Kisses and pinches — Don't make holes.

The Chief and the deputy returned to the case of the Swiss. The investigation was making no headway.

The theft had occurred a fortnight earlier.

The Swiss was on a camping holiday with his wife and three children, aged thirteen, fifteen and seventeen. They were travelling in an American car of a style already out of date, high-bodied and thick-tyred, which explained how they had succeeded in getting it as far as the beach of the isthmus separating the sea from don Cesare's salt lake.

They had arrived two days before the robbery. They had erected two tents beside the car, one for the man and wife, the other for the children.

On the first two days they had made some purchases from don Cesare's gardeners and fishermen.

At the time of the robbery, which was at noon, the Swiss and his three children were swimming together, about fifty yards from the shore and a hundred from their camp.

The wife was reading in her tent.

The man's jacket was on the back seat of the car, the wallet in the inside pocket of the jacket, and five hundred thousand lire in the wallet. The doors were shut, the windows open.

From eleven o'clock till twelve thirty neither the man nor the children nor the wife had seen anyone, either close to the camp or in the distance, along the whole stretch of beach.

The isthmus, locally known as such, was more precisely a *lido*, a sandbank formed in the course of centuries by the deposits swept down by the mountain torrents. It was several miles long, and in breadth it varied from a hundred and fifty to three hundred yards. The sand rose in dunes all along the lake and formed a beach beside the sea. There were only two means of approach: from the Porto Manacore end, a bridge across the outlet of the lake, at the foot of the house with the colonnades, the residence of don Cesare; at the other extremity, a customs post.

The evidence of don Cesare's people was categorical: nobody had crossed the bridge between dawn and midday, apart from two peasants from Calalunga who had come to cut

21

bamboo on the marsh and whose working routine had been supervised.

And no one had demanded entry from the customs men.

So the thief had not reached the isthmus overland — not unless he had hidden himself in the dunes before dawn.

The Chief of Police had examined the scene. By hiding in the dips between the dunes and behind the rosemary bushes, it was possible to make a concealed approach to within fifty yards of the camp. But how was it possible to reach the dunes without being spotted by don Cesare's people? This was the question the police were now asking themselves.

'All the same,' said the deputy, 'I wonder what the woman could have been reading — not to have seen or heard a thing? Something pretty dirty, I should think.'

'Swiss women are frigid,' the Chief said.

'If they were as frigid as all that they wouldn't come down here chasing after men.'

'Has she had an affair here?' the Chief demanded eagerly.

'Not that I know of,' said the deputy.

'These things get around in no time,' said the Chief. 'The moment a woman's involved, our men can't keep their tongues from wagging ...'

There was a gentle knock on the door and Judge Alessandro entered. He too was preoccupied with the case of the Swiss. The afternoon post had brought a sharp letter from the public prosecutor's office in Lucera, instructing him to 'expedite' inquiries into the action the camper had brought against persons unknown. The Swiss consulate had made representations to the Chigi Palace. The Swiss was on the board of a firm which had investments in the Italian petroleum industry ...

'A financier!' said the Chief with astonishment. 'And rather than stay at a decent hotel, he prefers to camp on a sand dune, right next to a malarial swamp. That's a Swiss notion for you ...'

'If you had arrested the thief,' the judge protested, 'I wouldn't have had my knuckles rapped by the prosecutor again.'

He had put on an old woollen jacket to come down to the police station. He paced up and down the office, his eyes shining, sweating and shivering.

'*Caro amico, carissimo,*' the Chief said. 'Sit down, I implore you.'

The judge sank into an armchair facing the desk.

The deputy went into the next room, leaving the door open.

The judge lit a cigarette. The fever gave the tobacco a bitter flavour. He stubbed out the cigarette.

The Chief summarized the investigation.

The informers had laid no information. In neither Manacore, nor the neighbouring towns, nor Porto Albanese, nor Foggia had any abnormal spending been reported; there was no news from either the brothels or the jewellers' shops.

'This is certainly the first time half a million lire have gone into circulation in Manacore without someone noticing ...'

'People shouldn't leave a fortune lying about on the seat of a car,' cried the judge.

'In Switzerland there's no stealing,' the Chief said.

'The Swiss have full bellies,' the judge said violently.

The Chief lowered his voice.

'Gently, *caro*, gently. My deputy is listening to every word you say. He'll go about saying you're a socialist.'

The judge lowered his voice.

'Isn't it an act of provocation,' he asked, 'to leave half a million lire lying about in a country full of starvelings and unemployed? It's the Swiss I'd like to arrest.'

'Maybe,' said the Chief, 'but it's my job to arrest the thief. Your friend don Cesare isn't making things easy for me ...'

He returned to his summary.

The thief could only have reached the camp by hiding himself in the sand dunes. All right. How did you get to the dunes? Either on foot or by boat. All right. The thief had not come on foot; he would have been seen. So he had come by boat. By using one in the swamps and on the lake and manœuvring carefully through the reeds it was possible to reach the dunes completely unobserved. All right. Don Cesare's people were the only ones who knew the passes through the reeds, and most of the boats belonged to them. So either the thief was a member of don Cesare's household or he had found an accomplice there. This was the Chief's reasoning.

Don Cesare had insisted on being present while his people were interrogated.

The interrogation had lasted a whole day, with don Cesare sitting in his monumental Neapolitan armchair with its grotesques of gilded wood, and the Chief and his subordinates sitting on benches.

When don Cesare considered that one of his men had answered enough questions, he said to him:

'Off with you.'

The police protested. They still had questions they wanted to ask.

'I know him,' don Cesare would say. 'He has nothing more to tell you.'

And he repeated to the man:

'Off with you.'

It had been impossible to interrogate the women. He had forbidden them to answer.

'I can vouch for the women and girls of my household.'

The following day he had closed his doors to the Chief of Police.

The police had done their best to pursue their work by going from one to another of the reed huts scattered over the marsh. The huts emptied themselves at their approach. Or else they were found to contain old women who had lost both sight and hearing: 'What can I tell, signori?' Moreover, the policemen were hardly fond of adventuring on to the marsh; many of the huts could only be reached aboard a punt; these were extremely frail, consisting of three assembled planks of wood, flat-bottomed, high in the water and narrow, so slender that it seemed only the act of propulsion kept them the right way up; the water was dead, and if you plunged your hand into it you touched

24

bottom right away — the immemorial mud which sucked, engulfed, extinguished.

In places the marsh was broken by narrow banks of beaten earth. Here they encountered don Cesare, walking with long, powerful strides, a rifle under his arm, followed by Tonio with the game-bag, in quest of the iron birds of Diomede's legend, the wild duck peculiar to the marsh and lake. He swept by without a word, without so much as a glance, and you had to balance yourself carefully on the side of the bank if he were not to send you flying. Tonio followed him, in his starched white jacket, as silent as his master. They walked soundlessly, rubber-booted. They disappeared behind the reeds. Suddenly you would hear a beating of wings, a report at close range, the gliding of a punt among the reeds.

'You must make allowances for don Cesare,' said the judge. 'He was brought up in the feudal tradition. He's too old to break away from it.'

'There you are,' cried the Chief. 'The moment one of the big landowners needs someone to speak in his defence, there's always some socialist ready to plead his cause.'

'Let's confiscate by all means!' cried the judge. 'But not just to swell the priest's pockets ...'

They embarked on one of their habitual arguments. The Chief was a Christian Democrat.

Tonio slowly circled the square on the Lambretta.

The unemployed followed Tonio's movements. Their eyes, like sunflowers drawn by the sun, ran round the square simultaneously with the Lambretta. This was the way they looked at everything. In the course of the time they had spent standing against the walls of the main square, they had lost the habit of moving their heads. The pupils moved slowly in the sockets of their eyes, like jellyfish which seem to be lying motionless between

25

two pools but which are really covering a lot of ground, and nothing escaped their notice.

Tonio had completed the errands with which don Cesare had entrusted him. He had two hundred lire in his pocket which he had managed to conceal from Maria. He wondered what he was going to do with the two hundred lire; it was half a day's wages for a woman worker, a third of a day's labour for a farm hand, the price of half a glass of Scotch in the bar of the Sports Café (no one in the Sports Café ever drank whisky; the bottle was there for the day when the Manacore beach 'caught on', as people put it). Two hundred lire — it was the price, also, of two hundred grammes of olive oil, of two litres of wine and of a quick visit to a brothel; but there was no brothel in Porto Manacore, and the bus fare to the nearest, in Porto Albanese, was six hundred lire.

The unemployed followed Tonio with their eyes, without moving their heads. Perhaps don Cesare needed someone to prune his orange and lemon trees. *Tonio won't look at us: he wants to prolong the pleasure it gives him to have to choose one of us, the sweet pleasure of a confidential man. If he remembers I'm a cousin of his wife's, he will choose me. Or perhaps what don Cesare really needs is a boy to help his fishermen? I'll go and fetch my son from the house.* But Tonio was riding round the square just for the pleasure of showing off the Lambretta. He was wondering what to do with the two hundred lire.

The sun was beginning to sink in the direction of the islands. The notary's daughter, lawyer Salgado's daughter and don Ottavio's daughter advanced in line abreast from the via Garibaldi; they began the *passeggiata*, the promenade, which consisted of walking clockwise all the way round the main square. They were wearing light linen dresses in lemon, emerald and geranium, each inflated by three superimposed petticoats; one of the three girls finding a pretext to run a few paces and then swing suddenly round, her dress, obeying the laws of gravitation, opened like a flower and showed the white lace of the three petticoats. These dresses came from the leading dressmaker in

26

Foggia, who bought her models in Rome. After don Cesare, it was don Ottavio who owned most land in Porto Manacore. But the notary's and lawyer Salgado's daughters could spend as much on their summer dresses as don Ottavio's daughter; their fathers owned estates too, though on a smaller scale, and could if need be live solely from the produce of their fields; if they continued to exercise their professions (liberal), it was from caution; while they were still students Mussolini had talked of collective farming; the Christian Democrats had, in their turn, added agrarian reform to their programme; a profession was an insurance policy against the demagogues.

The daughters and sons of summer residents and tourists followed in the *passeggiata*. They were Romans, the children of Manacoreans who had emigrated to the capital, where they worked in government offices. The girls wore sailor trousers and jerseys; the young men had knotted brightly coloured kerchiefs around their necks; they dressed as they had learned in *Oggi* that people dressed in St Tropez.

And now, in their turn, came the poorer people from the Old Town. They emerged from the alleys that fell steeply away behind the sanctuary of Santa Ursula of Uria, from the steps and slopes that rose from the harbour to the inner courtyards of the palace of Frederick II of Swabia. The girls, for the most part, wore home-made linen dresses but, thanks to the patterns published in the cheaper magazines, they were up-to-the-minute in style. The people of Manacore had impeccable taste; it was in their blood; Porto Manacore was already a town in the sixth century B.C.

The young girls of the Old Town walked arm-in-arm in threes and fours, slowly, in silence. The boys went round in groups, also slowly; they spoke only when they halted and without raising their voices. The unemployed, standing along the walls, followed the girls with their eyes, without moving their heads. Only the Romans spoke or laughed aloud.

On the look-out for a quick snatch the *guaglioni*, a gang of youths at the awkward age, hung around the workmen who were

27

engaged in draping from King Murat's pine electric-light globes for the evening ball. Pippo, their leader, and Balbo, his lieutenant, leaned nonchalantly against the terrace balustrade, hatching a plot which might turn the confusion of the ball to their advantage.

Tonio continued to ride around the square on his Lambretta. He wondered what he was going to do with his two hundred lire. Soon the crowd engaged in the *passeggiata* would be taking up all the available space, the traffic police would close the square to vehicles and Tonio would have to park the Lambretta. The sight of so many girls increased his desire for a woman who did not have a swollen belly like his Maria; he thought he should keep his two hundred lire till he'd had a chance to double them; then, if don Cesare again authorized him to use the Lambretta, he would go to the brothel in Porto Albanese; to the two hundred lire for the woman, add the price of the petrol and the extras (you couldn't refuse a prostitute a cigarette and you were morally obliged to give at least twenty lire to the *mammina* who guarded the door); four hundred lire would see him through all right, he could cover himself nicely. So reason commanded him not to spend the two hundred lire this evening. But he had come into Manacore on the Lambretta, and he could not return to the marsh without having done something exceptional; the day must end in luxury. A game of The Law would be a happy solution. It was early yet, but it was not impossible that a game would already be in progress in some café in the Old Town. With a bit of luck at The Law, Tonio would be able to drink as much wine as he wanted, without spending a lira. With a bit of luck he would be chief or deputy according to The Law.

Tonio thought that to play at The Law was as agreeable as making love to a woman who was unwilling but on whom you had claims. For that, it was worth risking two hundred lire.

It would soon be seven o'clock. In the via Garibaldi, the chemist's thermometer still registered 90° in the shade. There was no sea breeze. There had been no sea breeze all season. It was a summer of land winds, the sirocco which blew from Sicily, the libeccio which blew from Naples; you knew they were blowing, but you never felt them, because they struck the backs of the high rocky crests which overhung Porto Manacore, the lake and the marsh; the sirocco was deflected towards the east, the libeccio towards the west; they ran round the bay, one on the eastern side, one on the western, like two great protective arms, and they met out at sea, like the hands of two arms encircling a protected object. For months now the sirocco and the libeccio had been struggling off-shore from Porto Manacore. The libeccio, born in Morocco, had gathered clouds above the Mediterranean; the sirocco, born in Tunisia, whence it had blown direct to Sicily, had stayed dry. The clouds driven along by the libeccio were kept out at sea by the sirocco. When the sirocco got the better of the libeccio, the bank of clouds moved off towards the west; when the libeccio got the better of the sirocco, the bank of clouds covered the whole horizon; but not once since the end of spring had the libeccio been strong enough to drive the clouds as far as Porto Manacore. Day after day, the unemployed, standing along the walls of the main square, had followed every phase of the battle which was going on out at sea. But never had the slightest breeze reached Manacore, as though the warriors out at sea had exhausted all the air in the bay, as though the whole area between the high rocky crests and the open sea formed a hollow in the atmosphere, an air-pocket, the inside of an air-valve. Looking through a telescope from the top of the sanctuary of Santa Ursula of Uria, the highest point in the Old Town, you could see the crests of the great waves the sirocco and the libeccio hurled against one another. But within the bay of Porto Manacore, the sea was motionless; the waves deadened themselves against the sandbanks and on the ends of the beaches the sea stagnated like ditchwater; and when, very rarely, a particularly powerful wave succeeded in crossing all the sandbanks, it swelled slowly on the fringe of the shore, like lead rising in the crucible when it starts to melt — swelled like a blister and gently rose to burst on the surface.

Tonio parked the Lambretta near the terrace overlooking the

harbour and the bay, then went off through the alleys of the Old Town in search of a café where there was a game of The Law in progress.

From her window on the third floor of the court house, Anna, the wife of the Chief of Police, stood watching the *passeggiata*. In Porto Manacore the daughters of leading citizens took part in the *passeggiata*, but not their wives; in the small inland towns, only the young men. Signora Anna thought Porto Manacore was more 'advanced' than the inland towns, but less advanced than Lucera. She had been out of luck to marry a civil servant who had been posted to Porto Manacore. That's life, she thought.

Signora Anna looked beyond the main square to the port, where a number of fishing boats were moored. Before the war Porto Manacore had traded with the Dalmatian coast; steamers had arrived loaded with wood and gone back loaded with oranges and lemons; but the Italian government and the Yugoslav government had fallen out and now there was never a boat came into the harbour. From year to year the sand rose higher on the jetty. Anna watched the *vaporetto* which had stopped a few hundred yards beyond the pier; a small boat was pulling away from it to pick up the foreigners who had arrived during the afternoon and who were going to the islands for the underwater fishing. The *vaporetto* would reappear next morning, returning to its home port, Porto Albanese, a town which was identical with Porto Manacore, with this one difference: it contained a brothel, of which the menfolk never ceased to speak. As for the islands, they were three expanses of rock which provided a home for about a hundred fishermen who in summer let their houses to foreigners who came to fish under the sea; during these months, they slept in the stable with the donkey. Anna reflected that even the *vaporetto* no longer led anywhere.

Immediately above Anna, the wife of the Chief of Police, donna Lucrezia, Judge Alessandro's wife, had stationed herself behind the gap in the shutters. Her heavy head of hair was now wound in a neat bun. She wore a dress which had long sleeves

30

and a stand-up collar, in her customary style. But the discreet bodice rose and fell with her immoderate breathing. She was looking at Francesco Brigante, the law student, who had just sat down on the terrace of the Sports Café, opposite the court house, beneath the terrace of the post office. She repeated softly to herself: 'I love him, I love him.'

Francesco Brigante had chosen his table so that he could watch the gaping shutters on the fourth floor of the court house without the other customers being able to discover the direction of his glances. He murmured to himself: 'I love her, I love her.'

All afternoon the sirocco had slowly been getting the better of the libeccio, and the clouds, behind the islands, were no more than a fringe inflamed by the setting sun.

Judge Alessandro and Chief of Police Attilio continued their subdued discussion in the Chief's office.

Through the open door they could hear the deputy in the next room dealing with men and women who had come for administrative documents. To obtain a passport you had to present between ten and fifteen documents. In the cities there were rackets which specialized in the procurement of *documenti* — a prosperous business. In the main square the unemployed felt their pockets from time to time to make sure they had not lost their *documenti*: identity card, unemployment card, army record card, employers' certificates and many others, soiled, greasy dog-eared, split at the folds, infinitely precious. A man who had lost his *documenti* no longer had rights or a legal existence; he was abolished.

After the political skirmishing, in which he had joined without conviction, the Chief had — as usual — arrived at the major preoccupation of all civil servants in the South: the posting to a town in the North; it never came. Judge Alessandro was undoubtedly the only magistrate in the province of Foggia who had not asked to be transferred; the cult of Frederick II of

Swabia bound him to Apulia. Chief of Police Attilio had a new source of hope; his wife had made the acquaintance, down on the beach, of a woman from Rome who was the intimate friend of a Cardinal's niece.

The judge continued to shiver beneath his woollen jacket.

'You're still not on the right track,' he cut in. 'There are too many Cardinals' nieces in Italy. Almost as many as there are unemployed ...'

The deputy appeared in the doorway.

'It's Mario the bricklayer again. He insists on speaking to you.'

'I haven't got time,' the Chief said.

A loud voice rose in the next room.

'I've been waiting two years now. I demand my passport. I know my rights.'

'Come here!' shouted the Chief.

The man came into the room; he was tall and well-built, in duck trousers and cord-soled shoes. His shirt was frayed at the neck and wrists.

'Excuse me, *caro amico*,' the Chief said to the judge. 'Here is a man who has rights. In a democracy, a man who has rights is king.'

The judge did not answer. He lit another cigarette, took one puff, grimaced and stubbed the cigarette out.

The man came farther into the room. He held his hat in his hand. He remained standing in front of the Chief's desk.

'Well?' asked the Chief.

'Another week and it will be two years since I applied for a passport for France with all the necessary documents, including the certificate signed by my overseas employer.'

'Well then?'

'I still haven't had my passport.'

'What do you want me to do about it?'

'The Italian Constitution gives every citizen the right to travel freely abroad.'

'You know your Constitution well!'

'Yes, signor maresciallo.'

32

'You have never received a prison sentence?'

'I was sentenced to fifteen days for "squatting" on don Ottavio's waste ground on March 15th, 1949.'

'You were the ringleader.'

'It's true I encouraged the unemployed to move on to the waste ground. I admitted it before the tribunal. But the sentence was remitted. It doesn't appear on the police record I attached to my passport application. So I'm entitled to my passport.'

'Presumably that isn't the opinion of the prefecture.'

'I'm out of work. I've found a job in France. I demand my rights.'

'Go and demand your rights at the prefecture. The decision rests with them.'

'The prefecture have sent me to you,' the man said.

'There are some people who make a better job of things than you do,' the Chief said.

'I don't understand.'

'You remember Pietro the carpenter?'

'No.'

'The answer should be: no, signor maresciallo.'

'No, signor maresciallo,' the man repeated.

'If you ask me,' the Chief continued, 'I think you do remember.'

'No, signor maresciallo.'

'Pietro was a Red, the same as you.'

'I wouldn't know, signor maresciallo.'

'But I know. I know because he came here with his party card, the same as *your* party card, and he tore it up in front of me.'

'I wouldn't know, signor maresciallo.'

'The prefecture let him have his passport.'

'I demand my rights,' the man said.

The Chief of Police turned towards the judge.

'You see, *carissimo*, what a waste of time it is trying to help people.'

The judge played with the extinguished cigarette. He did not answer.

'I'll get a lawyer,' the man said.

'I advise you to get a good lawyer.'

'I won't get a lawyer from Porto Manacore.'

The Chief smiled. He was on bad terms with the two lawyers in Porto Manacore.

'I wish you luck,' he said.

The man made no move to go.

'I've nothing else to say to you.'

The deputy pulled the man towards the next room, arm over his shoulder. The man allowed himself to be pulled slowly away.

'Stubborn mule,' the deputy said to him, dragging him away. 'You damned stubborn mule. You were told quite plainly what you'd got to do. You don't know when you're on to a good thing ...'

They went through to the other room.

'You don't respect the law,' said the judge.

The Chief pushed back his chair.

'*Gentile amico* ...' he began.

'If those whose job it is to make the law respected,' interrupted the judge, 'if they of all people ...'

The Chief rose and ran on tiptoe to shut the door. He turned, his finger to his mouth. Then he raised his arms to heaven. He performed a whole charade of despair. Then he laughed.

'One would think, *carissimo amico*, that you had sworn to serve the rest of your time in Porto Manacore.'

'Why not?' asked the judge.

'The late lamented Frederick of Swabia won't get you a single rung up the ladder.'

'That man you're preventing from earning his living abroad,' said the judge, 'has children dying of hunger.'

The Chief of Police bent over the judge and seized him by the shoulders.

'And what about us, judge, what about us? Aren't we on our way to death, stuck in this town from which no one has ever managed to escape?'

★ ★ ★

34

Tonio, don Cesare's confidential man, was admitted as sixth member of a game which was starting up, on the initiative of Matteo Brigante, in one of the cafés of the Old Town. The Law can be played by five, six, seven or more; but six is a good number.

In Porto Manacore, Matteo Brigante controlled everything — including The Law. He was a former bosun's mate in the Royal Italian Navy. He had begun to control the town immediately upon his return to his native town in 1945, after the defeat. He was nearing his fifties, but he had retained the bosun's manner; you were always expecting to see him put a whistle brusquely to his mouth. It was a thin mouth, beneath a narrow, black, stiff moustache, and he always kept the lips pressed together, even when he laughed. Controlling everything, but doing nothing, he had never been convicted by the tribunals, except once, well before the war, which was for having *accoltellato*, knifed, a boy who had deprived one of his sisters of her virginity. It was a crime which did him honour, one of those crimes of honour for which the southern courts show every indulgence. He controlled the men who fished from boats, the men who fished with the *trabucco* and the men who fished with dynamite. He controlled the sellers of lemons, the buyers of lemons and the thieves of lemons. He controlled those who allowed themselves to be robbed in the olive-presses and those who robbed them. He controlled the smugglers who went out to meet yachts laden with American cigarettes and the customs men who prowled along the coast in their motor launches, suddenly throwing on searchlights that probed every cove, or not throwing them on if Brigante had made a deal so that they would turn a blind eye. He controlled those who made love and those who didn't, the cuckolds and those who made them cuckolds. He gave information to thieves and information to the police, which allowed him to control both the thieves and the police. People paid him to control and people paid him not to control; and thus he levied his tax on every operation, commercial or non-commercial, conducted within the bounds of Porto Manacore or the

35

neighbouring areas. Matteo Brigante had such a lot of controlling to do that he had enticed Pizzaccio, the assistant baker, away from the *pizzeria* and had taken him into his service as first assistant controller.

This evening, before going on to control the ball put on by the town corporation for the summer visitors, Brigante, the racketeer, had invited his lieutenant to play at The Law. Pizzaccio was the nickname of the former baker's assistant; it could be translated as 'dud Pizza'; similarly, in the heroic years of the city of Florence, Lorenzaccio had been the pejorative of Lorenzo.

The other players in the game were the American, a one-time emigrant to Guatemala who had returned to end his days in his home land, where he had bought a small olive plantation; the Australian, another one-time emigrant, who delivered fruit and fish in his light van; and lastly don Ruggero, don Ottavio's son, a student at Naples Law School, who preferred, during the vacations, to run after the wives of his father's peasants and get drunk in the cafés rather than flirt with the daughters of Manacore's leading citizens — a bunch of half-wits, in his opinion.

With his two hundred lire concealed from the vigilance of his wife Maria, Tonio was not on equal footing with his companions. But he could keep his end up for quite a time. The stake for each game was in fact fixed at a litre of Andria, a red wine $14°$ proof and costing a hundred and twenty lire. With six people playing, there were four losers. A hundred and twenty divided by four made thirty. Two hundred divided by thirty made six, with twenty left over. With two hundred lire, Tonio could chance his luck six times — or even seven times, for the landlord would certainly give him credit for ten lire. Besides, it was neither the amount of money risked nor the quantity of wine drunk which provided the point of the game of The Law, but the law itself, bitter when you had to bow to it, delectable when you imposed it.

The Law is played throughout southern Italy. It comprises two phases. The object of the first phase is to designate a winner, who is called *padrone*, chief; this is accomplished as rapidly as possible, sometimes with the cards, sometimes with the dice; the chief could equally well be chosen by drawing straws. This evening they chose tarot cards as the instrument of fate.

Pizzaccio won the first round of tarot and was thus designated chief.

The landlord produced a jug of wine which he placed beside Pizzaccio; a few men who were drinking at the bar came up and made a circle round the table. No one spoke.

It is after the designation of the chief that the second phase of the game of The Law begins. It comprises two episodes. First of all the chief chooses a *sotto-padrone*, a deputy.

Pizzaccio let his eyes rest successively on each of the other five players; then his attention returned to this one, to that one, feigning perplexity. He kept them waiting. He knew The Law well.

'Get on with it,' said the landlord. 'Your pizza's cooked.'

'It's not quite done yet,' said Pizzaccio.

At that moment he had his eyes on Tonio.

'Tonio,' he began, 'has a pretty sister-in-law ...'

Everyone's attention focused on Tonio who sat motionless, his eyes lowered, his hands spread flat on the table.

The winner, the chief, who dictates the law, has the right to speak and not to speak, to interrogate and to reply in place of the interrogated, to praise and to blame, to insult, to insinuate, to revile, to slander and to cast a slur on people's honour; the losers, who have to bow to the law, are bound to submit without sound or movement. Such is the fundamental rule of the game of The Law.

'There is something to be said,' Pizzaccio pursued, 'for choosing yourself a deputy with a pretty sister-in-law. If I made Tonio deputy, perhaps he would lend me la Marietta ...'

Attention remained fastened on Tonio. They knew he was hanging around Marietta, who did not want him. In Manacore, especially on the marsh, that false wilderness where relatives were always on the alert, the men became madly obsessed with the women of the family — sisters, sisters-in-law, daughters.

37

Pizzaccio's thrusts always found the mark; it was a real pleasure to listen to him playing at The Law. Tonio remained silent and motionless in his freshly starched white jacket. Bravo for him too!

'Come to think of it,' Pizzaccio said slowly, 'if I want to get la Marietta, Brigante's the one I ought to turn to …'

It was not unknown that Matteo Brigante, too, was hanging around Marietta, that he often paid visits to the house with the colonnades and that the girl replied with a provocative laugh to his double-edged remarks. Whenever Tonio saw him walking calmly across the bridge which spanned the outlet of the lake and heading for don Cesare's villa, his features froze and he made no reply to the visitor's greeting, even though he was scared of him. Brigante loved virgins. The fiancés, the suitors, the brothers and the fathers hesitated to attack the racketeer. But the need to avenge their honour can make people do silly things. So Brigante always carried his grafting knife with him, a formidable weapon, as sharp as a razor; a legal weapon too, the most common of working tools in a land of fruit growers, dangerous and on the right side of the law, like Brigante himself; he was the most artful of duellists with a grafting knife. Never would Tonio dare to defy him openly. None of this was unknown. Which was why everyone's attention remained fastened on Tonio.

'You'll pass Marietta on to me?' asked Pizzaccio of Matteo Brigante.

'After I have opened the way.'

'The going will be easier,' said Pizzaccio. 'I appoint you deputy.'

There was a murmur of approval. The game was developing well, straight and clean, without any blurring of the outlines.

Tonio had not batted an eyelid. Bravo for him too!

With the designation of the deputy the first episode of the second phase of the game of The Law ended.

The losers paid. The American, the Australian, don Ruggero and Tonio each gave thirty lire to the landlord.

Pizzaccio, chief of the game, poured himself a glass of wine

38

and put his lips to it. Thus began, according to rule, the second episode of the second phase of the game of The Law.

'A wine fit for a king!' exclaimed Pizzaccio. 'Taste it, deputy.'

It was piquant to hear Pizzaccio take the tone of chief to Matteo Brigante, his chief in real life. These reversals of the hierarchy, an echo of the saturnalia of ancient Rome, gave an added edge to the interest of The Law.

Brigante poured himself a glass of wine and tasted it.

'It would be a sin,' he said, 'to give such a wine to pigs.'

'Do as you like,' said Pizzaccio. 'You're the deputy.'

Brigante drained his glass.

'I could do with another,' he said.

'It is your right,' replied Pizzaccio.

Brigante poured himself a second glass. The jug held seven. There were only four left.

It sometimes happens that the chief and the deputy drink the whole jug, without offering a single glass to the losers. It is their right. This has point only last thing at night, and only then if fate and malignity have combined to prevent one or more players from being appointed, even once, chief or deputy; their exasperation is increased by the sight of those who dictate the law silently emptying the jug before their eyes. The sting of this gesture is not always negligible. But Pizzaccio and Brigante were too skilled to employ it early in the game, when everyone still had control of his nerves.

Brigante slowly emptied his second glass of wine.

'I'm dying of thirst,' said don Ruggero.

'Shall we stand him a glass?' asked Brigante.

'Do as you like,' said Pizzaccio.

Brigante filled don Ruggero's glass at once. There had been no point in keeping on tenterhooks a boy who spent the greater part of the year in Naples and who had become indifferent to the maliciousness of Porto Manacore; his heart was too lofty, by birth, to be humiliated by the shafts of the other players. Don Ruggero was a mediocre person to play against. They willingly admitted him, however, so as not to vex him, because he willingly lent his Vespa and his canoe and was always ready to stand drinks, and also because, once he warmed to the game, he was capable of malice, the most precious of virtues for The Law.

There were only three glasses left in the jug.

'You'll stand me a glass?' the American asked Brigante.

'You'll stand me a glass?' is the time-honoured formula and the request must be made to the deputy and not to the chief. Don Ruggero had therefore broken the rule by calling out: 'I'm dying of thirst.' For the reasons which have just been explained, no one had called attention to his crime.

'Shall we stand him a glass?' Brigante asked his chief, in accordance with The Law.

'Do as you like,' said Pizzaccio.

'I don't think we ought to stand him a glass,' said Matteo Brigante. 'He's too much of a niggard. We shouldn't encourage people to be niggards.'

'Is he really a niggard?' asked Pizzaccio.

'He's even more niggardly than his olives,' said Brigante.

The avarice of the American was as notorious as the poor state of his olive grove. The latter was undoubtedly the cause of the former. The American had returned in glory from Guatemala; he spoke of the miraculous orchards of the United Fruit Company, for whom he had worked as an area manager. He had forgotten the sly ways of the South; the land agent had made him pay a high price for olive trees which no longer yielded fruit; the transaction had left him permanently bitter. Brigante and Pizzaccio turned the blade in the wound for a long time. The eyes of the players and the spectators did not leave the American's face, which turned still greener. In the night he would have an attack of malaria. But he stood up to it well, not saying a word, not making a movement. An agreeable victim, but Tonio was preferable; the wounds which sprang from setbacks in love were the most diverting to see inflicted.

'You'll stand me a glass?' the Australian asked in turn.

He asked in an assured voice, being in business with Brigante, who had nothing to gain by persecuting him. In his van he transported, underneath the crates of fruit, the cartons of American cigarettes collected along the coastline; he always sent an exact tally to the racketeer, who was thus enabled to check the smugglers' declarations. In the case of the Australian, as in the case of don Ruggero, everyday considerations competed against the demands of The Law; reality modified the laws of good theatre; the game does not exist which is governed solely by its own rules; even in games of pure chance, like roulette, the player who can lose without feeling the pinch has a better chance of winning.

Pizzaccio and Brigante made a few nasty jokes, for the sake of form, and the Australian received his wine.

Then Pizzaccio poured himself a glass and drank it slowly, in silence. It was his privilege as chief. He turned to Tonio.

'You're not asking for any?'

'No,' replied Tonio.

'It is your right.'

Brigante emptied the last glass at a single gulp. Thus ended the first game of the evening.

The tarot cards designated the American as chief of the second game. He chose don Ruggero as deputy, considering him the one player who would have the nerve to humiliate Matteo Brigante if the occasion presented itself. But don Ruggero was growing bored. He was thinking of the hunt for foreign women in the streets of Naples when the boats arrived from Capri, of the English, the Swedes, the Americans (huntresses who hypocritically disguised themselves as game), of the French even, who had joined the horde for some years past — Frenchmen must have lost their proverbial virility; Mussolini, thought don Ruggero, had been right to speak of the decadence of that nation. He conducted the game distractedly, personally drinking three glasses one after another; the sooner he got drunk, the sooner this tedious provincial evening would be at an end. When Tonio asked him: 'You'll stand me a glass?', he said no, without giving any explanation; humiliating Tonio was not his idea of fun; he might equally well have said yes; it was almost by chance that he said no; or perhaps it was because Tonio's air of constraint had reminded him of a foreign woman who, the day after, had pretended to remember nothing.

They began the third game at once. The cards designated Brigante as chief, and he chose Pizzaccio as deputy.

Brigante attacked Tonio even before he had drunk his glass of honour.

'Aren't you going to ask my deputy for anything?'

'No,' replied Tonio.

He kept his hands flat on the table, his plump, white, personal attendant's hands, and his eyes fixed on his hands.

'Why,' insisted Brigante, 'don't you ask Pizzaccio to stand you a glass? You've already lost three games and you haven't had a single glass. As I see it, you'd be within your rights if you quenched your thirst.'

'It's my right not to ask for any.'

There was a murmur of approval. Tonio had not yielded to the provocation.

'Tonio doesn't crack in a hurry,' Brigante said to Pizzaccio. 'And yet I was told he was don Cesare's personal attendant, his deputy. A deputy ought to make himself respected ...'

'In don Cesare's house,' said Pizzaccio, 'it's the women who are the real deputies ...'

'You'd better explain that to me,' said Brigante.

'Thirty years ago,' Pizzaccio began, 'old Julia had a lovely pair of tits. When don Cesare had played with them to his heart's content, he married her off to some poor devil who died of shame.'

'I see,' said Brigante. 'This poor devil passed himself off as don Cesare's personal attendant, but it was la Julia who laid down the law.'

'At that time,' Pizzaccio continued, 'you were in the navy. You can't know what went on. But things turned out exactly as you guessed ... Before he died, the poor devil gave Julia three daughters. The eldest is named Maria.'

'Tonio's Maria!' exclaimed Brigante.

'Wait till I explain ... When Maria was sixteen, don Cesare

42

took a fancy to her. Her tits were even fuller than her mother's had been. Don Cesare led her on so nicely, she got big in the belly. There was nothing for it but to find some cuckold to marry her; Tonio came along ...'

Talk your heads off, thought Tonio. *When my turn comes to be chief or deputy, you'll hear plenty more. You play the gentleman, Matteo Brigante, now that you have an account with the Bank of Naples, but people haven't forgotten that every sailor in Ancona tumbled your wife, while you were sailing in the king's ships; it was with the money she put away in her stocking that you bought the flat you're living in today, in the old palace. And you, Pizzaccio, messed up pizza, who go with the male German tourists for five hundred lire ...*

Thus thought Tonio, preparing to make his tormentors swallow their own poison, sharpening the words he would hurl at them. All attention focused on him. But he remained silent and motionless, frozen, in his freshly starched white jacket. It was Matteo Brigante and Pizzaccio who were beginning to crack.

'If I understand you,' said Brigante, 'Tonio passes himself off as don Cesare's personal attendant, but it's Maria who has the whip hand ...'

'She's had the whip hand for a very long time,' said Pizzaccio.

He gave a little laugh, a chuckle. He bent towards Tonio to get a better look at him.

'But,' he continued, 'it was soon Elvira's, Maria's sister's, turn to be eighteen ...'

'Don Cesare passed the whip over to her,' said Brigante.

'It's Marietta's turn next,' said Pizzaccio.

'Don Cesare's a real bull.'

'Good bulls,' said Pizzaccio, 'never grow old. You should see how Marietta wriggles when he looks at her.'

Brigante, in turn, bent towards Tonio.

'As houses go,' he said, 'you might say your house is quite a house.'

'The door open and the shutters closed,' added Pizzaccio without a pause.

Talk your heads off, thought Tonio. In his mind he was sharpening terrible words for when his turn came to dictate the law. But at the same time he was calculating that he had already spent three times thirty lire; there were only four games left in which he could take his chance at being designated chief. With six people playing, you could sometimes lose fifteen or twenty times in a row. The Law is not a game which follows the course of justice, since the player who does not start off with a little capital cannot try his luck to the full.

Thus thought Tonio, without shifting his eyes from the plump, white hands resting flat on the table. His hands did not tremble, but the hollow of his chest began to tighten with anguish at the idea that he had only four chances left of becoming chief this evening.

Several spectators had withdrawn from the table and were debating the turn the game had taken, in lowered voices. Some considered Brigante was putting too much aggression into his game and Pizzaccio too much servility towards his chief; The Law demanded a greater detachment towards the victim and more variety in the choice of victims; the wounds should be inflicted as though in sport. Others, however, praised the two men warmly; the attack should be concentrated on a single objective and the mortification of the victim should be complete. Such were the two opposing schools of thought.

Matteo Brigante and Pizzaccio, realizing that their style was the cause of discussion, rapidly put an end to the series of exchanges. They each poured themselves a glass.

'To the health of don Cesare's women,' said Pizzaccio.

'You'll stand me a glass?' asked the Australian.

The game was under way again.

Beneath Murat's pine, the ball had just begun. The pale blue electric lamps, which had been hung from the main branches, violently illumined part of the main square and the approach from the via Garibaldi.

The dance floor, the orchestra stand, the buffet and the small collection of tables and chairs around the buffet were separated from the rest of the square by a barrier of green-painted wood. The price of admission was two hundred lire. Beyond the barrier the young men and girls who could not afford to spend two hundred lire on dancing continued the *passeggiata*, walking round the square in a clockwise direction. The unemployed had retreated to the Old Town, the houses juxtaposed and growing on to one another, *into* one another, the terrace of one forming the yard of another, each room forming the attic or cellar of another, all the way from the breakwater of the harbour to the sanctuary of Santa Ursula of Uria which dominated Porto Manacore; lying on a bed, on a palliasse or a counterpane according to their degree of poverty, they listened to the strains of jazz which rose or descended to them from the ball. In the via Garibaldi, the chemist's thermometer still registered 86°.

Chief of Police Attilio had invited the state agronomist to have a drink with him, on the terrace of the bar of the Sports Café, opposite the court house, on the corner of the main square. They had a clear view of the whole ball.

In honour of the ball (put on by the town corporation for the summer visitors) the Chief of Police had authorized the proprietor of the bar to extend the terrace on to the roadway of the via Garibaldi. The first row of tables was therefore almost within reach of the blinds of the prison, on the ground floor of the court house. There was hardly anyone apart from tourists on the terrace, the tourists whose sons and daughters were dancing round Murat's pine, tradespeople and minor officials from Foggia and the small towns of the interior; the rich families of the region spent their holidays on the beaches of the North or in the Abruzzi mountains. Some of the leading citizens of Manacore were present — notaries, lawyers, doctors — but without their wives; they sat in all-male groups. Some spared a thought, others did not, according to their hearts and opinions, to the prisoners

45

who were behind the blinds of the prison and who were listening
to the jazz band and to all the sounds of voices that indicated an
evening out of the ordinary. The prisoners no longer sang, for
they did not know the jazz tunes. They were petty prisoners,
detained or sentenced by Judge Alessandro within the limits of
his competence as judge of the lower court: orange and lemon
thieves, fishermen who used dynamite, heroes of minor knifing
incidents.

'You have a good jazz band here,' said the agronomist.

'An excellent jazz band for such a small town,' replied the
Chief.

He kept his eyes on Giuseppina, who was dancing under the
big pine, on the other side of the green barrier.

'When I was a student in Cremona,' the agronomist pursued,
'I was the drummer in the School of Agriculture jazz band.'

The government agronomist was a Northerner, very fair and
with a bulging forehead; a Lombard with rosy cheeks. He was
twenty-six and he had spent the last three years in Porto Manacore, his first post. He was particularly interested in the breeding
of goats. He lived in an isolated house on the dry hills to the
west of the lake and he had installed a model pen for the two
stud goats supplied by the government and a number of she-
goats of various races, certain of which he had imported from
Asia Minor at his own expense; he had set himself to create
a new race of goat, specially suited to the Manacorean coastline
and yielding two or three times more milk than the emaciated
beasts tended by don Cesare's shepherds. He reckoned to succeed
within twenty or thirty years. He was a conscientious technician,
born and bred in the North, a dogged Lombard.

'I'd like to be the drummer here too,' the agronomist went on.
'But when one's a civil servant, one must consider public
opinion.'

'We have our obligations,' said the Chief.

'I look young for my age,' continued the Lombard. 'The
peasants wouldn't take me seriously at all if they saw me on the
drums.'

46

'Reactionaries,' the Chief said distractedly.

'It isn't easy to make them realize that goats can be improved.'

'For the use they put them to ...' said the Chief.

He laughed, showing his teeth; he had fine teeth and was proud of them. The Lombard missed the allusion and went on:

'In the North, they have a jazz club in every town. A civil servant can't be condemned for joining the same club as lawyers and doctors. You still have only youngsters in your jazz club.'

'You were out of luck when they sent you to Manacore.'

'It's interesting,' said the Lombard.

'You'll have to wait a long time for another posting. I've known some civil servants here who've reached retirement without getting a transfer.'

'I haven't put in for a transfer. These goats interest me.'

'Oh yes ...' said the Chief.

He kept his eyes on Giuseppina who was dancing with one of the Romans. He was a tall boy with an easy manner. He had a very Roman mouth, heavy and with the lower lip turned up with disdain. Giuseppina was laughing. She had put her hand on the boy's chest and was pushing him away, laughing all the time. Her malaria-thin body was arched taut against the tall boy with the disdainful mouth.

'If I were in your shoes,' said the Chief, 'I wouldn't insist on don Cesare's Marietta coming to work for me.'

The agronomist had a couple of servants, the husband keeping the model pen in order, the wife looking after the house; but the pen was demanding more and more attention and he had asked old Julia to let him have her youngest daughter to keep house for him. They had reached agreement about the basic idea and the salary, but they were having to wait for don Cesare's approval; why, precisely? Wasn't Julia free to find a position for her daughter? And how did the Chief of Police come to know about it? Presumably it was his job to know everything ...

The Chief laughed, showing his teeth.

'Down here,' he said, 'everyone keeps a tail on everyone else.

What I do for a living, the others do for pleasure ... That's why I advise you not to take a virgin into your service.'

The Lombard's rosy cheeks flushed scarlet. He was indignant. What intentions were they ascribing to him?

'The virgins of the South,' said the Chief, 'are a pack of bitches.'

'No more so than those of the North,' said the agronomist.

'Those of the North end up by going to bed with you.'

'Not all of them. Not always.'

'When they've got a man into such a state that he's going crazy with it, they have the decency to go to bed with him.'

'It isn't a question of latitudes.'

'Either you'll sleep with Marietta,' the Chief continued, 'or you won't sleep with her. Either way, there'll be ten witnesses ready to swear that you've raped her or that you've tried to rape her. The whole parish will interfere — the priest ... You'll be dragged before the tribunal. The only choice you'll have is whether to marry her or make her an allowance ...'

The agronomist refused to believe in such baseness and protested the innocence of his intentions. The dance came to an end and Giuseppina went and sat down on a bench, next to lawyer Salgado's daughter. The Chief tried to convince the agronomist of the danger he was running by taking Marietta into his service.

'In the South you'll find nothing but jurists. Even a farm labourer who can't read or write is a great jurist ...'

The agronomist had a car. Right. Driving along the roads of the South, he must have been obliged time after time to jam on the brakes to avoid a cyclist who had suddenly turned to his left. Yes. What did the cyclist do? He held out his arm and immediately turned to the left, even if there was a car right behind him doing a hundred miles an hour. Why? Because it was his right. He had held out his arm, as the law demanded; so he had the right to turn. He did not stop to ask himself whether the driver of the car right behind him would be able to brake in time. That was up to the driver. As for himself, since he had the right to turn, it was a matter of honour for him to turn, even if it cost

48

him his life. If he gave way to the driver when the law gave him precedence over the driver, when he had right of way, he would lose his honour, which meant more to him than life.

The agronomist maintained, on the other hand, that it was not the South which made jurists of the poor, but their poverty. His right to a thing was all he could call his own; it meant more to him than did his poor life. A rich man had so many rights that he could afford not to make an issue of them.

Thus they argued. The band struck up another dance tune. Francesco, the law student, the son of Matteo Brigante, was handling the drums. Giuseppina was now in the arms of the young manager of the local branch of the Bank of Naples.

'How exactly,' asked the Chief, 'did you get the idea of taking don Cesare's Marietta into your service?'

How exactly had it started? The Lombard had called on don Cesare several times, to talk goats with him. He had not achieved much; these feudal landowners were not interested in turning things to their advantage; don Cesare seemed more concerned with the herdsmen of antiquity than with the improvement of his flock; they said he made excavations; he knew the recipe for making goat's cheeses in the third century B.C., but made no effort to ensure that his shepherds cooked their cheeses, his cheeses, in clean containers. In the course of these few visits, he had noticed little Marietta; he had found her cute — by which he meant lively, with a wide-awake look about her. And since he needed somebody ...

'No one suggested you should take her on?'

The agronomist remembered that, as it happened, a tall, well-built woman, a brunette he had been told was don Cesare's mistress, Elvira in fact, Marietta's sister, had expressed astonishment that he had only a goat-girl to keep house for him.

'You're caught in our web!' cried the Chief.

'Why not?' asked the agronomist.

'She owns him,' thought the Chief. He loved this expression. There were some human beings who owned others; the owners became owned in their turn; one condition led to another; there was no escape. He had owned many women, married women especially; his work offered him facilities which others did not have; it was always he who made the break, but usually the woman continued to be owned by him; she begged for one last meeting; it was always the last meeting; he took some pride in it. Now it was Giuseppina who owned him.

'Have you heard Marietta sing yet?'

'No,' replied the agronomist.

'She has a certain gift,' said the Chief. 'A very high-pitched voice which produces interesting effects in some of the local songs. You do sometimes find that type of voice among the peasant women of the region. Perhaps you have to be born on the Manacorean coast to appreciate it. You probably wouldn't like it. "The voice" is not so very different from the way Arab women sing through their noses.'

'The voice?' asked the Lombard.

'We say "the voice" when we're talking about that kind of voice. Women who have "the voice" are inclined to be witches.'

'You believe in witchcraft?' asked the Lombard.

The Chief reflected that the people of the North were decidedly slow-witted.

'Certainly not,' he replied. 'But there's a price for everything. From those who inherit a particular gift, nature withholds something else.'

'You Southerners,' said the agronomist. 'Always philosophizing.'

'Be careful,' the Chief continued. 'Talented people have no hearts. Marietta has a hard look about her. She'll own you ...'

'These girls brought up the hard way on your big southern estates make good housekeepers,' replied the agronomist.

The Law was definitely taking a pleasant turn. Seven games already, and the cards still hadn't made Tonio chief. And no one had chosen him as deputy. For The Law to be agreeable there had to be a victim, clearly designated, whom fate and the players could hound till he was exhausted; only thus did this poor man's game become as exciting as a hunt or a bullfight — still more exciting, the victim being a man.

For the eighth game the proprietor gave Tonio credit: he had already lost his two hundred lire and ten more besides. The cards were slow to reveal themselves and for a moment it seemed probable that don Cesare's servant would win. This would have been a matter for regret. Not that it need inevitably be regretted that fate should suddenly change its humour and begin to favour the victim. The turning of the tables can sometimes have piquant consequences. It all depends on the quality of the victim. When Matteo Brigante or Pizzaccio, after a long spell of losing, suddenly found themselves in a position to dictate The Law, the memory, still rankling, of the humiliations they had received gave fire to their natural spite and multiplied its resources; as when a bull of character which you think is finished suddenly charges, going for the man's body; there is no finer sight. But Tonio, by the eighth game, was already too mortified to raise much of a charge; by nature he was sly; but he had lost the cool-headedness which the best sly touches demand; concern over money, the idea of being in debt, also helped to weigh him down; had he won at this late hour, he would not have been able to carry victory to the point of annihilating the enemy, as should a good general and a good player at The Law. Luckily the cards finally pronounced for don Ruggero, who was proclaimed chief. He was beginning to take an interest in the game and appointed Matteo Brigante deputy, considering him the most vicious of his companions.

Tonio stood up.

'I owe you forty lire ...' he said to the proprietor.

He pushed back his chair and strode towards the door.

'... I'll pay you back next time.'

'He's running out on us,' cried Pizzaccio. 'He's got no guts.'

'Good night all,' said Tonio.

'Tonio!' shouted don Ruggero.

Tonio was already half out of the door.

'What do you want?' he asked don Ruggero.

'You haven't the right to leave,' said don Ruggero.

'You'd better listen to him,' said the proprietor to Tonio. 'He'll be a lawyer before long. He knows what he's talking about.'

'You haven't the right to leave,' continued don Ruggero, 'because you haven't fulfilled your part of the contract.'

There was a murmur of approval. Don Ruggero was getting the game off to an elegant start.

'Listen to me,' pursued don Ruggero. 'You're don Cesare's confidential man. Suppose you engaged a boy for him. You and the boy make a verbal contract with one another. You see what I'm driving at?'

Tonio listened with knitted brows, a set look on his face.

'Under the terms of this verbal agreement,' pursued don Ruggero, 'you haven't the right to dismiss the boy without notice. But neither has the boy the right to leave his job without notice. Do you agree?'

'Yes,' said Tonio, with hesitation.

'By starting the game, you made a verbal agreement with us. You haven't the right to leave without notice.'

'I don't feel up to it,' said Tonio. 'Good night all.'

But he hesitated to take the final stride.

Don Ruggero made a sweeping gesture with his arm.

'I call you all as witness. Don Cesare's confidential man is setting an example for breaking an agreement without notice.'

'Good night all,' repeated Tonio. But he still hesitated.

'I withdraw my credit,' said the proprietor. 'I don't give credit to a man who doesn't respect his agreements.'

'Here's a new situation,' proclaimed don Ruggero.

He shot out of his chair, went up to Tonio and put his hand on his shoulder.

'When one isn't allowed credit, one has to pay before leaving. Give him the forty lire you owe him.'

'I haven't got any money,' said Tonio.

'A clear case of sponging. This is a job for the courts.'

There was a renewed murmur of approval and some applause. A law student, when he was prepared to take the trouble, could add some neat trimmings to the game of The Law.

'It's true,' cried the Australian. 'I saw it happen one day in Foggia. The chap hadn't paid for his meal. The proprietor called the police and they arrested him.'

'I don't want to be awkward,' said the proprietor. 'If he promises to stay till the end of the game, I'll give him back his credit.'

They applauded the proprietor. They surrounded Tonio. They pushed him towards the table.

'You've got me,' he kept saying. 'I know you've got me.'

But he returned to his seat.

'You'll stand me a glass?' the Australian at once asked Matteo Brigante, the deputy.

'That depends,' replied Brigante. 'First let's see what your answers are like.'

'Go ahead and ask ...'

'I'd like to know why it is that Tonio can't take a joke.'

'Marietta's got under his skin.'

'A good answer. But tell me: why should Marietta get under his skin?'

'I was looking at her the other day, when I went to pick up supplies from don Cesare's fishermen. She'd got nothing on under her frock. The sweat was making the material stick to her skin. You could see the lot — breasts like lemons, a behind like a pair of pomegranates.'

'What does Tonio want from Marietta? That's what I'd like to know.'

'Her virginity,' replied the Australian. 'But Tonio isn't the only one who's after Marietta's virginity.'

'Who'll get it, do you think?'

'Don Cesare,' replied the Australian.

'No,' said Matteo Brigante.

'I tell you it will be don Cesare,' repeated the Australian.

'No,' Brigante repeated violently.

The Australian was insistent. Don Cesare was one of the real old noblemen. No one had ever heard of his not having the virginity of a girl from his household. His father, too, had been a real bull of an overlord. His grandfather the same. Certainly don Cesare was seventy-two now; but his mistress, Elvira, didn't complain. A family in which the men had always remained bulls up to a ripe old age. At eighty his grandfather had still been enjoying the girls of the marsh.

The Australian spoke with a kind of jubilation. Quite a number of drinkers had gradually grouped themselves around the table. The café was full. The jubilation spread to everyone. They repeated: 'An old bull! An old goat!' It was as though don Cesare's virility brought honour to the whole gathering.

'You gave the wrong answer,' said Matteo Brigante. 'You shan't have any wine.'

'You'll stand me a glass?' asked the American in his turn.

'First tell me who will get Marietta's virginity …'

'I know the answer to that,' said the American. 'My olives are on the edge of the marsh. I don't miss a thing. I know what don Cesare's women plan to do with Marietta's virginity.'

'Tell us.'

'Marietta is for the agronomist.'

'You're lying,' said Matteo Brigante.

He had drunk a good deal of wine since the start of the game, having been almost continually chief or deputy. His play now lacked finesse. This was not necessarily regrettable; there came a time, during a really animated game, when brutality brought a satisfying vigour to The Law. Most of the onlookers, too, had been drinking heavily; the laughter and the exclamations were growing louder.

The American related how Marietta's mother and her two sisters, Maria and Elvira, had lured the agronomist. Marietta was going to work for him. He wouldn't be able to keep his hands off the lemons and the pomegranates.

'Has Marietta got hooves, then?' asked don Ruggero.

54

There was an enormous laugh. The erection of the model pen had convinced the whole town that the agronomist shared the tastes of the men of the marsh. He was lodging his mistresses in a palace.

The onlookers imitated the bleating of the goat; each had his own way of bleating. Some scraped the ground with their feet, like the male goat when he is about to charge. Others lowered their heads and sketched imaginary horns in the air with their hands. No one now paid any attention to Tonio. Marietta was a splendid little she-goat. One character leaning across a corner of the table was waggling his rump and calling Marietta's name at every start. At this there was no end to the laughing and bleating.

When they had calmed down a little:

'You gave the wrong answer,' said Brigante to the American. 'You shan't have any wine.'

They booed Matteo Brigante.

'You'll stand me a glass?' asked Pizzaccio.

He smiled, looking very sure of himself.

'Tell us what your findings are?' asked Brigante.

'It's not don Cesare who will rape Marietta. Nor will it be the agronomist. It will be you, Matteo Brigante.'

They booed Pizzaccio. He was too servile with his chief-in-real-life. It was no longer a game.

'You have given a good answer,' Matteo Brigante said firmly.

They booed again.

Brigante filled a glass and offered it to Pizzaccio.

'If you like,' he said, 'you can ask me for a second glass of wine, for a third, for the whole jug if you like ...'

The booing redoubled. The café became a riot.

Brigante hammered his fist on the table.

'Listen to me,' he shouted.

It took some time to restore silence.

'Listen to me,' he went on, 'I'm going to tell you how I, Matteo Brigante, go about raping a virgin.'

There was a great silence.

Brigante bent towards Tonio.

'Listen carefully,' he said. 'I'm going to give yoú a lesson. But you won't be able to make use of it. You've got no guts.'

Attention fastened for a moment on Tonio, the victim selected by The Law. But it returned at once to Matteo Brigante who was now on his feet.

'Let's suppose,' he began, 'that Marietta was standing there, by the table ...'

He gave a clear, detailed and precise account of what each of them dreamed of accomplishing.

Tonio had turned as white as his freshly starched white jacket. Some of the characters were watching him out of the corner of their eyes, ready to collar him. But he made no move, all eyes for Brigante's mime.

Brigante was particularly insistent about the brutality with which he would rupture the hymen. Since he was thin, hard-boned and wiry, this was all the more impressive.

Tonio stared at him with the vacant expression of people watching television.

'And that's it,' concluded Brigante.

The silence was prolonged a moment more, and then the applause exploded. Several onlookers took their turn at miming the gestures of raping. Others began to bleat again; the bleats became ear-splitting. Still others clashed their heads together, miming the struggle of two male goats for the possession of a female.

Matteo Brigante returned to his seat, facing Tonio. He filled a glass with wine and offered it to him.

'Go ahead and drink,' he said.

Tonio took the glass, in silence, and emptied it at a gulp.

The Australian shuffled the cards for the ninth game. Tonio made no move to go.

'I'll give you credit,' the proprietor told him.

Tonio made no reply; he took the cards the Australian was dealing.

★ ★ ★

In the big downstairs room of the house with the colonnades, don Cesare, sitting in his usual armchair, had been staring all evening at a terracotta statuette which his fishermen had brought back for him and which he had stood on the table, in the light of the oil-lamp.

At the other end of the table, a long, massive table made of olive wood, the women of the household, old Julia and her three daughters, Maria, Elvira and Marietta, were conversing excitedly, in the light of another oil-lamp.

The women were sitting on benches, on both sides of the table, don Cesare in the big eighteenth-century Neapolitan armchair with the grotesquely carved gilt elbow-rests. This armchair and the light tones of the massive olive-wood table gave the room an air of pomp; don Cesare received his visitors here, since the rooms on the first floor were given over entirely to his collection of antiques.

In the shadows at the end of the room rose a monumental fireplace, of the kind they built in the North, a fantasy constructed by order of don Cesare's father, at the end of the last century. It was here the women cooked the meals, over a charcoal brazier, as in houses where there was no fireplace.

Don Cesare stared at the terracotta statuette standing in the light of the oil-lamp, a dancer with slender hips, whose slimness was accentuated by the hang of the tunic.

The women talked loud; they knew don Cesare paid no attention to what they said. For years now it had seemed likely that he no longer heard them. But sometimes, when they were shouting too much, he would strike the table with the flat of his hand and say:

'Women!'

They stopped. Soon they were whispering, then their voices grew louder, then they were shouting again, and he seemed not to notice.

When don Cesare, breaking with the fascist regime, resigned his commission in 1924, he was forty. He undertook the writing of the history of Uria, the prosperous Greek city, a colony of

Athens, built in the third century B.C. between the lake and the sea, where the marsh was today. His father before him, rebelling against the Bourbons of Naples, and his great-uncle, Archbishop of Benevento, who had been in disgrace for holding out against the terrible Pope Annibale della Genga, had started collecting and classifying the antiques found by the fishermen of the marsh and the labourers in the olive groves.

At the beginning of his retirement, don Cesare lived in the family palace in Calalunga, the little town perched on the crest of the rocky plateau which screened Porto Manacore from the land winds. Both father and son were liberal monarchists, in the freemason traditions of the House of Savoy. The father was quick enough to join the ranks of fascism. The two men hardly spoke to one another after the signing of the Concordat; for don Cesare, Mussolini, by coming to terms with the Pope, and the king, by allowing him to do so, had betrayed the great work of liberation undertaken by Victor Emmanuel II, Garibaldi and Cavour. He moved down to the house on the marsh, bringing with him a share of the antiques. He sent for everything that had been written on the subject of Greek colonization in southern Italy. He had been a keen student in Naples and read French and English fluently; he learned German in order to read Münch and Todt who were authorities of the Hellenistic era. During the first years he accumulated an enormous number of notes. He drew up a map of Uria. The terrace of the house with the colonnades had been the site of the agora. The Greek city was dedicated to Venus. The temple of the goddess rose on a rounded, rocky hillock at the mouth of the outlet of the lake. Don Cesare made excavations. The lake had been a large port.

When his father died, he continued to live on the marsh, to which he had grown thoroughly acclimatized. He fished, hunted and drank with the men of his household; he paid handsomely for the antiques they brought him. The men pretended not to know that he made love to their daughters and sisters; to get them into the house, he always made a pretext of work: washing, sewing, maize to be sifted, figs to be dried; in this way was the men's honour spared. When the girl continued to please him after the first night, he took her on as a servant; no one ever blackmailed him, because it was in the tradition of the lords of the marsh of Uria to show affection to the girls and women of their household. When a girl no longer pleased him, he married her off. He retained Julia after marrying her off because she was a good cook and because her husband took great care of the antiques; entrusted with the upkeep of the collection, he did not break a single piece, in ten years. Later he retained her because of her daughters.

He spent only a fortnight each year in the palace at Calalunga, just long enough to go through the books with the stewards of his estates. Wood formed a large part of his revenue; he owned most of the forest surrounding the rocky crest behind Porto Manacore. The olive groves and the orange and lemon orchards were scattered about the intermediate hills, the foothills of the mountain; he sold the crops when they were still standing, at the first blossom, to agents from Foggia who took over the risk of bad weather; certainly they fixed their prices so as to cover themselves against the wrath of the heavens; but don Cesare profited by not having to worry his head with business for the rest of the year. With the assistance of his 'confidential man', he personally managed the fishing in the lake and on the marsh; their yield was meagre, but they provided his hunting ground, his fishing ground, his pleasure ground.

As time passed and collusion spread, the stewards and the agents robbed him more and more. He did not care very much, not having the commitments of the landowners who spent part of their year in Rome or abroad. There was plenty left for the hunting and the antiques. He paid the contractors who did the excavating and the families of his mistresses with oil and corn, the dues from his stewards. The girls were content with baubles and the pride of rearing their families. So don Cesare found himself comfortably off, though robbed on a large scale. People respected him, even though they robbed him, because they knew that he knew that he was being robbed. He was not gullible, but magnanimous; to maintain this conviction, he had a habit of evicting one of his stewards from time to time, choosing at random; the man went and took his place among the unemployed, along the walls of the main square in Porto Manacore.

The palace at Calalunga had been an oil store in the seventeenth century, when don Cesare's ancestors had pressed olives for the whole region and had made enough money out of it to buy up their clients' estates one after another. It was a large building, far less noble in appearance than the villa on the marsh, which had been built round about 1830 with the colonnades fashionable at the time. The palace was perched right on top of the town, in a small square between an austere Romanesque church and a group of houses which had belonged to merchants at the time when Calalunga had been a centre of commerce. The millstone presses installed in the cellars had been out of use for a long time, the agents having installed a mechanical oil-mill with Diesel engines in the new square at the foot of the town. In the sales rooms on the ground floor, the fifty-litre clay jars were still ranged side by side, empty now — 'the statues of my ancestors,' said don Cesare when he entertained visitors in his palace. Three habitable floors, Venetian drawing-rooms, an English dining-room, French bedrooms, and a connecting attic on a level with the bell-tower, from which you could survey the whole region.

Every year, a few days before don Cesare's arrival, the managers of the estates sent their wives to clean out the palace. They took the dust-sheets from the armchairs, they washed, they swept, they dusted; the managers' families, their friends and their friends' friends came to look over the palace, exclaiming over the furniture; specially admired was the eighteenth-century Neapolitan room, with the huge mirrors in gilt frames, dating from the period of Chinese curios and giant grotesques. (The rich men of Naples had imitated the tax-farmers, in a bigger way, on the same scale as their palaces.) It was an armchair from this room that don Cesare had sent down to the marsh, after the death of his father.

During the fortnight he spent in Calalunga each year, don Cesare received his relations, offspring of junior branches who had not inherited estates, or only small estates, lawyers, teachers, doctors, chemists, especially lawyers. They came from Calalunga and the neighbouring towns, bringing their whole families with them. Don Cesare received them in the big Venetian drawing-room, into which he had introduced, just for himself, an English armchair; he made the others sit on uncomfortable chairs with hard, painted wooden backs, apart from a niece or a grand-niece, if she happened to be pretty, who sat on a stool at his feet.

Some years after the death of his father, when it had become quite clear he would not marry and when each relative could entertain hopes of being chosen as heir, he had entertained himself with their servility. He obliged the fascist bigwig to tell him the party dirt: Ciano's indiscretions, the Duce's sex-life. He interjected his narrative with graphic southern obscenities. He compelled the bigots to blaspheme.

'Now then, aunt, when are you going to bring this nun along for me? Come on, admit you'd be very glad to see me make a cuckold of the Holy Ghost!'

'Yes, nephew.'

'Admit you'd be very glad ...'

'I'd be very glad, nephew ...'

'To see me make a cuckold of the Holy Ghost,' he insisted.

'To see you make a cuckold, nephew ...'

'Of the Holy Ghost,' he insisted.

'Of the Holy Ghost,' the bigot repeated after him.

Everyone laughed.

That had been before the Second World War. Today don Cesare received his relatives in silence; he knew that human servility had no limits.

At the time when he was still not completely convinced, he used to touch the girls' thighs, in front of their parents sitting erect in the uncomfortable Venetian chairs; he felt the breasts and the buttocks; he appraised, gauged, judged with crude words. The fathers and brothers discreetly left their places and pre-tended to chat by the window, backs to the room, so that their honour did not compel them to intervene. The mothers cried:

'Ah, don Cesare! You don't change a bit. You'll never get old ...'

The girls concealed their annoyance less completely. If he had manœuvred them into an empty room, on some reasonable pretext, they would not have been offended; their whole up-bringing had schooled them to be flattered by men's desire, the one chance of escaping from that failure of life, spinsterhood. But it was a deliberate insult to finger them in public, like goats in a market place. Some blushed, others turned pale, according to temperament, but they did not make a scene; some for fear of maternal reprimand, others so as not to offend their fathers or their brothers by raising, when it was the men's place to do so and they were doing nothing about it, the question of honour, an entirely male province.

But one day one of the great-nieces got angry. It was im-mediately after the war, when the chaos of the successive occupa-tions and liberations gave girls new ideas of liberty and dignity. She freed herself violently.

'Dirty old swine!' she cried.

Don Cesare was enchanted beyond expression. He silenced the mother, who was accusing the girl of misinterpreting the paternal caresses of her great-uncle; she must (the mother said) have a very depraved imagination. On his return to the house with the colonnades he gave orders for her to be sent to him, to help him classify his antiques.

For a whole month he did not speak a word to her, except to explain the classification and labelling, the card index system. The girl, who had been a student of sorts, did not acquit herself at all badly; she did nothing to disturb the order of the collec-tions; but she did not ask a single question about the ancient city of Uria. He had a hundred stories ready; he had begun to have dreams of an intelligent assistant. She worked mechanically ten hours a day, on the first floor or in the attic, under the roof where the August sun, the lion-sun, flung its hottest beams. The rest of the time, Julia, Maria (it was then her reign), Elvira (who still had her husband) and even Marietta (who would soon be seven,

62

the age of reason) tormented her in every conceivable way; they polluted her food and they swore at her under their breath about the house, but worse things happened to her than that; every night she found on her bed, as a clear warning, a Carrara onion. The juice of a Carrara onion enflames the mucous membranes, makes them swell, sets fire to the whole body, and can even, they say, lead to death; it is inflicted like love; *I'll mate you with a Carrara onion* — the most feared of threats; it was the punishment inflicted on girls who upset happy homes. The Carrara onion flowered large and white among the dunes, an innocent perfumed star.

At night the girl heard bare feet running about the corridor, scratching on the door, the sound of women whispering.

One evening she went into don Cesare's bedroom, without knocking, silent, white in her white nightdress. He took her without pleasure and next day sent her home to her parents.

It was about this time that he gave up looking for any limit to human servility.

The grand-niece who had not preserved her pride, as he had hoped she would (and who had shown no interest in the noble city of Uria), counted less than political events. At the time of the liberation he had hoped for a reawakening of Italy; but the government of the priests had succeeded that of Mussolini, a change which brought, in his opinion, no improvement for human dignity.

In the early days of his voluntary exile he had evolved a philosophy of history. Every *uomo di cultura* in southern Italy evolved his personal philosophy of history. The kings triumphed over the Pope, the people overthrew the kings, but let power slip back into the hands of the priests; following the Italian model he had reconstructed the history of the world: the theocratic age, the heroic age and the democratic age engendering one another in a perpetual cycle. The heroic age was the age of kings and the high point of the system. The tyrants, false heroes of the common people, paved the way for the priests' return to power; Mussolini signing the Concordat, for example. Don Cesare's ideas had been moulded by reading Giambattista Vico, the eighteenth-century Neapolitan philosopher and precursor of Hegel and Nietzsche. Vico proclaimed the era of the hero-kings. It had been short-lived in Italy. Don Cesare was born on the wrong slope of the *perpetual cycle*. The plebiscite of 1946 and the proclamation of the Italian republic finally put paid to his hopes; Umberto, by leaving for Portugal, had left the door open for the mob and the priests.

Rome had already gone through the same thing; for don Cesare, the decline of Rome had begun with the end of the Punic Wars and Augustus had been the first of the Italian Popes. It was in the time of Augustus that Uria's harbour had begun to silt up. Don Cesare gave up reading the newspapers.

From then on, when representatives of the liberal monarchist party came to him for money, he made them sit down on the bench facing him as he reclined in the eighteenth-century Neapolitan armchair. He observed them through narrowed eye-lids. He listened to them in silence, without a word of approval or disapproval.

He had put on a little weight, but he was not corpulent. Tall, always very erect, rather thick-jowled. The face expressionless, apart from this attentive screwing up of the eye. Smooth cheeks; he shaved carefully every morning with the cut-throat razor which dated from his youth. The white hair neatly cut and combed; a barber came down from Calalunga twice a month. He sat there, in his armchair with the grotesque elbow-rests, motion-less, massive, attentive, in ponderous expectation of an event which he knew was never to happen. He behaved exactly as he did this evening, staring at a terracotta statuette his fishermen had brought back for him, while at the other end of the olive-wood table, the women of his household quarrelled in voices which grew louder and louder. The party representatives were forced to wonder whether it was really to themselves and to what they were saying that he was so attentive.

When they had said their piece, he held out to them without a word the envelope which he had sealed in advance. They left

64

stammering thanks, excuses, promises. Tonio accompanied them to the perron, and from the first step cried:

'Long live the King, gentlemen!'

They patted him on the back and gave him a tip, saying:

'Don Cesare is lucky to have a confidential man like you.'

They knew that Tonio was more a valet than a confidential man and that, furthermore, he voted Communist like all the working people in Manacore. But they said it for the sake of saying something — anything to efface the silence of don Cesare.

There he sat, in the light of the oil-lamp, massive, wedged in his armchair, his arms resting flat on the carved elbow-rests, staring at the Greek statuette, his eyes slightly screwed up in concentration.

The women were trying to persuade Marietta to go into service with the agronomist.

It was a week since the man had made his request and he would be back for an answer any day now. Julia had warned him that she would have to get don Cesare's approval. She had not foreseen that Marietta would turn down the chance she was being offered.

Marietta persisted in saying no. She wouldn't go and work for the Lombard with the blond hair. And if he came and asked for her again, she would send him packing straight back to his goats.

Julia had feared a refusal from don Cesare. Several times she had caught the old man's glance resting on her youngest, heavy and calculating; no doubt he wanted her for himself, as he had had the others. But don Cesare had smiled his ghost of a smile, his impish smile of the old days.

Marietta didn't want to go.

Her sisters described the model pen over which she would reign. The Palace of the Thousand and One Goats. Automatic troughs, mechanical milking machines, hoses to wash out the stalls, engine-driven mixing machines. People came to look at it from all over the province of Foggia, and even from Naples. They imagined Marietta reigning, receiving as a queen, distributing gifts; neither to her mother nor her sisters nor herself had it

E

occurred that by seeking her as a servant the agronomist might be taking the word 'servant' in its literal sense. To work as a servant was the honourable, accepted pretext. They had understood that the agronomist wanted Marietta for his bed but had no intention of marrying her; and they had immediately set up their counter-batteries so that he should have her — they had actually led him on — but should either be compelled to marry her or else pay dearly for her.

The Lombard had a Fiat Mille Cento, like the Chief of Police.

'He'll take you to Bologna,' said Elvira.

(It was the Bolognese, more than anyone else, who came hunting for duck on the marshes. For the Manacoreans, Bologna was the dream city of the North.)

'When I was young,' said Julia, 'don Cesare promised to take me to Bologna.'

'Me too,' said Maria. 'Don Cesare promised me a trip to Bologna. There are arcades you can walk under from one end of the town to the other.'

'Me too,' said Elvira. 'He's promised to take me there. It's a town where you can walk in the rain for hours without getting wet.'

'The agronomist will take Marietta there,' Maria went on. 'He'll do whatever she wants. She's got him under her spell.'

But Marietta shook her head. She no longer bothered to answer her mother and her sisters. She wasn't going to the agronomist's. She sat encased in her silence, as determined as that of don Cesare.

Each of the three women thought of the benefits of which Marietta's refusal was depriving her. Maria of the gifts a well-off lover showered on his mistress's family. Elvira of the removal of a rival who had reached an age to take her place beside don Cesare. Julia of the opportunity of stirring up the whole town against the man until he bowed to the law.

'If Marietta says no to the agronomist,' said old Julia, 'it's because she's got someone else.'

66

'I'm asking myself who it is she's got,' said Maria. 'Perhaps it's my Tonio?'

Elvira had moved next to Marietta. She looked her straight in the face and said:

'Tell us who it is!'

Marietta gave the ghost of a smile and said nothing.

'She's got someone!' repeated the three women.

They jumped to their feet and surrounded the girl.

'Tell us who it is!'

Elvira pinched her arm above the elbow, viciously, twisting the skin. Maria grabbed her wrist to twist it. Old Julia tugged at her hair.

'Tell us who it is!'

Marietta struck out to free herself. A butt with the head for her mother, a jab of the elbow for her sister. She got free, ran round the table and sat down near don Cesare's armchair, on the stool on which he sometimes rested his feet.

Don Cesare listened to the girl gradually gathering her breath.

The women screamed. Elvira had taken her sister's elbow on the chest; she was going to die of cancer of the breast, like don Ottavio's wife. Julia had a bleeding lip; her daughter had tried to kill her.

Don Cesare struck the table with the flat of his hand. The women stopped screaming and took cover among the shadows of the great fireplace at the end of the room. Marietta sat on the stool with her head cupped in her hands and kept watch on her mother and her two sisters, over the tops of don Cesare's knees.

The girl's breathing gradually steadied.

Don Cesare stared at the Greek statuette in the light of the oil-lamp.

In the shadows of the fireplace, at the other end of the room, the three women were whispering hurriedly. They were plotting a way to get their hands on Marietta, who had tried to kill her mother.

★ ★ ★

Matteo Brigante brought the game of The Law to an end; he had to go and control the ball. Besides, the pleasure had gone out of the game the moment Tonio had agreed to down the cup of his humiliation. Afterwards don Cesare's confidential man had lost another six games and run up a debt of two hundred and twenty lire, but people were not interested in him any longer. Fate should have chosen another victim. Perhaps not. Like tragedy, The Law demanded unity of action. Skilled players knew that it was best to stop playing when the victim had been thoroughly disposed of.

Tonio left the café and made his way up to the main square to collect the Lambretta.

Beneath King Murat's pine, Giuseppina was beginning a boogie-woogie with the Roman. Francesco, Matteo Brigante's son, gave the band a good, clear beat to follow. The trumpeter went into solos in the style of New Orleans. The Roman, despite his disdainful pout of a Caesar of the Byzantine Empire, found no cause for complaint in either the jazz band or his dancing partner. The Manacoreans were a city people; they had been a city people in the fourth century B.C., when Porto Manacore had competed with Uria, the city of Venus.

The Chief of Police had just taken leave of the agronomist. He went up to the green barrier and stood looking at the dancers. Sweat made Giuseppina's dress stick to the shoulders. The Chief saw, through the Roman's eyes, the dress sticking to the shoulders with sweat. He turned away and walked towards the other end of the square, the part which the big, pale blue electric lamps lit less violently.

The inhabitants of the Old Town stood about in groups and watched the ball from a distance. The tourists walked about the terrace in twos and threes, waiting for the sea breeze which never came. The *guaglioni*, the gang of youths led by Pippo and Balbo, roared round, tearing out of a side-street, cutting through the holiday-makers like buck-shot. The police stood with their hunting crops in their hands, keeping an eye on the *guaglioni*.

The Chief arrived at the darker side of the square and found

68

himself face to face with Tonio who had come for his Lambretta.

'Good evening, signor maresciallo,' said Tonio.

'Good evening,' said the Chief.

Tonio acted without premeditation. The words formed in his head at the sight of the Chief of Police. The Chief was not even looking at him: he had replied absentmindedly to his 'good evening'; he was staring over Tonio's head at the pale blue lamps of the ball.

'The morning the Swiss had his wallet stolen,' Tonio began, 'someone went on to the isthmus ... He reached it from the sea, by diving in from the top of the rocks where don Cesare is making his excavations ... he swam up the outlet of the lake ... quite a swimmer; when he was young they nicknamed him Master of the Sea ... he came out on the dune two hundred yards downstream from the bridge, in the shelter of the bamboos; that was how nobody came to see him ...'

'Except you,' said the Chief.

'Except me,' replied Tonio. 'I was up on the roof, putting the figs out to dry. From the roof you can see over the top of the bamboos.'

'And this only came back to you this evening?'

'I didn't dare tell you about it ... He's a dangerous man ... Matteo Brigante ...'

The Chief took a long look at Tonio, a little man, looking far too thin in the white jacket which was no longer fresh, a yellowed, malarial complexion, bilious eyes.

'Matteo Brigante,' repeated Tonio.

Chief of Police Attilio had a feeling of sadness.

'Now look,' he said, 'Marietta has ...'

'Marietta didn't see anything,' cried Tonio.

'Listen,' continued the Chief, 'Marietta has got under your skin.'

'I tell you it was Matteo Brigante who did the job!'

'Seeing her all day, waggling her behind, and not being able to touch her, that's what has got hold of you ...'

'I recognized Matteo Brigante even before he left the water ...

'I knew it was him by the way he was swimming ... He's got a very individual way of swimming ... anyone will tell you that ...'

'So,' continued the Chief, 'Matteo is after Marietta, too?'

'He came out of the water just on the other side of the bamboos and then slipped behind the rosemary bushes.'

'You saw him,' the Chief cut in. 'Perhaps he was on his way to meet your Marietta. But it wasn't the morning of the robbery.'

'The morning of the robbery,' repeated Tonio. 'I saw him, I swear I did.'

The Chief looked sadly at Tonio.

'The morning of the robbery,' he said, 'Matteo was in Foggia on business. I've checked.'

'I am ready to swear in court,' said Tonio, 'that I saw Matteo Brigante on the isthmus, the morning of the robbery.'

People had begun to stand round them in a circle, though at a distance. They wondered what don Cesare's Tonio could be talking about to the Chief of Police. Tonio had to gasp to get the words out, but spoke almost in a whisper. Pippo, the leader of the *guaglioni*, and Balbo, his lieutenant, eased themselves into the front row of onlookers.

'The thought of someone else pawing her about makes you feel brave,' said the Chief.

'But since I swear I saw him in the bushes, creeping towards the car ...'

'Go back to your Marietta,' said the Chief.

He made to walk away. Tonio planted himself in front of him and brought him to a halt.

'You'd think,' cried Tonio, 'you'd think it was Matteo Brigante who ran the law in Manacore!'

'Braver and braver,' murmured Chief of Police Attilio.

But he noticed the crowd which had formed around them, with Pippo and Balbo in the front row. He seized Tonio by the shoulders, spun him round and pushed him towards the Lambretta.

70

'*Vai via becco cornuto!*' he shouted at him, loud enough for everyone to hear. 'Clear off, you stupid little cuckold!'

Tonio reeled away and clutched the Lambretta.

The Chief strode away towards the pale blue lamps of the ball. The band was taking a rest. Francesco Brigante was explaining a new gimmick to his colleagues of the jazz circle of Porto Manacore. Giuseppina had sat down on the balustrade of the terrace which overlooked the harbour and the bay. The Roman was standing beside her, a pale blue jersey slung over his shoulders, the sleeves knotted round his neck in spite of the heat, because he had seen in a magazine that this was how jerseys were worn in St Tropez. Giuseppina was laughing, all red lips and feverish eyes. She was swinging her leg, and the lace of her three petticoats foamed beneath her dance frock. The Roman stood looking at her without smiling, his lips disdainful.

The Chief went up to the green barrier. Everyone was looking at him. Leading citizens saluted him. Wives of leading citizens smiled at him; he was a fine figure of a man, elegant, witty and gallant; people did not know yet that Giuseppina laid down the law to him. He turned away and went back into the court house.

Tonio was standing near the Lambretta. He told himself that in a few seconds he would be revving up the engine and driving through the night as fast as he liked; but the thought gave him no pleasure; for a moment he was surprised. He had a bitter taste in his mouth, as though he had smoked too much; this gave him a desire to smoke. He crossed the square and bought five cigarettes on credit in the tobacconist's, still open on account of the ball. As he came out of the shop he lit a cigarette.

The first wave of sickness hit him as he was standing right in the middle of the square. 'Has she got hooves, then?' don Ruggero had asked. 'You haven't the right, Tonio,' the proprietor had said. '*Becco cornuto,*' the Chief had just said. 'You gave the wrong answer,' Pizzaccio had said. 'This is how I go about it,' said Matteo Brigante. Tonio got as far as the Lambretta. He clung to the chromium-plated handlebars and vomited.

Two men who were passing saw him vomiting.

'Old Tonio's had a skinful. He must have had a run of luck at The Law.'

'He must have kept the whole jug for himself!'

'When you're not used to being chief ...'

Umberto II was driven from the throne. The grand-niece spent a month labelling the antiques without asking a single question about Uria. That same year the Bolognese came in such swarms to shoot on the lake that they massacred an immense number of duck. That was the year when don Cesare began to *lose interest*.

Superficially his habits had not changed. He had always spent his nights in a woman's company, now one, now another; he continued to do so; at the present time it was Elvira. At the end of the evening, when he got up to go to his bedroom on the first floor, Elvira rose as part of the same movement and detached herself from the other women; she followed him without a word. They undressed in silence. In bed, he assured himself that she was there by placing his hand on her breast or pressing his leg against hers; when he turned over in his sleep he sought her again, without waking; he felt the need to touch some part of her; things had been like this since he was twenty, in 1904; to sleep, he had always needed a woman beside him. But he never spoke to Elvira. He still took her sometimes, though more and more infrequently, and now always in silence, in the dark; she wondered whether he knew it was she, Elvira, that he was taking. Things had been like this since he had *lost interest*.

He still went out shooting and he always brought back a good deal of game, despite the Bolognese. He was a fine shot, age had made no difference to that, and he knew the marsh, the dunes and the hills better than the people of his household. But he no longer swore when he brought down a fine bird; his face did not even light up; he killed like a butcher in the slaughterhouse. For some years Tonio had accompanied him, carrying the game-bag and the second gun, without pleasure, with a kind of terror, as though he were in service with a statue, a huge statue which would march unendingly, with the same long, mechanical stride, through the bamboos and the reeds, the rosemaries on the dunes and the pines on the hills. Tonio imagined confusedly that the punishments of Purgatory were of this order; not of Hell, but of Purgatory, this same endless march in the service of a statue. Or Limbo, perhaps.

With the stewards, the agents or the rare visitors who came as far as the house with the colonnades, don Cesare had preserved the habits of other days. But his words resounded in a world without echo; his movements sketched themselves in an area without substance. Mention of a visit to the marsh produced thoughts of Limbo. This was the way things had been since he had *lost interest*.

Don Cesare had lost interest, the way the idle had lost their jobs. It was not their fault, and it was not his. He did not feel so very different from the unemployed who hung about all day, standing along the walls of the main square in Porto Manacore; but he did not even have the hope of something happening which would put him back in a job. In hope, too, he had *lost interest*.

With his habit of making a philosophy of history, he sometimes asked himself why he had *lost interest*, he, don Cesare, on the verge of the second half of the twentieth century, on the marsh of Uria. He asked himself this without attaching any further significance to it, because he had preserved the habit of asking himself questions, as he had preserved all his other habits.

Between 1904 and 1914, between his twentieth and his thirtieth years, he had travelled throughout Europe, during the university vacations, to complete his education, in accordance with his father's wishes. One summer, returning from London and on his way to Valencia where he was to embark for Naples, he had stayed for a time in Portugal. He had asked himself a thousand

73

questions about the decline of this nation whose empire had extended all the way round the globe. He had come to know writers who wrote for nobody; politicians who governed for the British; businessmen who wound up their businesses in Brazil and lived aimlessly, on small incomes, in provincial towns. He had thought it the worst of misfortunes to be born a Portuguese. In Lisbon, for the first time in his life, he had made the acquaintance of a people who had *lost interest*.

Today he reflected that it had been the turn of the Italians, the French and the English to *lose interest*. Interest had emigrated to the United States, Russia, China, India. He lived in a country which had *lost interest*, except superficially the provinces of the North; but it *was* only superficially — the Italians of the North, like the French, concealing their loss of interest with the noise of their cars and their scooters. The Italians and the French had begun to *portugalize* themselves after the Second World War. This was what he thought, without attaching very much interest to it.

Even the attention he continued to give to the antiques had changed its character. If he still preserved an interest in anything, it was in the antiques. You cannot *lose interest* absolutely, except in death, which amounts exactly to a total severing of bonds, an absolute loss of interest. So he continued to give attention to his collection and to the new pieces which were brought to him, as and when they happened to find them, by the men of his household and the labourers on the neighbouring estates. But he no longer made notes and he no longer wrote articles for the archaeological reviews. The manuscript of his great work on the city of Uria had been completed several years ago: one thousand five hundred pages of close writing, shut away in the drawer of a cabinet. He had never offered it to a publisher; he would have had to cut it, condense it, bring it into focus (for the good of whom and of what?) or else publish it at his own expense, six large quarto volumes, with illustrations, a few copies of a monumental study run off for specialists in the history of the Greek colonies in southern Italy in the Hellenistic era; the idea had attracted him, but not enough for him not to shrink from the tediousness of coming to terms with the printer, correcting the proofs, receiving strangers.

Every afternoon, between siesta and supper, he gave orders that he was not to be disturbed. People said he was working. He observed the vases, the oil-lamps, the statuettes, the coins displayed in the rooms on the first floor and in the attics, labelled and classified, as this evening he observed the statuette which his fishermen had brought in for him and which now stood on the long olive-wood table, in the light of the oil-lamp — with Marietta sitting at his feet, on the stool, her elbows on her knees and her face between her closed fists.

It can be said that he observed, although it is incorrect to use the active form of the verb to define his observation. It was not that don Cesare was passive in his attitude to the statuette. Not only did he see it, but he observed it, although his observation was not exactly active. He considered it, although his consideration was not exactly active. He considered the statuette and he considered at the same time all the other items in his collection, and he considered at the same time the whole town of Uria, the prosperous Hellenistic city of Uria re-emerging from the marsh, the agora on the terrace where the nets hung to dry, the white houses, the porticoes and the colonnades, the citizens who had not *lost interest* in anything which was happening in the world, that air of intelligence which vibrated in Ancient Greece, the fountains, the pitcher bearers, the harbour with the ships bringing merchandise from the orient, and the temple of Venus on the tip of the promontory, rising from the sea. But to say that he considered is not quite exact, the active form opposing the subject to the object, presupposing an influence by the subject over the object, whereas don Cesare had so *lost interest*, from one year to another, that he had become his own object; don Cesare confronting don Cesare considering the terracotta statuette and the intelligent city of Uria, but as foreign to don Cesare as to the terracotta statuette and to the dead city of Uria; without love, without hate, without any further desire either to love or to hate,

75

as destitute of any kind of desire as the deceased city of Uria. That was loss of interest.

Marietta, however, sitting at don Cesare's feet, was keeping a watch, over the tops of the old man's knees, on her mother and her two sisters, whispering in the shadows of the tall fireplace. The three women were plotting to get their hands on her as soon as don Cesare had left the room, to punish her for striking her mother and make her reveal the name of the man for love of whom she was refusing to go into service with the Lombard. Marietta was not greatly worried, fearing only Elvira, a strong woman in her thirties; now, Elvira would have to follow don Cesare up to his bedroom. But she remained on her guard, knowing that all three of them were sly.

Normally Marietta slept in the same room as old Julia, her mother. She counted on making her escape as soon as don Cesare was in his bedroom, and spending the night in the shed attached to one of the orange and lemon orchards. It wouldn't be the first time. She had often been obliged to run from the house so as to escape the women of the household.

Don Cesare rose, took the terracotta statuette and came round the table, making for the door which led out to the corridor. Elvira rose in the same movement, took the oil-lamp from the table near the armchair, and followed don Cesare. At the same moment, Maria went to the door which gave on to the perron, locked it and put the key in her pocket.

Marietta was unconcerned to see herself denied exit by way of the perron. She had planned to rush out into the corridor as soon as don Cesare and Elvira were in their room on the floor above. At the end of the corridor French windows opened on to a balcony supported by pilasters. That was where she would make her escape; more than once she had jumped from the balcony on to the terrace of the villa; her method was to hold on to one of the pilasters and let herself drop; she rebounded on her bare feet and was at once running down the paths, between the bamboos.

Don Cesare went out into the corridor, followed by Elvira with the oil-lamp. Old Julia, from the direction of the fireplace,

76

and Maria, from the direction of the perron door, advanced on Marietta, sitting on the stool at the foot of the monumental Neapolitan eighteenth-century armchair.

Marietta sat ready to make a run for it; but she was not worried. She was only really afraid of Elvira, who did not have children like Maria, who had the energy of young widows, a strong, swarthy woman who had wielded the flail like a man when her husband had farmed an arid mountain estate; he had left his bones up there. Marietta recalled Elvira with the flail in her hand, striking the threshing-floor, in a cloud of dust and noise, striking like a blacksmith, as she had seen her when she had been taken to her sister's home in the mountains at the age of eight.

The heavy stride of don Cesare, the wooden soles of Elvira receded slowly along the corridor. The heavy stride of don Cesare, the wooden soles of Elvira. There was a bend in the staircase and the sounds approached again, overhead now.

Maria advanced rapidly towards Marietta, who shot off the stool and began to dodge around the armchair. She wanted to avoid coming to grips with her sister. She was waiting to rush out into the corridor as soon as don Cesare and Elvira were in their room.

Don Cesare opened the bedroom door, Elvira's wooden soles behind him. Marietta dodged round the armchair again, Maria behind her.

The heavy stride of don Cesare reached the bedroom, immediately above the big ground-floor room. The wooden soles of Elvira advanced as far as the chest of drawers. Marietta thought Elvira was about to stand the oil-lamp on the chest of drawers.

But the wooden soles of Elvira had gone into reverse. There they were in the corridor. Hurrying, like castanets at the end of a dance. There they were on the stairs.

Mariette had run out into the corridor. But Elvira was there already, barring the way.

Elvira was bigger, more robust than Marietta; she had the strength of her maturity. She knocked Marietta back into the room, slapping her face with all her strength and jabbing her

77

knee into her stomach. Maria caught her and held her arms behind her. Old Julia closed the door, so that don Cesare should not hear.

The women had prepared the cords, in the shadows of the fireplace. Julia had hidden them under her skirt. They bound Marietta to the back of the chair, tying her ankles to the acanthus leaves on the legs, pulling her arms round in front of her and tying them to the grotesquely carved gilt elbow-rests. Thus the girl found herself doubled up, her face and breasts pressed against the rough material of the back of the chair, her buttocks in the air.

Elvira unhooked one of the shotguns attached to the wall. She unscrewed the steel cleaning rod.

Don Cesare was growing impatient; it was normally Elvira who got into bed first; or perhaps he had heard the slaps in the corridor. He stamped his foot loudly, several times, on the floor-boards of the bedroom, immediately above the ground-floor room.

Elvira approached the armchair, rod in hand. She raised her head towards the ceiling:

'The old man's getting irritable,' she said.

Don Cesare stamped again.

'Get irritable,' said Elvira. 'I'm going to take my time over marking the girl.'

The steel rod whistled through the air. Marietta was naked beneath the linen frock.

'For your mother,' said Elvira.

Marietta clenched her teeth.

'For me,' said Elvira.

'For your mother.'

'For me.'

Marietta let out a long groan. The rod cut again. The women heard the heavy stride of don Cesare, who had got out of bed and was heading for the door of his room.

Elvira hurriedly passed the rod to Maria.

'Your turn,' she said. 'Mark her for life.'

She ran towards the door.

78

They heard the wooden soles in the corridor, on the stairs. There was a long moment of silence. Elvira and don Cesare must be talking things over. Then they heard the heavy stride of don Cesare returning to his room.

Maria went up to Marietta, crucified across the heavy arm-chair with the gilt wood.

'And now,' she said, 'you are going to tell us your lover's name.'

Marietta clenched her teeth.

Maria took a step backwards. The rod cut again.

'I'll refresh your memory for you,' said Maria.

At that moment they heard the engine of the Lambretta, under the window.

'Tonio,' screamed Marietta. 'Tonio, help!'

'So you admit it's him,' cried Maria.

Tonio was in the room in a flash.

'Untie her,' he said.

In his shoes, facing the women in their bare feet, in his white, confidential man's jacket, facing the women, he felt very sure of himself.

'Quicker than that,' he said.

Julia protested that she had the right to thrash her daughter.

'Who lays down the law in this house?' demanded Tonio. 'The women?'

He added:

'I ought to go and wake don Cesare. He has forbidden beatings in his house. He'll throw you out ...'

The two women untied Marietta.

Marietta went and leaned against the wall, her elbows a little raised, her hands flat, ready to spring.

Julia and Maria stood in front of the armchair. They looked at Tonio.

'You haven't the right, Tonio,' the proprietor had said. 'You gave the wrong answer,' Pizzaccio had said. 'This is how I go about it,' Matteo Brigante had said.

'*Ecco*,' said Tonio. 'The youngster will keep the marks of the

79

rod for a long time ... I'll put you in your place, you vipers ...
And now, get to bed ...'

Marietta, crouched against the wall, began to laugh.

'It's you she's laughing at,' said Julia.

'Go to bed, you old hag,' cried Tonio.

The two women backed out of the room. Reaching the door:
'It's you she's laughing at, man,' repeated Julia.

Tonio slammed the door and was alone with Marietta. She was
still laughing.

Tonio went up to the girl.

'Now,' he said, 'now Marietta, you're going to give me a big
kiss ...'

'Yes,' said Marietta.

She took the stride which separated them.

She put her hands on Tonio's arms, whether out of tenderness
or to check his movements he did not immediately grasp.

She leaned forward and planted a kiss on his forehead.

He did not have time to realize what was happening. In a
flash she had made her escape, running on the tips of her bare
feet. Already she was on the perron. There she paused for a
moment.

'I really love you, Tonio,' she said. 'I really love you, you
know.'

She disappeared into the night.

As they came out of the café, Matteo Brigante invited Pizzaccio to take a glass of wine with him, at the ball. He paid their
entrance fee with a five-thousand lire note. The two men took a
table near the bar. Brigante ordered a bottle of Asti spumanti.

He ran his little eyes, with their hard expression, over the ball,
the square and the surroundings. He noted everything (in his
memory) in a split second. It was a habit he had preserved from
the time when he had been a bosun's mate in the Royal Navy and

which was very useful to him now that he controlled Porto Manacore.

A shutter moved, on the fourth floor of the court house. Donna Lucrezia was not asleep. The woman from Naples staying at the Belvedere Hotel was not at the ball; she was probably taking a stroll on the beach — who with? Giuseppina was dancing with the Roman — uninteresting. The secretary of the chair manufacturers' co-operative had brought his three daughters to the dance and was drinking French brandy — where had he got the money from?

Scanning the terrain, his terrain, the racketeer played with his grafting knife. A handsome tool, stamped with the trade mark of the *Due Buoi*, the Two Oxen, the best money could buy in the way of a grafting knife; the whole thing fitted into the palm of the hand; the handle was black and shiny, with copper pins set in the wood, broader at the base, shaped to suit the palm, comfortable. The retracted blade lay in the hollow of the handle, clean, smooth, brilliant, dangerous, as delightful to look at as an oyster in its shell, as luxurious as a pearl in its setting.

At a neighbouring table, a couple of tow-headed tourists were making eyes at the waiters. They had left their car, a Volkswagen with Bavarian registration plates, at the top of the new road which wound down to the beach. Brigante noted this (in his memory); he also controlled the arrangements which the waiters made with foreigners.

He gently released the blade of the grafting knife, then retracted it: it slid back into the handle with a firm snap. He loved the crispness of this noise, like the snapping of a young jaw.

Beyond the dance enclosure, Pippo and Balbo were leaning against the café railings. Pippo was looking at Matteo Brigante.

Pippo's trousers were holed, torn and tattered. Men, youths and *guaglioni*, everyone in the Old Town wore ragged trousers; patched rags, darned rags, rags of shame. Pippo wore his rags with glory, like the fringes of foam with which the old masters surrounded Venus. His shirt was a rag too, without buttons, not even knotted at the waist as many of the *guaglioni* were wearing

F   81

their shirts this year in imitation of the summer visitors. The shreds of his shirt flowed from his shoulders like the sash of St Michael the Archangel. His black hair fell in curls on his forehead. Sixteen years old, chief of the *guaglioni*, a fearless expression.

Balbo was ginger-headed, stocky and wore his rags neatly; when there was booty to be shared out, he apportioned the lots — he was the gang's bureaucrat. Pippo was watching Matteo Brigante, Balbo was surveying the square. When they were together, it was like a single head taking in the four points of the compass at a glance.

The other *guaglioni* had suddenly disappeared. The orchestra was taking a rest. The silence was oppressive. The youths' shouts had filled out the earlier interludes.

'The *guaglioni* are up to something,' said Brigante.

'They've gone home to bed,' said Pizzaccio.

'That Pippo is over there, like a captain on his bridge. He's getting ready for a job ...'

Brigante raised his finger and beckoned Pippo. He wanted to talk to him across the green barrier.

Pippo replied with a brief grimace, a distortion of the jaws, a wrinkling of the brows. Already he had assumed his impassive archangel's expression again.

Brigante turned his head away. Pizzaccio was exultant: Pippo's antics marked the limits of his chief's power. It was always pleasant to see his chief make a false move.

In the whole territory of Manacore, Pippo and his *guaglioni* were the only ones to escape the control of Matteo Brigante. One day battle would be joined: two gangs cannot coexist in the same territory. But at the present time the *guaglioni* were as elusive as the dust which rose from the floor when the men, or women like Elvira, threshed the corn. A tradesman because he owned a shop, a fisherman his boat, a driver his lorry, a pedlar his tricycle, a gardener his blossoming trees, a local celebrity a reputation, a civil servant a career, the unfortunate because they owned unfortunate wives could not escape the control of Matteo

82

Brigante. A man out of work who collected his dole from the town hall, a goatherd responsible for someone else's goats, a cripple who needed a hospital bed, a convict who wanted a message passed on had to pay their tax to Brigante. But the *guaglioni* owned nothing; the proceeds of their petty thefts were shared, eaten and smoked without delay; and they had as many hiding places as there were houses in Manacore, sheds on the marsh, huts on the hills; nobody noticed an extra boy in houses where they slept ten or twelve together.

One of the finest jobs the *guaglioni* had pulled was to steal a policeman's Lambretta. It was immediately stripped, as completely, as absolutely as a machine can be stripped, and each piece was sold separately. Even the bolts were the subject of separate deals. Brigante let it be known that he proposed to levy his tax; he found the registration plate of the police Lambretta attached to his front door, C.S.C.R., Corpo Speciale Carabinieri della Republica, in red letters on a black ground. For some days the *pizzerie* sold more pizzas, the ice-cream vendors more ice-creams; this was the only sign left on the surface by the wreck of the Lambretta.

Brigante had half-opened the grafting knife. Pizzaccio was watching Pippo and Balbo out of the corner of his eye.

'Perhaps it was the *guaglioni*,' he said, 'who did the Swiss job.'

'Too big for them,' said Brigante.

He let the blade slap back into place.

The orchestra began a slow foxtrot. Francesco had abandoned the drums for the electric guitar. Brigante noted (in his memory) that Giuseppina was dancing with the branch manager of the Bank of Naples, a young manager who had just got married. And that the Germans had struck up a conversation with the chemist's son; they were telling him about the engine of the forthcoming Mercedes; one of them drew a sketch of the turbine; their next move would be to invite the boy to a drive in the Volkswagen; they were using an old tactic.

The *guaglioni* suddenly swarmed into the square. They had smeared their faces with mulberries. Dark eyes in the middle of red masks seemed to be everywhere. The whole gang, a score of them, all between twelve and fifteen. They tore across the square, letting forth howls and brandishing imaginary axes. They were playing Redskins.

Brigante laughed, screwing up his eyes without relaxing his lips; it was his manner of laughing, his cold laugh.

'Idiot,' he said to Pizzaccio. 'If the *guaglioni* had pulled off the Swiss job, there'd be no lollipops left in the shops.'

He placed the grafting knife on the table.

Pippo and Balbo had made no move.

The *guaglioni* swept by again, at full gallop, clinging to the manes of their imaginary horses.

Pippo and Balbo walked slowly away, in the direction of the via Garibaldi. Brigante noted that they went into the bar of the Sports Café. The Redskins disappeared down a side street, at the other end of the square.

Pippo propped himself against the bar.

'Two glasses of twenty lire,' he said.

Balbo placed two twenty-lire pieces on the counter.

The holidaymakers stared at Pippo in his glorious rags.

'I don't serve tramps,' said Justo, the bartender.

Balbo, in turn, propped himself against the bar.

'We've paid our money,' he said.

'*Vai via*, clear out,' said Justo.

The Deputy Chief of Police was sitting at a table near by.

'Signor commisario,' said Pippo, 'we've paid our money.'

A great uproar spread across the square. The Redskins were returning to the attack.

'These children are right,' a customer said. 'These children have paid their money. Why aren't they being served?'

'Probably because they're poor,' said a woman visitor with advanced ideas.

At the same moment the pale blue lamps of the ball and all the other lamps in the square went out. The crescent moon had set. Only the pale light of the stars remained.

'Signor commisario,' said Pippo, 'we demand our rights.'

The Redskins jumped over the green barriers and dispersed, screaming, among the dancers. The police, hunting crops in hand, hurried towards the dance enclosure.

Three Redskins surrounded the Germans.

'Is this a southern Italian custom?' one of the Germans asked the chemist's son.

Their table toppled over. They stood up, uneasy.

The red masks were everywhere at once. Suddenly they disappeared. There was an enormous silence.

The electric current was restored ten minutes later. A witness reported that a Redskin who had passed the porter's lodge of the town hall just before the attack had simply thrown the switch which controlled the lighting in the main square.

The police reckoned up the damage. Two women on their holidays had lost their handbags. One of the Germans had had his wallet stolen from the pocket of his jacket, spread on the back of his chair. Some girls had lost items of cheap jewellery.

Pippo and Balbo slowly ate the ices which Justo had served them on the explicit orders of the woman visitor. When the first account of the raid on the ball to reach the bar of the Sports Café was given by a witness:

'Did they at least manage to arrest one of these *guaglioni?*' asked Pippo.

'No,' said the man.

'Adios,' said Pippo.

'Good night all,' said Balbo.

The deputy was already out collecting evidence from witnesses.

Pippo and Balbo strolled slowly down the via Garibaldi, turned into a side street of the Old Town and entered the rendezvous fixed for the distribution of loot.

At the moment the lights had gone out, Matteo Brigante's grafting knife had been lying on the table, beside the bottle of Asti. When the pale blue lamps had again thrown their glaring light over the dance enclosure the knife had disappeared.

'Eight hundred lire in the hardware store,' said Brigante. 'Not worth talking about ...'

85

He bit his thin lip. Pizzaccio was delighted that the *guaglioni* had defied his chief.

When Marietta started to sing, nobody was asleep, apart from Elvira.

Yet don Cesare, his hand resting on Elvira's breast, was not completely awake. From year to year his sleep, like his waking hours, had *lost interest*. For years now he had been deprived of the deepest sleep, parent of metamorphoses, in the depths of which man assimilates and elaborates his set-backs and humiliations and from them derives a renewed vigour, like the larva in the darkness of the cocoon, and from which he awakes triumphantly, stretching his reborn limbs with joy in the morning light. Don Cesare's nights, like his days, were now uniformly cheerless. Bereft also of the sleep which exists immediately above the deepest sleep and which engenders prophetic and warning dreams. Not for a long time had don Cesare dreamed any but disjointed and fragile dreams, those futile images which confusedly intermingle memories of the petty events of the day, scarcely distinct from the perceptions of the waking state. At the moment Marietta started to sing, don Cesare's musing was turning to dreaming, he wavered between musing and dreaming; this was how he spent most of his nights.

Old Julia was chasing the mosquitoes which were humming round her bed. She waited for them to come to rest on her face and killed them with a sharp smack. She seldom missed. On her right, under the window, the pale brightness of the stars lit Marietta's empty bed. The old woman associated the mosquitoes with the girl who had defied her. At each smack:

'For you, you hussy!'

'For you, you slut!'

'For you, *troia*!'

In the next room, Maria lay huddled on the far side of the bed, against the wall, leaving Tonio's side conspicuously empty. She

86

was praying. *Pater Noster, Ave Maria*, she went right through the rosary. Holy Mother of God, give me back my husband. St Joseph, *beatissimo sposso*, blessed spouse, awaken remorse in the heart of the adulterous man. Holy Mary of Capua, patron saint of the South, show compassion for the most wretched of your servants. St Michael the Archangel, drive the devil from the heart of my sister who has taken my husband away from me. Santa Ursula of Uria, virgin and martyr, bring their father back to my children.

Maria was not certain that her sister had yielded to her husband. She had caught her putting him in his place more than once. And the neighbours, the inhabitants of the reed huts scattered among the bamboos, from where you could see everything, had never surprised them together; they would have spread the news at once. But at this moment Tonio and Marietta were (she thought) alone together in the big room. Marietta still quivering (she thought) from the strokes they had given her. Tonio more assured than his wife had ever seen him; what could have happened to him in Porto Manacore tonight? A note of such tranquil authority when he had ordered the women to untie Marietta, that Maria did not now have the courage to go and confront him in the big room; she believed him capable of protecting his isolation with the girl with as much force as would a real man. This was enough to create the semblance of unhappiness. Maria exulted as though the doctor had just disclosed to her that she had cancer. And she took heaven to witness to assure herself of the propriety of her chosen unhappiness.

Meanwhile Tonio, standing at the top of the flight of steps, was keeping his eyes fastened on the dark line of bamboos into which Marietta had vanished. He had a bitter taste in his mouth, as if he had smoked too much, just as when he had vomited, a little earlier, in the main square of Porto Manacore.

Marietta started singing from behind the reeds, near the outlet of the lake. She took her bearings from an old olive-gatherers' song. She began on a tone of joy, as if her intention were simply to make a mockery of the women from whom she had just escaped.

But the song was one of those which sometimes permit 'the voice' to take shape; don Cesare was at once awake and attentive. Tonio scanned the darkness.

Marietta moved all the way round the house, behind the bamboos and the reeds which hid her from the brightness which shines from the night sky of the South even after the young moon has gone down. She repeated the same verses in a tone which became ever more joyous.

Elvira woke up. The challenge circled round the whole house. Marietta began the same refrain, a scale higher. Don Cesare rose silently and went over to the window. Elvira sat on the bed. She was violently aware that she hated her sister with all her heart.

Marietta was settling down to the new scale. She sang only the refrain until she had really settled down to the new scale.

Then she went several notes higher. Several times she went several notes higher. Then she fell back into the scale to which she had settled.

Tonio, leaning against the balustrade of the perron, his body thrust forward, his arms raised above the darkness, clapped his hands silently, keeping time with the song, passionately murmuring:

'Go, oh! Go, go!'

This is how people encourage 'the voice', when it is on the point of taking wing. It rarely happens at night, and after dramatic ups and downs, like tonight. Rather towards the end of the afternoon, on a public holiday, when all the guests have already sung, when the whole company has warmed to hearing songs and to singing everything there is to be sung: comic songs, ritornellos, stornelli, airs from operettas and operas. The man (or woman) who has the gift of 'the voice' has hung back, a disgruntled look on his face. The others have asked him to take his turn, but without insisting. When he (or she) indicates that he wishes to sing, everyone is silent. He starts up an old song which will allow 'the voice' to blossom, but at first he sings it just like anyone else. When he (or she) tries to sing higher, opening the door to 'the voice' (just as the real gambler joining a roulette table will haphazardly

88

back first one number, then another, without any system, so as to open the door to luck), when he begins to jump from one scale to another, like a fountain trying to gain a hold in the air, in the sky, the others stand up and surround him. He is still only feeling his way, but he is getting higher and higher. Then everyone accompanies him in silence, helps him in silence, by silently clapping their hands; they surround him with a silent, united clapping of hands and they implore him with passionate murmurs of:

'Go, oh! Go, go!'

As Tonio did now, stretching his arms beyond the darkness. As don Cesare murmured now, on the balcony of his room, between the colonnades.

'The voice' had suddenly reached its full pitch.

Don Cesare, at the time when he was still entertaining foreigners and explaining Manacorean folklore to them, used to claim that 'the voice' was that of the priestesses of the Venus of Uria when they went into trances. But that the tradition went back still further, to the Phrygians who had themselves inherited it from the fire-worshippers.

Others, pouncing on analogies with certain Arabian songs, were convinced that the Manacoreans had acquired it from the Saracens who conquered Uria, after the silting up of the harbour.

Albanians having several times settled on the coast, still others accorded 'the voice' an Illyrian origin. But all these hypotheses were all the more fragile in that musicologists had seldom had a chance to hear it and no recording had yet been made of it. Manacoreans were far from anxious for strangers to hear 'the voice'; they equally disliked the idea of strangers taking part in the game of The Law. As though out of modesty or shame for their song and their game, their most intimate possessions. But with this difference, that The Law is played throughout southern Italy, whereas 'the voice' is the special attribute of a small portion of the Adriatic coast.

There was no further need to murmur:

'Go, oh! Go, go!'

The girl had reached the height of her song.

A musician would have noted the very high pitch of her voice. But it could also be described as coming from the depths of her stomach. This was the basic paradox of 'the voice'.

A vertiginous song, that is to say at once very precisely positioned and careering wildly out of position. This is the basic paradox of 'vertigo'.

An inhuman song which could only be sung with a human voice. A virtuoso's song, in the least practised throat in the world. This was the basic paradox of Marietta.

When she had finished singing — 'the voice' broke suddenly and cleanly — Marietta disappeared so lightly that not one of the attentive ears which populated the false solitude of the marsh heard the rustle of her linen frock among the bamboos and reeds through which she fought her way.

She untied a fisherman's dinghy, sat down in the stern and, pulling gently at the two short oars (shorter than her arms), glided rapidly through the reeds, using the channels she knew so well, so easily that she did not disturb the aquatic birds.

Tonio went back into the house and got silently into bed beside his wife, Maria, whose belly was deformed by childbirth. Don Cesare returned to his canopied bed. Elvira was sitting erect in her white nightdress, which fastened high in the old-fashioned style: he saw that she was looking at him with hatred; he thought it would soon be time for him to dispense with her. Old Julia, stretching out her thumb and forefinger, continued to cast spells and to curse her youngest daughter.

Marietta landed at the foot of the mass of rock on which Manacore was built (the harbour was at the other end of the town, the opposite end from the marsh). She made her way round the town through the olive groves, treading lightly on her bare feet, without hurrying. She came out on to the highway and followed it until she came to the nearest milepost to the town. With a piece of chalk which was hidden there she drew a red circle on the sign and, inside the circle, a cross. She climbed up the embankment, made her way back to the olive groves and soon reached the first foothills of the mountain which screened Porto Manacore from the land winds. Here began the zone of orange and lemon trees.

Each orchard was surrounded by a high fence, a protection against thieves and also against the winter winds, which blew in from the sea. Without hesitation Marietta plunged into the maze of sunken paths which ran between the high fences of the orchards. The slopes were steep. Soon she could see at her feet the pale blue lamps of the ball, the red beacon at the entrance to the harbour, the whole expanse of the bay in the brightness of the southern night and the lighthouse on the tallest of the islands. She stopped beside a gate, raised herself on tiptoe, slipped her hand on to the supporting wall, searched blindly beneath one of the tiles and produced a large key. She opened the gate and, once inside the orchard, replaced the key in its hiding place.

It was very dark beneath the dense foliage of the orange, lemon and fig trees. Marietta took her bearings from the sound of the springs. Three of them came murmuring out of a hollow in the mountain and joined up at the far end of the orchard after flowing through the bark conduits from which the water was directed, when needed, into the basins hollowed out at the foot of each tree; then the stream fed from the three springs cascaded down into another orchard, where it was trapped in a reservoir and again distributed from tree to tree, from basin to basin by a complex system of bark conduits. And so on and so on all the way down the mountain foothills.

Even in the heart of August it was fresh in the orchards, interlaced with so much running water.

Near the uppermost of the three springs, a shed, hastily knocked together. Inside the shed, gardening tools, a table, a wooden chair, figs on the table and a pitcher of water; in one corner, a pile of sacks.

Marietta went into the shed, ate a fig, lay down on the sacks and fell asleep at once.

* * *

Matteo Brigante left some instructions with Pizzaccio and went home. It was not yet three in the morning. The ball was still on.

Brigante lived in the palace of Frederick II of Swabia. This was an enormous block of ill-assorted buildings linked by corridors, spiral staircases and hanging bridges, and stretching from the via Garibaldi to the side streets of the Old Town, at the foot of the sanctuary of Santa Ursula of Uria. The Emperor built the octagonal tower which today formed the corner of the main square and the via Garibaldi; he used to go there for a rest after hunting on the marsh. The Angevins added a porticoed palace, the present town hall, facing on to the main square. The kings of Naples perched a number of baroque edifices on top of it and built outhouses, stables and store-rooms at the back; this was at the time when Porto Manacore was doing an extensive trade with the Dalmatian coast. The present-day post office was one of the buildings of the baroque period, leaning against the Frederickan tower on which climbed the convolvuluses donna Lucrezia could see from her window. The other buildings had been turned into flats, housing more than a hundred families. The women hung their washing out in the yards where once sovereigns' horses had pranced; the *guaglioni* joined battle on the bridges of sighs. Matteo Brigante lived in one of these flats, one of the most happily situated, above the town hall, rather at an angle, with a little terrace with eighteenth-century arches where his wife had planted geranium creepers and potted pinks. He had rented the Frederick II tower from the town corporation: it was uninhabitable. He had sublet the lower floors to the police; it was here that Chief Attilio stored his files on cases that had been written off unsolved. He had kept the upper floors for himself; 'My attic,' he said, 'my junk room.'

Matteo Brigante's wife was born in a suburb of Trieste; she was blonde and taller than he was; no doubt she had Slav blood in her. He had met her in Ancona, where she had been working as a barmaid when he was a sailor in the Royal Navy. She was only twenty, already rather flabby; but he was flattered to have a northern girl as his mistress. When he put her in the family way, the Trieste family compelled him to marry her; she had originally come from Venezia Giulia with a whole tribe which owned and ran the bars, the restaurants and the hotels. Matteo Brigante was not then in a position to dictate the law, especially to men of Trieste; and so Francesco acquired a father. Now the wife lived like a recluse; the leading citizens of Manacore did not receive her and her husband forbade her to have anything to do with the poor; she had no other children, Brigante not wishing to divide what he left when he died.

He returned to his flat. His wife was asleep. When she was not sleeping, she kept house for him, very efficiently, in the Trieste tradition. He took several files from the sideboard, which was full of papers, and spread them out on the dining-room table. He began going through accounts and writing to his agents in Foggia, in a large, painstaking hand, very neat, very clear. The money he earned from controlling Porto Manacore was at once invested in all kinds of businesses, all over the province of Foggia; he had a part-ownership in the Calalunga oil-store and he had shares in the transportation of bauxite, in Manfredonia; he had just acquired some land near Margherita di Savoia which Montecatini would have to buy back at a high price when they wanted to extend the area of their salt-marshes — as they were bound to. Nowadays his business affairs brought him in more than the control of Porto Manacore. Francesco would be rich. That was why his father had made him become a law student. When you had a fortune to look after, you had to know the law. Lawyers were the only people who had ever got the better of Brigante.

The ball ended at three o'clock in the morning. Francesco Brigante disconnected his electric guitar and put it away in the big black case with the mauve silk lining. He declined to go to the bar of the Sports Café with his colleagues of the jazz circle, first of all because he had no money and secondly because he had a vague impression that by staying out drinking with other young men and perhaps talking women with them he would be guilty of a wrong towards donna Lucrezia, who was no doubt watching

93

him through the gap in the shutters on the fourth floor of the court house.

Donna Lucrezia was indeed watching him as he said goodbye to the young men. She told herself again that she loved him. She was exultant at having the courage to say it almost aloud to herself; she was in the act of triumphing over her southern up-bringing. She repeated to herself the decisions which she had taken and which she had decided to communicate to him in the course of the meeting they had arranged for the coming morning. He would be proud of her, she thought.

Francesco went home and placed the guitar case on the side-board; this was its regular place; the Brigantes always ate in the kitchen.

Matteo Brigante threw a glance at his son. The boy was taller than he was, broader in the shoulders, sandy-haired and well-covered, like his mother. Brigante returned to his writing.

Francesco did not say good evening to his father. The Brig-antes never wished one another good morning or good evening. He was not sleepy, still feeling excited at having played so much jazz and a little uneasy about this meeting with donna Lucrezia next morning and all that would probably result from it. He went through to the ante-room and took some music scores from the racks on which they were carefully arranged, near some gramo-phone records and books — very few books. He went back into the dining-room, sat down opposite his father and began reading the scores, going from one to another, returning now to this one, now to that.

Matteo Brigante, going on with his letters to his business agents, thought with satisfaction that his son was taciturn. He did not like it that his son was fair, sandy-haired and well-covered like his wife, but he liked it that he was silent, with a perpetual air of guarding some secret. Francesco would know how to stand up to the lawyers, he thought.

He gave him hardly any pocket money; he had made it a rule, so long as the boy had not begun to earn his living. He paid for his studies, in the Law School at Naples, and for his board and lodgings with a relative of his mother's, one of the Trieste crowd who had become a priest; Francesco lived in the rectory, at Santa Lucia. He had offered him the guitar, a jewel of a guitar, the best money could buy, so that he could hold his own with the sons of the leading citizens of Porto Manacore, students like himself, who had formed the jazz circle. This was how Francesco had come to be invited to the home of Judge Alessandro, whose wife was interested in music.

Francesco had spread a blank sheet of music in front of him and was rapidly sketching notes on the staves. At the last Naples festival he had received a silver medal, for the composition of a light ballad. Brigante watched him with pleasure. He hesitated to disturb such a studious hobby. But he thought this was a good moment to catch his son off-guard with a sudden attack and get the truth out of him.

'Why do you have letters sent to you poste restante?' asked Brigante.

Francesco slowly raised his eyes. He thought: 'This had to happen. The clerk in the post office has told him. He always knows everything. I should have thought of that, I should have gone about it some other way.'

He had slowly lifted his head.

'Yes, Father,' he said.

'I'm not asking you *if* you were getting mail poste restante. I know you are. I'm asking you *why?*'

Brigante stared fixedly at his son. Francesco did not bat an eyelid. He had big, prominent, pale blue eyes. He looked at his father for a moment in silence. Then:

'It's nothing important,' he said.

Matteo Brigante's hard little eyes bored into the large liquid eyes of his son. He had no more chance of plumbing their depths than have the peaks of the Dolomites, however high they stand, of piercing the sky. This inaccessibility did not displease the father. The wiles of businessmen would smash vainly against this Olympus.

'Have you got a girl in Naples, then?' asked Brigante.

95

Francesco reflected for a moment. A trap or a way out? he wondered. A trap maybe, but best foster a delusion that can't be checked. Nothing of what he was thinking showed, in his eyes, where the pupils merged with the irises, or in his face, with its rounded jaw, reposing on a long, broad neck like that of the Olympian Jupiter.

'Yes, Father,' he said.

'I don't see any harm in you having a girl in Naples. You can tell her to write to you at home.'

'I'll tell her.'

'Is she on holiday?'

'Yes, Father.'

'She's spending her holidays in Turin?'

'No, Father.'

'But the envelope was stamped with a Turin postmark.'

'I didn't look.'

'Take a look now.'

'I've thrown away the envelope.'

'Look and see where she's dated the letter from.'

'I've thrown the letter away.'

'You do know where this girl is?'

'Yes, Father.'

'Would you mind telling me where she is?'

'She's on holiday in Piedmont.'

'With relations of hers?'

'Yes, Father.'

'I see,' said Matteo Brigante. 'She got someone to take the letter to Turin so that her relations shouldn't know she was writing to you.'

'Probably.'

'Is she with her parents?'

'I think so.'

'You don't know much about her ...'

'No, Father.'

'Why does she use a typewriter?'

'She works as a secretary.'

96

'She's taken her typewriter away on holiday with her?'

'I don't know.'

'He'll stand up marvellously to the lawyers,' thought Brigante. But he was careful not to show his delight. He started writing again.

'If he has read the letter,' thought Francesco, 'he's keeping me on tenterhooks, he's leading me on, he's preparing his trap. But if he hasn't handled the letter, if the clerk has simply given him a description of the envelope and the stamp, then I've won. I'd better stay on my guard.'

Brigante raised his head.

'I hope you're not writing anything silly to this girl ...'

'No, Father.'

'You remember what I've said to you on this subject.'

'Yes, Father. I never write without thinking of the law.'

'You remember that there's only one way of making sure girls don't have babies?'

'Yes, Father.'

'She agrees?'

'Yes, Father.'

Brigante laughed silently, without breaking off writing.

'Just like these secretaries,' he said. 'Girls in service don't give way so easily.'

He said nothing more. Francesco returned to sketching notes on the blank staves.

At the end of the ball, the branch manager of the Bank of Naples had gone home with his wife. She was sulking because he had danced several times with Giuseppina. He had sat in a chair while she undressed in silence. When she was in bed, he had said:

'I'm going out to smoke a cigarette in the square.'

'You're going to meet that girl again,' she had cried.

'I tell you I'm going out to smoke a cigarette in the square. I'm entitled to some fresh air, aren't I?'

He had gone to meet Giuseppina. Now they were kissing, in the shadows of an arcade along the Angevin wing of the palace.

Pizzaccio prowled about the town, in accordance with Matteo Brigante's instructions. He saw Giuseppina and the branch manager of the Bank of Naples. 'Always after the married men, that one,' he thought; he noted it casually (in his memory), just in case. But it was not those two Brigante had briefed him to control.

On the fourth floor of the court house, Judge Alessandro was awake in his study, which had been his bedroom, too, since donna Lucrezia had insisted on sleeping alone. At dawn he would fall asleep on a divan under the bookshelves.

He wrote in a notebook, his private journal, in a hand which rose and fell unevenly, for the attack of malaria was not quite over.

... I shall never complete my *Frederick II, Lay Legislator*, of which I used to talk to my fiancée Lucrezia. I am one of ten thousand Italian magistrates who have embarked on a work full of original ideas, on some point of legal history, and who will never complete it. I lack resourcefulness.

Just seven hundred and fifty years ago, Frederick II, back from Rhodes, was disembarking at Porto Manacore. In his absence, the Papal army had invaded his kingdom. He stayed for only two hours in the octagonal tower I can see from my window, time enough to have some of his unfaithful subjects hanged. That same night he reached Lucera by a roundabout route. He made his way secretly into the citadel and resumed command of his Saracens, whose leader had allowed himself to be bought by the Pope. A week later he was defeating the pontifical army under the walls of Foggia and pursuing it to Benevento. Another two months and he had recaptured Naples and Palermo and was threatening Rome. Frederick II was a man of great resourcefulness. The judges he appointed to reframe the legal code were men of great resourcefulness. Lucrezia was made for one of those judges.

Frederick II was a tyrant. But he fought against the feudal overlords who had allied themselves with the Pope and imposed a little more justice in southern Italy. Can it be that tyranny is essential for a little more justice?...

Etc. etc. ... Judge Alessandro went on writing in his notebook for a long time.

The walls bore witness to his preoccupations at the beginning of his career. Several portraits of Frederick II of Swabia. And, framed in passe-partout, photographs he had personally taken of some of the castles the great king had built in Apulia. Beneath each picture, typed on a narrow slip of paper, a brief commentary by the judge. For example:

'Castel del Monte, or Gothic Rationalized.'

'Lucera, five hundred years before Voltaire: the Saracens in the service of Reason.'

'Benevento: the Reiters rescue Roman law.'

It was ten years since Judge Alessandro had typed these captions in the form of maxims. He had just been posted to Porto Manacore and was moving into the fourth floor of the court house, with his young bride, donna Lucrezia. He proclaimed proudly: I am a man of culture of the South of Italy. The strips of paper pasted to the passe-partouts had turned yellow and the ink of the captions was discoloured.

Now he devoted most of his free time to what he called his dictionary of imbecility. This was housed in tall, shining tins given him by the hardware dealer, Giuseppina's father. A collection of picture postcards, sold in stationers' shops and tobacconists'; the series set in the little car (two lovers smiled at one another, sulked with one another, kissed one another, read poems to one another, all without leaving the wheel), the Vespa series, the series portraying the young couple in an American-style 'home', without children, with children, playing cards, watching television. He had several boxes full of them. When he was not having an attack of malaria, he needed only to look at his collection to get hot under the collar.

The band had long stopped playing and the pale blue lamps of the ball had long been extinguished. Dawn was beginning to brighten the sky. Judge Alessandro still wrote:

> If a Frederick II (of Swabia) were to emerge from the ranks of any of the political parties in present-day Italy, he would have no difficulty in procuring a Fiat and a television set for every worker. In which case, there would not be a single man left with sufficient time on his hands to indulge in reflection. Imbecility is necessarily the price of justice.

He re-read the last phrase, transposed 'is' and 'imbecility' and changed the full stop to a question mark. He was a scrupulous man. Then he shut the notebook and went and lay down on the narrow little divan, under the books he now so seldom read.

He generally left his private journal lying about on the work table, hoping that in his absence donna Lucrezia would be indiscreet enough to read it. It would show her that he still had ideas. But she never had sufficient curiosity to open the notebook.

Judge Alessandro fell into the clammy sleep of those afflicted with malaria. The sun rose from behind the promontory which enclosed the eastern side of the bay of Porto Manacore. Don Ottavio's *guaglione* errand boy set out on his motor tricycle to collect the goat's milk from the hills beyond the lake.

Pizzaccio had fallen asleep on a bench on the terrace. The tricycle engine woke him up. Soon the whole town would be active. He went and posted himself under King Murat's pine, from which he could survey the main square and the whole of the via Garibaldi.

Don Ottavio's *guaglione* pulled up beside the first milepost out of the town. He stopped there every morning. On Pippo's orders. Usually there was nothing chalked on the sign. Today someone had chalked a red cross in a red circle. He absorbed this and returned at full speed to Manacore. He left the tricycle at the foot of the Old Town and ran through the side streets till he came to the house he was seeking.

Pizzaccio saw the *guaglione* abandon his tricycle and turn down into the Old Town. He followed him, without showing himself, hiding on the corners.

The *guaglione* roused Pippo:

'A circle,' he said, 'and a cross inside the circle.'

'I get it,' said Pippo.

The *guaglione* returned to his tricycle. Pippo rose, stretched himself and shot a glance out of the window. He did not see Pizzaccio. He left the house and made his way to the highway, which he crossed slowly. It was still deserted. Out at sea, the sirocco and the libeccio continued their titanic struggle. During the night the libeccio had got the upper hand to the extent of a few miles and the bank of clouds had advanced sufficiently to seal off the entrance to the bay. The sun was rising rapidly over the pine woods on the promontory. The chemist's thermometer registered 82°.

Pippo left the town behind him and made towards the mountain. He quickly reached the foothills, the orchard zone. There were so many orange and lemon trees on the first foothills of the mountain that in spring the sailors on ships out at sea could smell the heady perfume of the orange and lemon blossom even before they sighted land; as if the white horses had turned into an endless orchard.

Without hesitation, Pippo plunged into the maze of sunken paths between the high walls which enclosed the green fruit in process of filling out (like Marietta's breasts) and soon to turn to gold. He took the key from the hiding place, opened and shut the gate, put the key back in the hiding place and made his way up towards the shed, running agilely, barefooted, among the bark conduits through which the running water murmured.

He found Marietta in the act of bathing her face in the little pool of the top spring, near the shed in which she had slept. Now they were face to face. She in her white linen frock, with the sleeves rolled up, naked beneath the frock, her hair in disorder and drops of water on her face and arms. He, the rags of his shirt hanging across his shoulders like a sash, his black curls falling on to his forehead.

'What have they done to you now?'

'They beat me.'

'Does it hurt much?'

'No,' she said. 'My turn will come.'

'Are you going back to the marsh?'

'I don't know,' she replied. 'I'll have to think about it.'

'When is the agronomist calling for his answer?'

'Today or tomorrow ... It doesn't much matter, since I don't intend going ...'

The two of them sat side by side on the small mound beside the pool.

Already the sun was burning. But here, in the orchard with the springs, under the dome of fat-leaved orange and lemon and fig trees, in the shelter of the laurel hedges which intersected the orchard, lining the walls, to protect the trees from the winter winds which blew in from the sea, in the murmur of running water, in the perfume of the blossom which made ready the fruits of winter while the fruits of autumn were already turning gold, the shade was fresh, almost cold. It was a joy to be sitting in the cool shade, while the sky, the earth and the sea all burned.

Marietta was not quite seventeen. Pippo just a little over sixteen. They had never read a thing, being hardly able to read or write. They sat in the fresh shade, feeling in good spirits, hand in hand, listening to the running water streaming by at their feet, each enjoying the freshness of the other's hand.

'I've brought something for you ...'

Pippo held out a grafting knife to Marietta. The blade was retracted in the black, shiny handle with copper pins embedded in the wood. The extremity of the blade jutted out, shaped rather like a spur; this was the part which was inserted beneath the bark, once it had been pierced, so as to prise it up. When you held the knife closed in your fist, between the thumb and the four clenched fingers, the spur projected like the spur of a fighting cock.

Marietta opened the knife. She looked at the trade mark engraved at the base of the blade: the heads of two long-horned oxen and the inscription: *Due Buoi*.

'It must have cost at least eight hundred lire,' she said.

She tested the edge of the blade against her finger.

'Well ground. A fine blade, beautifully ground, like a razor ...'

She shut the knife; the spring was strong; the blade slapped back into place like a pistol shot. A stranger using the tool without instruction would cut his finger on it. But, in the land of orchards, Marietta had been born with the slap of grafting knives all around her.

'A fine knife,' she said. 'What do you want me to do with it?'

She stared mockingly at Pippo.

'I'll keep it for you to shave with, when you have a beard ...'

'It's Matteo Brigante's knife,' Pippo said.

Marietta jumped to her feet.

'Is that true?' she asked.

'Yes,' said Pippo.

'Bravo!' cried Marietta.

Pippo told her about the Redskins' coup. How he had planned the affair with Balbo. That the *guaglioni* had carried it off well. That he had been astute enough to attract attention to himself in the bar of the Sports Café at the very moment of the attack — a perfect alibi. He listed the booty captured from the Germans, the two women, Brigante himself.

Marietta held the grafting knife in her clenched fist, spur outwards, and followed every step of the story with excitement.

'Bravo for the *guaglioni*! Bravo for Pippo!'

A sudden concern darkened her expression.

'It means war with Brigante ...'

'We've been at war for a long time,' said Pippo.

'You've flung a challenge in his face.'

'Let's fight it out, Brigante!' said Pippo.

Marietta stretched her fist towards the town.

'*Avanti guaglioni!* Death to Matteo Brigante!'

Then, turning back towards Pippo:

'We'll get Brigante where we want him,' she said. 'I feel it.'

For some little time they went on chattering about their affairs.

'Well,' Pippo asked, 'what have you decided?'

'I still don't know,' she said. 'Perhaps I shall have to go down to the marsh again …'

'When are we going to make a run for it?'

'Perhaps sooner than I thought.'

'As soon as you like,' he said.

'You'll leave the *guaglioni* behind?'

'We'll send for them,' he said. 'Gradually, one by one …'

'I'll think about it,' said Marietta. 'I'll think about it all day. I shall have to think of some excuse …'

'I'll come back and see you tonight,' said Pippo.

On his way back to Manacore, he ran into two *guaglioni*, employees of don Cesare who were going up to the orchard to put in some maintenance work on the bark conduits.

'There's nobody in the shed,' said Pippo.

'We know who "nobody" is.'

'There's nobody there,' Pippo repeated severely.

'Nobody … nobody …' the *guaglioni* repeated, smiling.

Marietta had gone back into the shed and sat down on the sacks, her elbows on her knees, her head between her hands. She was going to stay there all day, laying plans.

At eight in the morning, Francesco was ready to leave.

In the kitchen, his mother was serving Brigante with his breakfast.

'Are you going already?' asked his mother.

He had anticipated she would ask this.

'Yes,' he replied, 'I'm going to Schiavona.'

Schiavona was a small fishing village, on the other side of the pine-covered promontory which seals off the eastern approach to Manacore Bay (looking across to the marsh and the lake).

Brigante did not ask his son what he was going to Schiavona for. Francesco was rather put out of his stride. He had anticipated this question. But after their conversation overnight, Matteo Brigante had decided to treat his son more as a man, to give him a little more liberty.

Francesco hung about in the kitchen, nibbling a biscuit.

'Schiavona's a long way,' said the mother.

'Hardly ten miles. It won't take me long. Don Ruggero is lending me his Vespa.'

'Why do you have to borrow don Ruggero's Vespa?' asked the mother.

'I have to go and see about getting a trumpeter from Schiavona … Their jazz band has an excellent trumpeter … I wasn't satisfied with our trumpeter last night …'

'If he isn't satisfied with his trumpeter,' Brigante intervened, 'he's quite right to make a change.'

Then:

'Have you got the money for the petrol?' he asked his son.

'Twenty miles there and back … Don Ruggero isn't pushed for a couple of litres of petrol.'

'I'm just as well off as Ruggero's father,' said Brigante.

He gave a thousand-lire note to his son, who did not reveal his astonishment. But the fear which had been gripping his stomach for several weeks was heightened by the unexpectedness of the gesture. Did Father know? If Father knew, he would certainly not have made him this present of a thousand lire. Could it be a trap? But what kind of trap? Francesco could not see it. Everything had turned out this morning as he had predicted, except that it had been his mother who had asked the questions he had expected from his father (and except, too, for this surprising present of a thousand lire). It mattered little who had asked the questions, since Francesco had been able to give the answers he had prepared, answers which would prevent

Brigante from being surprised when he learned from one of his deputy controllers that his son had been seen in the pine woods, on the road to Schiavona, riding don Ruggero's Vespa. The desired result had been obtained. Yet Francesco's fear increased; for several weeks he had been caught up in a series of events beyond his control, and each day he grew more afraid.

'He might have spent today with us,' said the mother, 'considering he's leaving tomorrow to spend a week with his uncle in Benevento ...'

'He's old enough to know what he ought to do,' said Brigante.

Francesco walked slowly out of the house, tall, broad-shouldered, with a measured stride it seemed nothing could impede. This is often the case: those who no longer control their destiny assume the countenance and bearing of destiny itself. Brigante admired the inexorability of his son's bearing.

Francesco was now riding towards Schiavona, on the Vespa lent him by his colleague from Law School.

It was the previous winter, during the Christmas vacation, that he had met donna Lucrezia for the first time — at the house of don Ottavio the great landowner, don Ruggero's father, in the course of a small reception of the kind given several times a year by every person of standing in Manacore. Matteo Brigante was never invited; he was richer and more influential than most of the persons of standing, but this richness and influence were his by acquisition, not by right; to bridge the gap, he would have to be elected mayor of the town or receive some decoration, like being made a *cavaliere* or a *commandatore* by the government, as one day he certainly would be; but his acceptance among persons of standing was retarded not so much because he had once knifed a boy for robbing one of his sisters of her virginity or because of his universal racket, which everyone was prepared to tolerate, as by the fact that he had served in the navy for years without ever getting beyond the rank of bosun's mate. But Francesco was reading for his law degree in Naples, just like the sons of persons of standing; he ran the jazz circle; there was no difficulty about him. Last year don Ottavio had agreed at once when his son had suggested inviting Francesco. After that he had received invitations from all the other families.

And so, during the Christmas vacation, he had met donna Lucrezia several times in various people's houses, once in her own home, at the party she gave once a year, and only once a year, to fulfil her obligations; later she had explained to him that she did not care for a social life, least of all in Porto Manacore.

Since, like him, she did not play bridge, since, like him, she did not dance, they had often found themselves together, near the record player. They had discussed the records they selected together; he had told her that he composed, occasionally. She had ideas about music; he had listened to them. She loved novels, too; he had never heard the names of most of the writers she talked about; he had admired her.

At twenty-two, he knew very little about women. He sometimes went into the brothels in Foggia and Naples; as he had little money, he stayed only 'a moment' in the room painted white like a hospital ward; the hygiene instructions were posted on the wall, near the wash-basin, in accordance with police regulations, the more important recommendations appearing in bold type; on the glass shelf above the bidet, the permanganate of potash, mouth-wash and skin ointment, use of which was optional but advised; such was the setting of his amours. 'A little present for me', 'Wouldn't you like to stay for half an hour? It would only cost you two thousand lire', 'You couldn't let me have another fifty lire?', 'Get a move on!': this was all he knew of the language of love. Already the madam's assistant was hammering on the door: 'Let's hurry it up.' Each time he promised himself he was through with this fool's game, solitude and imagination providing him with sharper pleasures. But time went by and slowly but surely he persuaded himself that women imagined in solitude were only a foretaste of real women; he wanted to check his impressions; he needed to make contact, to touch. Between the ages of sixteen and twenty-two, he had paid ten or a dozen quick visits to a brothel.

He was convinced that the girls in Naples, the students he

met at Law School were inaccessible, like all girls in the South. The Neapolitans made fun of the Apulian accent, which he had never succeeded in shaking off. With the result that he did not even flirt, as his companions claimed to do.

The only women he really knew were those who figured in his daydreams. At different times he gave them the features of a foreigner glimpsed as she stepped off the *vaporetto* from Capri, of a waitress who had served him an *espresso* with a tender smile, of a woman he had followed in the street without daring to speak to her; sometimes it was a woman he would never have thought it possible to desire, but who forced herself into his dreams, a matron seen from the window of his cousin the vicar of Santa Lucia, deformed, enormous, ruling all her brood with a rod of iron.

Donna Lucrezia, even now, was never the accomplice of his daydreams.

The first thing he had admired about donna Lucrezia was her easy manner, what he later called her *disinvoltura*, when she had proffered the word in connection with the heroine of a novel she had made him read, translated from the French, *La Chartreuse de Parme*. Of jazz, of the hunt for duck, of Beethoven, of French novels, of love as it figured in French novels, the women of the South, or those at least whom he had met, never spoke; donna Lucrezia spoke easily on any subject, as though it were absolutely natural for the wife of the judge of Porto Manacore to talk about all these things. It was the same with the way she moved: if during a party she walked from one group to another, from a chair to a sofa, from the refreshment table to the window, you could not conclude (as it was so easy to conclude with the other women) that she was seeking to show herself off in a better light or that she wanted an audience for some slanderous remark; no, her movements were constantly unpredictable, giving the impression that she moved only for her personal pleasure, without a thought for others. She changed her position the way a torrent flows, following her own laws.

He had never yet met a woman who had a character of her

own and behaved with natural ease. It took a springtime illness which kept him convalescent in Porto Manacore for two months to make him realize the full extent of his feelings. At first he had thought he was only in love with her *disinvoltura*.

Today they were going to meet alone for the first time. They had not yet exchanged a single kiss.

They had arranged to meet in the pine woods at the foot of the promontory. But first Francesco had to go on to Schiavona and back, so that his alibi should be complete.

At ten o'clock donna Lucrezia went into the study of her husband, Judge Alessandro.

'I'm ready,' she said.

'You really persist in going?' he asked.

'I told them I'd be coming.'

'I'm feverish again,' said the judge.

'The inspectress will be there this morning, specially to see me.'

The judge sweated and shook. He looked at her, tall and erect in her long-sleeved dress which buttoned at the neck.

'Frigid women,' he said, 'take up charitable work at an early age.'

It took him a quarter of an hour to get the Topolino going. This, too, she had anticipated and was not late in starting. She silently took her seat beside him; she was a good half head taller than he was.

It was her family, in Foggia, who had planned the marriage. She had offered no resistance, having only one desire at the time, to leave the flat where the fifteen of them lived in four rooms. Until she was eighteen she had never been alone, night or day. Her mother's parents, her father's mother, her sister's husband, her brothers and her sisters had never ceased to love and hate one another 'all around her', she said. If by any chance the girls who shared her room were either out or busy in another part of the flat, it did not even occur to her to shut the door; someone would have said: 'You've got something to hide, then.' A lower middle-class family, civil servants, tradespeople, bank clerks; all the men were out at work; they were quite comfortably off. Among the poor, fifteen people would not have had four rooms to live in. The towns of the South were overpopulated. In some quarters of Taranto, there were as many as eight to a room.

Contrary to what was written at the end of the last century, 'promiscuity' did not make love any easier. You were watched all the time. Incest was more exceptional than you might think from the questionable gestures of fathers towards their daughters, brothers towards their sisters, brothers towards their brothers; even in the same bed; it would require too much silence and underhandedness. Promiscuity teased the imagination, but prevented its appeasement. And the fear of sin, familiar even to atheists, made agony of frustration.

Lucrezia was proud, pure-minded; the girls' whisperings disgusted her as much as the men's glances and stealthy caresses; the mumbling and fumbling of the obsessed, impotence, failure — these sickened her. She arrived at the age of eighteen completely ignorant of matters of love, in a town where little enough was made, but where people never stopped thinking about it and talking about it.

She had had a secondary education, without passing the final examination. She had read a few nineteenth-century French and Italian novels, twenty pages here, twenty pages there, constantly interrupted, constantly called upon to intervene in the quarrels which erupted among her fourteen companions from one minute to the next. She had established no connection between the love described to her in the novels she idly read and the grossness incessantly alluded to all round her, present always in men's looks directed at her breasts and thighs. The one aspiration of her adolescence: to get away and cut herself free from the men's eyes. It was only after her marriage that she found the peace and quiet to read seriously. Through novels, she began to imagine passion, but as a privilege denied to the women of the South of Italy and to herself.

In the early years of marriage, she had enjoyed her husband's conversation. He talked to her of Frederick II of Swabia, of Manfred, of the kings of Anjou, of Spanish captains, of General Choderlos de Laclos bringing to Taranto, at the head of the soldiers of the French republic, new ideas of liberty and happiness. Thanks to the judge's stories, she had ceased to live solely in that fleeting thing, her own life. Her country, the South of Italy, had not always been the same drab, distressing place where the unemployed stood along the walls waiting for an employer who never came, where the men planned clever manœuvres to run their hands over virgins they would not possess.

In bed she gave herself without pleasure, but without resistance. Being obliged to submit was one of the inconveniences to which women were subject.

But in the Topolino, bought the day after their wedding, they had visited Apulia, Romanesque basilicas, Trani, San Nicolas-de-Bari, fortresses and palaces, white in the midday light, pink at dawn and dusk, tall, hard, 'pure as you are', Alessandro told her; all the palaces of Frederick II of Swabia, the Emperor wild about building and legislation; Lecce, the town of soft stone where, by submitting to discipline, the baroque, like poetry in the hexameter, had not got out of hand, the portal of Santa Croce, 'volubile like your breasts', Alessandro told her. Romanesque, Frederickan or baroque, the stone bore witness to the luxurious minds of their ancestors; for centuries the South had put forth harvests far beyond essential needs; man had flourished, now he vegetated, but since the past had been different, the present could be transformed; this was what the judge explained to his young wife.

He called himself an independent socialist. She could have wished for something more, to collaborate actively in the transformation of the present; but a southern education had convinced her, firstly that politics were no concern of women, and secondly that it was not in the South that the fate of the South would be decided. They read socialist and communist periodicals and tried to divine the shape of the fate which was being prepared elsewhere for their country and for themselves.

Her two confinements, which she had neither wanted nor resisted, told her nothing new about herself. The servant spared her the bother of keeping the children clean and washing the nappies. She nursed them, then brought them up punctiliously and conscientiously, in exactly the same way as, in the comfortless room on the fourth floor of the court house, she washed herself daily from head to foot. This precision in the physical attentions she gave the children and herself took the place, although she was not consciously aware of this, of the religion in which she did not believe and the heroism which circumstances denied her. But she did not pass on to the children the vague hopes which had not come true for her; this was why she did not regard them as her own flesh and blood, feeling astonished at times at her attitude, but without attaching much importance to it. Now the elder child was nine, the younger five, herself twenty-eight.

The marriage had been a step-up for Lucrezia. The four rooms of the court house were preferable to the four rooms in Foggia; her husband, the servant, the two children and herself — there were only five of them, compared with the fifteen back there. In spite of the obligations, now surmounted, of the double bed, the company of an intelligent man was preferable to that of the Foggia family. The young woman's father and brother-in-law had clubbed together to buy a car; they devoted all their out-of-office hours to keeping it clean; the judge never washed his Topolino and forgot to fill it with oil; he was preferable to the father and brother-in-law, he was a man of culture.

But Judge Alessandro was guilty of two wrongs towards donna Lucrezia.

When their elder child was six he insisted that she should send him to catechism. Now, he had spent their honeymoon and the years that had followed ridding the young woman of the few superstitions which had escaped the anvil of her adolescence. He was passionately faithful to the rationalist tradition of southern intellectuals; Croce had been his master. But the civil authorities would have taken it as a manifestation against the government if the judge of Porto Manacore had not let his children make their First Holy Communion. Already he was frowned on for not going to Mass, still more so since his wife did not go either; thus he showed a real courage which he did not carry to the point of not sending his children to catechism. Lucrezia asked herself if he wasn't a coward.

When people began to 'squat' on the landlords' estates, the judge, in his own home, in the secrecy of the flat on the fourth floor of the court house, sided violently with the agricultural workers; but two floors down, in the court room, he condemned them, as the government demanded. Donna Lucrezia decided that she could no longer love a man who had lost her respect. In fact, she had never loved him; at that time she still had no experience of passion; she could quite sincerely give the name of love to the pleasure of conversation with a man of culture.

'I give the minimum sentences. People know it only too well ...'

'You do everything by minimums. I know that only too well.'

When she insisted on sleeping alone, he became abusive: 'frigid woman', 'iceberg', 'block of wood'. He spoke of his 'rights as a husband'. She eyed him contemptuously.

'You're worse than my father. He talked nothing but smut, but at least he didn't try to impose it in the name of the law.'

After a year of arguments, they reached a compromise. She got her separate room but she agreed to receive him there sometimes. Each time, he had to alternate between prayers and demands.

He had just dropped her at the far end of the bay, on the edge of the pine woods, outside the gate of the post office workers' holiday camp.

He manœuvred to head back to Porto Manacore. He made three unsuccessful attempts at turning in the entry to a gravel path. Some years before, she had been grateful for his shortcomings as a driver, which distinguished him from the other men of their acquaintance, always self-conscious about their skill in handling cars, as though virtuosity at the wheel was proof enough of the virile exploits of which they never ceased to boast. Now that she thought him weak and incapable, his awkwardness aggravated her too.

She was standing near the Topolino. He was pressed against the back of the seat, preparing for another attempt at turning.

'Have I got room?' he asked.

'Go on ... Stop ... Now turn for all you're worth.'

The turn was accomplished. He was beside her again, the bonnet towards Porto Manacore.

'You really don't want me to come and pick you up?'

'I've already told you I'm being given a lift back.'

'Goodbye, *carissima*.'

'Goodbye.'

The holiday camp gates, marble columns and wrought iron railings, had been built in Mussolini's time on behalf of the post office authorities. There was an official opening, but the work was never continued. The pine woods began immediately behind the marble columns. The children camped on the shore, in military tents. The huts, between sea and gates, were the administrative offices.

Donna Lucrezia called on the supervisor.

'My dear friend, I just happened to be passing. I have some matters to attend to with the doctor.'

In the doctor's hut, she found only a nurse.

'Always so much to do, my dear ... You can tell the doctor I looked in. The head sister is waiting to see me.'

In the head sister's office:

'I don't want to disturb you, the supervisor is waiting to see me.'

On the far side of the hutments she continued down the gravel path. She looked round. 'I can't see anyone, but there are at least ten pairs of eyes watching me. What a country!' She compelled herself to walk with nonchalance. She slowly climbed and cleared a stretch of rising ground, beyond which a path led down on to the promontory. A clump of briars hid her from view. She hurried down the path with a thudding heart. She was keeping a lover's rendezvous for the first time in her life.

On don Ruggero's Vespa, Francesco had made the rounds of Schiavona. He had stopped off at the post office café and drunk an *espresso*, chatting with some young men he knew. Now he was on his way back towards the pine woods.

It was at the end of his convalescence, in the spring, that he had found himself alone with donna Lucrezia for the first time. He had called to return some records and books — including this French novel, *La Chartreuse de Parme*.

She asked him for his impressions.

'I myself,' she said, 'have read *La Chartreuse* ten times.'

He said little in reply. Even with his fellow students, in Naples, he was sparing of his words, a habit he had acquired in his dealings with his father, of whom he always fought shy. He listened to donna Lucrezia and watched her as she moved unpredictably about the room, from the bookcase to the gramophone, from the bar (' a glass of French brandy?') to the standard lamp, which she lit, to the switch of the chandelier, which she turned off, to the leather armchair, which she pushed under the lamp, the whole time talking about this novel, so completely at her ease, a fine-looking woman, well-built, but not at all overweight like the fine-looking women of the South, majestic and simple, simply majestic.

He had suddenly realized that it was with the looks of donna Lucrezia that he had pictured la Sanseverina, all the time he had been reading the French novel.

'I should have thought,' she said, 'you would have had more liking for Stendhal, that he would have been a shock, a revelation ...'

'I can't understand Fabrice,' he said.

'What do you mean?' she asked quickly.

'It seems to me ... ' he began.

He had not put it into words yet, even for himself. He left the sentence unfinished.

'It seems to you …?' she insisted.

'It seems to me,' he said, 'that if I'd been in Fabrice's place, it wouldn't have been Clélia I'd have loved.'

She looked at him with curiosity.

'Don't you like young girls?'

'I don't know,' he said.

'I see,' she said. 'You'd have preferred little Marietta.'

'Marietta?'

'Yes,' she said, 'the actress whose protector Fabrice wounded in a sword-fight.'

'I'd forgotten,' said Francesco.

His eyes met Lucrezia's.

'No,' he insisted. 'I'd have loved la Sanseverina.'

He had immediately felt himself blush.

Reaching the Schiavona side of the pine woods, he changed down to second and turned off on to a path which he followed for some three hundred yards, jolting across the mounds of beaten earth. Then he hid the Vespa in a bush and proceeded on foot.

The pine woods covered the whole length of the promontory which sealed off the eastern side of Porto Manacore Bay. The road cut through it at the base. On the point, the fishermen had built a *trabucco*. The woods were frequented only by resiners and crossed only by the fishermen on their way to the *trabucco*. The tourists stayed on the beaches, within reach of Schiavona and Porto Manacore. The fishermen always took the same path and, in the month of August, the resin jars were empty — no resiners. The isthmus and the pine woods were the only deserted places in the region; to reach the isthmus, you had to cross the outlet of the lake, using the one and only bridge, at the foot of don Cesare's villa, under the eyes of his people — and immediately the whole town knew about it; which was why Francesco Brigante and donna Lucrezia had chosen the pine woods for their first lovers' rendezvous.

At first Francesco followed the edge of the pine woods, on the Schiavona side, skirting a field of stubble. He came on a band of wild donkeys, then a herd of goats. Some gad-flies left the donkeys to attach themselves to him. He cut himself a myrtle branch to drive the gad-flies off. The sun was rapidly climbing towards its zenith.

That first tête-à-tête he had had with donna Lucrezia, in the course of which he had said that if he had been Fabrice he would have preferred la Sanseverina, had lasted only half an hour. In that same moment he had said to himself: 'I love donna Lucrezia.' Three months before, he would never have thought it possible that a boy like himself could love a woman like donna Lucrezia. This was what came from reading French novels.

After which, he had been incapable of offering a word in answer to the easy-mannered questions of the judge's wife. She looked at him with curiosity, 'an intense curiosity', he thought; donna Lucrezia's looks always intensely expressed what she was thinking and feeling.

He had stood up and for a moment retained in his the hand which had been held out to him.

'You'd better go,' she had said.

During the three weeks that had followed, he had loved her as the heroes of the novels of the last century loved. He met her in the drawing-rooms of Porto Manacore; they had never met so often; he spoke less than ever, she fell into the same silences as he did, they went on sitting side by side, near the record player, while the others danced or played bridge, uttering only the names of the records which one suggested the other should hear. But he was constantly thinking of her, imagining walks together through the streets of Milan, declarations of love on the banks of the Arno, in Florence, kisses in the Bois de Boulogne, in Paris, never anything in Porto Manacore or even in Naples; their love was only imaginable in a different world from the world he knew, in a different time and space, in the last century or north of the Tiber.

At the end of the third week he had to go back to Naples; he called to say goodbye and found her alone. They remained silent, standing facing one another. He spoke without premeditation.

'I love you,' he said.

'Me too,' she said.

She leaned against him and rested her head on his shoulder.

Donna Lucrezia and Francesco Brigante had arranged to meet at the entrance of a cave near the *trabucco*. The promontory was humped in the centre; on the Schiavona side, the woods descended in layers to a cornfield, which Francesco was skirting at the moment on the Manacore Bay side, the woods ended flush with the top of a tall cliff which fell straight into the sea. Several winter torrents had hollowed out an abrupt bed in the woods and cliff; it was on a small beach, at the fall-out of one of these torrents, that the cave had its opening.

Starting from the holiday camp, that is to say from the base of the promontory, on the Manacore side, donna Lucrezia had therefore first to climb the pine woods till she was level with the top of the cliff.

She climbed slowly because the slope was steep. The sun was approaching its zenith. The pine needles crackled underfoot. The perfumes — thyme, lavender, peppermints, marjoram (which clung to the skin like an oil) — were so dense that they appeared to acquire substance; they slowed her down as though she were having to fight her way through a thick undergrowth. She climbed from tree to tree, sometimes clinging to a scaly trunk, sometimes slipping on the pine needles, but recovering at once, tingling from the heat beneath the pines, facing up to the heat, the exertion, the onslaught of the perfumes, as it was in her nature always to face up to things.

The first time Francesco had found himself alone with her, when he had told her that in Fabrice's place he would have preferred la Sanseverina to Clélia, her curiosity had been aroused. Having never even thought of imagining herself as Sanseverina, she had not seen a disguised declaration in the young man's preference. But, having acquired a taste for intelligent conversation from her husband, she had tried to get him to explain his reasons.

It was in the minutes which followed that something new began. He did not answer her questions. She was not surprised. Silence was one of the attributes of Brigante's son, just as much as his broad shoulders, his prominent blue eyes, his reserved behaviour, his air of grave assurance. But suddenly his silence had changed its nature. It had become anguished and anguishing, like the lack of air in Manacore Bay, the vacuum between the mountain and the enfolding arms of the libeccio and the sirocco battling out at sea, like the silence of the bay behind the offshore storm, facing the hollow of the storm which, in the distance, shook invisible hairs over invisible ships.

Till now, Lucrezia had never judged human actions with anything but her head; but she had felt this silence in the hollow of her chest, the home of anguish. When Francesco, taking his leave, had retained her hand for a moment, the anguish had suddenly descended to her stomach. She had become a woman.

'You'd better go,' she had said.

She had at once reproached herself for this silly phrase, like a provincialism. Francesco had already gone.

In the course of the three weeks which followed, she had courageously faced up to the new situation. She was a woman now, with a woman's body capable of being aroused, and she was in love, exactly as if she had been born not in a country where there was never any work, but in the North of Italy, in France, in the Russia of Anna Karenina, in the England of Mansfield. She at once deduced the consequences, not in the manner of one or other of the heroines whom she admired but who served only to enlighten her as to her feelings, but in her own style. She had absolutely no intention of making arrangements to meet Francesco Brigante in secret, to have him as her lover, to be his mistress, to make shift with an adulterous affair. No. Since she loved him, she would live with him; since the South of Italy was opposed to illicit affairs, they would go North together; and since they had no money, they would work.

She did not ask herself: does he love me too? Is he ready to go away with me? Since she loved, it was clear that she was loved. At eighteen, she would probably not have been so sure of herself. At twenty-eight she expended on her love all the energy of a tall, robust and idle woman.

That she coldly deduced the consequences of her love did not prevent her from loving with elation. Quite the contrary. All day long she repeated to herself with exaltation: 'I love Francesco Brigante, his face is full of strong-mindedness, he is good-looking, he walks with the quiet assurance of real men, his discretion reveals a sensitive and delicate heart, I'll make him happy.' She congratulated herself on being prepared to leave her children, without regret, in order to make her lover happy. During those three weeks she was happy to a degree she would never again achieve.

She had no scruples about the grief Judge Alessandro, her husband, would probably experience. It was the books on which he had nourished her, and his conversation, which had schooled her to all the nuances of passion; it was to the peace and quiet which he had procured for her, when she had left the Foggia flat, that she owed the increased strength which nourished her elation. Besides, reflection would not have altered her decision in the least. Without knowing it, Judge Alessandro had shaped her for the love she was to feel for another; for ten years he had reared Lucrezia, and now that she was of age she felt an overpowering need to leave him; she detested her tutor for reminding her of her conquered weakness.

When next she found herself alone with Francesco, three weeks after he had held her hand a little longer than usual and this slightly prolonged pressure of Francesco's hand had revealed to her that she was a woman like other women, with the same sudden surges of the blood which made them long to give themselves to the man in question, she found it absolutely natural that he should say to her:

'I love you.'

And she replied, quite calmly:

'Me too.'

Then she rested her head in the hollow of his shoulder. He was a little taller than she was. Everything was as it should be.

She had finished scaling the woods and was now following a path which ran along the top of the cliff. Now that she had put a safe distance between herself and the eyes of the men of the South she walked with a long, serene stride in the eleven o'clock August sun, the *solleone*, the sun-lion.

The whole of Manacore Bay lay before her, enclosed and classified.

As to the classifications: to the west, the lake, the marsh, the goat hills, the olive plantations, every shade of green; the isthmus, straight as a line drawn with a ruler, divided them from the sea. To the south, white against white, the terraces of Porto Manacore, perched one on top of another, the sanctuary of Santa Ursula of Uria at the top of the town, the long, straight jetty at the foot. Between south and east, the roll of the hills where the orange and lemon trees grew, a dark green, almost black.

As to the enclosure: seawards the horizon was completely sealed off by the bank of clouds driven along by the libeccio and held back by the sirocco, grey, dark grey, light grey, lead, copper. Landwards, the mountain rose relentlessly, behind the goat hills, the orchards and the pine woods, a monumental cliff with reddish streaks, surmounted, three thousand feet up, by a darker patch, an ancient ghost of a forest with trees many hundreds of years old, the forest which was majestically named *Umbra*, Shadow.

Nor was there any escape skywards. The sun, now almost perpendicularly above the bay, sealed off exit from above, enveloping his daughter, donna Lucrezia, in his burning gold.

Francesco Brigante had plunged into the pine woods and was

panting his way towards the top of the promontory, burnt by the rays of the sun-lion, bitten by gad-flies from the goats and mules.

After he had told donna Lucrezia that he loved her and she had replied 'Me too', they had stood beside one another for a long moment, she with her head resting on his shoulder, he not daring to embrace her, encumbered by her arms. The servant had made a noise in the next room, they had separated, she had opened the door. Judge Alessandro had arrived home and asked his wife to offer them a glass of French brandy; they had talked jazz. Lucrezia preferred New Orleans, Francesco bop and the judge Beethoven. Francesco had gone home without hearing donna Lucrezia repeat that she loved him and the following day he had returned to Naples, without seeing her again.

In Naples, he made no further bones about a passion which brought him the greater honour by being shared and which had such extensive literary backing. As chance would have it, in the loft in the priest's house he came upon a translation of *Anna Karenina*, which he read at a sitting, discovering that adultery guaranteed great ladies a tragic fate; he felt sorry for donna Lucrezia, but his vanity was gratified.

All the time he was preparing for his law examination he was constantly searching his mind. There could be no question of having the judge's wife as his mistress in Porto Manacore. In the whole town there would not be a single door they could lock behind them; this was the rule in every big city where the number of inhabitants was several times larger than the number of habitable rooms. The beach was exposed to the eyes on the road, the orchards to the eyes in the other orchards, and the olive plantations to the eyes of the whole world. The foresters who rode on horseback through the Shadow forest, mountain men and men of the shadows, when they came upon lovers beat the man in the name of God and took the woman in the name of the devil; there was no question of complaining to the police, adultery being not only a sin but also a crime punishable by law; besides, the police were careful not to oppose the men of the forest. The hills were exposed to the eyes of the goatherds, the marsh to the eyes of the fishermen and the boats which put to sea to all the eyes along the coast. They could meet one another in the pine woods, on condition they went there separately, all the paths which led there being exposed to all sorts of eyes, and only once — for a second time the coincidence would be remarked upon. Francesco, who had never been beyond Naples, had never seen a countryside without eyes; this deprived him of a complete understanding of many French novels: how could the lovers find solitude in woods, meadows and fields? How could a hedge not have eyes?

Therefore, he thought, he would have to meet his mistress somewhere away from the South. But he was dependent on his father for money, time and travel. He turned the problem over and over in his mind. The only solutions he could find seemed to him neither reasonable nor practicable; for example, getting donna Lucrezia to elope with him, taking her to the North, living with her in Genoa, Turin or Milan and working to earn a living for the two of them; he was strong, he could mix mortar for bricklayers, unload trucks, load ships, work on the roads breaking stones

He made Corpus Christi, a public holiday in the Christian Democrat republic, an excuse to visit Porto Manacore. He succeeded in spending half an hour alone with Lucrezia, in her flat. It was their third tête-à-tête. In the course of the first he had compared her with la Sanseverina and pressed her hand. In the course of the second they had confessed their love to one another.

He explained that he could not live without her, that she was to follow him, he didn't know where — it didn't matter where.

She listened to him in silence, fixing her fiery eyes upon him.

Then he recounted his wild dreams, his plans of eloping, of a life together in the North, of manual labour. She declared the project perfectly reasonable, apart from his choice of job. He had two law certificates, he would soon have three, it would be easy for him to earn a little money as a solicitor's or notary's clerk or as a legal adviser, while continuing his studies. She had already given some thought to the matter and told him how to set about it. Judge Alessandro was on intimate terms (the friendship had lasted through childhood, school and college) with the Naples agent of a large Turin firm; Francesco would look this man up on behalf of the judge (people never checked up on these things); he would tell him that he suddenly found himself compelled to start earning his living, that his family had suddenly emigrated to Piedmont, that he had a widowed mother, younger sisters, anything, whatever he liked, but that he was compelled to earn his living in Turin. A few days later, donna Lucrezia herself would write to the man, again on the judge's behalf, insisting that he should do something for Francesco; afterwards she would go through the mail the postman brought up to the fourth floor while her husband was in court. If this scheme did not succeed, she would think of something else; she was not without alternative solutions.

Francesco was so astonished that he forgot to clasp in his arms the woman he already called his mistress, although he had not yet given her so much as a kiss.

He climbed, sweating and puffing, among the pines which offered a poor protection against the sun-lion, in the heady perfumes, pursued by the gad-flies. He had stupidly chosen the steepest slope. He was not built for running through pine woods in the midday sun. He was a studious boy, with white skin like his mother. He wondered why donna Lucrezia had arranged to meet him in, of all the caves in the riddled, limestone cliff, the cave nearest the tip of the promontory — the one, that was to say, which obliged both of them to cover the greatest distance on foot. Panting made him lose his assurance because he had long since adopted the habit, out of mistrust of his father, of speaking slowly, not wasting breath.

When he came away from his third tête-à-tête with his mistress, still without getting a kiss from her, his fate was determined.

In Naples he called on the judge's friend, who greeted him with kindness and was favourably impressed by his silence and placidity, so foreign to Neapolitan behaviour. Three weeks later the man sent for him; by the same post he had received donna Lucrezia's recommendation, a few words she had succeeded in obtaining from the Bishop of Foggia through the mediation of a relative, and a reply from Turin, favourable in principle, but asking for details of the young man's education. Everything was turning out exactly as his mistress had predicted.

It was in that same month she began to make an appearance in his night dreams — still not in his daydreams. Since his early childhood, his night dreams had followed the same theme — pursuit — with all kinds of variants; he was on a staircase and the steps gave way under his feet; he was on a plateau, and each stride brought him closer to a dizzy drop; he could be anywhere, and his legs turned to jelly and refused to obey him. He seldom saw the face of his pursuer, but somehow he knew, the way you know these things in dreams, that it was his father, Matteo Brigante. Sometimes he caught a glimpse of him — just the two hard little eyes and the thin black moustache. At the very moment when his persecutor, his father, seen or unseen, was on the point of catching him, the anguish which had been with him throughout the dream swelled out of all proportion. It was a two-sided terror, mixed with pleasure, comparable with what he had felt when his father — this had gone on until he was thirteen — had punished him by thrashing him with a leather strap, coolly, counting the strokes, or making Francesco count them, as he considered you should chastise a child to bring him up the right way, so that one day he should be master of himself, capable of defending his heritage against the lawyers; it was essential to hammer the law into his hide. At its unbearable climax the terror awakened him, sometimes with the same start as did love, painful and delicious.

Now that month (following Corpus Christi and his third tête-à-tête with the woman to whom he accorded the name of mistress) his dream persecutor assumed an ambiguous face, donna Lucrezia now taking shape in the features of Matteo Brigante, like the winged insect forming in the chrysalis, both distinct and consubstantial, the way it happens in dreams, the cold and imperious eyes of his father, the burning and imperious eyes of his mistress, the cold-burning eyes of his father and his mistress.

He had reached the peak of the promontory. He walked with long strides, under the sun-lion, along the upper path. He was filled with rage against donna Lucrezia who had made an absurd choice of rendezvous. The gad-flies still pursued him; he was filled with rage against the gad-flies, against his father who obliged him to take so many precautions and against his mistress who, by obliging him to walk in this exhausting fashion, had robbed him of his breath, his carefully measured breath, that illusion of self-control.

As soon as Francesco had left her, at the end of their third and last tête-à-tête, without clasping her in his arms but approving all her plans, donna Lucrezia had exclaimed:

'He loves me, just as I love him!'

She walked with long, serene strides towards the cave where she had arranged to meet him, along the path which followed the top of the cliff and which at times dipped towards the small shingly beaches she could see at her feet between the branches of the strawberry trees, and at others rose towards the pine woods. He walked with long, panting strides, parallel to her but higher, on the upper path of the promontory.

At the beginning of July, when he had returned to Porto Manacore for the university vacation, donna Lucrezia had looked around for a go-between. Impossible to build their future by relying on chance tête-à-têtes or whispering near the gramophone in leading citizens' drawing-rooms or on the beach, around the sunshades of leading citizens' wives. Even to arrange a meeting like the one they were making for at the moment, they had first to write to one another. And there could be no question of writing poste restante — still less for her than for him. The whole town would know at once that the judge's wife was carrying on a secret correspondence.

Her instinct, since she had made her decision, would have led her to inform her husband she was going to leave him and demand, before she went, at least the right to correspond freely. She would not allow herself to be swayed by his objections. She had often heard him show temper at the fact that Italian legislation refused the right to divorce, a shameful example of the priest's dictatorship. She would remind him of that. She was not afraid of an argument, but she had mistrusted him ever since he had insisted she should send their children to catechism and sentenced the agricultural workers for 'squatting'. He was quite capable, she reckoned, of employing legal means, direct or indirect, to prevent her from leaving or to persecute Francesco; the Italian law was full of pitfalls for lovers; and there were police regulations to stop a man from the South working in the North. She was also afraid he might inform Matteo Brigante, who would certainly be disinclined to have his son taken away from him by an adulteress. Herself, she felt capable of surmounting all obstacles. But she was afraid Francesco would be caught in the triple nets of the judge, the Chief of Police and Matteo Brigante, in the equivocal machinery of legal, illegal and paralegal powers. So she must stay silent.

The alternative was to find a go-between to keep her in touch with Francesco. She had run through the women with whom she was acquainted, deciding to confide in none of them; she distrusted them all equally. Besides, the wives of the other leading citizens were subject to a no less strict surveillance than herself.

She had chosen Giuseppina, the hardware dealer's daughter, because she had immediately discovered how to buy her.

At twenty-five Giuseppina could no longer hope to marry, especially without a dowry (her father had not yet finished paying off his mortgage). She was compelled to limit her ambitions to becoming the regular mistress, accepted if not received, of a widower, of a younger son anxious not to have legitimate children who might one day dispute the inheritance of the elder branch (it was on this condition that the head of the family made him an allowance) or of a man who was already married but who was either rich enough to keep two homes going or astute enough to get his wife to take a back seat. If Anna Attilio were to go back to Lucera, she would yield to the Chief; he would set her up in a flat which he would visit as often as he liked, but she would no longer be allowed in the court house; all this accorded with convention. These prospects marked Giuseppina's special place in Porto Manacore society; there were no scandals she could be reproached with and, since the men were unanimous in calling her a flirt and a little bitch, it was legitimate to suppose her a virgin; so people accepted her on the same terms as other tradesmen's daughters, but already a little as a subordinate, as an advance reflection of her future marginal position. They came to her for various small services: baby sitting, shopping, acting as a companion. In return for these services, she enjoyed more liberty than the other girls; they were never surprised to see her leaving or entering a house or walking about the town at any hour of the day or night. She also looked after the sick. She was never suspected of anything foolish, the whole town being convinced that she would give up her virginity only on the best possible terms and with everything guaranteed. This foolish virgin was the most rational creature in the world.

So as not to damage her own particular kind of respectability, Giuseppina accepted presents only from women, in exchange for her small services. They did not amount to much. And the hardware dealer, obsessed with the payments due at the end of the month, cavilled at her dressmakers' bills. She could not rival in elegance the daughters of the leading citizens. Since she was clever with her hands, most men failed to notice this. She wore three superimposed petticoats, like don Ottavio's daughter, but only one row of lace.

Donna Lucrezia, too, had found Giuseppina useful, to look after the children, for example, when their servant went home to see her parents. But she had never confided in her (what would she have had to confide?) not even listening to the girl's gossip.

Her haughtiness bore out her title of *donna*, but she was not liked. It cost her a great deal to have to ask Giuseppina to act as messenger between her and a boy of twenty-two. It was the first sacrifice her pride had allowed her love. This was the way she went about it.

She found an excuse to go down and see Anna Attilio, the Chief of Police's wife and her downstairs neighbour, late in the afternoon, at the time when Giuseppina was normally there. Donna Lucrezia and Anna Attilio were good neighbours to one another, nothing more. After a few remarks about the children:

'I'm going along to Fidelia's ...'

Fidelia, the linen draper, had the finest shop-window in the via Garibaldi.

'Will you come with me?' she asked Giuseppina.

Up to this point, everything was quite normal. It was among Giuseppina's functions to go about with people. Donna Lucrezia did not say a word to her on the way from the court house to Fidelia's shop. Her heart beat harder than it had this morning as she had turned into the path through the pine woods, behind the gates of the holiday camp, to meet her lover. To avoid the complicity which it sickened her simply to think of, she had made up her mind to buy Giuseppina before asking her services.

A few days earlier, at Anna Attilio's, she had heard Giuseppina complain that she could not afford to buy a Lastex swimsuit. To her shame, the girl, a contemporary of Lollobrigida and Sophia Loren, had small breasts. Now there was no better material than Lastex, she thought, for concealing the frames which tautened and expanded the breasts. But a Lastex swimsuit cost anything from six to twelve thousand lire, which meant from sixty to a hundred and twenty litres of wine, an agricultural worker's wages for a fortnight or a month, far too much for the hardware dealer's daughter.

At Fidelia's donna Lucrezia chose a Lastex swimsuit at random.

'Do you like it?' she asked Giuseppina.

'*Stupendo*,' Giuseppina replied. 'But it's certainly a bit on the small side for you.'

'It's your size.'

Giuseppina stared at her with her large, black, rather wild malarial eyes.

'I'd be glad if you'd accept it,' said Lucrezia.

She thought she detected a note of humbleness in her voice, which made her furious.

'Make your mind up!' she went on, with a note of anger.

Giuseppina was studying her face.

'Wrap it up for us,' Lucrezia said to Fidelia.

'No,' said Giuseppina, 'I prefer the pale blue.'

She continued to stare at donna Lucrezia.

'I'm darker than you,' she said. 'Blue shows a tan to its advantage.'

Giuseppina tried the pale blue swimsuit against her figure and decided it was too big. She tried another, then returned to the first.

Donna Lucrezia stood waiting, motionless, erect, without a word. Giuseppina could not make her mind up. Fidelia watched them. Giuseppina chattered about colours and complexions and scrutinized Lucrezia's face. At last she made her choice. The judge's wife handed over eight thousand lire. Giuseppina took the package.

As soon as they were in the street:

'You know Francesco Brigante?' asked Lucrezia.

'Of course.'

'Can you see him alone?'

'I'll arrange it.'

'You'll take a letter to him and bring me the answer.'

'Whenever you like.'

'You'll come up to my flat for the letter tomorrow morning.'

'Yes,' said Giuseppina. 'Before twelve. Before Judge Alessandro gets back.'

'Yes,' said Lucrezia.

They walked the rest of the way in silence. When they reached the court house, Giuseppina said:

'We'll tell everyone it was my father who gave me the swimsuit.'

130

'Yes,' said Lucrezia. 'Thank you.'

When, that same evening, donna Lucrezia gave a rapid account of her exploit to Francesco, whom she had run into by chance in the main square, surrounded by a dozen people who were trying to catch what she was saying:

'An eight-thousand lire swimsuit,' he whispered. 'It's far too much. You could have bought her for life with a three-thousand lire brassière. Now she'll think she's got you in her pocket.'

'Poor boy,' she said to herself, 'he still hasn't shaken off the Porto Manacore way of looking at things.'

The judge and his wife spent little money. They had never thought of changing the Topolino, they seldom went out and they ate anything, neither of them thinking it important. Dress-makers irritated donna Lucrezia and a ready-made frock, bought in five minutes in Foggia, looked stylish on her. Books, gramophone records and French brandy were supplied by the judge's parents, who drew a decent income from some property in the Tavoliere; oil and wine came out of the rents from the farmers on their land. Thus, despite the modest salary of a judge of the lowest order, at the end of the month there were sometimes a few notes left in the drawer into which Lucrezia casually threw the household money. When the fresh supply of money arrived, she placed the residue of the previous month, without counting it, in a tin similar to those in which the judge collected the evidence of contemporary imbecility. When she had made up her mind to leave, she had opened the tin and counted a hundred and ninety-two thousand lire — enough to buy two dozen Lastex swimsuits. She felt she was sitting pretty.

On the point of the promontory, not far from the cave where Donna Lucrezia had arranged to meet Francesco, the fishermen had built a *trabucco*, some thousand or two thousand years before.

A *trabucco* is a fishing machine composed, in its essentials, of

131

a group of masts projecting out over the sea, spread in a fan parallel to the water, and supporting from the tips (in the air when the machine is at rest, in the water when it is in motion) an immense polygonal net.

Movement of the net is controlled by cables running over pulleys and wound on winches. The number of masts is equal to the number of sides of the net. A master cable, knotted to each corner of the net, runs over a pulley attached to the end of each mast, and is wound on a winch.

The *trabucco* on Manacore Point is one of the most imposing on the Adriatic coast: seven long masts, a seven-sided net, a team of a dozen men.

When the net is immersed — the fish-trap set — one of the seven sides of the polygon rests flat on the rocky bottom; two sides are held at a slant; the other four are kept on the surface.

Thus at the beginning of the operation the net lies open in the sea, like a jaw. When the winches pull in the cables, the submerged portion rises to the surface: the jaw closes.

The winches are operated by the men, without any mechanical aid. The men exert their weight on the handles of the winches, treading the ground, in a circular march, like the blind horses which used to turn the old mills; the cables slide over the pulleys; the jaw closes with a speed which depends on the rapidity of the men's rotation.

A look-out is posted half-way along the central mast, either standing with his hand on a rope, or sitting astride the mast with his trunk bent forward, as though he were riding at a gallop. There he perches, directly over the centre of the net, sixty feet above the water. The sea is transparent as it is transparent only in the South, with a rocky bed, in a calm bay; so the look-out has a clear view of every detail on the bed; he can see the whole expanse of net and the full depths of the sea, within and without the gaping jaw. He keeps his eyes open. When he sees a shoal of fish swimming towards the net, he gives the signal and the land trawler's crew take up their positions around the winches. While he waits, he can take his time following the slow progress of the jelly-fish and the starfish and the mullets at play down on the rocks. Fishing with the *trabucco* means fishing with the eyes.

The seven long masts spread in a fan above the sea are anchored to the bottom by cables weighted with rocks, and to the shore by other cables tied to stakes. Ropes connect the ends of the masts, holding them at a constant distance from one another. There are cords controlling subsidiary apparatus and a giant landing net which it takes four hands to control. Cables, ropes and cords are interwoven in a thousand different ways and form, as it were, a second net, hanging in the air, a reflection in the sky of the fishing net, stretched beneath the waves, an open jaw.

The *trabucco* extends a long way back on to the shore: white, dome-shaped structures, shelters for the fishermen on days of bad weather and store-rooms for the crates of fish; earthworks for the winches, stakes, pegs, cement bollards; and a wooden gallery, suspended in a circle round the rocks on the point, sixty feet above the sea, its shape reminiscent of the poop on old sailing ships.

Greek and Latin texts mention the existence on this part of the Adriatic coast of gigantic fishing machines, the description of which corresponds with that of the *trabucco*. Certain technologists trace its origin back to the Phrygians, others to the Pelasgians; it probably dates back to the invention of the net, the pulley and the winch.

Every year the *trabucco* comes in for a little renovation. After heavy storms, the fishermen replace a mast, change one of the cables. But neither the technique nor the shape changes. Different each year and always the same, like a human being who grows old and remains as he always has been, the *trabucco* has stood there for hundreds and probably thousands of years.

Francesco was now running down from the top of the promontory, through the woods.

The cave in which donna Lucrezia had arranged to meet him opened at the foot of the cove nearest the point; its entrance, on a

133

small beach, was at the back of the *trabucco*, out of sight from the fishermen, screened from the eyes of the look-out by the pile of rocks in which it was lodged. The small beach could be reached through a clearing in the woods, the bed of a winter torrent.

Francesco ran down towards the cove. He thought Lucrezia's choice absurd. Of all the caves there were along the coast, why did she have to choose the one nearest the *trabucco*, the one which meant the longest trudge in the sun, the one which afforded them the biggest chance of being seen? Looking out through the pines on his way down to the cove, he had a clear view of the fishermen, who could not see him because he was hidden by the pines. All the same, it was absurd to come so close to them. At moments he hung back; he would have liked to retrace his steps. But the thought of having walked so far and of being now on the downward slope carried him on.

From where Francesco stood the *trabucco* resembled the war-machines of antiquity, as they are shown on engravings in military academies. A gigantic siege-machine erected on the tip of the promontory, directed against the bank of clouds which were driven along by the libeccio and sealed off the horizon.

Donna Lucrezia, a few minutes behind her lover, walked with long, serene strides along the top of the cliff, hidden from view by the strawberry trees.

She had chosen this particular cave rather than another because she knew its name. It was called the cave of the Tuscans because some archaeologists from Pisa had come there to make excavations. They supposed it had served as a shelter for Greek navigators, before the foundation of the port of Uria, and they hoped to find urns, coins, tools. They had found nothing but bones. Lucrezia had gone there with her husband and don Cesare during the time the Tuscans were making their excavations and they had talked to them about Polyphemus and Ulysses; that had been immediately after their marriage; they took an interest in such things.

The other caves had no names, for Lucrezia at least. They

134

could not run the risk of Francesco waiting for her in one cave while she was waiting in another. So she had written: 'The Cave of the Tuscans, near the *trabucco*, the one where the archaeologists made excavations.' She had underlined 'near the *trabucco*' once, 'the one where the archaeologists made excavations' twice. Underlining key words was yet another habit she had taken from her husband, but it tallied with her own personal preference for precision. Then she had sent the letter through Giuseppina.

Francesco was the first to reach the small beach at the foot of the cove. The torrent bed ended precipitously; you had to descend the last three hundred feet with your face to the rock, picking your steps carefully, as though you were on the rungs of a ladder, holding on to projecting pieces of rock and caper bushes. He had growled to himself: 'I'm not a mountaineer'; he smiled grimly at the thought that donna Lucrezia would have to negotiate this bit too; then he reproached himself for his malice, unworthy of his love.

A small beach, fifty paces long, fifteen paces deep. When you hugged the shore in a boat, you had to know it was there to be able to pick it out, a slender strip of white sand wedged against the cliff at the back of the cove.

The entrance of the cave was enormous in proportion to the size of the beach. It occupied the whole wall of the creek at the back of the *trabucco*. It was like the mouth of the cliff, a gaping jaw.

From the beach, Francesco had the impression of being able to take in the whole interior of the cave at a glance. He knew of others which afforded far greater concealment. He thought Lucrezia had shown a lack of common sense in choosing this jaw open to all eyes. A boat might come out from the coast.

It was only when he went inside the cave that he distinguished further depths, shadowy recesses. His eyes had first of all to become accustomed to the dark.

To his left, the ground was uneven, rising steeply, with projections, crevices, sudden peaks, terraces dimly lit by a light which seemed to come out of the rock. To the right, on the other hand, the ground fell away to reveal a second chamber, hollowed deep in the bowels of the promontory, closed at the top by a chaotic mass of rocks forming a dome, which was lost in darkness; farther in you could just about pick out the opening of a third chamber, on the far side of a trench dug by the Tuscan archaeologists.

From the rear of the first chamber Francesco turned back towards the light. The whole bay was inscribed in the jagged opening, drowned in a kind of mist by the reflection of the sun, the isthmus, don Cesare's olive plantations, the white terraces of Porto Manacore surmounted by the sanctuary of Santa Ursula of Uria, the beach, the orange and lemon orchards. It was from this heat haze donna Lucrezia would emerge.

It was cold inside the cave. The ground was damp, uncertain underfoot. A dubious smell seeped from the walls.

Francesco was drawn to the left by the light which seemed to come from the rocks. He climbed among crevices and projections till he reached a ledge, a miniature balcony. He then discovered a hole in the wall of the rock; it was from there the light was coming.

From this opening, to the left and at the back of the cave, a little above sea level, he could see the *trabucco* two or three hundred yards away. He could see the undersides of the fan of masts spread above the sea and the whole machinery of cables, ropes and cords. The look-out was standing in the middle of the central mast, his arms spread in a cross on the supporting rope, his head bent forward, watching everything that was happening in the underwater depths.

Squatting on the wooden planks which formed a balcony round the rocks on the point, the two boys in the crew were also studying the sea-bed.

The others were at action stations beside the winches.

Francesco might have thought that the look-out and the boys, their faces inclined towards the sea, that is in his direction, were watching him. But he knew they could not see him since they were in the blaze of the sun-lion and he was in the darkness of the cave.

Beneath the look-out's feet a line was attached to something moving about in the depths of the water. In response to whatever was moving down in the water, the line hung at a greater or smaller angle to the vertical and described on the surface circles, ovals, arabesques, returned to its position directly below where it was tied at the look-out's feet, then went off at an angle again.

Francesco had been down to the *trabucco* often enough to find an immediate explanation of what he was seeing. They were fishing for mullet by attraction. This was one of the numerous methods of fishing practised from the height of the land trawler and undoubtedly the most fascinating. Francesco was all attention.

At the beginning of the morning or perhaps the night before, the fishermen had been lucky enough to trap in their net one of those fish which in Italian are called *cefalo* and, in French, *mulet* on the Mediterranean coast, *muge* on the Atlantic.

Mullets attract one another. The difficulty lies only in catching the first and in the chances of its being plump, robust, full of life, full of attraction. This first mullet, which is known as the *richiamo*, the bait, is thrown back into the sea, attached to a line long enough for it to move freely about inside the net, but too short to allow it to reach the wall of the cliff.

Francesco, like the other young men of Manacore, had been down to the *trabucco* often enough to have a very clear picture of what was happening.

A second mullet would come along (or had already come along) to join the first — the one attached to the line, the bait — and attach himself to him, slightly to the rear, his head level with the dorsal fins, in exactly the same way as, in the course of a race, one cyclist attaches himself to another cyclist, his front wheel against the other's back wheel. The second mullet would describe the same circles, ovals, arabesques, zigzags as the bait, heading towards the rocks with him, returning with him vertically below the look-out, slowing and accelerating with him, attached to him.

Then a third mullet would come along and attach himself to the second, his head level with the dorsal fin. Then a fourth, a fifth, then a whole shoal of mullets running in the wake of the bait, wheel against wheel, describing interminably the same circles, ovals, arabesques, zigzags.

It was for the look-out to know and decide, uniting in the judgment of a moment the experience of a lifetime's fishing on the *trabucco*, the moment at which to shout 'Hoist away! Hoist away!' not till all the latecomers had joined the gang (but how could you tell how many there were in the gang?), not after the bait, exhausted by its futile movements, was suddenly left abandoned at the end of the line, inert at the look-out's feet while the whole gang dispersed; there was no time then for the look-out to shout 'Hoist away! Hoist away!', all the fish were already out of the net.

From the hole hollowed in the wall of the cave by the winter waves, Francesco followed every movement of the bait line. How many fish in the gang? In his mind's eyes he saw the plump black fish, glistening, with their flat heads and large jaws, where a white line carved out an up-turned lip. Francesco's head swung from right to left, from left to right, like the look-out's head, like the boys' heads as they attentively followed the bait's movements. Wasn't the look-out leaving it too late?

It came to Francesco that he would rather be up on the *trabucco* following the movements of the gang of mullets, with a thudding heart, holding his breath as he waited for the shout which would snap the jaw of the net shut, and then the men would tear round the winches, and he would help them — that he would rather do that than stand about in this cave waiting for his mistress.

138

He at once rejected the idea as unworthy of the passion on which he prided himself.

He drew back. He turned. Donna Lucrezia was walking across the beach, tall and erect in her dress with the stand-up collar, completely enveloped in the blaze of the sun-lion. She came into the cave.

There they were, face to face, in the entrance to the cave, in the sun reflected by the sea and the white sand of the little beach.

They looked at one another in silence.

Francesco was wearing a pair of blue jeans, narrow in the legs, with broad, obvious seams at the hips sewn with white cotton, cowboy fashion; a shirt in the very latest summer style, without a button to fasten the neck, since no one ever wore a tie at the seaside, but fastened all the same, with a kind of frill, as in the great periods of history; the sleeves were long, rolled up over the elbows, giving a casual effect.

Donna Lucrezia reflected that when, in the near future, they were living together in the North of Italy, she would have to break him of the habit of dressing in the latest fashion, especially the latest Naples fashion.

He was suffering agonies. He reflected that this was the first time he had found himself alone with his mistress in a quiet spot, and that he ought to take her in his arms and cover her with kisses. But she was looking at him, motionless, silent, severely dressed. What was he to do? Which way did his duty lie?

'I was watching the *trabucco*,' he said.

'How could you see the *trabucco*?'

'You can see it from up there.'

'They can't see us?' she asked.

'How could they see us?'

'Had you been up there long?'

'No,' he replied.

139

He was standing in front of her, displaying his big, blue, prominent eyes.

She thought with satisfaction that he was not like the other men of the South, whose eyes lit up the moment they were in the presence of a woman or, if she were placed in a situation in which she could not defend herself, became condescending, superior. She imagined him in a drawing-room in Turin. It pleased her that he was reserved, not at all southern (apart from his clothes), almost English.

For him, this prolonged silence and immobility were becoming unbearable. He was failing in his duties: he had not the courage to take his mistress.

'They're fishing by attraction,' he said.

'By attraction?' she asked.

He explained how people fished by attraction. His voice was grave, very steady, slow. He spoke in short phrases, with silences between them.

She reflected that Judge Alessandro, her husband, cared only for intellectual discussions, general ideas and the heroes of other days. Francesco was speaking of something technical, with quiet assurance and a working knowledge of what he was discussing; he was a real man. She imagined him to be good with his hands (he wasn't).

He reflected that it was his duty as a man to clasp her in his arms, pull her down and take her. The floor of the cave was wet and lined with mould. He did not dare to throw the tall, handsome and faultlessly dressed woman to the ground. But the idea of the spotted dress disturbed him.

The look-out shouted:

'Hoist away! Hoist away!'

The full-chested cry carried to within the cave.

'They're pulling in the net,' he said.

She stood facing him, but out of reach. She stayed where she was, as though she wanted to hold back in order to view him better. She's not helping me, he thought.

'Do you want to see them?' he asked. 'It's very interesting.'

She thought: How tactful he is.

'But of course I want to see them,' she said. 'It's certainly very interesting.'

He took her hand to help her climb the slope, near the hole worn in the wall of rock by the winter storms.

'Have you never seen them fish from the *trabucco*?' he asked.

'Only from a distance,' she replied.

He sat down on the rock. She stood close beside him.

'I once saw them net ten hundredweight of fish in one go.'

'That must have made them happy.'

'But it doesn't often happen,' he said.

Placed as they were — he sitting, she standing — it was difficult for Lucrezia to follow the movements of the *trabucco*; she came closer, so that he should not think she was indifferent to the fishermen's exploits; her long thigh rested against the boy's shoulder. The shelf in the rock was a little longer than it was broad, as long as a body stretched full-length, as broad as two bodies lying side by side. It had a loose surface, formed of the dry dust of rocks pulverized by the action of the sea in winter. This is where I must take her, thought Francesco. He remembered students' conversations, how you went about awakening a woman's desire, preparing her for the act, possessing her; he was afraid of failing in so many ways.

The look-out repeated with more and more urgency:

'Hoist away! Hoist away!'

The fishermen tramped round the winches, some in a clockwise, others in an anti-clockwise direction, depending on the winch.

Francesco put his arm round Lucrezia's knees, embraced them and squeezed them.

Lucrezia pushed the boy's arm away.

'Don't move,' she said.

She took hold of his head and held it against her side.

'Don't move,' she repeated.

On their wooden gallery, the two boys pranced about with excitement.

'Hoist away! Hoist away!' they shouted in the same rhythm as the look-out.

The pulleys creaked, the cables rasped, the cords quivered. The net rose slowly above the waves. The entire crew of the land trawler shouted:

'Hoist away! Hoist away!'

The ends of the net were already high in the air, but the middle, with its load of fish, was still level with the water.

Lucrezia held the boy's head against her side.

Francesco hesitated to embrace his mistress's knees again. He did not know what to do with the arm she had pushed away, but he was afraid to take up a more comfortable position. If I move, she'll think I'm pushing her away, to get my own back.

She caressed his temples, his brow. She was hardly touching him. This was not how he had imagined the fires of passion. But he stopped thinking of his duties. He shut his eyes.

She put her hand over his closed eyes and pressed lightly on the lids.

He embraced her knees again, but this time without squeezing them. He drew her tenderly against him. She did not push his arm away. But, in return for so much tenderness, he did not feel obliged to 'ram home his advantage', as his colleagues at Law School put it.

They remained like this for quite a time.

'You're not like the others,' said Lucrezia. 'They only think of dirt. How I love you for being so kind and patient with me. I love you, Francesco.'

He rubbed his head against the side of the tall woman, his tender mistress. How relaxingly she spoke! He abandoned his head to the light caress of Lucrezia's hand, against the warmth of her stomach. He felt all his unhappiness dissolve within him.

The *trabucco* team had locked the winches. The bottom of the net was now at water level. The big fish used the impetus of the last wave breaking beneath them to leap high against the sides of the lifted net; they hung in the air; then they fell back on top of one another, in a shuddering mass of gleaming skins and fins.

142

The men mopped away their sweat, weighed the haul with their eyes and calculated their earnings. The boys began to manœuvre the giant landing net.

Not so long ago, it had been one of Francesco's major pleasures to see the *trabucco* net rising from the sea. As a child, he had pranced around like the crew's two boys, shouting with them: 'Hoist away! Hoist away!' As a youth, he had helped manipulate the winches; he would take over from the man he saw sweating the hardest. He was strong and hefty, and he put plenty of weight into turning the winch handles.

Today he shut his eyes and abandoned his forehead to the warmth of Lucrezia, that tall and handsome woman. He had heard the leap of the big fish, vainly struggling against the sides of the net; he had not opened half an eye. He was a man from now on; he no longer belonged to the young, chaste band of heroes who indulged in violent play; he abandoned them, he abandoned himself.

He, the boy who had learned in a hard school, in opposition to his father Matteo Brigante, to control every gesture, every word, the expression on his face, now let fall from his lips words which followed no pattern.

'Holy Mother of God ...' he murmured.

Twenty-two years of unhappiness dissolved within him.

'I love you, donna Lucrezia. How I love you!'

She said in her turn: 'I love you, Francesco darling,' pressing the boy's head against her stomach. She repeated it several times, until he summoned up enough courage to call her darling.

'I love you, Lucrezia darling.'

His eyes closed, his muscles relaxed, with no further thought of any kind of duty, for the first time in his life, he hung like a man in the arms of his mistress.

Thus they remained for a long time, without moving, without speaking except to say the same words over and over. When he reopened his eyes, the net was submerged again, the look-out was astride the mast and the other men lay sleeping on the bank.

'I've had an answer from the head of the Turin firm,' he said.

143

He handed Lucrezia the letter which he had asked to be addressed poste restante and which had let him in for so many questions from his father. The director agreed to employ him on the terms explained by his agent in Naples. But he wanted to see him first, and he asked him to take advantage of the university vacation to call on him. If, as seemed likely, they found they suited one another, the young man could start work in October, while continuing his studies at Turin University.

'You must go,' she said.

'Yes,' he said. 'I can get away from my uncle's for a couple of days while I'm staying in Benevento. My father won't know. But I haven't the money for the journey.'

He had dreaded telling her this. But now that she had made him relax, he mentioned it quite naturally.

'I have money,' she said.

It was tomorrow he was leaving for Benevento. They agreed that she should send him the money that evening, in a sealed envelope, through Giuseppina.

At noon Matteo Brigante and Pizzaccio had taken their usual seats, over Coca-Colas, on the open-air veranda of the Beach Bar. The wooden planks, supported by slender cement bases sunk into the sand, had a hollow ring; when you stamped on them a grey dust seeped from between the joints; a disagreeable sensation; Matteo Brigante preferred solidity, the ceramics in the Sports Bar, the marble work in the bars in Foggia. In winter, life in Porto Manacore centred on the main square; there was no point in leaving the Sports, where everything that happened out on the main square — for example, a deal concluded by a sign passed between two men who immediately separated, without anyone appearing to have noticed they had ever met — had immediate repercussions which were almost imperceptible but which Brigante picked up and knew how to interpret. Winter was more accommodating. But from July 15th to August 30th, between twelve noon and two in the afternoon, it was on the beach that the controlling had to be done.

Ten bathing huts on either side of the bar. A loudspeaker perched on a mast broadcast the songs on the Italian Radio. On the veranda, metal tables and chairs, painted green, already occupied.

The beach was long and narrow, at the side of the road which wound down from the main square. Near the harbour, the sand was covered with fishing boats and drying nets. At the other end, towards the promontory, the beach came to rest against the supporting wall of a large orange orchard belonging to don Ottavio. Breadth: about twenty yards. Length: something like twelve hundred. The bar and the beach huts somewhere near the centre. The loudspeaker was powerful and the radio could be heard from one end of the beach to the other.

From the veranda of the bar, you could take in the whole narrow strip of sand and, beyond, the whole bay, a flat expanse of water of no interest to anyone, except between the shore and the first sandbank, a marine park for swimmers, rubber dinghies and pedal boats. No one ever glanced up at the horizon, except to assure himself that the libeccio was not getting the upper hand over the sirocco, in which case the bank of clouds would advance on the coast and turn to rain the moment it touched the top of the mountain; but this had not happened once that year. If you looked towards Manacore Point, which sealed off the bay to the east, you could see the outlines of the *trabucco* (close to which Francesco Brigante and Lucrezia were confessing their love for one another), looking like a great ship rounding the point; but most of the bathers were uninterested in the *trabucco*.

Quite a small beach, running in a straight line from the harbour breakwater to don Ottavio's orange trees. From the sea you could pick out only the supporting walls of the orange and lemon orchards bordering on to the road. Yet there was room for three different levels of society, each with its strictly defined area, though no barrier or line of any sort marked out the boundaries.

From the harbour to within about fifty yards of the bathing

huts the sand belonged to the working class. It was something quite new for the working class to come on to the beach, a conquest made immediately after the war by an advanced guard of thirteen- to fifteen-year-old boys who were taught the crawl stroke and how to dive off the top of the breakwater by a schoolmaster from Genoa who (a minor disgrace) had been transferred to Manacore. Then a few girls had appeared, the same brave band of girls who, in the chaos of the immediate post-war years, had dared to go about on bicycles, despite the abuse of the old women and the stones of the *guaglioni*, incited by the priest, and who had forced Manacore to accept their use of the bicycle, despite the obscenities shouted at them by the men of the town, who compared the cycle saddle with other pointed objects and cycles in general with everything else which could be straddled, despite another schoolmaster, who was a Red but who said it was necessary to seize power first and *then* change standards of behaviour, who maintained that women's claims to ride bicycles, like Klara Zetkin's claim to free love, formed part of the bourgeois demands condemned by Lenin in a famous letter. These same girls, having conquered the bicycle, then braved the beach, in the same swimming costumes they still wore today, extending over the shoulders and descending to half-way down the thigh, with a brassière underneath and a skirt covering the stomach and thighs. The first two seasons, their brothers protected them, standing guard up on the road, their hands in their pockets, wrapped round grafting knives, while the girls bathed or lay in the sun, glorious in defiance, drunk with audacity.

Since then, progress had spread at a giant's pace. Mothers now came down to the beach with their daughters, descending from the Old Town with their whole brood in tow, chattering in groups, crouching on the sand, advancing into the sea till the water was over their knees, in their long white linen chemises, advancing into the sea with timid little steps, but asserting their freedom, in twos, in threes, laughing a little nervously and, to give themselves courage, slapping one another noisily on the back with one wet hand — the mothers! — while with the other they drew their long white linen chemises tight around their legs, letting them balloon out at the hips, so as not to show their buttocks.

Mothers, daughters, kids — the lower classes took up the beach from the rim of the harbour (where the nets lay drying among the boats drawn up on the sand) to within fifty yards of the bathing huts. The men did not come down to the beach, either because they were working or because they were idle, at their posts, along the walls of the main square; on Sundays they preferred fishing, football or playing at The Law in the cafés.

The sand on either side of the bathing huts belonged to the leading citizens of Porto Manacore and the successful emigrants, who had returned to spend their holidays in their native region.

By tacit agreement, an empty space, a no-man's-land, separated the leading citizens' sand from the sand of the lower classes.

On the leading citizens' side, the women lay in deck-chairs, under sunshades, the mothers and wives in beach dresses, the girls in swimsuits. The men took an apéritif on the bar veranda; from time to time one of them would get up and go and talk to the women, standing beside the deck-chairs.

Social life was very intense in this zone which extended scarcely fifty yards on either side of the bathing huts but which was subdivided into several territories, into clans and coteries, with enclaves and divisions within the subdivisions and occasionally irredentisms under the same sunshade, arising from political, religious or anti-religious affiliations or ideas more or less 'advanced' with regard to behaviour and all sorts of other things, interfering with the innumerable nuances of social standing.

Five or six young women belonging to the 'advanced' set wore swimsuits like the younger girls, swam and took apéritifs on the veranda with their husbands. The other women regarded them with envy or contempt — it depended on their conception of morality, good behaviour and progress.

The third zone, which extended to the supporting wall of don Ottavio's orange orchard, was left to the summer visitors, families headed by civil servants, clerks and tradesmen from Foggia, wives and children of notaries, lawyers and chemists from the small mountain towns; they would rather have gone to the real beaches whose names appeared in the annual resort guides, where you could see foreigners in shorts dancing in night clubs; but they were too expensive; they were embittered, particularly the girls; they sat in families, in tribes; they undressed in canvas tents or in their cars that lined the edge of the road; they were a horde without hierarchy, foreign to Porto Manacore life, an accident of summer.

Don Ottavio owned a private beach, a patch of white sand in a creek below his orange trees. He never used it.

Up on the road, the sons of leading citizens came and went on their scooters looking for a girl who would agree to go for a ride with them; they never found one, for the summer visitors, too, had mothers, brothers, sisters, fiancés.

From one end of the beach to the other, ignoring frontiers, indifferently trampling the sand of the three zones, the *guaglioni* ran about on the look-out for a quick snatch.

On the road at the back of the beach the police walked up and down, hunting crops in hand, keeping their eye on the *guaglioni*.

On the road foreigners swept by in their large cars. They did not stop on this beach swarming with Italians. They drove on to the other side of Schiavona, making for the lovely resorts they hoped to find deserted, but where they would find encampments of Germans, Swedes, Swiss, every kind of Nordic clan seeking blue skies and romantic memories, four hours' bathing a day and red, peeling skin. Solitude is a luxury ever harder to come by in the world of men, begetters of children.

At half-past twelve, Chief of Police Attilio pulled up opposite the beach in his Mille Cento. Anna, his wife, was sitting beside him, Giuseppina and the three children in the back seat. The women and children got out. The Chief turned the car in its own length, two forward movements, two backward movements, neat, precise, the wheel fully locked, then he parked flush with the ramp; he was a man. He got out himself.

148

'The Chief's coming down on to the beach,' announced Pizzaccio.

It was unusual to see the Chief on the beach, except on Sundays. This was why Pizzaccio drew attention to his arrival.

Anna, Giuseppina and the children shut themselves in the hut they had rented for the season. The Chief hung about on the veranda of the bar, going from table to table, chatting with friends. Brigante saluted him from a distance, with a nod of the head. He replied without looking at him, raising his hand shoulder high, no higher. They did not make a show of being good friends, which they were.

Matteo Brigante was considering the report Pizzaccio had just made to him: Pippo, the leader of the *guaglioni*, had gone out at dawn to meet don Cesare's Marietta in the shed in one of the old man's orchards. Pippo, Balbo and their gang were not big enough to worry him; they had stolen his grafting knife at the end of the ball; he wanted to teach them a lesson, that was all; it was to find an opportunity of doing so, and a little in the heat of the moment, that last thing the night before he had instructed Pizzaccio to control Pippo. Now, Pizzaccio's shadowing had brought a new fact to light: Marietta had not slept in the house with the colonnades; she was hiding in the orchard shed, where she had received a visit from Pippo at dawn. Brigante did not think Marietta foolish enough to have chosen Pippo as her lover; she was a smart girl; when Brigante found an excuse to call at don Cesare's she examined him furtively with a coldness, a hardness he admired; if he'd had a daughter, he would have liked to see her wear this inscrutable, intelligent expression, in which the intelligence was concealed with a mastery astonishing on the part of a seventeen-year-old girl.

He cast about for the right explanation for this morning rendezvous between Marietta and Pippo. He thought there was something special to ferret out. He turned the incident over in his mind, abandoning it, returning to it, looking at it from every point of view, patiently, deliberately allowing his mind to

149

wander; this was how he habitually reflected until he had found a link, an analogy, and then the isolated incidents suddenly made sense; such was his apparently nonchalant method of analysing what went on; it allowed him to ascertain many things which the reports of Pizzaccio and all his other informers did not reveal to him.

Chief Attilio's children came out of the hut, then Anna and Giuseppina. The latter, as for several days past, was wearing the Lastex swimsuit given her by donna Lucrezia (but no one knew how she had come by it, apart from Brigante who had been told by Fidelia and had noted it, in his memory — it might always come in useful). The Chief's wife was also in a swimsuit; it was the event of the day; during the ten years she had lived in Manacore, during the ten seasons she had been coming to the beach, people had always seen her in a beach dress, never in a swimsuit — it was the event of the season; was one to understand that the Chief of Police was going over to the 'advanced' set?

To reach the beach from the huts, you had to walk across the bar. Anna and Giuseppina stepped on to the veranda.

All eyes turned on Anna. Even the men who were at that moment chatting with the Chief could not conceal their surprise.

'Now it's my turn to change,' said the Chief. 'I shan't be long ...'

He laughed with the assurance of a handsome, elegant man in the pink of condition. He shut the door of the hut after him.

Anna felt every man's eyes upon her. The children had already gone; there was nothing for her to fasten on to. She quickened her step to reach the three steps which led down from the veranda on to the beach. But Giuseppina cornered her in the narrow gangway between the tables.

'Don't blush, signora Anna,' whispered Giuseppina. 'Lift your head up. Don't let them think you're ashamed ... You aren't the first married woman to show herself in a swimsuit ... You're a fine figure of a woman, don't be afraid ... Show them you're not afraid of them.'

Anna was fat and white, Giuseppina slender and sunburnt;

150

she had taken the sun every day, from twelve till two, since the beginning of the season.

Anna was wearing the garnet-red swimsuit purchased for her honeymoon, which she had spent in a resort in Tuscany, ten years before. She had never been to a real resort since. In Tuscany, she had not been the wife of a leading citizen, but a holidaymaker; besides, in the North the problem did not present itself. She had put on a lot of weight in the course of ten years and three confinements, and the swimsuit made rolls of fat appear. She had not given a moment's thought to this aspect of the question during all the days and weeks when she had been so insistent that her husband should allow her to bathe, to go on the beach in a swimsuit, as did the five or six women of the 'advanced' set, forgetting that she was not athletic like them, that she ate too much, that she was limp and idle, already shapeless at thirty, as women were before the timid emergence of the new fashions, the new style of living. Like all other daughters of genteel southern families, she had brought a triple trousseau with her as a dowry: underclothes to fit the slender young girl she had then been, underclothes free of clips and folds for the robust mother she was at present, enormous underclothes for the matron she would be after the change of life. Giuseppina had so fed her desire to take the beach in a swimsuit that she had given no thought to anything beyond that desire for emancipation which all women, even those of the South, bear within them; it had not even occurred to her that she would find herself exposed, half-naked, to the eyes of the whole town, with her formless, deformed body.

The Chief had firmly resisted the idea, laughing at times, making a joke of it, with the easy superiority of a man dealing with women, at others putting his foot down ('There's nothing more to be said') with the authority of a man used to giving orders in the name of the government. He had given way only the night before, hastily persuaded by Giuseppina. Anna did not know that her husband's sudden acquiescence had been bought by a kiss and a few caresses on the court house landing.

She was not, however, without her suspicions of something of this kind. For several months now, Attilio had been replying to Giuseppina's provocations with special glances, special inflections of the voice, his whole lady-killer's charade; Anna had not missed a trick; when she was alone she counted her grievances as the wife of a lady's man; it only made her invite Giuseppina still more often; she was afraid that by keeping her away she would irritate Attilio, who would then meet her elsewhere; she preferred to have her rival where she could see her; she was not without hopes of disarming her with kindness, apparent confidence; indeed, she considered her less dangerous than some of the others, she supposed her to be naively flattered by the Chief's attentions, and hence of no value to him; she had absolutely no suspicions that it was the foolish virgin who laid down the law to don Juan. And now Giuseppina was cornering her between the tables, on the veranda of the Beach Bar, in front of all the leading citizens, increasing her shame by telling her not to show it.

'Let me pass,' whispered Anna, flushed with shame and anger.

She was ashamed and angry to such a pitch that the flush spread right down on to her shoulders, furrowed by the straps of the swimsuit.

She slowly fought her way between the tables, with Giuseppina clinging to her arm, slowing her down as much as she could and shouting at the top of her voice:

'You'll pick up a tan right away, out in that sun. In three days you'll be as dark as I am, signora Anna!'

The Chief came out of the hut, wearing a pair of black trunks. He was a tall, good-looking, muscular man, so naturally brown of skin that you could have supposed he was sunburnt, although he only came to the beach once a week, on Sundays.

He saw Anna stumbling on the steps which led down to the beach, assisted, pushed, impeded by Giuseppina, flushed to the shoulders. Attention switched to him. He was an official accustomed to controlling his expression and he did not show his displeasure.

'Last night,' said Pizzaccio, 'it was the manager of the Bank of Naples Giuseppina was after ...'

'The branch manager,' Brigante corrected.

The Chief advanced rapidly and separated the two women, putting an arm round each of them and hustling them towards the sea.

'Into the water, ladies!' he shouted playfully. 'Straight into the water!'

The glances of leading citizens' wives and daughters, lying in deck-chairs beneath the sunshades, converged upon them.

'That's it,' cried Giuseppina. 'We'll teach signora Anna to swim!'

She detached herself and ran on ahead. She had a very good figure. In Manacore, women were either too heavy or too thin, straight as a board. Giuseppina, with her rounded buttocks, small waist, and breasts enlarged by a wire structure invisible beneath the Lastex swimsuit, was really *formosa*, shapely, slender and well-covered.

She ran a few yards and then turned, her arms raised to the sky, the points (artificial) of her breasts taut beneath the swimsuit.

'Come on, signora Anna!' she called. 'Come on, we'll teach you to swim.'

She ran towards the sea again, splashed lightly in, ran till the water came to above her knees, stopped dead, raised herself on tiptoe and then dived, with a jerk of the back. Her body arched itself above the water, then you saw just her legs, taut, sinewy, feet together, then there was nothing. She reappeared fifteen strokes farther on, level with the first sandbank, where she was again in her depth. She came out of the water facing the snore, displaying above the sea (standing on the sandbank, with the water only up to her knees) her long, slender, gleaming body, polished by the sun and sea.

The Chief, in full view of the leading citizens — the men sitting in the bar, the women beneath the sunshades — pushed his wife, Anna, firmly towards the sea. He was gripping Anna so tight that his fingers drew furrows, white edged with red, on her fleshy arms — just as the straps of the swimsuit drew furrows on her fleshy shoulders. The eyes of Manacore, trained to infinitely perspicacious observation, saw this. And people whispered, sneered, rejoiced.

'Leave me alone,' said Anna. 'I want to take the sun under our sunshade first.'

'You can't take the sun under a sunshade,' growled Attilio. 'Come on.'

'Take it easy,' she said. 'Let me get used to the water. I'm cold.'

'The water is warm,' he said. 'Come on.'

They advanced into the sea till the water was up to their knees.

'I'm so cold,' she said. 'Let me get my breath.'

'Haven't you made yourself ridiculous enough? Pull yourself together. Come on.'

The water reached the tops of her thighs.

'I'd rather dive straight in,' she said.

He stopped, let go of her, looked at her.

'Go ahead,' he said. 'Go ahead and dive! Don't be afraid. Your fat will make you float.'

Giuseppina returned, swimming on her back, the points of her breasts level with the water. She straightened up two paces away from them. She called:

'Get right in, signora Anna! The water's lovely. Santa Maria of Capua, how lovely the water is.'

Anna looked at them in turn. She suddenly squatted on the bottom and was up to her neck in water.

'Bravo, signora Anna,' cried Giuseppina. 'Bravo! You're a real athletic type.'

Anna's pale head seemed to float on the sea. The Chief spoke to her in an undertone.

'Well, now are you happy? You wanted to come bathing; well, now you're in the water. Stay there. Enjoy yourself ...'

He flung himself into the water and swam easily out to sea.

154

'Signor maresciallo,' called Giuseppina, 'you're not very polite. It isn't nice to leave signora Anna all by herself ...'

Then she turned to address Anna's pale head, floating on the sea.

'Don't move, signora Anna,' Giuseppina cried. 'I'll go and tell him what we think of him ...'

She broke into a rapid crawl in the wake of the Chief. She could swim, when she liked, faster than he did. She was in training, practising the crawl every day, from beginning to end of the season. She had calculated in advance that when he tired and turned back towards the shore, she would take the lead, so that he would appear to be chasing her.

Signora Anna stood up, the water streaming from her body, and walked heavily back towards the beach, under the eyes of the leading citizens.

'You know,' said Pizzaccio, 'if I was Chief Attilio I'd slap that Giuseppina's ears back ...'

'Would you?' said Matteo Brigante. 'I'd give her a yellow swimsuit.'

'Why a yellow one?'

'Like the winner of the Tour de France.'

'Why the winner?'

'Because she's champion.'

'She swims well,' said Pizzaccio. 'That's true.'

'Idiot,' said Matteo Brigante.

The Chief of Police entertained his mistresses in the tower of Frederick II of Swabia, which Matteo Brigante rented from the town corporation. There were three ways of entering it. In one corner of the terrace of the post office, immediately opposite the court house, a door gave access to the second floor, a large octagonal room which Brigante allowed the police station personnel to use; here the files on unsolved cases were stored, so no one was surprised to see the Chief entering or leaving; another door, set in the wall, opened on to a stone staircase which led up to the third floor, the bachelor quarters shared by the Chief and Matteo Brigante. It could also be reached from

Brigante's flat by a passage through the loft of the Renaissance part of the building, above the corporation's offices. Finally, you could get into the tower from the palace chapel. The keys of the three entrances were held by Brigante, to whom the Chief had to apply when he wanted to meet his mistresses.

The third floor of the tower, like the second, consisted of a single, vast, octagonal room. The Gothic windows had been walled up, apart from a hole introduced above the arch for ventilation. One corner had been sealed off with tapestries bought from a second-hand dealer in Foggia and furnished with an iron bedstead, painted with garlands of flowers in imitation of Venetian woodwork, and with a dressing-table, with all accessories, behind a cretonne screen. A mirror on the wall, behind the bed, a carpet of the Moorish style, of the kind brought back from Libya by army N.C.O.s, at the foot of the bed. A small lamp with a bead shade, on a marquetry pedestal table, in the same Libyan style as the carpet.

The women generally came through the chapel, which was open for worship; they climbed the spiral staircase, built into the old wall and leading to the top of the tower, a stopping-place for tourists; on the third landing they found the door to which Chief of Police Attilio had given them the key, borrowed from Brigante.

Sometimes they came through Brigante's flat. The latter's wife had till recently undertaken small items of dressmaking, which gave them an excuse to call on her. They trusted to her discretion, knowing that she was terrorized by Brigante; she was so afraid of her husband accusing her of having betrayed one of his innumerable secrets that she never spoke to anyone.

The Chief's love affairs were thus controlled by Matteo Brigante (just as Lucrezia's was controlled by Giuseppina). In small, densely populated towns, illicit love affairs are impossible without collusion (hence the role of pimps and procuresses in Italian literature).

Only the great landowners could make do with pretexts so plausible that they deceived nobody. If the girl or the woman were poor, they took her on for a time as a servant. If it were a woman of some standing, they invited the couple down to one of their villas, and then sent the husband out hunting or asked him to go and supervise the olive presses or to settle some tedious business which would be to his profit.

There was as great a gulf between the great landowners, like don Cesare or don Ottavio, and the town's leading citizens as between the leading citizens and the common people. On a still higher plane, Matteo Brigante had met the directors of la Montecatini, with whom he was negotiating the sale of his land in Margherita di Savoia, or those of the Bauxite Ore Corporation, to whom he had submitted a tender for transport; these firms could have bought up all don Cesare's or don Ottavio's estates without any appreciable difference to their annual returns.

The world was made in the image of the Royal Fleet, of the period when Matteo Brigante had served as a bosun's mate. The seamen: the common people. The petty officers: himself, the Foggia lawyers. The junior officers: the leading citizens of Porto Manacore or Foggia, the Foggia lawyers when they had been called to the Bar. The senior officers: don Cesare, don Ruggero. The General Staff: la Montecatini, the Bauxite Corporation. And, higher still, the king whose name people no longer remembered now they were living in a republic, the limited company of State authority. At the summit: God.

Although he was perpetually in a state of mortal sin, apart from one night a year, between confession on Holy Saturday and communion on Easter Sunday, Matteo Brigante firmly believed in God and His Holy Church. Human society, as he knew it, rigidly shaped and graded, constituted, in his eyes, an irrefutable proof of the existence of God, who crowned it and sealed it, just as, at noon, the sun-lion crowned and sealed Manacore Bay.

If Matteo Brigante was compelled to commit so many mortal sins, it was because God, who had allowed him to become a petty officer, and controller of Porto Manacore, prevented him from penetrating the superior caste (lawyers, notaries, doctors, judges, Chief of Police, signor dottore, signor professore, the university titles). This was reserved for his son. As if he paid with his sins for his son's promotion. Everything had its price; that was The Law.

Money itself was not sufficient to explain the rigidity of the classes. Matteo Brigante had far more money at his disposal than Chief Attilio. Incomparably more. The Chief was buying his Mille Cento on the instalment plan; if Brigante were to buy a car, he would simply have to draw a cheque on his account at the Bank of Naples; if he did not buy a car, it was because he did not wish to lose the interest on capital a car represented, and also because he found it more amusing to use the cars of the people he controlled, especially when they showed temper about it. The Chief was an official, a word which Brigante was already rich enough to pronounce with contempt. But however rich Brigante became, thanks to the interest derived from a carefully managed capital, and whatever services he rendered the Chief, he would continue to say 'signor maresciallo' and *lei* (the third person in Italian, equivalent to the French *vous*) and the Chief, in reply, would call him 'Brigante' and *tu*. To enjoy the privileges of the senior officers, with whom his fortune now allied him, Matteo Brigante would have to leave Porto Manacore, as he might when the time came for him to retire, when his son had become a lawyer, a landowner and had been trained by him to defend their fortune. In a province other than Foggia, in the North or abroad, people would accord him those privileges of rank to which the money he expended made believe he belonged. Was that certain? He himself distrusted the foreigners who swept through Porto Manacore in big American cars (or German or French cars) and who sometimes lunched in the *trattoria* down by the harbour; perhaps they were only bosun's mates back in their own lands, driving through Italy in their big cars, visiting the museums, having church doors unlocked for them, sweating their way round basilicas in the heat of the day, beneath the sun-lion, and staying in the ritzy hotels where all the guests had the right to the same respect — perhaps they were only doing all that to give themselves the illusion of being senior officers? From the back of the *trattoria*, Matteo Brigante spied on them; he watched for the gesture, the tone of voice, the lack of ease or the too prominently displayed ease which would furnish the proof that the foreigner was a fraud, just as he himself would be a fraud if he went into exile. The Brigante in his chosen place of exile would find out in no time that he was a fraud. In God's world, there was no escape from the controllers whom God had distributed and who, by levying their taxes on disorder, contributed in their own way to the maintenance of order. It was of this Matteo Brigante was thinking — a man of meditative nature, accustomed by his profession as a racketeer to meditating on social inequalities — it was of this he was thinking as he sat and watched the Chief and Giuseppina swimming on the far side of the first sandbank.

Giuseppina was a faster swimmer than the Chief, and whatever manœuvre he planned she was able to stay a little ahead of him, so that the leading citizens and their wives, following them from the beach, should think that it was the Chief who was chasing Giuseppina. And from time to time she turned in the water and laughed very loudly, so that they should hear her on the beach — the laugh a girl gives to a man who is provoking her, whose provocation she does not entirely repulse but of whom she is making fun; *lo fa caminare*, she was leading him on.

Anna had returned to the beach and stretched herself in the deck-chair, beneath her sunshade, with a towel over her thighs to hide the rolls of fat escaping from under her tight swimsuit. For as long as she could, she held back the tears which had welled into her eyes and been observed by all the women. When she had felt she was on the point of not being able to hold them back any longer, she had gone and shut herself in her hut. Now, behind the closed door, sitting on a small wooden bench, the shoulder straps of the swimsuit pulled down in front of her, her big white breasts exposed, she wept silently.

The Chief continued to swim on the far side of the first sandbank, manœuvring this way and that way, followed by Giuseppina and appearing to follow her. Perhaps he was calling her names. He had certainly begun by calling her names. Now, probably, he was begging her to come one day soon to his room in the tower of Frederick II of Swabia; in which case, Giuseppina was certainly replying: 'First send signora Anna back to her parents in Lucera.' From the beach they could not hear what they were saying, only the shrill, provoking-provocative laugh of Giuseppina.

The leading citizens, taking their apéritif in the Beach Bar, and their wives, lying in deck-chairs, were not taken in. They knew it was not Chief of Police Attilio who was chasing Giuseppina, that he might be calling her names, that it was the girl, who, profiting from being a stronger swimmer, was manœuvring so as to make it seem that she was being chased by the Chief. Before a public so experienced in all the nuances of social life, Giuseppina was playing an open game. She knew it as well as her public. What excited and delighted the leading citizens of Porto Manacore was that Chief Attilio had let himself be talked first of all into permitting his wife, the fat and respectable-respected Anna to come on to the beach in a swimsuit; secondly into making a show of himself on the beach between his wife the now shapeless Anna (misshapen by her childbirth and greed) and the slender and shapely Giuseppina (kept thin by malaria), the most brazen of all virgins in Manacore; and thirdly into making himself, on the far side of the first sandbank but within full view of the beach, the plaything of the quick, alert and provoking Giuseppina. He was delaying the moment of setting foot on the beach again, continuing to manœuvre this way and that, because he could not yet bring himself to face the mocking stares of the leading citizens (and the cold stare of Matteo Brigante); his ease as a man accustomed to pleasing women was of no use to him in this test; it was suddenly shattered, precisely because he was letting himself be made a fool of in front of the wives of all the leading citizens, his past and, he had hoped, his future mistresses, by the most brazen foolish virgin in Porto Manacore.

It was not curiosity which lit up the spectators' faces. To most of them Giuseppina was revealing nothing new; they had known for ages that the Chief was after Giuseppina, his wife's best friend, and that he had compelled his wife to receive her as her best friend. It was an excitement of another kind which lit up the spectators' faces, livelier, crueller, closer to the pleasure inspired by an assize trial or a bullfight. They were watching the execution of Chief of Police Attilio by Giuseppina, the daughter of the hardware dealer in the via Garibaldi.

Pizzaccio had finally grasped the situation.

'Giuseppina,' he said, 'is laying down the law to the Chief.'

'It was bound to end that way,' said Brigante.

'Why?' asked Pizzaccio.

'He's not as tough as he makes out,' replied Brigante.

Because of the room they shared, the Chief and Matteo Brigante often talked of love, either in the seclusion of the Chief's office or in the room itself, when they exchanged keys. They talked openly about it, as men who, in the circumstances, could hide nothing from one another. When they were talking about love, just the two of them, and only on these occasions, Brigante called the Chief by his name, Attilio, without any mention of a title, and the Chief called Brigante *caro* Matteo. Broadly speaking, the two men both had the same conception of love: what gave it value was to impose the law on your partner, the woman or the girl.

As for pleasure, the girls in certain Foggia houses, houses of pleasure to be precise, those at from two to five thousand lire a half-hour, ten thousand lire an hour, were more expert than any mistress. But it was another kind of pleasure, less totally exciting than imposing the law on a mistress. In certain cases, however, the prostitute could surpass any mistress. The relationship between prostitutes and their clients was, in fact, complex: by paying the girl, you imposed the law on her; by demanding to be paid, she imposed the law; she was thus able to provide the double pleasure of imposing and submitting to the law at the same moment; this was the height of liberty in love. Success depended on the girl's skill in making clear, with every gesture, this double dependence-liberty of the two partners with regard to the law they imposed on one another. But if the girl were not skilled in this game, in which lay the essence of her profession, the two laws cancelled one another out (instead of multiplying, of transcending their reciprocal effect) and there was nothing left but the pleasure of copulating, no matter what the respective instruments and positions, the dullest of pleasures, which others enjoyed equally well with a goat or by themselves or with their wives, who had grown so used to submitting to the law that there was now no point in imposing it on them. This was more or less what Matteo Brigante thought of girls — in other terms, but very clearly, because of his experience at the game of The Law; and the Chief too, though more confusedly.

Matteo Brigante and the Chief were therefore agreed that what gave love its value was to impose the law. But they chose different objectives.

Chief Attilio courted the wife of a leading citizen, surrounded her with attentions and snares, wheedled her, pampered her, coaxed her, fondled her, persuaded her to come to his bachelor quarters in the octagonal tower of Frederick II of Swabia. He put everything he had into his love-making, determined to provide the adulteress with a pleasure she did not find, she said, in the arms of her husband; he triumphed: 'You're mine.' In Christian countries men are readily convinced that when a woman says: 'I'm so happy,' she is thinking: 'You've branded me, I've become your property'; unconsciously metaphysicians, instinctively proprietors and jurists, they consider the pleasure of love in absolute terms: it is the hot iron which brands the acquired beast for ever. When Attilio was quite convinced that his mistress belonged unreservedly to him, he taught her the gestures, the poses, the practices of the Foggia prostitutes. 'I've degraded her,' he said. Then he made the break and passed on to another.

Seduction, possession, depravation, break-away: these were the four phases of the Chief's licentiousness, a far more religious business than he thought. And now he was subject to Giuseppina's law. Brigante was overjoyed.

As for Matteo Brigante, he preferred raping virgins.

★ ★ ★

The pleasures of the beach came to an end at two in the afternoon. People returned to Manacore for lunch and their siesta. The Chief drove his wife, Anna, Giuseppina and the three children back in his Mille Cento. On the point of the promontory, near the *trabucco*, donna Lucrezia and Francesco had just separated and were walking through the pine woods, he making for the spot where he had hidden don Ruggero's Vespa, she for the gates of the holiday camp, both repeating to themselves the words of love they had just heard from one another.

Matteo Brigante slept till five, at home, in his flat in the palace of Frederick II of Swabia. He took a shower and dressed; he was always impeccable. He chose, for this second part of the day which began after the siesta, a petrol blue alpaca jacket, a turquoise blue shirt and a navy blue butterfly bow. The butterfly bow was seldom worn these days in Italy; Brigante had accepted it when he had started up his racket, after being demobilized; at that time he had considered the butterfly bow more imposing than the narrow, sailor-knot tie; he would not look himself now, without a butterfly bow.

'Will you be back to supper?' asked signora Brigante.

'I don't know,' he replied.

He turned the corner of the main square and the via Garibaldi. On the ground floor of the court house, behind the blinds with their slats tilted towards the sky, the prisoners were singing:

Tourne, ma beauté, tourne ...

But he was no more conscious of them than a fisherman is conscious of the engine of his boat. Then he headed for the first foothills of the mountain, the zone of the orange and lemon orchards.

He took a different path from the one chosen first by Marietta, and then by Pippo, followed, without knowing it, by Pizzaccio.

In this way he came to an orchard close to don Cesare's (where Marietta was hiding), but approached differently on the opposite slope of the valley with the three springs. The overseer,

163

a friend of his, was supervising ten or a dozen women who were weeding the basins hollowed out at the foot of each tree.

They stood chatting for a moment.

'A pack of shirkers,' said the overseer. 'I've only to shut one eye for them to stand around with their arms folded.'

'If you don't look after your own property,' replied Brigante, 'nobody else will.'

'They make a mint out of me,' continued the overseer.

'The hand is nothing without the brain behind it,' replied Brigante ...

Etc. Petty officers' civilities.

'I'll take a rest for a moment,' said Brigante.

'Suit yourself.'

People never asked Brigante questions. If he stopped in the orchard, it was because he had something to control in the neighbourhood. That was his business.

He sat in the shade of a fig tree and waited for the overseer and the workwomen to go.

Brigante's father had been an agricultural worker, paid by the day (when he was not out of work). His mother had also worked by the day, weeding the orchards or drawing water from the well to water the trees; she was out of work even more often than his father. They also did all kinds of jobs, free of charge, for the overseer or steward who had been kind enough to find them work.

Italo Barbone, one of don Ottavio's overseers, had a weakness for his father and often employed him. He lived in the orchard zone, two hundred yards from the road, along a path interspersed with steps. When he went into Porto Manacore, Matteo's father waited for him at the corner of the road, with a lamp in his hand, from nightfall till he returned, so as to guide him along the path; he walked in front of him, practically sideways, like a crab, so as not to get between the lamp and Barbone's feet. The overseer was a great lover of the game of The Law and often did not get back much before dawn. Matteo's father used to wait all night, never daring to say to the man who had been kind enough to find work for him: 'I'll leave the lamp at the end of the path

164

and then go home to bed.' Had he in fact left the lamp, someone would certainly have come along and stolen it; a lamp was an article of value in a land of unemployed. And if he had hidden it (they could have agreed on a hiding-place), Barbone, who generally came back drunk, would not have found the hiding-place or would not have been capable of lighting the lamp. So there was no other solution but to wait, sitting on the ground, at the corner of the road, until the overseer made up his mind to come home.

Barbone also had some waiting to do. At that time, don Ottavio used to spend most of the year in Rome. He would write to his overseer: 'Wait for me on Monday at Villanuova station.' Barbone would harness a pair of horses to the coach and go and wait for his landlord at Villanuova, twelve miles from Porto Manacore. Often don Ottavio did not come on Monday, as he had announced, or on Tuesday, or on Wednesday; sometimes the overseer had to wait a whole week, outside the station, on a bundle of straw, in the back of the carriage. Today don Ottavio no longer took the train; he had several cars. But old Italo Barbone continued to wait, on countless occasions, for all sorts of reasons, in many different places.

Don Ottavio kept his overseer waiting who kept his agricultural worker waiting. The King probably kept don Ottavio waiting, and God the King. This was the first idea young Matteo conceived of the social hierarchy. Everyone waited for someone and kept someone else waiting. Only God waited for no one and only the agricultural worker had no one to keep waiting. Thus were defined for him two absolutes at the opposite ends of the hierarchy (although he did not see it in these words): God and the agricultural worker. For this son of an agricultural worker, the agricultural worker's lot constituted absolute wretchedness.

Others, like Mario the bricklayer (whom Chief of Police Attilio had refused a passport because he had refused to tear up his party card), wanted to throw down the whole structure and erect another in which the hierarchy would be founded on different criteria (no hierarchy at all, demanded the anarchists,

165

still numerous in the South). These conceptions presupposed the reading of newspapers and books, or at least the companionship of people who *did* read newspapers and books, things which were out of the question for young Matteo (besides, this was during the fascist regime). But by the time he was ten he had made the decision to escape at any price, from absolute wretchedness — from the lot, that was to say, of the agricultural worker. It was all right to wait, since waiting was inevitable, but at least you should acquire the power to make others wait. It was all right to submit to the law; but you should also impose the law; this was how the child conceived human dignity.

Despite severe hidings, he refused to go weeding, even once, with the women, or to draw water from the well and carry it, two buckets at a time, on a yoke, into the orchards which were not irrigated, as agricultural workers' children normally did on the fortunate occasions when the overseer needed them. Today he considered that his father's blows had hardened him. When he thought of it now, he was equally content to have been beaten by his father and not to have given way under his blows; that was how he had grown hard, as it so pleased him to be. And that was why, when the time came, he had beaten his own son, Francesco, not in anger, as his father had beaten him, which diminished the effect of the punishment, conferring on it the inexorability of natural catastrophes, storms, earthquakes, malaria, but coldly, so many strokes with the strap, counting the strokes or making Francesco count them, and he had rejoiced to see the boy clench his teeth without crying out, to feel that the boy hated him but that already he had sufficient self-control not to shout his hate aloud, to control his hate so well that it did not even show in his eyes, to feel that he was toughening, hardening, becoming a man.

As soon as he was old enough Matteo Brigante had worked with the fishermen, as a ship's boy. The fisherman was wretched too, and he had many masters: the ship owner, the fish merchant, the wind, the sea and the migrations of fish. But the multiplicity of his masters offered him some defence: the owner and the merchant kept him waiting, but he could make an excuse of the wind, the sea or the migration of fish, and he could play one merchant against the other, obliging them to wait. It was a calling which demanded and exercised intelligence. To use the wind to sail against the wind defined not only the art of sailing but also that power which man was given by his intelligence to bend natural and social laws to his service; it was the measure of his liberty. Although he was often as poor as the agricultural worker, the fisherman was not, like him, in a state of absolute wretchedness. The fisherman sold his fish, which were bought from him; the moment there is trade, slavery ceases to be absolute. The relative liberty of the master fisherman reflects on the sailor, and even on the ship's boy, the reward of their complicity in the struggle against nature and against men.

At fifteen Matteo Brigante could swim well and dive even better. The mussels the others tore up with hooks, he went down to look for with his eyes wide open, among the underwater reefs, bringing them up in armfuls. He received small bonuses, in kind and in hard cash, but the praise meant more to him. Along the whole of the Manacore coast, he was known as Matteo the Master of the Sea.

Today a boy of fifteen who was nicknamed the Master of the Sea would not remain a mere ship's boy in the service of a master fisherman. He would go to the islands, he would act as guide to the foreigners who went in for underwater fishing; he would become a master swimmer, a master diver; the door would be open for all kinds of adventures, not just the splendour of national and international underwater fishing contests, but also the chance that some rich foreigner might take an interest in him, and all the advantages that might be derived from that.

But Matteo, the Master of the Sea, did not leave Porto Manacore, such opportunities not existing in those days. When he was sixteen, a boy from Schiavona deprived one of his sisters of her virginity and refused to marry her. Matteo knifed him. The Court was indulgent, as it generally was in dealing with crimes of honour, especially since the boy from Schiavona, although

167

well and truly knifed, survived. Matteo was sent to prison until he was eighteen; they then allowed him to join the Royal Navy.

Now he sat under a fig tree, in the orchard of his friend the overseer. He had removed his petrol blue alpaca jacket and placed it, neatly folded, beside him. He looked at the sea, the sun going down over the islands, the bank of clouds thrust forward by the libeccio, thrust back by the sirocco, retiring slowly westwards. He felt in good form. He was waiting for the overseers and the women weeders to go before he jumped the wall and entered don Cesare's orchard. He had decided to rape Marietta.

At two o'clock, a *guaglione*, on Pippo's orders, had brought Marietta a pitcher of oil, some bread and tomatoes. She had gone to the spring, near the shed, to refill the water jug. So much for her meal. Then she had slept until five.

Sitting on the sacks, she was laying plans. Her forehead was creased with concentration. She had been playing with some lengths of straw and had broken them in the tension of her thought, and the pieces had fallen on to her knees; now she manœuvred them like pieces on a chessboard, shifting them about on her knees, imaginary people, symbolizing those who could aid or obstruct her. She was formulating a long-term plan, using the pieces of straw as an accountant used his abacus.

The slanting rays of the sinking sun came through the dormer window and enveloped her in pale light.

The overseer and the women weeders left the neighbouring orchard and returned to Manacore, along the sunken paths between the high walls.

Matteo Brigante jumped over the wall, adroitly, without catching his petrol blue alpaca jacket, as agile as when he had dived for mussels and, later, clambered up the masts of the training ship.

168

He made his way to the window of the shed and stood watching Marietta, who did not see him. He paused in this way, not to lay his plans, which were perfectly simple and always the same in such cases, nor to savour his pleasure in advance; it was a momentary, absolute pleasure, which you could not savour in advance (except by telling it in public, in the presence of someone it would pain, as he had in front of Tonio; another's pain brought reality to the imaginary act). He paused for a moment, before pushing the door open and going into the hut, because, the moment he had been about to swoop on his prey, he had thought of Chief Attilio, another beast of prey, often his accomplice, but whom a few hours earlier he had seen bowed beneath the yoke, by Giuseppina. He made a brief comparison between Chief Attilio's conduct and his own.

Chief Attilio, that grand seducer who had brought into their shared quarters the wives of practically all the leading citizens of Manacore, had finally accepted the absurdity, that was to say the humiliation, of submitting to Giuseppina's law in front of his past and, he had hoped, future mistresses. If Brigante had wanted Giuseppina, he would have had her. But foolish virgins did not interest him. He liked only wise virgins, whom he took by force. He considered himself more virile than Chief Attilio.

When they talked about love together, either in the Chief's office or in their shared room, they often contrasted their points of view.

Brigante pretended to believe in his friend's technical prowess.

'But,' he said, 'I can't understand you. You teach them everything, you, you make fine little cats of them, very playful, very loving and affectionate, and then you send them away. It's the husbands who profit from you.'

'I'll even have donna Lucrezia!' cried the Chief.

'She won't be easy to thaw out ...'

'The same as the rest,' rejoiced the Chief.

Then he laughed, to give his show of conceit the appearance of levity.

169

'The husbands of Manacore,' he laughed, 'ought to erect a monument to me, to show their gratitude.'

But he could not account for Brigante's taste. What made it still harder was that the latter had once stabbed his sister's seducer. Rape and vengeance of rape could, he considered, be ascribed to the same fetishism.

Once, when a crime of honour had just been committed in the territory which came under his jurisdiction, the Chief said to Brigante:

'Another poor fool like you who'll do a stretch for his sister's virtue.'

To Brigante's mind there was no contradiction between rape and knifing: it was the same business. He executed what he had to execute.

In the navy, the men of Chief Attilio's rank (senior or junior officers) devised plans, gave orders. The petty officers executed (using the sailors as the operative hand). The hangman also executed. It was no accident that the same word was used in both cases.

The Chief tripped witnesses and accused alike in the tangle of his questions, in the nets of his reasoning. He seduced the wives of the leading citizens. Brainwork, officers' business.

But officers were awkward when circumstances obliged them to execute. Brigante was convinced that Attilio was not half as good in bed as he boasted and to crown it all he had let himself fall into the hands of a foolish virgin.

He, Brigante, raped and knifed. He tested himself, he proved himself, to himself, in the moment of execution. This was why he considered himself more virile than Chief Attilio.

Even in his body, he gloried in being more virile than the Chief. The latter was built athletically, like Jupiter, tall, with rounded muscles. Matteo Brigante was small, stocky, all triangles; the black line of the eyebrows, the black smudge of the moustache; the broad shoulders, the narrow hips; a knife.

Marietta pleased him, laying plans, sitting on the sacks,

manœuvring the pieces of straw on her knees, with an air of concentration, a wise virgin.

He let himself into the shed and shut the door after him without a word.

Marietta asked no questions. She sprang to her feet and propped herself against the wall, her hands in the pockets of her frock, her eyes as hard as Brigante's.

Brigante was entranced by her expression.

Quietly and deliberately he drew off his petrol blue alpaca jacket and placed it, carefully spreading the shoulders, on the back of the chair.

Then he came towards her with light, sure steps.

'Lie down,' he said.

She stood her ground and made no reply. The hard eyes stared at him. No sign of fear. He liked that.

He took another two steps and slapped her hard across both cheeks. This was his regular procedure: you could do nothing with an obstinate virgin if you didn't start by beating her up.

Again she made no movement, except to sway from the force of each blow, and she did not drop her eyes. He repeated:

'Lie down!'

Marietta took one step forward. He was surprised. Could she be going to lie down? He had not expected that of her.

She took another step forward and stood with her body pressed against his.

'Your grafting knife,' she said.

Brigante did not have time to grasp her meaning. The girl's hand flashed out of the frock clasping a steel spur and slashed his cheek twice to form a cross. She took two steps back and stood, once more, leaning against the wall.

He put his hand to his face and withdrew it, dripping with blood. At the same moment he heard the slap of metal. Marietta had opened the grafting knife and was holding it pointed firmly towards him. He saw the blade, as keen as a razor, and at the back of the blade he saw the spur (which served to lift the bark

171

after incision), stained red with his blood. He backed hurriedly towards the door.

Marietta walked slowly towards him, grafting knife in hand. She took short paces to give him time to open the door, but she advanced on him steadfastly, her head slightly lowered, as though about to charge, her eyes furtively watching him, her arm bent at the elbow in a boxer's guard, aiming the blade throat-high.

Brigante turned his back and scurried through the doorway. Marietta rapidly shut the door behind him and turned the key in the lock. Then she went and posted herself at the dormer window. He was down on his knees beside the spring, bathing his wound. He got to his feet and she was able to see the cross she had carved on his cheek, two distinct lines intersecting at a right angle, just deep enough to last as long as Matteo Brigante.

Marietta removed herself from the window and examined the door. The posts were worm-eaten, the hinges rusted, daylight showed between the planks; any form of leverage — one of the forks, say, lying about in the garden — would have been sufficient to tear them out. On the floor of beaten earth, the blood from Matteo Brigante's cheek retained the bright red of blood which has still to dry. Her eye lighted on the petrol blue alpaca jacket spread on the back of the chair.

She acted entirely without thinking. In a flash she had reached into the pile of cloth sacks, produced a buff-coloured leather wallet inlaid with gold initials, taken a black leather wallet from the inside pocket of Brigante's jacket and transposed the two, putting the buff-coloured wallet in the jacket pocket and hiding the black one under the sacks. Then she returned to the window and waited.

Brigante turned back towards the shed and stopped opposite the window. Marietta was careful not to stand too close. For a moment they stared at one another in silence. The cross on his cheek hardly bled at all now, except for a few drops which slowly swelled between the lips of the wound, like blisters.

'*Dio boia*,' swore Brigante. 'Executioner god! You've marked me for life.'

172

There was a small glint in her eyes which might have been amusement.

'You haven't seen the last of me,' he said.

'I did it with your own knife,' she said. 'The one with the trade mark of the Two Oxen ...'

'*Porco Giuda*,' he swore. 'Pig of Judas! I've never met such a wench.'

'I'll keep it,' she said. 'I may need it again.'

'Let me come in,' he asked, 'and get my jacket.'

She raised the blade level with his eyes.

'Try coming through that door,' she said, 'and I'll slit your throat.'

'You're quite capable of it,' he said.

He looked furtively at her, as she had looked at him.

'Try me,' she said.

'I won't touch you,' he said. 'Just let me in long enough to get my jacket.'

'I'm watching you,' she said. 'You're coming closer.'

'What have you got to lose? I've nothing in my hands ...'

He pulled out his trouser pockets.

'... and nothing in my pockets. I'm the one who ought to be scared.'

'It would pay you,' she said.

They observed one another in silence.

'It would be better for both of us,' he said, 'if we were friends.'

'Why don't you shut up and wipe your cheek?'

Several of the liquid blisters had burst between the lips of the two cuts and now flowed down his face in thin red lines. Brigante wiped his face with the handkerchief he had already several times rinsed at the spring.

'Now you listen to me ...' he said.

His voice had become hard again.

'You've marked me and you're going to pay for it. There's only one way you can buy me off. Let me in and lie down ...'

She laughed soundlessly.

'Open this door!'

'I'll fetch your jacket,' she said.

She took the coat from the back of the chair and returned to the window. In one hand she held the jacket, in the other the open grafting knife.

'I'm going to pass it to you,' she said. 'But be very careful. If you try reaching for it, I'll use the knife.'

She held the jacket out of the window for him and he took it without attempting to seize her arm.

'You're beginning to get the idea,' she said.

He put on his coat.

'If you liked ...' he said.

His voice had softened.

'... I've never met such a wench ...'

His voice had become almost tender.

'... Just the two of us ... We'd go to the North together. A girl like you ... we'd have the world at our feet. I'm rich, you know ... there's no limit to what we could do ...'

Again she laughed soundlessly. Then, quietly and coolly, she shut the window by pulling across the wooden shutter that opened inwards into the shed.

Brigante tapped gently on the wooden shutter.

'I'm rich, you know, Marietta. I'm rich. Very rich.'

No answer. He went away.

In the morning don Cesare had gone out shooting moorhen on the marsh. He had walked for a long time, with his long, silent stride, followed by Tonio who was carrying the game bag, sweating.

When the moorhen rose from among the reeds, he fired without taking aim, as if he meant to hurl the gun; he went through the motions of hurling it, the tip of the barrel described a curve, came to a halt, and the lead shot — projected less, it seemed, by the explosion of the powder in the case than by the neat, crisp and entirely precise and elegant movement — streaked

174

through the air and — more in response, it seemed, to don Cesare's will-power than to the laws of kinetics — scored a direct hit on the heavy bird, which continued to fly for a moment, but falling back towards the reeds, still flapping its wings, but without assurance, less as if he had received a direct hit with the lead shot than as if don Cesare's will-power, materialized in that sudden movement of the arm raising the gun, had seized it by the throat, among the down, beneath the large spread wings, and were gradually strangling it, forcing it back on to the marsh.

As he killed his third moorhen, at the very moment he fired, don Cesare had felt a stiffness in the arm. This had happened to him several times in the course of the last few years. He attributed it to his manner of shooting without taking aim, neat, crisp, resolute and entirely elegant, the style of which had perhaps become exaggerated as he had grown older, the neatness turning to abruptness, the muscle objecting to the strain. The arm, the shoulder, and several times the hip, remained numb for some hours; Elvira covered them with hot compresses. Old Julia, convinced that stiffness in any part of the body sprang from a spell and could be relieved by a counter-spell, would produce a bowl filled with water and oil.

'Look at the eye, don Cesare!'

And she pronounced the incantation which obliged the evil eye to depart, in the guise of one or more *eyes* on the surface of the bowl. Don Cesare believed neither in spells nor in counter-spells, although, as he often said, he considered sorcery less irrational than religion and medicine. And so he watched the liquid in the bowl until the eye formed, a little to please Julia, a little in defiance of medicine and religion, a little out of homage to the ancient city of Uria, where this rite had already been practised, a little because, if he had not been incredulous as a matter of principle, he would have yielded to these superstitions, rather than to the superstitions of religion or of politics, because they were in the tradition of the ancient territory of Uria, of which he was the last lord. Later that evening or the following day his arm, his shoulder would lose their stiffness — robust old man

175

that he was, the most successful and elegant shot in the whole region.

He arrived back in the house with the colonnades at about noon (at the same time as Francesco Brigante and donna Lucrezia were beginning to declare their love for one another, in the cave down on Manacore Point, near the *trabucco*). His siesta at an end, he had come down to the big ground-floor room and sat down in the eighteenth-century Neapolitan armchair with the grotesquely carved gilt elbow-rests, with compresses around his arm and hip, wearing a navy blue silk dressing-gown (the corners of a white silk handkerchief protruding from a pocket), surrounded by three women of his household — old Julia, Maria, Tonio's wife, and Elvira, Maria's sister, his mistress. The agronomist knocked on the open door and entered.

Maria hurriedly bore down on him, to prevent him from speaking to don Cesare.

'I'm calling to see,' said the agronomist, 'whether you're still agreed about Marietta.'

'We're still agreed,' replied Maria.

Old Julia had approached in her turn.

'Is it about my daughter?' she asked.

There he stood facing the two women, with his pink, delicate cheeks of a man of the North and that false ease of manner, the at once awkward and self-confident air of all agronomists; they knew much more about the use of the land than the peasants did, but they also knew that the peasants were spying on them, ready to seize on the smallest error, the smallest slip, to challenge all their learning. This gave a stiffness to all their dealings, even those which had no connection with agricultural techniques.

'I've called to see,' he said, 'whether we're still agreed.'

'We're agreed,' replied Julia, 'on the same conditions.'

'Good,' he said, 'then she can start this evening. I'll take her things over in the car.'

'It's just that today ...' said Julia.

'She's gone to her aunt's ...' said Maria. 'In Foggia ...'

'Her aunt in Foggia who is sick,' said Julia.

176

'Oh well,' said the agronomist, 'it isn't important. She can start tomorrow. I'll come and fetch her in the afternoon.'

'She might not be back tomorrow night ...' said Julia.

'Because her aunt is ill,' added Maria.

Elvira, too, had come to say her piece.

'It might be better,' she said, 'if Marietta didn't start till next week.'

Don Cesare's voice rang out, dominating all the others.

'You!' he shouted. 'Come and sit here!'

The women were silent. The agronomist looked questioningly at Maria.

'He wants to talk to you,' she said.

'I'm telling you to come and sit down,' repeated don Cesare.

'Don Cesare wants to talk to you,' said Elvira quickly.

The agronomist advanced slowly towards the armchair. He did not like the manner of the great southern landlords who talked down to young officials as though they were members of their staff.

Don Cesare pointed to the bench, facing the armchair.

'Sit down there,' he said.

The Lombard sat down. The women had followed him.

'You women,' said don Cesare, 'leave us in peace.'

Maria and Julia made their way towards the far end of the room, near the fireplace.

'You too,' said don Cesare to Elvira.

Elvira went and joined the two others.

'How old are you?' asked don Cesare.

'Twenty-eight,' the Lombard replied.

'Don't you understand that they've set a trap to make you marry Marietta?'

'So I've been told.'

'You don't know the South,' said don Cesare. 'You won't be able to get out of it.'

'We'll see.'

'Why don't you get married?'

'I don't say no.'

'You have money?'

'I've my salary.'

'It wasn't the government that paid for the palace you built for your goats.'

'I came into a bit of money. I've put everything into my installations.'

'You believe in them?'

'I love my work.'

'You could marry a landowner's daughter.'

'I hadn't thought about it.'

'Our landowners' sons are only fit to become lawyers or deputies. That's the South for you. An agronomist could be of service to a landowner. I think don Ottavio would give you one of his daughters. Would you like me to talk to him about it?'

'I'm no fortune-hunter,' said the agronomist.

Don Cesare looked at him: that bulging forehead, those rosy, Northerner's cheeks, that childishly stubborn head of a boy who had gone on to college.

'Here,' said don Cesare, 'we had agronomists in the fifth century before Christ. The goat-hills on the other side of the lake were irrigated …'

'I don't see the connection,' said the other.

Don Cesare thought: Peasant, thinking your peasant's science is enough to earn you city rights among us. To be accepted by us, the oldest city people in the world, you have to know how to live. But he also thought: Our *savoir-vivre* sank into the marsh and dunes with the noble city of Uria; all that's left are superstitions. He had no wish to humiliate the boy.

'You're right,' he said.

'You don't want Marietta to go into service with me?' the agronomist demanded aggressively.

'She will do as she likes.'

'If anyone's entitled to interfere, it's her mother. Not you.'

'What do you know about it?' asked don Cesare.

'The *droit de seigneur* is a thing of the past!'

You great Lombard idiot, thought don Cesare.

178

'So you want to marry her?' he asked.

'That's her business and mine — at a pinch, her mother's.'

'I see,' said don Cesare. 'You'd prefer to have her without marrying her. But if you're compelled to take her to church, you'll take her to church.'

'That's my business,' said the Lombard.

He stood up.

'I think our discussion is over.'

'Sit down,' said don Cesare.

'I've nothing more to say to you,' the Lombard protested.

But he sat down.

Don Cesare reflected that whenever he had happened to desire the virginity of a girl from his household, he had taken it, without anyone making an issue of it. That if he let the Lombard have Marietta, his people would think him within his rights to demand that she should first spend one night, or as many nights as she wished, with him. Afterwards his women would fabricate a new virginity for the girl for the stranger's benefit (as had happened to Santa Ursula of Uria). But since he was *uomo di cultura*, he thought, at the same time, of all the historical, sociological, biological and psychoanalytical explanations which could be given for the veneration of virginity and the accompanying desire to ravish it, an obsession in the South. That he did not share these superstitions. That he had not demanded the virginity of all the girls of his household. That he took girls and women, according to taste, without caring, from the point of view of his enjoyment, whether they were or were not virgins. That it would be both laborious and useless to explain to the agronomist, imbued with his double superiority as a technician and as a man of the North, the unwritten but strict jurisdiction of the South, a land of jurists. That this Christian Democrat government official would be violently indignant that the noble feudal jurisdiction should still be recognized in the South, tacitly but absolutely. But that, whatever his, don Cesare's, personal tastes or his opinions on virginity, he was determined, with regard to Marietta, to make use of his privilege.

The Lombard was losing his patience, confronted by the old man silently turning over his thoughts.

'What is it that you have to say to me?'

Don Cesare reflected that it was only that morning, while he was out shooting, just before he had felt the stiffness in his arm, that he had come to the decision to demand Marietta's virginity for himself. Walking along, with his eyes open for the heavy birds, he had recalled the events of the previous evening, Marietta sitting at his feet, on the little wooden stool, watching her mother and her sisters over the tops of his knees, then the girl singing round the house; he had suddenly realized that his decision was taken.

'I have nothing to say to you,' he replied to the Lombard.

'You asked me to sit down.'

'Marietta doesn't want to go and work for you.'

'Her mother has just told me the opposite.'

'Ask the girl.'

'Where is she?'

'Nobody has any idea,' replied don Cesare.

The agronomist strode out of the house, muttering at his misfortune in being obliged to live among the reactionary peasants of the South, and the even more reactionary big landowners.

'Elvira!' called don Cesare.

Elvira approached.

'Change my compresses.'

Elvira ran to the fireplace, where the water was heating over a charcoal brazier.

Julia and Maria moved closer to the armchair. Tonio came in and stood by to see that the women did their duty properly. Maria's and Tonio's children appeared in their turn and formed a circle. Don Cesare had the impression that the muscles of his thigh were beginning to stiffen, now; but he did not mention it. The compresses were changed.

'Elvira,' said don Cesare, 'as from tonight you will sleep in Julia's room.'

This had always been the household formula for disgrace.

180

Elvira turned pale. It had been bound to happen, she had always known it. Reduced to the status of a servant like her mother, old Julia!

'My room's full as it is,' protested Julia.

'Elvira will sleep in Marietta's bed.'

'Marietta will come back.'

'Marietta,' said don Cesare, 'has never gone away. She doesn't show herself because she's afraid of you. When you see her, you will tell her to come and talk to me.'

He raised himself from the low seat of the Neapolitan arm-chair, supporting himself on the gilt grotesques. Stiffness gripped the muscles of his thigh.

'My cane,' he said.

Tonio ran to find the gold-knobbed cane. Don Cesare waited, gripping the grotesques, eyeing the women with an expression which robbed them of the courage to speak.

'I am going to work,' he said. 'I don't wish to be disturbed.'

He reached the inner door, resting his weight on the cane. For a long time they could hear the noise of his footsteps and the cane, in the corridor, on the stairs, then in the rooms which housed his collection of antiques.

Matteo Brigante made his way back to Porto Manacore, along the sunken paths, between the high walls of the orange and lemon orchards.

He was marked. He reflected on this new fact of being marked, till now so improbable that he had never envisaged the possibility of its happening, so extraordinary, in connection with him, that he had been far from realizing all the consequences when it had happened to him, a matter of minutes ago, at the hands of Marietta, with his own grafting knife with the trade mark of the Two Oxen, this cross indelibly cut into his cheek.

Few men would dare to ask him questions, or even indeed to make any allusion which would show they had seen the mark.

But some would dare to. His partners, for example, at the game of The Law last night — how would they behave? Neither Tonio nor the American would dare to, but the Australian would ask about it, certainly without wishing to offend him, with deference in his tone, but he would ask about it. Pizzaccio, too, would ask about it, in his own way, offering his assistance: 'If you're in trouble, I'm with you,' 'If someone wants working over and you don't want to be involved, I'll do it for you,' but he would be only too pleased, on the sly. To the Australian Brigante would reply: 'The man who did that to me is dead.' No, it was a poor reply which would deceive no one. Yes, it was a good reply which would stop people from wanting to ask further questions. As for Pizzaccio, he would only have to look at him to shut him up.

But suppose don Ruggero were to laugh and say:

'Have you taken up cock fighting?'

How would he reply? He would want to kill him, but a man who owned a fortune, as Brigante now did, did not kill lightly. And if he replied to don Ruggero that the man who had done it was dead, as he ought to be, don Ruggero would laugh with still more insolence.

'The news would have got around,' he would say.

'The man who did that, the man who marked Matteo Brigante ...' It was a chit of a girl and she would shout her head off about it. He stopped short at this idea, which only now presented itself to him in this form. He had been slashed by a girl who would be sure to boast of her exploit before the whole town. He must return to the orchard and ask Marietta to keep it a secret, demand under threat of death that she should not boast of having slashed him, beg her, move her heart, offer her money, whatever she liked. But in his imagination he saw Marietta's reply, a little laugh, a flash of amusement. She was like him, inflexible.

So the whole town, the whole province was going to learn that he had been marked by a girl. And even if he decided, rich as he was, to regain his honour by killing, who could he kill? —

182

not a chit of a girl or a *guaglione*, they were too small, dispropor-
tionate with the honour of Matteo Brigante.

Go away. Leave Manacore at once, he could keep in touch
with his son to make sure he was defending their fortune. With
all his money he would be treated, wherever he went, as a
member of the upper classes. No. He was marked. An indelible
cross on the cheek was not just another wound, an honourable
duelling scar, as some of the German tourists bore who came to
the southern ports in search of young boys, but a mark of
ignominy, like the cleft ears of tricksters in a country the name
of which had slipped his mind.

He walked on again, turning the question over and over. He
was Matteo Brigante, the man who had always clenched his teeth.
In prison, he had taken the warders' blows without flinching; he
had not replied to the provocations of the other prisoners. He had
put his honour in parentheses the whole time he was in prison, because he had set his mind on being released before his sentence
was finished. In the navy, which he had joined so as to get out
of prison before the end of his sentence, he had again been
obliged to put his honour in parentheses, until he became a
bosun's mate; only then, on some feeble pretext, had he fought,
with a *sciabola*, a bosun's mate who had insulted him while he
was a seaman. The apparent motive of his challenge had con-
formed with the military code of honour, which he thought
laughable, but he had chosen a pretext of this kind so that the
officers should shut their eyes to the fight, indulgently, favouring
a petty officer who seemed to be trying to raise himself to their
level, vainly it was true, but with a praiseworthy good will, going
so far as to risk giving or receiving death in order to show himself worthy of their conception of honour. But the true reason
(unknown to the officers) sprang from the Manacorean sense of
honour, the bosun's mate having, two years beforehand, abused
the right his rank gave him of dictating the law to an ordinary seaman, to humiliate Brigante in his position as son and lover by
insulting his mother and his mistress (whom later he was to
marry, when she was expecting Francesco), before the whole

183

crew lined up on deck. The man was marked for life with great gashes on his face and chest. Brigante was placed under arrest without losing his stripes, exactly as he had foreseen.

Now it was he who was marked — and by a girl. This was the mortifying thought which bored into him while he walked back to Porto Manacore.

'But,' he said to himself, recalling his sabre duel, 'a girl's insult is too small to touch the honour of a man like me.' Besides he could make anyone eat his words who dared to doubt that the disproportion between the offence and the offended was so great that it annulled the act. He should not hide his mishap but, on the contrary, draw attention to it, boast so much that it became laughable.

He decided to test his plan at once. Instead of going home as he had at first intended, he went straight to the Sports Bar.

He stopped in the middle of the middle gangway, took out his stained handkerchief and slowly wiped the drops of blood which were swelling between the lips of the double wound. At the same time he sought the customers' eyes; as his eyes rested on them, they turned their heads away.

He went up to the counter and ordered a French brandy. He sought Justo's, the bartender's eyes, then touched the wound with his finger to invite a question.

Justo raised his eyebrows inquiringly.

'It was a virgin who slashed me,' said Matteo Brigante, 'while I was raping her.'

He said this in a very loud voice, so that everyone should hear.

'*Sangue per sangue*,' replied Justo, 'blood for blood, no offence, signor Brigante.'

'Blood for blood,' repeated Matteo Brigante.

He turned to face the room, running his eyes over the customers' faces.

'Blood for blood,' he added. 'That's my motto.'

'And may one ask who this girl is?' asked Justo.

'No,' replied Brigante, 'I'm a man of honour.'

He laughed, then he added:

184

'But it's quite likely she'll be boasting about it herself.'

He took out his wallet to pay.

It was not the black leather wallet, well known to Justo and the regulars of the Sports Bar, into which every Manacorean had poured his dues; but a buff-coloured leather wallet with gold initials inlaid in the leather.

Despite the self-control to which he had trained himself, first of all in the years spent in clenching his teeth and later in the practice of his racket, he turned the strange wallet over in his hands several times; he glanced inside; one of the pockets was empty; in the other, papers he had never seen before. He saw that Justo had turned his eyes away but was watching him in the mirror. He slowly replaced the wallet in the pocket of his petrol blue alpaca jacket.

'Charge it up,' he said to the bartender.

'*Prego*,' replied Justo, 'gladly, signor Brigante.'

Marietta was waiting for Pippo, near the hollow of the spring. A little before the sun disappeared behind the islands, he appeared among the bark conduits through which the running water flowed.

'I've slashed Matteo Brigante,' Marietta said gravely.

She told him everything that had happened, apart from the exchange of wallets. He listened, his eyes sparkling beneath the black curls which fell forward on to his forehead.

'Fine,' he said, 'fine …'

They went into the hut, so that she could show him the topography of the battle. She pointed out the spots of blood, which had darkened and were now rust-coloured.

They discussed the many questions which presented themselves. For example: how had Brigante discovered Marietta's hiding-place? Pippo refused to believe in a betrayal by the *guaglioni* working on the bark conduits. Several times already,

185

after quarrels with her mother, Julia, or her sisters, Maria and Elvira, the girl had taken refuge in the shed in don Cesare's orchard; but she could equally well have taken refuge in the sheds of don Cesare's other orchards, in the stone shanties on his goat-hills, in the cabins in his olive groves, in the straw huts on the marsh. Once she had spent the night in the tower of Charles V, on the edge of the isthmus, a survival of that belt of towers which the Emperor built along the shores of the South, now a store-place for fodder. If she had come to this particular orchard, it was precisely because she had agreed to do so with Pippo, who was so sure of the *guaglioni* working on the conduits. Could it be the milk-boy who had betrayed them? Impossible, since the milk-boy did not know the significance of the signs drawn on the signpost (a circle and a cross within the circle), by means of which, it had been agreed, Marietta would inform Pippo if a new dispute with her mother and sisters or some other unexpected event, disturbing the plans they had laid together, compelled her to flee from the house with the colonnades.

They discussed these problems with seriousness, warmth too, a kind of restrained passion, a shimmer of joy covering every-thing they said, since they were victors of Matteo Brigante.

'He might come back,' said Pippo. 'You shouldn't stay here.'

'With the knife, I've nothing to risk.'

'Even with the knife. He's crafty. He'll find some way of get-ting hold of it.'

'Stay with me,' said Marietta.

He had not thought of that.

'Of course,' he said.

They were silent. They sat down on the cloth sacks, hand in hand, as they had sat hand in hand that morning, beside the spring, while Pippo related the nocturnal exploits of their *guaglioni*. But now in silence. Both were thinking of this long night they were going to spend close to one another. She had not premeditated asking him to stay; the idea had grown quite naturally out of their discussion. And now, for the first time, they hesitated to look one another in the eye.

In the past they had often been alone together, by day and night, on the marsh, on the hills, in the dunes, in the orchards, and even in the forest of the Shadow. But that had been to poach and steal. He always consulted her before going into action with the *guaglioni*, but although their coups had occasionally been of some size, such as the theft of the policeman's Vespa or that other, much bigger job, one of the consequences of which had been (though Pippo still did not know of this) the exchange of Brigante's wallet for a wallet of buff-coloured leather, they had spoken of these things always in the language of childhood.

They had already told one another they were in love. They would never leave one another; that went without saying. They would marry; that was a natural consequence. More recently they had decided to escape from Manacore together, and chance, assisted by a little wiliness, had provided them with the means; Marietta was to fix the date of departure; they were in no hurry. But they had never yet exchanged either caresses or lovers' kisses. And they had not had to curb the wish to do so. They were not at all puritanical. If they had had the desire to kiss one another on the lips, to touch one another, to make love, they would have done so without scruples of any kind, leaders as they were of the *guaglioni*, accustomed to violating all the laws. But they had not yet had the desire to do so.

Pippo was not ignorant of the gestures of love, which he had practised with other boys, with the goats, by himself and even, on several occasions, by lying about his age, with the girls in the brothel in Porto Albanese. It had usually given him pleasure, larger or smaller, rather smaller with the girls, who were always in too much of a hurry, except once, when he had had enough money to stay half an hour and the girl had taught him all kinds of ways of using her body and his own. But he had not yet established any connection between the pleasures of love and his love for Marietta. He enjoyed her company, he made her the confidante, often the supervisor of his games and exploits, and it was agreed that she would become his wife, that their complicity

187

should last till the end of their lives. But he did not associate the idea that she was to be his wife with the idea of her as a partner in the pleasures of love; that, he knew, was what she would become, but he did not linger over the idea; he preferred to avoid thinking about it.

Leader of the *guaglioni*, at war with all the adults of Manacore, he had, of necessity, closely observed them. The rich gave their wives children, but for the pleasures of love they went to the brothels in Foggia or to a mistress specialized in pleasure, as Giuseppina would become for the Chief of Police or for someone else. It was only the poor who made love only to their own wives, not having the money to pay others. Although he had never admitted it to himself in clear terms, it had been a luxury for him up to the present not to think of the gestures of love in connection with Marietta, his present accomplice and future wife.

As for Marietta, fully grown for four years now, a fine looking girl, her breasts pointed sharp beneath the linen dress, she was constantly obliged to defend herself from men brushing against her, touching her, making no attempt to hide their obsession with her virginity. Even don Cesare she sometimes caught looking at her with a sultry expression, neither lewd nor excited, but enveloping her heavily; she was not revolted at the idea of having to give him her virginity if he demanded it, since that was the law of the South, which she had become accustomed to finding natural; if she thought of it at all — and she rarely did — it was not as some dire changing-point in her life, but as one of those innumerable minor tribulations which it was not always possible to avoid; there was nothing you could do about them, you immediately turned your mind to something else.

But this evening, in the shed in the orange and lemon orchard, with the prospect of spending the whole night side by side on the cloth sacks, in the exciting complicity of the victorious battle against Matteo Brigante, they began to embrace.

As soon as they began to embrace, the law of the South, the habits of the South and everything which, more or less clearly, the two of them had thought till now about love and the business of love was totally forgotten. Religion having never been more to them than a superstition shared by others, it did not occur to them that they were committing a sin; a morality which has no doctrinal basis collapses in a moment. They suddenly found themselves exactly like the herdsmen on the hills behind the prosperous city of Uria.

They had no thought for anything now but to mingle their breaths, to touch every part of their bodies, to press themselves against one another, to excite one another, to seek, in its very excess, the appeasement of their passion. Marietta lost her virginity without even noticing it, as is usually the case with girls used to violent exercise.

They were without any kind of remorse; to them it was the most foreign of emotions.

From dusk till dawn they did nothing but take one another, release one another and take one another again, with ever-increasing pleasure. They uttered not a word, only the stammerings, the exclamations and the sighs of love. When one was tired, the other revived him; it was the work of a moment. At dawn they fell asleep on the cloth sacks, their legs intertwined, their hands united and their hearts beating with the same rhythm.

Donna Lucrezia and Francesco Brigante had separated above the small, white, sandy beach near the *trabucco*, he climbing and descending through the pine woods towards the bush where he had hidden don Ruggero's Vespa, and she following the path along the top of the cliff, tall and erect in her discreet dress with the stand-up collar and long sleeves, walking slowly with her long, serene stride, feeling at ease in the blaze of the sun-lion which had still not begun to sink towards the islands.

She had not given a single glance to Manacore Bay, enclosed between the tall mountain crowned by the forest of the Shadow

189

and the bank of clouds driven along by the libeccio, kept out at sea by the sirocco; she no longer loved these places, as she had loved them ten years before, when she had arrived with her young husband, Judge Alessandro; nor did she hate them, as later she had come to; the decision to leave taken, the material conditions (she believed) realized, she already felt herself to be a stranger, like a woman from Turin down here on holiday who was soon to leave, who had already left because she knew that, back there, her loved one had need of her.

Thus, with thoughts only for the future, she had arrived at the empty gates of the holiday camp. She had rapidly found the supervisor, who had supposed her to be spending her time in the canvas village, dealing with the group leaders and the children, and had offered to drive her home — an offer she had accepted. She had taken it as a good omen that her ruse, childish as it was, should have been so successful.

To her husband, Judge Alessandro, she had said: 'I had lunch with the group leaders,' and she had at once shut herself in her room. Lying on her bed, her head flat on the counterpane, her eyes wide open, she had given endless thought as to how to organize Francesco's life in Turin so that he should be happy.

At five o'clock — when the prisoners started to sing again; the song rose straight from the prison blinds to her half-open shutters four floors above — she wrote to Francesco. She gave him the address and a brief letter of introduction to a friend of her family's and her own, whom she had just remembered, a former official in the prefecture in Foggia who was now working in Turin and might possibly be of service to him. She advised him to take advantage of his journey to reserve the room or, better still, the small furnished flat where they would live in October. She reminded him to wear a white shirt and a quiet tie when he called on his future employer. She hardly mentioned their love which seemed to her self-evident. She concluded: 'Thank you for being so good,' thinking of the vilenesses he could have demanded of her in the cave and which she would not have thought herself

190

entitled to refuse. In the envelope, as they had agreed, she placed thirty thousand lire for the journey. Then she went out to find Giuseppina, to get her to deliver the letter.

From the Sports Bar, Matteo Brigante had gone to have his wound dressed by his friend the chemist. The latter had asked no questions. The treatment over, a rectangular dressing over the cheek, attached to the wing of the nose and the cheekbone by strips of adhesive plaster, the chemist had said:

'Perhaps you don't know ... the recent advances in surgery ... grafting, electrical treatment ... It's simply a question of money ... I'll go to Naples with you, you'll come back with a girl's complexion.'

'When?' Brigante had asked.

'You have to let the first skin form.'

Brigante reproached himself for not having thought, as soon as he had received the wound, of the marvels of plastic surgery. Walking down towards Porto Manacore, still bleeding from the ignominious wound inscribed in his flesh by Marietta, his mind had wandered like a child's; he had even come near to begging the girl to hold her tongue. He was astonished that he should have lost his sang-froid so easily; it was unlike him.

He hurried home, doubly relieved about the wound by the bartender's '*sangue per sangue*' and the chemist's promise. Now he had to solve the problem posed by the exchange of wallets.

'Have you hurt yourself?' asked his wife.

'Only a scratch,' he said. 'Leave me alone. I've got work to do.'

He shut himself in the dining-room and placed in front of him the buff-coloured object with the gold initials. Its appearance corresponded with the description given by the Swiss after the theft of the five hundred thousand lire. He cautiously turned it over and over.

Then he opened it and examined everything, minutely. The pockets were empty, except one which contained insurance forms and a customs paper, in the Swiss's name, the photograph of a woman with some children against a background of snow, two ten-franc notes. With these spread before him, he reflected.

Only Marietta could have made the exchange.

So Marietta was tied up with the thieves, probably the *guaglioni*, or was the thief herself; but it was surprising that they (or she) should have taken on a job of that size. She had hidden the money; so far she had spent nothing; this tallied with the mental maturity he suspected and admired in her.

But why the exchange of wallets? Had she planned to have her revenge on him by accusing him of the theft? She could not have failed to foresee that he would get rid of the wallet before she had time to accuse him.

He was tempted to interpret the girl's gesture as a kind of wink, a discreet call for help; that would have meant: 'I robbed the Swiss, the money is hidden, I've got this far alone, but to complete the job I need the help of a man of experience and maturity.' He rejected this interpretation, because it seemed to him to be dictated by the penchant he felt for Marietta, even greater since she had defended herself so well and so viciously; viciousness, in which he believed he had found the source of his own strength, always inspired him with respect, for himself and for others; respect reinforcing desire, he was on the verge of passion; he did not know it yet. For the moment he was determined to mistrust the excessive penchant he felt for Marietta. He was accustomed to resisting his penchants; he had always clenched his teeth. So he left till later the task of understanding Marietta's motive. For the time being he simply fastened on to the fact that she was in possession, directly or indirectly, of the half-million lire stolen from the Swiss; this affected him in his role as controller; he would have to find a way of levying his tax.

He was not afraid of being compromised by the possession of the wallet, even if Marietta were trying to throw the blame on to him for a robbery committed by herself or by someone she intended to protect; besides, he did not believe she would actually go so far as to accuse him; he found it hard to imagine her as an informer and he did not see what she could hope to get out of it; nor did he believe she would hold a grudge against him for his attack; it had, he thought, been rather flattering, and she had already taken her revenge, and more, by marking him. Justo, the bartender at the Sports, would certainly make a report to Chief of Police Attilio, who had given a detailed description of the wallet to all his spies (and to Matteo Brigante); gold initials were highly uncommon in Manacore; Brigante might be obliged to give the Chief to understand that he was on to something, had found the wallet but not — so far — the money, and could not say any more for the moment. He was not afraid of Chief Attilio, who would not be insistent. Yet out of basic caution he decided not to keep the wallet in his flat. He wanted to hold on to it, though; you do not part with securities, and it was a kind of security against Marietta he now possessed. He went and hid it on the third floor of the tower of Frederick II of Swabia, in the room which he shared with the Chief, but the keys of which he kept himself. He attached it with two strips of adhesive tape to the underside of the marquetry pedestal table. A ghost of a smile flickered round his eyes; he thought it elegant (without using that word to himself) to have chosen the hiding-place so astutely.

As he was making his way back to his flat through the loft, under the roof of the Renaissance wing of the palace, above the municipal offices, he caught sight of Giuseppina climbing the open-air staircase to his flat which ran down to the inner court-yard; she had some gramophone records under her arm.

Brigante's flat was composed of four rooms in a row, part of what had once been a princely suite running all the way round the courtyard; at the rear, the bedroom, then the kitchen, where the Brigantes ate their meals, the dining-room which Matteo used as his office and Francesco as his study, and finally an old-fashioned ante-room, where Francesco slept and where, on shelves along the walls, he displayed his books and records. The front door (opening on to a stone balcony where the open-air staircase terminated) and the attic door, the first folding, the second made of a single stout plank of wood with a wrought iron lock (to which only Matteo had a key) were embedded side by side in the same wall of the ante-room.

Signora Brigante had just gone out to buy some food for dinner, without locking the double door.

The bell rang, then Giuseppina turned the handle and came in. She waited in the ante-room for a moment.

'Francesco!' she called, several times.

Matteo Brigante, still in the passage through the loft, heard her calling 'Francesco!' He crept to the door and stood there motionless, without opening it.

He heard Giuseppina make her way through the other four rooms, then return to the ante-room. A wicker chair creaked near the gramophone. Then silence.

Brigante gently pushed the door open. Giuseppina was sitting in the wicker chair, one hand on a pile of records, presumably those she had been carrying on the stairs, which now lay on the lid of the gramophone. Her eyes half-shut, she waited.

'What are you doing here?' asked Brigante.

She started and drew the pile of records hurriedly on to her knees.

'I'm waiting for Francesco,' she said.

She straightened her back and stared at Brigante with her brilliant, rather wild, malarial eyes.

'What do you want with him?'

'I'm bringing him back some records he lent me.'

'Leave them there. He'll find them.'

'But I wanted,' she said, 'to borrow some others.'

'You can come back.'

He stared at her attentively. He always saw everything. The pile of records was not level. The one on the top was not exactly parallel with the one on the bottom. The third was not exactly flush with the fourth. Some foreign matter had been concealed there.

'Yes,' she said, 'I'll come back.'

She shot out of the chair and made for the door, the records under her arm.

194

As she passed, Brigante put his hand on the records.

'Leave me alone,' she said.

He screwed up his eyes to laugh, without relaxing his lips.

'I am,' he said. 'I am leaving you alone ...'

With a short, quick movement, he snatched the record which had caught his attention, the one with an uneven surface.

'But I'll take that ...'

Beneath the sleeve of the record, he found a white envelope, unaddressed, with something bulky inside.

'That's mine,' said Giuseppina, 'I forbid you to ... '

He gave another of his half-laughs.

'The girl who'll forbid Matteo Brigante anything has yet to be born.'

He turned the envelope over several times in his hand, examining it from every point of view, as was his manner; then he opened it, taking great care not to tear or crease the contents. He drew out several pages of close writing and three ten-thousand lire notes.

Giuseppina made another move to reach the door. He barred the way, standing with his back to it.

'You're not in any hurry,' he said. 'You were going to wait for Francesco ...'

He pushed her till she sank into a chair at the other end of the ante-room.

'Let me go,' she said.

'Stay where you are and shut up ...'

He sat down in the wicker chair, unfolded the letter, first glanced at the signature, Lucrezia, then began attentively to read the long, precise and tender chit-chat of, it seemed, his son's mistress.

Signora Brigante returned, a basket under her arm.

Giuseppina stood up.

'Signora!' she began.

'Shut up!' repeated Brigante.

And to his wife:

'Go into the kitchen and shut the doors. I've something to say to Giuseppina.'

Signora Brigante went through to the dining-room, shutting the door behind her. She could be heard shutting the other doors. Brigante returned to his reading of donna Lucrezia's letter to his son, then he reflected, re-read the letter, reflected again. He rose, went into the dining-room (leaving the door open so as to keep an eye on Giuseppina), took a white envelope from the side-board where he kept his papers, folded the letter, put it in the new envelope, added the three ten-thousand lire notes, sealed the envelope.

He came back into the ante-room and placed the new letter, exactly the same as the old one with the exception of the envelope, in the sleeve of the record, and the record in the pile.

'You see,' he said to Giuseppina, 'nothing has happened.'

She stared at him fixedly.

'I didn't find the letter, I didn't read it, I don't know anything about it. You understand?'

'Yes, signor Brigante.'

'You're going to go away and take your records with you. Francesco won't be in except for his supper. You'll come back at supper-time and you'll give him the letter, so that I don't see. I don't know anything and I won't see anything.'

'You don't know anything,' repeated Giuseppina.

He went up to her — she was still sitting — and took the tips of her breasts between the thumb and index finger of each hand. He pulled and obliged her to stand. Under his fingers he had felt only the structure of the brassière.

'They're false,' he said.

He had not let go; he pinched harder and she groaned.

'You end up by finding something, though ...'

Very close to her she saw the little eyes with the hard expression, and the dressing on the cheek. Asymmetry — a bandaged eye, a scar or a dressing — gives a terrible air to a severe face.

Her feverish expression (feverish from malaria) became

196

panic-stricken. She fluttered her eyelashes precipitately, the way a bat beats his wings when surprised by light.

He ran his hand over her. The girl's legs trembled. He felt her as a veterinary surgeon feels a heifer, attentively.

'It's true then,' he said, 'you've managed to preserve it ...'

His hand insisted. Her legs gave way. He let her sit down.

He walked a few paces away from her and looked at her, his eyes screwed up in a half-smile.

'I don't want to rob you of it. Matteo Brigante takes virgins, not old maids ... But if you betray me, if ever you let Francesco or the Lucrezia know I've read this letter, I warn you: I'll mate you with the Carrara onion. You know what a Carrara onion is?'

'Yes,' murmured Giuseppina.

'People have told you how it inflames? — how there's no remedy for that kind of heat?'

'Yes,' she whispered.

'You know that a girl who's been mated with a Carrara onion is more worn, more ravaged, more open than an old prostitute? Answer me!'

'I know, signor Brigante.'

'Then get out. Take your records and do as I've told you.'

Giuseppina tried to get up, but her legs were still shaking and she fell back on to the chair.

'You've understood me,' said Brigante.

He went through to the dining-room and returned with a bottle of brandy and a liqueur glass.

'Drink,' he said.

She drank and again tried to get up. But her legs were still shaking. He refilled the glass.

'That gives courage,' he said, 'even to a wet rag.'

She drank, got up, took the records and staggered towards the door. Brigante let her pass and, from the top of the balcony, watched her descend the stone staircase, slowly at first, then faster and faster. She crossed the courtyard with a firm gait.

He came back into the flat and poured himself two glasses of brandy, which he drained at a gulp.

In the evening, at supper-time, Giuseppina called to return Francesco the records she had borrowed from him. They chatted for a moment in the ante-room, then Francesco returned to his place at table. Towards the end of the meal:

'It is tomorrow, isn't it,' Matteo Brigante asked, 'that you're leaving for your uncle's in Benevento?'

'Yes,' replied Francesco.

The impenetrable expression of his large, prominent blue eyes rested on his father.

'What time are you going?'

Francesco considered for a moment, without taking his eyes off his father.

'On the nine o'clock bus,' he replied.

'I'll come with you as far as Foggia ... I have to go and see a business contact. I'll take you to lunch at the Hotel Sarti ...'

He continued to observe his son, who did not bat an eyelid.

'It's only right,' he continued, 'that at your age you should know what it is to eat, really eat, in a good restaurant.'

'Thank you very much, Father,' said Francesco.

'You'll find a bus in the afternoon to take you on to Benevento.'

'I shall certainly find one,' replied Francesco.

At ten to nine the following morning when the Porto Albanese–Porto Manacore–Foggia bus arrived, Justo, the bartender from the Sports Café, was in Chief of Police Attilio's office. The deputy had just brought him in to his superior and was staying on for the interview.

The bus stopped on the corner of the via Garibaldi and the main square, outside the court house. Some peasants got out, laden with boxes, baskets, sacks. Manacoreans were waiting, ready to take their seats by storm; the last aboard would have to stand the whole way. The driver and his assistant, one standing on the roof of the bus, the other on the ladder at the back, passed cases and parcels to one another.

The unemployed had left their posts along the walls of the square and stood round in a circle, partly out of curiosity and also in the hope that each of them would be the first to catch the eye of an overseer who might have come into town for a labourer (between Porto Albanese and Manacore, the bus called at the mountain villages and the orchard zone).

The leading citizens' sons stood in a group in the doorway of the Sports Café, on the look-out for some peasant girl who might have come into town to do some shopping and whom they would pursue from street to street. Little chance of touching her, except by arranging to run into her, swinging your arms, and brush against her, as though by accident (by swinging the arms adroitly you could sometimes catch her between the thighs — this was known as 'the dead hand'); you withdrew saying 'sorry, signorina' and the whole band of boys would laugh very loudly. But what was even nicer, and even a little disturbing, was to follow her whispering enormous obscenities; these country wenches were so nervous that they did not dare either to put their persecutors in their places or to call a policeman. They blushed and hurried on. The young men passed them on to one another.

The *guaglioni* prowled about in the crowd, anxious to profit from the bewilderment of a mountain shepherd who had come into town for some shopping. The police, hunting crops in hand, kept their eyes on the *guaglioni*. The prisoners, behind the ground-floor blinds of the court house, were singing the latest radio tune.

The scene was the same every time a bus came through the town.

From his office immediately above the prison, Chief of Police Attilio could follow all the phases of this spectacle, sometimes full of clues, always amusing, especially in the evening when the Foggia bus arrived, connecting with the trains from Rome and Naples, bringing the new batch of tourists (he would know next morning, through his normal working routine, in which hotel or

199

with whom the women were staying; it was wonderful for a lady's man to have an office with a good view and well-organized contacts; in this way he was always the first to sight the game and to know where it lay; but now that Giuseppina dictated the law to him, the Chief had lost his taste for hunting, or almost lost it; he did just enough to prove to himself that he was still a man).

'Buff-coloured leather,' specified Justo, 'with the initials M. B. inlaid in gold on the leather.'

'The Swiss's wallet,' stressed the deputy.

'Absurd,' replied Chief Attilio. 'In the first place, Brigante isn't the man to meddle with a job like this. In the second place, he was in Foggia on the day of the robbery. In the third place, he wouldn't have amused himself by holding the wallet under your nose.'

'I tell you I saw it,' insisted Justo. 'I saw it right on the other side of my counter, closer than I stand to you now ...'

All the peasants had got out of the bus. The Manacoreans stormed the seats. Matteo Brigante and his son came out of the little courtyard of the palace of Frederick II of Swabia and made their way slowly towards the bus.

Francesco in a light grey linen suit, the quietest he had, white shirt and black tie. His mother had shown her surprise at so much austerity. 'Benevento,' he had explained, 'is a real town; you can't go about looking as though you were dressed to go on the beach.' In fact, it had struck him that Lucrezia would watch him leave, through the gap in her shutters, and he had wanted to make her happy by showing himself, in advance, ready to follow her advice. But since he had foreseen that after presenting himself to the director, his future employer, he would enjoy taking part in the *passeggiata*, under the arcades of Turin, which were said to be so full of life, he had filled the case he was carrying with clothing and shirts better suited to his conception of elegance.

Matteo Brigante walked beside his son, shorter, stockier, wearing a pair of impeccably creased white ducks, a double-breasted blue jacket and the habitual butterfly bow. This was his usual rig, inspired by his memories of the navy, when he went to see his business contacts.

'You see,' said Justo. 'He knows he's done for. He's making a run for it.'

'Ought we to arrest him?' asked the deputy.

'Don't be a fool!' exclaimed the Chief.

'It really does look as though he's making a run for it,' insisted the deputy. 'He's even taking a case — he's got his son to carry it for him.'

'A man with the property he's got,' the Chief said, 'doesn't run away because of a wallet which isn't his in the first place.'

'Precisely *because* the wallet isn't his!' cried the deputy. 'You've said it, Chief.'

It seemed as though he would never stop laughing.

'I'm the one who'll pay for it,' said Justo. 'If he ever finds out I gave him away ...'

'That's enough,' the Chief said. 'You can go. And keep quiet about it! I'll question Brigante myself when he gets back.'

The two men went into the next room.

'You bet your life on it,' said the deputy. 'If Brigante ran into trouble, the Chief wouldn't have anywhere to take his birds.'

'I'm the one who'll pay for it,' groaned Justo.

'Brigante must know a lot about the Chief.'

'He'll slash me,' groaned Justo. 'He's been slashed, he'll have to have his revenge on someone.'

'Let me get on with my work,' said the deputy.

Matteo Brigante and Francesco were the last to board the bus. The driver made room for the case. Two men who were under Brigante's thumb stood up to offer their seats to the father and son, who accepted them. The bus started up. The unemployed returned to their places along the walls of the main square. The prisoners were signing '*Parlez-moi d'amour ...*'

The deputy Chief of Police climbed the stairs to Judge Alessandro's office.

★ ★ ★

Towards eleven o'clock Chief Attilio, in turn, climbed the stairs up to the court room to discuss with Judge Alessandro the cases that were under investigation.

'And the Swiss camper?' asked the judge.

'Nothing new.'

The judge was now in the third day of his attack of malaria. His eyes yellow, shining with fever, his forehead covered with sweat, his shirt unbuttoned, he sat shivering in his woollen jacket.

'I was told someone had seen the wallet.'

'Mere gossip, *caro amico* ...'

'I was told,' the judge cut in, 'I was told quite clearly that the bartender in the Sports had seen the Swiss's wallet in Matteo Brigante's hands last night.'

'My deputy's talking nonsense,' the Chief replied. 'Let the dogs bark. The story doesn't hold water.'

The judge rose from his chair, gripping the table for support, his arms trembling.

'You're making a mockery of justice, maresciallo ...'

The Chief was sitting on the other side of the table, in an armchair, with his legs crossed. He raised his arms to the sky.

'Gently, Alessandro, gently ...'

'The day before yesterday you applied political blackmail to an honest workman asking for the passport to which he was entitled. Today you're trying to cover up the crime of a gaol-bird, a racketeer, your friend, your ...'

'Careful, Alessandro ...'

Cuckold, thought the Chief of the judge, irritable like all cuckolds. Already he knew that donna Lucrezia, the day before, had spent four hours in the pine woods. He did not yet know with whom. But it would not take him long to find out. A young woman did not spend four hours alone in the pine woods.

Lecher, thought the judge of the Chief, letting yourself be made a fool of by a little whore. He had already been told of Attilio's execution by Giuseppina in front of the whole town

202

assembled on the beach. Corrupt, rotten, double-dealing, like all lechers.

The judge sat down again.

'Listen to me, maresciallo ... As judge appointed by the public prosecutor to investigate the charge of robbery against X ...'

He had prepared a search warrant for Matteo Brigante's residence, where they were to search for the wallet seen in his hands the night before.

The Chief protested that they were going to make fools of themselves. The judge warned him that if the warrant were not executed at once, he would inform the prosecutor's office in Lucera.

The search was carried out early in the afternoon by the Chief, his deputy and two policemen. They offered lengthy apologies to signora Brigante; she was to tell her husband that they were only carrying out the orders of Judge Alessandro. They made a superficial tour of the flat, taking care not to disturb anything and drawing attention to their tact. In their own minds they were certain that even if Matteo Brigante had committed the robbery, which they doubted, he would not have kept the wallet in his flat.

'It only remains for me to say how sorry I am,' the Chief said to signora Brigante.

'Excuse me, Chief,' the deputy interrupted. 'The warrant stipulates we should search the tower which is also occupied by signor Brigante.'

The Chief shrugged his shoulders. The policemen exchanged winks. It was they who had suggested the judge should mention the tower; they were itching to visit their superior's bachelor quarters, the existence of which the whole town suspected and concerning which they had managed to gather a few details from various women, but which no one had ever seen.

'I think we can get to it through here,' said the deputy, pointing to the oak door with the wrought iron fittings.

Signora Brigante did not have the key. They had to send for a locksmith. The Chief sat down in the wicker chair and put a

Chopin prelude on the turntable, as a means of emphasizing the gulf between himself and his subordinates, who liked only opera and *canzonettas*. At last the four men made their way along the passage through the loft, the deputy leading the way, the Chief bringing up the rear, followed by signora Brigante and the two witnesses required by law.

Thus they reached the octagonal room on the third floor of the tower of Frederick II of Swabia and, behind the tapestries bought from a second-hand dealer in Foggia, that scantily furnished skeleton of a room where Brigante raped his virgins and Chief Attilio corrupted, or so he thought, the wives of leading citizens.

They at once came across a cigarette case which the Chief had left behind and which they all seen him use.

'Brigante's been robbing you, too, Chief!' exclaimed the deputy.

This was just talk. Nobody believed the cigarette case had been stolen. Its presence was the confirmation of Attilio's secret debauchery.

Confronted by this long awaited piece of evidence, the deputy and the two policemen could not conceal their joy. As if it were their superior himself they held in their hands. Now it was his turn to submit to the law to which he had made them submit for years. They forgot signora Brigante's presence and Matteo's future revenge. Pretending to make fun of Brigante, they could make fun of their superior, in his presence. They made play of the iron bedstead, painted with Venetian garlands:

'Ah, the old devil! What he must have got up to on this.'

They named all the mistresses the Chief had been suspected of, pretending to attribute them to Brigante: he had done this to them, he had done that to them, they had …

They could hardly contain themselves.

On pretext of searching for the wallet, they tampered with everything, especially the toilet articles, imagining aloud the erotic uses to which they might have been put.

In his obscene enthusiasm the deputy, climbing on the

204

marquetry pedestal table, manipulated the mirror 'to see how much you could see from the bed'. He tripped and fell, knocking the table over on to its side.

Thus it was that the Swiss's wallet, hidden against the underside of the table-top, was revealed to all eyes.

Impossible not to see it. Attached by two strips of adhesive tape, in the shape of a cross (like the dressing on Brigante's gashed cheek), to the centre of the overturned table. Buff-coloured leather with gold initials, M. B., inlaid in the leather, exactly as described on the search warrant.

There was a great silence. Now the policemen were thinking of the vengeance Matteo Brigante would not fail to exact in full. There was not one of them whose career could not be smashed by an indiscretion on the part of the racketeer.

Chief Attilio broke the silence.

'What's done,' he said, 'can't be undone.'

The moment he had the wallet in his possession, Judge Alessandro drew up a warrant for Brigante's arrest and telephoned the police in Foggia, where the racketeer was probably to be found, and the public prosecutor's office in Lucera.

Matteo Brigante and his son lunched face to face at a small table in the air-conditioned dining-room of the Sarti Hotel in Foggia.

The other tables were taken by foreigners, the men in shorts and sleeveless, open-necked shirts, most of the women in jeans. It pained Francesco to look provincial, with his white collar and dark tie, accompanied by his father, with his buttoned jacket and his tightly knotted butterfly bow. Then he reflected that if, in a few years' time, he took it into his head to come south as a tourist, with Lucrezia, they would be free, as citizens of Turin, to be as insolently casual as foreigners.

Brigante ordered the dearest food and French wines. Francesco did not care for wine, but he drank some, so as not to appear insensitive to his father's liberality or incapable of appreciating

205

the delicacy of his manners. He felt a tightening of the bowels. The feeling of abandon which he had experienced with Lucrezia the day before, letting slip the words of love which welled up inside him, had not survived the moment of finding himself once more face to face with his father. During the night, the persecutor of his habitual nightmare had appeared, with the same ambiguous features it had assumed in recent weeks, his father's eyes and donna Lucrezia's eyes merging in the same demanding expression. His terror had not left him when he woke, and it was with him now.

After the meal, Brigante pushed his son into a taxi.

'Where are we going?' asked Francesco, who had not caught the name of their destination.

'That's something else you ought to know,' said Brigante.

Francesco raised his large, impenetrable eyes to meet his father's.

'It isn't exactly a brothel,' said Brigante. 'It isn't open to just anyone ... Madame is an old acquaintance of mine.'

Brigante fixed his hard little eyes on the large liquid eyes of his son.

'I know you haven't got any money,' he said. 'You'll be my guest. Madame's house isn't quite like the others. The girl you choose won't ask you for anything; it's up to you whether you give her a little present. In first-class houses, like this one, you come to terms with Madame, go with the girl and pay the sub-manageress (or sub-mistress). It's like the Sarti Hotel; you probably noticed I settled the bill, not with the waiter who'd served us, but with the head waiter; before sitting down to table, I went and discussed the menu with the proprietor; as we were going I left a small tip for the waiter. That's the way these things are done ...'

He added:

'Don't you worry. I'll arrange with signorina Cynthia, the sub-mistress, the cost of the time you spend with the girl you've chosen.'

'Thank you, Father,' said Francesco.

The taxi deposited them at an isolated villa on the outskirts of Foggia. Madame received them in a small drawing-room with light leather armchairs and a citron-wood pedestal table.

'May I introduce my son?' said Brigante.

Madame took Francesco in at a quick glance, then, turning towards the father, with the ghost of a smile:

'How did you manage to produce such a good-looking boy?'

She said this lightly, as a compliment which did not need expressing. A woman in her forties, tall, slender, wearing a discreet jersey wool dress. Francesco thought she had the same air of breeding as the matron of a smart Naples nursing home where he had once visited a sick comrade.

'I thought of Fulvia for him,' said Brigante.

'Fulvia's free,' replied Madame.

'But he might prefer one of the others,' replied Brigante.

'I've seven or eight waiting in the main room at the moment,' said Madame.

She turned to Francesco:

'But probably you'd prefer me to introduce them to you one after another. You can let me know your choice afterwards.'

'You see what a difference style makes,' said Brigante to his son.

'I'd like to talk to you,' he said to Madame.

'Let's go to my office,' she said.

She led the way to the door.

'Wait for us,' he said to Francesco.

As they were going out:

'By the way, what's his name?' asked Madame.

'Francesco,' replied Brigante.

She turned.

'Till later, Francesco,' she said.

He was left alone. From a neighbouring room came the muffled sounds of several voices in conversation, women's voices, a sudden slight swell of laughter, then a confused out-break of exclamations, as if some newcomer were being greeted — perhaps my father, thought Francesco.

The small drawing-room with its leather armchairs also

reminded him of the Naples nursing home. The prints on the wall, Fragonards, were scarcely indecent; the chemist in Porto Manacore had the same ones in his bedroom. But here the frames were prettier, in citron wood, like the table.

His terror persisted but, helped by the wine he had drunk in the Sarti Hotel, it now took the form of torpor. Francesco sank into a drowsiness neither less painful nor more easily surmountable than terror.

The door opened.

A tall dark girl stood in the opening, in a high-necked black silk gown, in a tight sheath style which emphasized the thinness of her body, extended at the neck by a strip of material wound asymmetrically over her shoulders.

'My name is Fulvia,' she said.

She looked at him without, he thought, any provocation. He had not in the least expected this kind of detachment. It rather intensified his terror. She examined him. He shook his head to drive away his drowsiness. She gave an amused smile. He thought she looked very sure of herself; such a thin girl, he thought with astonishment. She stood in the doorway, her arms by her sides, without provoking him with either her eyes or her hips or her bust or her lips, examining him calmly, a mocking light in her expression. He was keenly aware of this mockery and rose to his feet.

'Follow me,' she said.

She led the way into the corridor; he followed her. When they were in the room (grey velvet, grey wallpaper, a large bed folded back to reveal white sheets, still crisply folded):

'Make yourself comfortable,' she said.

She helped him off with his jacket and draped it from a hanger. He stood where he was, motionless, following her with his eyes. She came back to him and undid his tie which she went and spread over the shoulder of the jacket. Again she went up to him. He stretched his hand — thinking this was what the situation demanded — towards the thin breast which thrust below the gown. She gently repulsed his hand.

208

'Let me get on,' she said.

The mocking expression sharpened.

'For the moment,' she said, 'I'm the boss.'

She undid the buttons of his shirt and helped him out of the sleeves. She went and placed the shirt on the hanger, over the top of the jacket. He remained standing, in his trousers, stripped to the waist.

'Lie down,' she said.

He stretched out on the bed.

She unfastened something beneath the kind of scarf in which the top of her gown terminated, the black sheath slid to the floor and suddenly she was naked, above him.

She was even thinner than he had thought, her breasts drooping a little, but so small that they were still sharply pointed — like the nails, he thought, in the hand of the great wooden Christ in the entrance to the sanctuary of Santa Ursula of Uria. Again he wanted to touch her; she stopped him. She took hold of his arms and spread them in a cross on the bed and caressed them with the points of her nails, first in the bend of the arm, gently, with a grating of the nails against the skin, but without marking him, with a slow, regular movement, like that of a rake. He relaxed.

The sharp-sweet, tender, cutting caress descended towards the wrists, rose towards the shoulders. He thrust towards the girl his big, bosomy, sandy-haired chest, arching himself to meet the thin breasts with the hard points. The nails began to work at the hollow of the shoulder, the hollow of the groin. He began to groan with pleasure and anguish.

Meanwhile Matteo Brigante was talking business with Madame. A former inmate, now associated with the management side of the business, signorina Cynthia, joined in the conversation. They had installed themselves in the office, around a big, glass-topped table, near a bureau in which were stored invoices, bills, contracts.

Business was not bad this season; the influx of tourists on the via Adriatica swelled the pockets of the restaurateurs and hotel keepers, which had happy consequences for the other tradesmen. Madame was thinking of opening another establishment, on the

o

coast this time, at Siponte, a resort frequented by foreigners and the Foggia bourgeoisie. They would have to interest the hotel porters in scouting for tourists. The initial expenses would be heavy, but the profits high, the returns quick. While Madame revealed her plans, Brigante was calculating that a girl like Fulvia would bring in at least fifty thousand lire a day, more than a small hotel, a medium-sized garage, a large olive grove or three lorries carrying bauxite. The difficult part was to determine the percentage of everyday expenses: what figure, for example, could be placed on police tolerance? Anxious to lure her possible associate with the prospect of a large profit, Madame was probably underestimating costs of this kind. Brigante decided to make personal inquiries with friends of his in the provincial police.

Madame explained that Cynthia would manage the new establishment. She was serious and capable. But a woman was a woman. She needed the backing of a man of substance and experience, not only for the expense of starting up, but also for negotiating with the police, the corporation, the racketeers.

Someone tapped on the door. Fulvia entered, in her black silk gown. In her hand she had a ten-thousand lire note which she held out to Brigante.

'First instalment,' she said.

Madame smiled. Cynthia knitted her brow.

'The rest later,' said Fulvia.

She made for the door.

'How did you get on?' asked Brigante.

Fulvia turned.

'Your son's a pansy,' she said.

'Cut it out,' said Brigante.

'He hasn't got what it takes,' she said.

'Shut up,' he said.

'I left him,' she said. 'He begged me to go back. If I'd wanted, I could have taken the three notes from him in one go.'

Cynthia pursed her lips as a sign of disapproval.

'I'll knock your head off,' said Brigante.

Fulvia looked mockingly at him.

210

'Don't get so worked up about it,' she said. 'Eight men out of every ten are like your kid. It isn't what you think that gets them.'

She went out, quietly closing the door behind her.

Brigante held the ten-thousand lire note between the tips of his fingers, folded lengthwise in two.

'I don't understand,' Cynthia said drily, 'fleecing customers isn't our style.'

'It's an arrangement between Matteo and Fulvia, with my consent,' said Madame.

'We shouldn't set the staff a bad example,' said Cynthia.

'You can see she's a woman of principle,' Madame said to Brigante.

'Tell her,' said Brigante.

'You don't mind?'

'Since I asked you to ...'

'This is it then,' explained Madame. 'Matteo's son has planned to run away with a lady. We've put the boy in Fulvia's hands, for her to cure him.'

'That doesn't explain the money,' said Cynthia.

'The lady gave the youngster thirty thousand lire so that he could pay for his train fare, find a nest for the two of them and all kinds of other nonsense. We've instructed Fulvia to get the three notes out of him. The boy won't be able to make the journey, the good woman will call him to account about the money, and he'll come home to papa with his tail between his legs.'

'Who is this good woman?' asked Cynthia.

'A judge's wife,' replied Brigante.

'We don't want any trouble with judges,' said Cynthia.

'We're giving the judge his wife back,' said Brigante.

He gave a half-smile, screwing up his eyes.

'The judge will thank us.'

'It's all in order,' said Madame. 'Fulvia is returning to the father the money she takes from the son.'

'Which he gives her,' said Brigante.

Cynthia still pursed her lips.

'She's stubborn,' said Madame.

'No,' said Brigante. 'She means to show me that she'd be a conscientious manageress. How much do you need for your Siponte scheme?'

'We're going to look into that,' said Madame. 'You're not in any hurry ...'

Brigante handed the note to Cynthia.

'Champagne all round,' he said.

Cynthia left them and went into the main room. It was dark and cool. Sunbeams, filtering through the shutters, flashed here and there on the gold of the armchairs. One girl was knitting. Others were reading illustrated magazines.

'Signor Brigante is standing you all champagne,' said Cynthia.

'What's happened to him?' a voice asked.

'His daughter's getting married,' said Cynthia.

'Who to?' asked another voice.

'To a judge,' said Cynthia.

She returned to the office with a bottle of champagne in an ice bucket. A maid brought in some glasses. Madame asked Brigante:

'Is the judge's wife an old woman?'

'Twenty-eight,' replied Brigante, 'and nicely rounded. Much better than your Fulvia.'

'Fulvia brings in more business than anyone else in the house.'

'So you've told me. How do you explain her success? If you saw her out in the street you wouldn't look twice.'

'She's intelligent,' Madame said.

'She can guess at a glance,' Cynthia said, 'what a man's vice is.'

'I can do that too,' said Brigante. 'I can't ever have taken a good look at my son.'

'To get back to business,' said Madame, 'let's go over the figures ...'

She searched in the bureau. There was a tap on the door. Fulvia reappeared and held two ten-thousand lire notes out to Brigante, who took them.

'How did you manage it this time?'

'You can ask the kid.'

He stood up and gave her back the two notes, pressing them, folded, into the palm of her hand.

'That's for you,' he said. 'You've earned it.'

'Thanks.'

'I've stood a round of champagne. Go and have a glass with your pals.'

'Later,' she said. 'I must go and finish off your brat. I'm an honest girl.'

'He let you leave him?'

She looked him straight in the eye, mocking him.

'He's very docile,' she said. 'You must have been severe with him. He's picked up some bad habits. He likes having the law laid down to him.'

He went up to her and touched her.

'So you get to know everything about everybody?'

'About you, too,' she said.

'Me?' he said. 'No one ever laid down the law to me.'

He turned back to Madame and Cynthia.

'Wait for me,' he said. 'I'm going with Fulvia for a moment.'

Fulvia laughed.

'No Matteo,' she said. 'Not today.'

'Why not?'

She put her mouth close to his ear.

'To make you wait. You'll crawl just like the others.'

She had spoken so that the others should not hear.

'I'm a man,' he said.

He pressed his hardened body against her.

'There's nothing I can do about it,' she said. 'Pimps and coppers, I make them all crawl to me. It's what they expect of me.'

She moved away, pausing at the door to say, aloud:

'See you later, Matteo. Another five minutes and I'll send you back your son.'

Brigante returned to his seat at the glass-topped table.

'Let's see the figures,' he said.

'What do you think about having Fulvia for our house in

Siponte?' asked Cynthia. 'If Madame were willing to let us have her, it would give us a wonderful send-off.'

'Don't let's get bogged down with details,' said Madame.

An hour passed in the discussion of figures.

'What about your son?' asked Madame.

'He must be sleeping,' said Brigante. 'Fulvia's exhausted him.'

Cynthia sent for Fulvia. The latter had left him dressing in the bedroom, after showing him the way to the small drawing-room where he could wait for his father; then she had gone to meet a client who had asked for her. Cynthia questioned the maid; the boy had come out of the room a few moments after Fulvia and had immediately left the villa. They sent for the gardener, who remembered seeing the tall young man they described to him, three-quarters of an hour earlier; he had left the villa, gone out on to the road and started walking towards Foggia.

'Did he look as though he were in a hurry?' asked Madame. 'Or in a bad way? Did he seem to know where he was going?'

'I don't know,' said the gardener.

During the three-quarters of an hour which had elapsed since his departure from the villa, Francesco had had plenty of time to reach the town centre. A bus would shortly be leaving for Benevento; the boy would probably catch it, to go to his uncle, as they had arranged. But Brigante did not feel patient enough to wait till evening came before he telephoned one of his uncle's neighbours to see whether his son had arrived.

'Call me a taxi,' he asked Madame.

She telephoned: the taxi arrived almost at once. Brigante told the driver to take him to the bus station. The last bus for Benevento was on the point of leaving. Francesco was not in it.

Brigante made the rounds of the bars where he was known. He gave his son's description, asked whether anyone had seen him. No. Certainly not. They had served no one like him.

214

The bus for Porto Manacore left at half-past six. At a quarter past, Brigante again headed for the station. Perhaps Francesco, after wandering about the town, had simply decided to take himself home.

No Francesco at the station.

At twenty-five minutes past Brigante saw two plain-clothes policemen of his acquaintance heading towards him.

He rushed to meet them.

'My son?' he asked.

He was convinced they were there to inform him of some untoward event.

'It's nothing to do with your son,' said one of the policemen.

'We have a warrant for your arrest,' said the other.

'Forgive us,' added the first. 'But we have a warrant for your arrest.'

'Let's see it,' said Brigante.

He read the paper attentively. It made no mention of the discovery of the wallet. He thought Judge Alessandro must have become delirious, during a bad attack of marsh fever. Or else someone had told him of the intrigue between donna Lucrezia and Francesco and he had wanted vengeance — another kind of delirium. The judge had blundered; he would have to think of a way of turning it to his advantage.

'We're to take you to Porto Manacore,' said one of the policemen.

'We'll have to handcuff you,' said the other.

'Get on the bus with us,' added the first. 'We won't handcuff you till you get there.'

'I'll pay for a taxi,' said Brigante.

Just as he liked.

'But I arranged to meet my son on the bus. Let's wait a little longer.'

The policemen were in no hurry.

The bus left without any sign of Francesco. The three men went off together to find a taxi.

Just before Porto Manacore, the taxi was overtaken by a red

car, a Giulietta, conveying a Foggia doctor down to the marsh; he had been called to don Cesare's bedside.

Brigante entered the court house handcuffed. He was immediately taken to the judge's office. He said little in answer to the questions which were put to him. He had never seen the Swiss's wallet. He could not understand what series of circumstances could have led to its discovery in an extension of his flat. He had never had it in his pocket. The bartender had been lying.

The judge told him he would be confronted with Justo next morning, and had him taken down to the prison, to the one separate cell.

A quarter of an hour later, Chief of Police Attilio had him brought to his office and left alone with him.

'Explain yourself ...'

'In a minute or two,' replied Brigante. 'We'll go into all that together ... My son Francesco has disappeared. I'm afraid he might do something silly ...'

He related the whole affair: the intercepted letter, donna Lucrezia's and Francesco's love for one another, their plan to run off together, the handing over of thirty thousand lire; how he had taken his son to Madame, how Fulvia had got the money out of him and how the boy, ashamed and possibly thinking himself dishonoured, might give way to despair.

The Chief at once alerted the provincial police by telephone.

'The lesson was a good one,' he said. 'But perhaps you carried it rather far ...'

'I just heard,' he added, 'that donna Lucrezia met your son in the Cave of the Tuscans yesterday, near the *trabucco*. A fisherman saw them together on the little beach below the pine woods. La Lucrezia! — I wouldn't have believed it ... I was wrong not to attend to her sooner; she can't be without her charms and I would have spared you and your son a good deal of trouble ... Now let's talk about this wallet.'

'Brigante's word for it, my word as a man, I had nothing to do with the robbery, either directly or indirectly.'

'I always thought you were too intelligent to get mixed up in a thing like this. But it was you who hid the wallet in … your room in the tower.'

'It was me.'

'You know where the money is?'

'Not yet.'

'What made you let Justo see the wallet last night?'

'I didn't know it was in my pocket.'

'Who put it in your pocket?'

'I don't know yet.'

'You're shielding someone.'

Brigante thought for a moment.

'I can't answer that question yet.'

'If you know the thief, you might just be able to prove you aren't his accomplice.'

'I don't believe it was the thief who put the wallet in my pocket.'

'I always thought you were pretty shrewd. But I have a feeling that at the moment you're letting yourself be led by the tail. By whom, I wonder …?'

'I can't fit it all together yet,' replied Brigante.

'You can't explain it to me, just between ourselves?'

'Not yet.'

'Who scratched your cheek?'

'That's got nothing to do with it.'

'Did you get into a fight?'

'No,' said Brigante. 'It was a virgin I was raping.'

'We don't have much luck with virgins,' the Chief said.

'Get Giuseppina in a corner,' said Brigante. 'Knock hell out of her and then rape her. After that, you won't think any more about her.'

'That's not my way of doing things,' said the Chief.

'Then find yourself another woman.'

'I'm trying to. La Lucrezia is going to take it badly when she hears how your son …'

Brigante wrinkled his forehead.

He loves his son, the Chief thought. A wave of pleasure swept through him at the discovery of a chink in Brigante's armour. He asked himself whether Francesco had not somehow been involved in the theft of the half-million lire; that would account for the father's reticence.

'La Lucrezia ...' he continued.

Brigante hastily brought his hand to his groin; it was thus you summoned the evil eye. He was trying to convince himself that the judge's wife had cast a spell on Francesco. The Chief reproached himself for seeming to make light of grief which was making the most sensible man he had ever known behave nonsensically.

'Has your boy got any other money on him?' he asked.

'About five thousand lire that I gave him for pocket money ...'

'He'll come back when he's spent it. We're used to escapades like this.'

Brigante's forehead wrinkled again.

'Francesco isn't as tough as I'd thought,' he said.

'What makes you think that?' the Chief asked quickly.

'Fulvia took him in too easily.'

The Chief was disappointed. He had hoped they were getting back to the Swiss affair.

'It's just his age,' he said.

'I'll get the better of him,' said Brigante. 'No more studying. I'll put him on one of my lorries at the bauxite mine. Twelve hours work a day. He'll eat in the miners' canteen. Sleep on a straw mattress, in a shack. Lose weight. He's too fat for his age. I should have noticed it before.'

'Before what?'

'Before Fulvia.'

The Chief looked questioningly at him. Suddenly, for the first time during the ten years that they had been in daily contact, he saw Brigante's eyes soften.

'I beg you,' said Brigante. 'Look for him. Fetch him back.'

'I have telephoned,' said the Chief.

'If he finds out I've been arrested ... He might think himself even more dishonoured. I'm afraid ...'

'No, no,' the Chief said. 'By this time he'll be blind drunk in some café. We know all about runaways; they all behave exactly the same ...'

The Chief rose to his feet.

'I'll ring Foggia again in a few minutes, and get them to hurry up their search ... I shall have to send you back to your cell. We've already been talking too long. My deputy will go about saying we've been preparing your defence together.'

'No,' said Brigante. 'You've been interrogating me. It's perfectly normal.'

He stood up. His expression had reassumed its customary firmness.

'What have you told me?'

'The same as I told the judge: I haven't set eyes on the wallet. I didn't have it in my pocket last night. Justo is lying.'

'He was the only one who saw it?'

'Yes,' said Brigante. 'I was standing with my back to the customers: they couldn't have seen anything. Besides, no one would dare testify against me.'

The Chief smiled.

'I see,' he said. 'Justo framed you.'

'If I were the police, that's what I'd think.'

'How did he get into the tower to hide the wallet?'

Brigante thought for a second or two.

'That's it ...' he said. 'Justo stole the key of the tower from me ... one evening last week ... It was in the pocket of my petrol blue jacket ... which I'd left on the back of a chair ... I went over to talk to Pizzaccio ... When I looked for the key later, it wasn't there ... I thought the *guaglioni* must have taken it ... Pizzaccio is the only person I've mentioned it to ... I'd completely forgotten it ... I'll remember it all when the police find the key and question me ... Pizzaccio will remember it all, too.'

'Where will the police find the key?'

'On the floor, in the bar,' replied Brigante. 'Tomorrow morning at about eleven ... it will fall out of Justo's pocket while he is serving Pizzaccio.'

'No,' said the Chief. 'Even the judge knows Pizzaccio is your number one.'

'While Justo is serving the Australian ... The police sitting at the next table will pick up the key ... They will be intrigued by a label attached to the key, on which they will read the words: "Door to tower storeroom".'

'They'll put in a report to me,' said the Chief, 'and take the key to the judge.'

'And now,' said Brigante, 'I've got all night to think things over. I'd like to help you catch the man who stole the half-million lire. It would look good on your record. You might even end up by getting that transfer ...'

'You know more than you've told me.'

'I'm on the track of something,' said Brigante. 'That's all.'

'You'd make a better policeman than me.'

'Yes. Because I'm not so pleasant. That comes from working for myself.'

'I'll have some dinner taken along to your cell,' said the Chief. 'Would you like some wine?'

'No,' replied Brigante. 'I need a clear head tonight.'

He gave his half-smile, screwing up his eyes.

'Tonight,' he said, 'I'm going to work for you.'

The Chief called his deputy.

'Take the accused back to his cell,' he said.

'Follow me,' said the deputy to Brigante.

'Signor maresciallo,' said Brigante, 'I beg you not to forget ...'

The two men looked at one another.

'... the kid.'

He braced himself and followed the deputy.

When he was back in his cell, alone with the head warder, who was under his thumb, he asked:

'What time do you go off duty?'

'I'm off duty now,' replied the gaoler. 'I only stayed because of you.'

'I must talk to Pizzaccio.'

'I'll go and tell him. But he can't come before midnight.

There's one warder I'm not sure of; I'll go and buy him some drink; you'll have to give me time to put him to sleep.'

'Midnight will do,' said Brigante.

From the window of his office, Chief of Police Attilio saw Judge Alessandro leaving the court house for his usual after-dinner walk. He sent word to donna Lucrezia, asking her, despite the lateness of the hour, to call down at his office. She had just learned of Matteo Brigante's arrest and came down at once.

'My dear friend,' the Chief said to her, 'police officers can't help stumbling upon many secrets of private life. Their sense of honour, and sometimes their friendship, compel them to pretend they do not know them. But tonight honour and friendship demand that I should speak quite openly to you ... You have entrusted money to a boy who does not deserve your trust ...'

He related his own version of the events, without telling her of Matteo Brigante's confession. This boiled down to a kind of police report, to which he added no commentary. Francesco Brigante had spent the afternoon in a Foggia brothel, spending above his means. A letter from donna Lucrezia had been found on him from which it had been concluded that she was his mistress, that they had planned to run off to a northern town together and that he had received some thirty thousand lire of hers, which he had just given to a prostitute.

Donna Lucrezia, sitting across the table from Chief Attilio, listened in silence, impassive, straight-backed.

Francesco had disappeared — taking the letter with him, unfortunately. The police were searching for him. The Chief had already taken precautions, so that the letter, if it were still in the boy's possession when he was found, should be destroyed or returned personally to donna Lucrezia.

'Why,' she asked, 'are the police looking for him?'

The Chief preserved the same note of detachment, of 'objectivity', with which he had 'delivered' his (misleading) report.

'The embarrassment of meeting you again, the distress of learning that his father has been arrested and accused of robbery ...'

She stood up.

'He's killed himself?' she asked.

'No.'

'You're afraid to tell me.'

'No,' the Chief repeated firmly, 'no. He has disappeared and we are looking for him. That's all there is to it.'

'You're not hiding anything from me?'

'I give you my word.'

'Attilio,' she said, 'you must find him. You must. He's only a child.'

'I'm putting a constant stream of calls through to the whole province.'

'Perhaps this girl knows where he is.'

'We don't think so.'

'You have some idea of what he might have done?'

'We're looking for him.'

She was insistent.

'Let me know the moment you find out where he is. No matter what time it is. Wake the whole household.'

'But … ' he protested.

'Ah!' she cried, 'I'll shout my love from the housetops.'

'*Carissima amica …*'

'Find him,' she said.

She left the office. He heard her hurrying up the stairs. The fourth-floor door slammed shut.

He reproached himself with having spent so many years close to donna Lucrezia, meeting her practically every day, without ever suspecting the ardour of which she was capable. Such violence and natural abandon in passion placed her far above all his past mistresses. He at once drew up a plan of action. Preserve, tomorrow and during the days that followed, the same note as this evening — the note of discretion, the note, he thought, of a high official — but hint at the depth of his feelings with small details, eagerness to pass on news, haste to repel intruders, warmth in a handshake, scrupulous discretion. Methodically gain her confidence, the right to her confidences. Francesco would probably be found, return sheepishly to Manacore; defend him rather than abuse him, wait till her own experience had convinced donna Lucrezia of her lover's weakness and cowardice. To whom would she then turn for protection if not to her one friend, to the one real man of her acquaintance, to himself? Then, switch over to the attack, conquer.

He rose from his seat, strode to the middle of the office and performed a few gymnastic exercises: touching the toes of his left foot with his right hand without bending the knees; knee bends without bending the trunk. 'I'm in the pink of condition. The South possesses a treasure, I shall have her. I'm hungry.'

He left his office, went up to his flat, two floors higher. Anna was knitting in Giuseppina's company.

'Good evening, signor,' said Giuseppina.

'Good evening,' he replied, without looking at her.

He reflected that he would have this one, too, after three months' aloofness. The other would give him the patience to wait.

'Shall we eat?' he asked.

'I must be going, then,' said Giuseppina.

'Good night to you,' the Chief said.

And to his wife:

'I'm hungry, *carissima*. Ravenously hungry.'

At about eleven in the morning, Marietta and Pippo had woken, in the shed in the orange and lemon orchard, lying on the cloth sacks, their legs intertwined and their hands united, as they had fallen asleep at dawn.

Pippo had sent the two *guaglioni* at work on the bark conduits to buy some bread and Bologna sausage in Manacore. He himself had climbed a fig tree and plucked the first ripe fruit of the season. Marietta had filled a jug of water from the spring.

During the night, the sirocco had got the upper hand over the libeccio and the bank of clouds had moved away from the coast, well beyond the islands; it merged with the sea on the horizon, now no more than a bold, unbroken line, a rim which emphasized the separation of the sky and sea. But beneath the orange, the lemon and the fig trees, amid the murmur of the orchard's three springs, it was almost cool.

Marietta and Pippo had eaten with the best of appetites. Then they had returned to the shed, shut themselves in and began once more to nibble, touch, take and release one another, never ceasing to wonder that such simple gestures should procure them so much pleasure.

Pippo had not returned to Porto Manacore till nightfall. He had learned at once, from *guaglioni* who lived on the marsh, that don Cesare's right leg and arm had been paralysed since the evening before, and that a Foggia doctor had just arrived at his bedside, a famous doctor who would only visit a patient in return for thousands of lire and who had come in an Alfa-Romeo, a red Giulietta driven by a very young man; he was certainly a lucky boy.

The *guaglioni* from the marsh also told him that don Cesare was asking for Marietta the whole time; that it was she he wished to nurse him.

Finally Pippo learned that Matteo Brigante had been seen getting out of a taxi, handcuffed between two plain-clothes policemen. That he had been denounced by Justo, the bartender at the Sports Café. That a search had been carried out at his home in the afternoon and the police had found the wallet stolen from the Swiss camper, but not the five hundred thousand lire.

Pippo returned to the orchard and reported these events to Marietta. He concluded:

'Someone has framed Brigante. Why should they say they found the wallet at his place?'

'Because it was there,' said Marietta.

Pippo ran to the sacks, lifted them, searched. No wallet.

'Explain,' he demanded.

Marietta related how she had switched the wallets before returning Brigante's petrol blue alpaca jacket, after she had slashed him.

'Why didn't you tell me about it before?'

'I had an idea.'

'You're always having ideas,' Pippo protested. 'There's only one thing I'm certain of: Brigante knows now that it was us who did the Swiss job.'

'Dimwit,' said Marietta. 'Who was it the police arrested? Us or Brigante?'

'He'll denounce you.'

'I haven't got the Swiss's wallet.'

'They'll find the money.'

'Let them look for it,' said Marietta.

'You're not going to tell me where you've hidden it?'

'You're too stupid.'

'And what have you done with Brigante's wallet?'

'Buried it.'

'I don't understand,' Pippo said over and over again, 'I don't understand you ...'

How, without leaving the shed — and he knew perfectly well she had not left it, had Marietta been able to set the wheels in motion which had led to the search of Brigante's flat in Manacore and his arrest in Foggia? Besides, he did not really know what to make of this police intervention. Why had Marietta done all this? — and how?

'Explain it to me,' he insisted.

She passed her hand through the boy's black curls.

'I'm not like you,' she said, 'I've got something in my skull.'

Then she decided:

'I must go back to the house. You're going to come with me. We'll go round by the olive plantations so as to avoid Manacore: we mustn't be seen there for a few days. You will hide in the Charles V tower. I'll fetch you your food.'

The doctor from Foggia was a humanist, such as are still to be found in the South of Italy, where specialization is not carried so far that it prevents a doctor from forming his own conception of the world. He had known don Cesare, and been on visiting terms with him, twenty years before and recognized in him an *uomo di alta cultura* like himself. He did not think it necessary to lie to him. A certain level of culture, he considered, presupposed the conquest of the fear of truth and the terror of death. They were both freemasons — members of the Scottish order, but atheists.

From the limbs, the paralysis had spread to the whole of the right side, except the face. A slight numbness impeded the movements of the jaw, but without preventing don Cesare from speaking quite normally.

The doctor sounded his heart without establishing either stricture of the mitral valve or any other condition capable of giving rise to cerebral thrombosis.

He shone a lamp in the eyes; the pupil no longer contracted at the light. He made don Cesare read, gradually drawing the page away from him; the pupil continued to respond to the demands of distance.

Temperature: 100.7°.

The doctor asked the sick man if he had ever contracted syphilis. He had, twenty-five years before; he had treated himself in accordance with the therapeutics current at the time. Had there been any relapses? He supposed not, he could not be sure about it, he had noticed nothing, he had never consulted a doctor; when he felt out of sorts, he took quinine, just as he made his peasants and fishermen take it; on the marsh, they put every physical ailment down to the fever.

Yes, he had suffered from numbness before now; his right leg and arm had sometimes given way, but not often. No, he had never had the tremors; until the day before, he had remained the best shot in the district. Yes, he sometimes had pins and needles in the foot or hand.

The doctor made a lumbar puncture and took a blood test. He could only give his verdict after analysis.

'But you've come to a hypothesis?' asked don Cesare.

'Yes,' said the doctor. 'Gradual hemiplegia, of syphilitic origin.'

'Your prognosis?'

'There's little hope of recovery.'

226

He explained why, using the medical language of the early years of the century, the terms and dialectics of which were within the comprehension of every man of culture.

The idea of approaching death produced a certain excitement in don Cesare. For the first time in years, for the first time since he had *lost interest*, he philosophized aloud. The pleasure of intercourse with women had never disappointed him; his appetite for them had never weakened; the very moment the paralysis had struck him he had been planning to take the youngest and most beautiful girl of his household to bed with him. Like a soldier falling on the field of battle, he was dying of wounds received in the hand-to-hand fighting of love, the battle of his choice; a glorious death, he thought. The ancient city of Uria had been dedicated to Venus; the last lord of Uria, after years of salvaging the remains of the noble city from the sand and marshes, was dying of the disease of Venus; his life was ending without discord.

Privately the doctor considered that the pox did not merit such lyricism. But he was happy to see his friend firm in the face of death. It is only at the very end that you can be quite sure of a man's quality. Don Cesare was confirming now that he was indeed a man of quality.

He asked how much time he could count on to put his household affairs in order. The disease was rapidly tightening its hold; the temperature had begun to rise. The doctor could not promise more than twenty-four hours' lucidity and power of speech. In fact, he could not promise anything. Aphasia might set in at any moment. He would return next morning, with the results of his analysis.

Meanwhile, in the big room beneath don Cesare's, old Julia, Elvira, Maria, Tonio and several of their children were saying the rosary to help their master recover his health. They stood round the big olive-wood table, Tonio with his arms folded, the women with their hands joined in prayer.

'*Ave Maria piena di grazia,*' began Julia. '*Il signore è teco e benedetto è il frutto del ventre tuo, Gesù.*'

She stopped and the others droned on:

227

'*Santa Maria, madre di Dio, prega per noi peccatori, adesso e nell'ora della nostra morte.*'

And all together, Julia and the others:

'*Così sia*, so be it.'

Then Julia would begin alone again: '*Ave Maria ...*'

The large eighteenth-century Neapolitan armchair with the grotesquely carved gilt elbow-rests had been pulled away from the table. Empty, it held the centre of the room.

Out on the terrace, in front of the perron of the house with the colonnades, the men and children from the reed huts formed a circle round the doctor's Giulietta, pressing the young chauffeur for details of the vehicle.

The fishermen's wives were waiting in a group at the foot of the staircase.

Marietta appeared suddenly from behind the bamboos, skirted the group of men, pushed her way through the women, hurried up the steps of the perron and slipped between Tonio and one of the children, in front of the big table. She joined her hands.

'*Il frutto del ventre tuo, Gesù,*' concluded old Julia.

Marietta responded with the others:

'*Santa Maria, madre di Dio ...*'

They heard the doctor coming down the stairs. They stopped praying and turned towards the door which opened into the corridor.

The doctor looked at them, searching for the girl don Cesare had been planning to take to bed with him when the disease of Venus had gripped his limbs. His eyes halted when they reached Marietta and it was to her that he addressed himself:

'I shall return tomorrow morning,' he said. 'I can't give any verdict yet.'

He was silent for a moment, then he added:

'There's very little hope.'

He went out. Elvira broke into a long wail.

'Be quiet,' said old Julia.

She touched the trumpet-shell, a counter-charm, which hung from her neck beside the Virgin's medallion.

'Be quiet. It is wrong to cry before death has entered the house.'

They mounted the stairs to don Cesare's bedroom and grouped themselves round the canopied bed. He ran his eyes over them, in silence, until he caught sight of Marietta.

'So you're back,' he said.

He was sitting up in bed, supported by pillows. His right arm, from which all movement had gone, rested on a brocade cushion of white and gold. He had been shaved by Tonio, very close, as on every other day. His white hair had been parted and brushed by Elvira, and it crowned his forehead evenly, as it always did. A white lawn handkerchief projected from the pocket of his dark blue silk pyjamas.

Marietta threw herself down on her knees, close to the bed, and kissed his right hand.

'Forgive me, don Cesare, forgive me!'

She covered his hand with tears.

He smiled down at her.

'Here are my orders,' he said. 'Marietta is going to nurse me. Marietta alone. The rest of you will wait downstairs. Tonio will go and get the Lambretta out and hold himself ready all night to drive wherever I say. Marietta will tell you what you are to do and whether I need you.'

They went out in silence. Old Julia paused in the doorway:

'Don Cesare,' she said, 'we must send for a priest.'

'Listen carefully, Julia …'

He spoke without anger, but stressed the words so that he should not be bothered with this question again.

'… I still have one good arm and it never bothered me to shoot left-handed. If any priest sets foot in my house while I have life in me, I'll empty both barrels up his backside.'

Julia crossed herself and went out. He was alone with Marietta, still kneeling beside the bed, her lips pressed against his right hand, weeping and repeating: 'Forgive me, don Cesare!'

He would have liked to withdraw his hand, rest it on the girl's head, stroke her brow. But the hand no longer obeyed him.

'Get up,' he said, 'and come round to the other side of the bed.'

229

She got up and went round to the other side of the bed, on don Cesare's left.

'Draw up an armchair and sit down.'

She drew up an armchair and sat down at his bedside.

'Give me your hand.'

She gave him her cool hand and he took it in his burning hand.

'And now,' he said, 'tell me what you did with those two days.'

She looked him straight in the eye.

'I made love,' she replied.

He smiled at her.

'What better can a girl do?'

He squeezed her hand.

'Give me a smile,' he said.

She smiled at him through her tears. He felt the cool hand relax in his burning hand.

'I had hoped,' he said, 'that I would be the one to teach you the ways of love. I made up my mind too late ... But tell me who you've chosen as your boy friend.'

'Pippo the *guaglione*.'

'The boy with the black curls falling on to his forehead?'

'Yes.'

'He's good-looking and he's sure to be passionate. You've gained by my taking so long to make up my mind.'

'But I love you, don Cesare!' Marietta exclaimed violently.

She bent her trunk towards him, her eyes wide open, unrestrained.

Don Cesare looked at her in silence.

He thought that she was sincere and insincere. That there were many ways of loving. That not for a great many years had he given the word the absolute, and in a way sacramental, meaning which young lovers conferred on it. That not for decades had he said to himself 'I love', using the word intransitively, as he had joyously repeated it to himself the first time he had experienced the passion of love. But that it was perfectly true that Marietta might love him, in a certain manner. That he had been

230

the very image of what the girl had been taught to respect, fear and love, from her earliest childhood, a God-like figure; he would have preferred to resemble Zeus, Apollo and Hermes, but Marietta had been instructed in the other mythology. That even today, sitting up in his large bed, half paralysed by the disease of Venus, he inspired fear, veneration and love, three faces of a single emotion which had no name but which embraced much more than any of the others and came closest to that absolute love to which young lovers aspired in vain. That the love which Marietta now confessed to him was far closer to the absolute and unattainable love to which lovers aspired than was the purely temporary love which bound her to her young boy friend, but that she did not know this.

This was what don Cesare thought, examining Marietta as she sat silently crying by his bedside and examining himself, through the eyes of thought, as was his habit, his right arm resting on the brocade cushion, his left hand holding the girl's hand and his eyes focused on her.

As for the pleasures of love, he thought, he could have aroused the girl more splendidly than her young lover — he, don Cesare, he thought, as terrible and as wheedling as thundering Zeus, whose every movement made the earth tremble. But the cruel Venus had struck him down with paralysis at the very moment when he had decided to take the girl to bed with him.

Marietta, meanwhile, went on crying.

'You're hiding something from me,' he said.

'I'm afraid of Matteo Brigante,' Marietta replied briskly.

'You hadn't promised yourself to him?'

'No,' said Marietta. 'No.'

Don Cesare released the cool hand which he held in his burning hand.

'Wipe your eyes,' he said, 'and tell me what you've been up to.'

She dried her tears and began to say what she had decided to say, her expression firm again, her voice assured.

* * *

It was she who had stolen the Swiss's wallet, with Pippo's help. Using her regular punt and steering within the shelter of the reeds, she had taken him out on to the isthmus, not far from the camp. She had kept look-out. Pippo had advanced from one rosemary bush to another until he was as close as he could get to the two tents. Then in a few quick strides he had reached the car, which screened him from the eyes of bathers just as the tents screened him from the woman. He had returned just as smartly. She had taken him in the punt to within reach of the Charles V tower, where they had all kinds of hiding-places.

It was she, too, the day before, who, prowling round the camp and then getting into conversation with the Swiss woman, had noticed the jacket lying folded on the back seat and spotted the wallet projecting from the pocket; to tell the truth, she had not hoped to find so much money in it. She had hidden the half-million lire, refusing to allow either herself or Pippo to touch a single note, having often noticed that thieves were always getting caught because they attracted police attention by spending too much. She had promised herself she would not break into their hoard until sufficient time had gone by for her and Pippo to leave Manacore for a town in the North, without arousing suspicions.

Don Cesare listened to her with enchantment. So there were still a few adventurous children left in this Italy which he had supposed no longer interested in anything but scooters and television! He was happy that it should be a girl from his household who should revive the traditions of banditry. Perhaps she was his daughter? He had still been sleeping with Julia occasionally at the time Marietta was conceived.

He smiled at her.

'Then you're rich,' he said.

'No,' she said, 'because Matteo Brigante will denounce me.'

'You don't mean to say you told Brigante about the wallet?'

'No,' she said, 'but ...'

She recounted the fight in the shed and how she had slashed Brigante.

Don Cesare was more and more delighted with her. He grew

convinced that she was his daughter. He considered the dates; he promised himself that he would question Julia.

Then Marietta came to the exchange of wallets.

'But why did you do that?'

'I don't know,' she replied. 'I didn't have time to think about it. I was pleased with myself. Brigante, always so cautious — he was carrying the Swiss's wallet about in his pocket, enough to put him in gaol for months. I could have laughed aloud.'

Finally she related how the police had found the wallet on Brigante's premises and he had been arrested. What was he going to say? What had he already said? The fact that he had been slashed would make him all the more malicious.

Why had she put the Swiss's wallet in Brigante's pocket? don Cesare wondered. Hadn't she, without completely realizing it (as her embarrassed explanation revealed), wished to rid herself, by symbolically passing it on to Brigante, of the responsibility of a theft more cumbersome than she had first imagined? He rejected this explanation, which diminished Marietta's boldness. She was never afraid of anything, the bandit! She had not even hinted at wanting the racketeer's collaboration. She was strong-willed. But in his mind's eye he saw Matteo Brigante's triangular face, his broad shoulders, his narrow hips, his air of quiet assurance; he rediscovered jealousy (an emotion forgotten, suppressed so long ago).

'Now,' he said, 'I can see only one solution for you: you must give the money back.'

'No,' said Marietta.

'I'm not telling you to go and hand it to the Chief of Police. We'll find some way which will keep you out of it.'

'I don't like the idea,' said Marietta.

'I shall send for the judge,' went on don Cesare. 'I shall give him the bundle of notes and tell him that one of my men found it hidden while he was working on the marsh. As it's me, he won't ask for any other explanation.'

'I don't want to,' said Marietta.

'Just think,' added don Cesare. 'Matteo Brigante is bound to have denounced you already. They'll come here looking for you. They'll question you. They'll torment you until the money is found. If I return it and formally exonerate you, they'll drop the whole business. You have only to say that Brigante is lying, that he's trying to get his revenge for being slashed.'

'I don't want to give the money back,' said Marietta.

Marietta's obstinacy restored don Cesare to his enchantment. As unyielding as a gentleman bandit. Impervious to fear. He was tempted to explain the exchange of wallets by the desire to mark Brigante a second time: I have inscribed a cross on your cheek and now, to add to that, I saddle you with a crime you haven't committed. Not for decades had any human being, in such a short space of time, made don Cesare feel such keen and contradictory emotions.

'If I had five hundred thousand lire in the house in ready cash,' he said, 'I would hand them over for you, and you would have nothing to worry about. I can send Tonio to the bank tomorrow morning. But I'm afraid they'll come for you before tomorrow morning.'

'I can hide until Tonio has been to the bank.'

'No,' said don Cesare, 'I want to keep you with me.'

But he adored it that she should be so irrationally obstinate.

'Go and find something to write with,' he said.

He dictated a codicil to his will. She wrote with care, in an ungainly but clear hand, using large characters and carefully joining up the loops. He spelt out each word, knowing that she had little book learning. He bequeathed her a large olive plantation and several orange and lemon orchards.

'The land I'm giving you,' he explained, 'brings me in something like six hundred thousand lire, whether it's a good year or a bad one. It's as though I were giving you twelve million lire.'

Pen poised, she stared at him in silence.

With his left hand, he dated and signed.

'When they're yours,' he said, 'they'll bring in much more, because you'll be harder than I've been with bailiffs and overseers.'

234

'I won't let them rob me,' she said.

She had the same look as Matteo Brigante. But he was so well disposed towards her that he did not love her any the less. She had always been too poor to be able to be kind. It was the law. And come to think of it, he thought, I haven't been kind but indifferent.

'Now, tell me where you've hidden this half-million lire.'

A gleam of malice appeared in Marietta's eyes.

She stood up and plunged her arm into a Greek vase resting on the chest of drawers. It was the only vase from the ancient city of Uria which, in the course of the excavations, had been re-covered perfectly intact. From it she produced, wrapped in an old newspaper, the fifty ten-thousand lire notes. She put them on the bed.

'They would never have thought,' she said, 'of coming to poke about in your room.'

How much pleasure you give me, thought don Cesare.

He sent her to find Tonio, whom he instructed to drive to Judge Alessandro's, find him wherever he was, get him out of bed if necessary, tell him that he was dying and bring him straight back.

They waited for the judge. Marietta was thinking of the fortune she was going to inherit, don Cesare of the hard look of poor girls.

After tough campaigns on the Piave, he had finished the First World War as a captain of cavalry. When the armistice came, he was sent on detachment to Paris to work with a commission which prepared the peace treaty and then drew up the clauses of application.

The French officer with whom he most frequently worked, a staff major, was no more than five feet three inches from head to foot and suffered from myopia; he wore pince-nez. Having no fortune, he had married the daughter of a draughtsman in the

Seine prefecture, who had no dowry but was beautiful. He would travel home on the Metro and find Lucienne altering her last year's dresses, to bring them into fashion.

On several occasions don Cesare ran his colleague home in the vast Fiat of the Italian Armistice Commission. They made him stay to dinner. He sent the rarest flowers and returned their hospitality in the Café de Paris, complete with champagne. He had no financial cares, having his father's allowance in addition to his officer's salary and his living-out allowance. Lucienne did not resist his advances for long. Being in love, he did not want to leave the husband anything and he installed her in a pair of rooms in the rue Spontini.

They spent the nights going from bar to bar, from club to club, in the company of officers of the English and American expeditionary corps, French airmen and diplomats of all the victorious nations. They made an admirable couple, she almost as tall as he was, as fair as he was dark, with one of those devil-may-care faces which went with the times; she was one of the first Frenchwomen to cut her hair short.

Lucienne had a grasping nature. She disappeared for whole days, returning with a new hat, a fur, a dress, a flower. The air-men took her to the Bois in their Voisin sports cars. For the first time in his life, don Cesare was jealous. In front of the others he kept his impassive and smiling mask, the fruit of good breeding, but when they got back to the rue Spontini, at sunrise, he re-proached her for hours on end. He tore to shreds the dresses for which she could not produce bills. She gave him her hard look:

'When you're back in Italy you won't bother yourself about who dresses me.'

'I'll take you with me.'

'Never. I don't want to spend the best years of my life eating macaroni in Apulia.' When he had worn himself out insulting her, she allowed herself to be taken, coldly, without softening the look on her face. This coldness prevented him from leaving her, as he believed his honour required of him. Sure of his virility, he was convinced that he would end by making her experience the

236

pleasure she persisted in not even pretending to feel. Only then, according to his Manacorean conception of love, would he possess her; it would be her turn to be jealous. In the meantime, like a gambler ruining himself by following an impossible system, he suffered ever greater humiliations every night.

'Once,' said don Cesare to Marietta, 'once a woman dictated the law to me ... That was a very long time ago; your mother was still only fourteen and I was living in a foreign capital, in *Parigi* ...'

Marietta looked at him in astonishment. It was not like don Cesare to confide in a girl of his household. She thought he was weakening, the inevitable effect of the illness which had just paralysed his limbs. She felt the tears come into her eyes again.

Don Cesare tried to tell the girl the story of his one unhappy passion. It was not easy. She had never left Porto Manacore or seen her master's supremacy contested.

She reacted strongly when he described Lucienne's infidelities.

'You should have sent her packing!' she cried.

And in fact he had sent Lucienne packing. The day it happened she had not hurt him any more cruelly than usual. To his face, speaking on the telephone to someone he did not know, she had replied teasingly and provocatively. It was by far the smallest humiliation she had inflicted on him. But at that moment it had come to him that he no longer submitted to her law. Quite suddenly he had seen her and himself beside her, in their shared rooms in the rue Spontini, he sitting on the bed and she at the telephone, just as they really were, but exactly as he would have seen two lovers who were neither he nor she, on a theatre stage, for example, or in the manner of Le Sage's devil on two sticks, by lifting the roof off a house. On the Piave he had received an Austrian bullet in the thigh; two days had passed before they could collect him in an ambulance; during those two days, the bullet, with all the suffering which radiated from it, had become the most personal part of him; at times he identified himself completely with this throbbing metallic flesh embedded in his human flesh; they put him to sleep; when he woke, the bullet was

237

on his bedside table, a disarmed, harmless foreign body. Thus it had suddenly been with his passion, in the moment he had ceased to submit to its law. He had stared with astonishment at Lucienne and this man who had loved Lucienne with passion, he and she, two strangers now. He had immediately sent his unfaithful mistress packing.

He had watched her going down the stairs, dragging her belongings after her. She had looked back, her face bathed in tears, that face every expression of which, only yesterday, had inscribed itself in the hollow of his chest, filling him with pain or happiness; it was the first time he had seen her cry. But he had already *lost interest* in her.

She had returned sometimes in his night dreams, punishing him with jealousy, as in the days of his passion. He saw her going down the stairs again, as on the day she had left, but it was a joyous face she turned towards him: 'I'm going to live with my lover,' she said. Then he had effaced her from his dreams, too.

'Heaven knows if she's still alive,' said Marietta.

'I've never thought of her since then,' said don Cesare.

He thought of her only in the hour of death, because the hard look of Marietta had reminded him of the hard look of Lucienne.

Why had Marietta slipped the Swiss's wallet into Matteo Brigante's pocket? Pippo had a look of passion and tenderness; he was the romantic bandit leader. The day would come, thought don Cesare, and come soon, probably, when Marietta would ask Matteo Brigante to go into partnership with her, to impose her law more pitilessly on the workers in her orchards and olive plantations.

They waited for the judge. Marietta thought of all the money don Cesare had spent on Lucienne; don Cesare thought of the successive renunciations on which he had constructed his life.

He had been a gambler and a drunkard, like most of the officers in his regiment. Why should he not have gambled and drunk?

Even the strict code of military honour forbade neither cards nor wine. But one day he had seen himself with a gambler's features, the features of a man whose whole behaviour was conditioned by the habit of gambling, for whom gambling was the law. But having once seen himself in this light, the figure he had seen was already a stranger. That same day, he had given up gambling.

His one moral rule — which had, however, been the inviolable law of his whole life — had been to preserve himself for a task which he had never had to accomplish. Each time he had found himself on the point of being completely 'engaged' in something he did not feel to be his essential task (which, in the end, he had never had to accomplish) he had abruptly and cleanly 'disengaged', as a well-born and well-trained swordsman disengages.

He had found it relatively less simple to free himself of drunkenness. Men of honour abandon themselves more easily to alcohol than to humiliating love affairs or the mechanical skill of gambling, which involves exposing oneself to all kinds of bad company, and often boredom. Alcohol left one just as played out (a gambler's expression), but one was left with the illusion of engaging only oneself and the smallest part of oneself. He reached the stage where he needed a glass of brandy the moment he woke in the mornings. He did not have the strength to break himself of it alone; he had to place himself in the hands of a doctor.

That had been in Florence. An iron bed and chair, a white wooden table; a room like a cell; sometimes they lodged lunatics there, too. The building stood on a hill overlooking the Arno, with terraced gardens leading down to the river; but from his bed he could only see the sky.

Small banks of dappled clouds, turned pink by the light and the late afternoon, sailed very slowly across the sky framed by the window. It was as if he were dead. He felt himself dissolve, exactly as those fragile clouds dissolved when the very light wind which had brought them above the southern horizon of the window and slowly accentuated the curve of the arc they drew

239

in the sky, gradually, as they drew closer to the northern horizon, dispersed them in a golden mist. So this, he had thought, without grief or happiness, as though he were an inanimate object, so this, he had thought, is death, my death. But if you can see your death, you must be alive, man! And suddenly he had begun to cherish this tender May sky, his life, stretching above the Arno which he sensed beneath him, a slow moving river which, like his eyes, reflected the sky.

But the passion of which he had most difficulty of freeing himself had been the passion of politics. From childhood he had devoted himself to the House of Savoy and the concept of royalty, to the hero-kings. As an adult, he had killed and risked death a hundred times, during the First World War, to win back Trente and Trieste for Victor Emmanuel III. He had even assumed the tics of the little man, his king. But Victor Emmanuel had let Mussolini seize the real power; the dictator, the usurper, filled the world with the echoes of his vaudeville voice, threw out his muscles to buy the votes of the masses. The *buffone* had installed himself on the throne of the *baffone*![1]

The time of the hero-kings had drawn to an end.

Don Cesare had retired to the house with the colonnades. Then, again, he had thought: if you can see your death, you must be alive, man. But this time it took him more than a year to return to the land of the living. He had started excavations to reconstruct the history of the noble city of Uria. But he had never again identified his motive for living with the task he had undertaken.

Don Cesare was sitting up in bed, propped up by pillows, his dead arm resting on a brocade cushion. Marietta was sitting at his bedside, in her linen frock tight across the breasts, her ears open for sounds of the car which did not come. They were waiting for Judge Alessandro. It made Marietta uneasy that the judge should take so long to come; she was afraid the police would get

---

[1] An untranslatable play on words. *Baffone*: moustached. *Il baffone*: the moustached one, an affectionate nickname for the monarchs of Savoy, who all wore moustaches. *Buffone*: buffoon.

there first and take her away. Don Cesare was thinking of his death.

He did not wonder whether there was another world, whether he would find God there, whether God would judge him and whether at the Last Judgment he would be resurrected in his body for eternal reward or eternal punishment. He knew the answer was no.

He did not wonder whether death would mean suffering or the suffering of all sufferings. He knew that suffering was one of the multiple aspects of life and that death was, by definition, nothing.

He thought that he had been born where he had been born, that he had lived as well as a man of quality could live, in accordance with the quality which it was possible for a man of his birth and upbringing to show in that particular time, in that particular place and in those particular circumstances.

He said aloud:

'*Così sia*, so be it.'

By these words he did not mean to proclaim his submission to the divine law, as Christians did, or to a biological or social or personal law, as did the faithful of all kinds of sects. He was testifying on his own behalf. It had been so. He regretted nothing; he was ashamed of nothing; he wanted nothing; he was acknowledging himself, he was proclaiming himself (to himself) as he had been and as he remained in the hour of death. That was what he meant by saying: 'So be it.'

'*Così sia*,' replied Marietta.

She thought she was replying as a Christian to a Christian's prayer in the hour of death. But fundamentally she was so pagan that the sense she gave to her *amen* was not (although she did not define it to herself) so very different from the sense which don Cesare gave to his.

Several times in his lifetime, a man of quality was called upon to make war. This had been the case in every period of history. The rest of the time, he kept his distance. Don Cesare had certainly made war and certainly kept his distance.

He thought that if he had been an Athenian before Pericles, a

Roman citizen at the time of the Punic Wars, or a Member of the National Convention in 1793, his refusal to submit to the law would have made him a member of that small community which throw down outworn social structures and open up new avenues of life. In certain countries, in certain periods, the man of quality found support in the movement of History and asserted his quality by transforming the world.

He thought, too, that if he had been born in the reign of Augustus or Tiberius, Lorenzo de Medici or Ivan the Terrible, his refusal to submit to the law would have obliged him to commit suicide, as men of quality did when it was impossible for them personally to escape from tyranny. The right to suicide, which the most conscientious gaolers, the cleverest torturers are only able to suspend for a time, had always seemed to him the only, but the irrefutable, proof of the liberty of man.

Thus, he considered, depending on the circumstances, the man of quality felt himself compelled now to action, now to suicide, but most often simply to a succession of engagements and disengagements, one giving rise to the other. It was precisely in this impulse, which led him now to engage himself, now to disengage himself, that his quality resided.

Born in 1884, in western Europe and more precisely in southern Italy, he had committed suicide slowly, by successive phases, keeping time with his period. This had taken seventy-two years and had not always been disagreeable. So be it.

The pleasures of study, love and the hunt had amusingly filled in the long hours of leisure which circumstances had forced on him. He had been born rich and blessed with the gifts which enabled one to become *uomo di alta cultura* (as the Italians of the South put it) and an *homme de plaiser* (as the French of the great years put it), in a time and a country which had obliged him slowly to commit suicide (but not without pleasures) so as not to destroy his quality. So be it.

He gave himself up to what he had been and what he remained at the hour of his death. This acquiescence was of value only for himself, in relation to himself, but in the hour of his death, of his lucid death of an atheist accepting death, this acquiescence acquired an absolute value. So be it. He said aloud:

'*Così sia.*'

'*Così sia,*' replied Marietta.

They heard the judge's Topolino crossing the bridge across the inlet of the lake. Marietta went downstairs to the main room and took her place among the women praying round the olive-wood table. Tonio led the judge to don Cesare's bedroom.

'My dear Alessandro,' said don Cesare, 'I have a request to make of you ...'

As historian of the city of Uria, he addressed himself to the historian of Frederick II of Swabia. He was about to die, sooner than he had supposed. He asked him to see that the antiques he had collected were not dispersed and that his manuscript on the Greek colonies in the regions of Manacore in the Hellenistic age were placed at the disposal of scholars. He would like the house with the colonnades to be turned into a museum; he had set a small sum aside for this purpose in his will; if this were not possible, collection, manuscript, notices, notes and money were to be offered to the Foggia provincial museum; this eventuality had also been dealt with in the will. He would be grateful to the judge, a man of culture, a man of learning, if he would see that these clauses were scrupulously respected.

He wondered, in fact, why he was attaching so much importance to these trifles. Once he was dead, the entire universe would be obliterated for him. Anyway he had considered himself to be dead for many years. But in the very moment of his absolute death, he found it not unpleasing to ensure a kind of perenniality to the remains of the ancient city of Uria, gathered by him from the sand, the marsh and oblivion. His friend Alessandro must forgive him this last-minute fancy.

The judge thanked him effusively, overwhelmed that don Cesare should be so ready to trust him.

Don Cesare, who was not, he explained, without his fears of the people of his household and, still more, of the relatives who would come haring down from Calalunga, entrusted to the judge both his will and the codicils which had just been drawn up, so that he should place them in the notary's hands. Then he gave him the fifty ten-thousand lire notes wrapped in a newspaper.

'One of my fishermen found this money in a hiding-place on the marsh. Presumably they're the notes which were stolen from the Swiss ...'

'I shall have to see this fisherman of yours,' said the judge.

'You know how they are,' replied don Cesare. 'They don't like having any dealings with the law. He asked me not to disclose his name. I complimented him on his honesty and gave him my word that he wouldn't be troubled.'

'But a man has been arrested!' the judge exclaimed. 'I have overwhelming proof against him ...'

'All the more reason for not upsetting my fisherman.'

'I must confront the prisoner with him!'

'Alessandro,' protested don Cesare, 'I've other things to worry about ...'

'Forgive me,' the judge said hurriedly.

He left with the will, the five hundred thousand lire and, for donna Lucrezia, as the final homage of a dying man for a wonderful woman, a terracotta oil-lamp dating from the third century B.C., ornamented with naked figurines.

Marietta returned to her place at the invalid's bedside.

Beneath his bedroom, around the olive-wood table, the local fishermen had come to join the women. The whole room was filled with a dense mass of people reciting prayers for the cure of sickness.

Marietta soon dropped off into a doze, occasionally launching into a sigh, a movement of the lips, a hollowing of the stomach, into one or other of those delicious gestures she had learned from Pippo, last night and this afternoon, on the cloth sacks, in the shed of the orchard with the three springs.

Don Cesare passed the night, sometimes dozing, sometimes lying awake, as he had passed the preceding nights. When he opened his eyes, the first thing he saw was Marietta, in the light of the oil-lamp, her head thrust back against the armchair she had pulled up to the bed, her lips half open and her eyes ringed with darkness from long hours of loving.

At daybreak he woke her, to get her to open the shutters.

The familiar landscape lay before him, the inlet of the lake cutting its way through the reeds and bamboos till, soon, it reached its mouth, to the left the dunes of the isthmus, to the right the rocky hillock, looking as though it had been planted in the sea, on which the temple of the Venus of Uria had been built and from which nothing rose now but rosemary bushes, and beyond those the whole of Manacore Bay and the promontory which sealed it off, prolonged by the masts of the *trabucco* — gigantic erections, but, from don Cesare's bed, the *trabucco* looked no bigger than a fishing boat rounding the point of the promontory. The sun climbed above the pine woods and turned the sands of the isthmus to gold. The sirocco, throughout the night, had got the upper hand over the libeccio and held the bank of clouds far out to sea.

Don Cesare asked Marietta to change the pillow slips and the top sheet. He loved the feel of fresh linen when the folds were still crisp.

'A little later,' he said, 'we'll ask Tonio to shave me.'

He saw one of his fishermen heading up the inlet of the lake, silently pulling on his short oars, sitting in the stern of a narrow punt. A flight of ducks took wing behind him and headed towards the lake.

Don Cesare thought that never again would he go out shooting in the cool of the dawn. He had a feeling someone was depriving him of something, and it made him sad. Then he ridiculed his feeling: there was no 'someone' and he had shot until the exercise left him limp with boredom. What he had really loved had been the walk over the paths of beaten earth across the marsh and on the beach of the isthmus, in the cool of the dawn. He would never again feel underfoot the suppleness of the beaten earth, hard and not-hard from the dampness of the marsh. That was how it was, *così sia.* Trees finished up by dying when they had spread all their branches, even the olives which lived longer than all the others; four men linking hands could not encircle with their arms the trunks of certain olives in his groves, and their knurs kept alive the memory of the storms which had twisted them into being during the last years of the Roman Empire; but occasionally one of them would die; the leaves would suddenly wither, for no apparent reason; when they cut into the trunk, they found nothing but dead wood all the way to the heart.

Don Cesare thought, too, that no one would ever again be capable of seeing this view with the same eyes as himself: the marsh, the isthmus, the mound on which the temple of Venus had stood, the gulf and the promontory; of taking in, as he could, past and present at a glance, the noble city of Uria, of which he had drawn up a map and recovered the remains; the drab, second-century Roman town, with its garrison of Teutons; the sand and mud which had covered everything over again, through Christian negligence, when the priests of the foreign god had seized the Venus of Uria, dragged her to the top of Manacore and, robbing her even of her name, imprisoned her in the sanctuary of their Ursula, foolish virgin and martyr, saint of darkness; the stone harbours rebuilt for a few decades by Frederick II of Swabia; then sand and mud again under the besotted Bourbons of Naples; and finally don Cesare's shooting and pleasure grounds, the straw huts of his fishermen — he had known all their wives. No one would ever again be capable of taking in, at a glance, the whole of this past and present, the past made up of the history of men and the history of one man closely linked in the solemnly present present of a man dying in full possession of his mental powers. Only to him would all this have appeared as it did, gathered together in this one moment. *Così sia.*

A fishing boat heading in towards Porto Manacore entered his field of vision. The echo of the engine reached the room through the wide-open bay window, one of those heavy Diesel engines with a slow rhythm, the muffled sound of which reverberates in the depths of the sea and the hollow of the listener's chest.

Marietta and don Cesare followed the fishing boat with their eyes as it crossed the bay of the window from west to east.

The engine misfired, hiccupped, then stopped, the boat continued to make headway, more and more slowly. Hurriedly Marietta made the sign of the horns with her index finger and thumb. Don Cesare realized that she was casting a spell for him: the engine stopping, the heart ceasing to beat; she was defending him.

'Marietta …' he began.

She turned her head towards him.

'Marietta,' he continued, 'I wish you so much happiness …'

He wanted to pronounce the girl's name again but at that moment his throat and mouth seized up. He made a great effort to free his throat and mouth, but the maxillary muscles no longer responded. The effort, he thought, must have contracted his features, for Marietta was staring at him with horror. She was on her feet, leaning over him, crying:

'Don Cesare! Don Cesare!'

The left arm and the left hand still responded. He lifted his finger to his lips to signal the girl to silence. She was silent.

He signalled to her to lie down on the bed, beside him. She lay down beside him, on the fresh sheets, still crisply folded.

She looked at him with an impassioned expression. He thought that in this moment she loved him with a kind of love which was worth all the others put together.

He placed his hand on the girl's breast, on the linen frock.

247

Marietta lifted don Cesare's hand away, quickly undid her dress (which buttoned down the front), then replaced his hand on her bare breast. The breast was small, round and hard, and the master's broad hand enveloped it completely.

The women of the household were waiting outside in the corridor. They did not dare to enter, don Cesare having said the night before that they were only to come to him on Marietta's orders. They had heard the girl's cries of 'Don Cesare! Don Cesare!' and they were surprised not to have heard anything more. A long time passed in this fashion.

Marietta stared passionately at don Cesare, who stared back at her with smiling eyes. Then she noticed that his stare no longer had any expression. The pressure of his hand on her breast relaxed; the palm grew cold.

Marietta stretched don Cesare's arm out alongside his body. She closed his lids. She placed a light kiss on his cold lips.

'*Così sia*,' she said.

She buttoned her frock and went and opened the door.

'Don Cesare is dead,' she said.

The women began to lament. The wails filled the whole of the house, spread across the marsh and carried right down to the sea, to assail the ears of the fishermen whose boat had come to a standstill at the mouth of the inlet of the lake, at the entry of what had once been the harbour of the noble and intelligent city of Uria.

The half-million lire stolen from the Swiss camper had been returned, not a centime short; the wallet had been recovered, not a paper missing. But Judge Alessandro spent the whole morning obstinately refusing to free Matteo Brigante; restitution did not cancel out the theft; the crime still existed; the investigation continued; the law must be respected.

At noon, two policemen brought into the judge's office the key to Brigante's bachelor quarters, which they had just impounded, on the wing so to speak, as it fell, right in front of their eyes, from the apron of Justo, the bartender at the Sports Café. Justo was the only witness who claimed to have seen the Swiss's wallet in Brigante's hands. The fact that he should be in possession of the key to the place where the article had been found turned suspicion on to him.

The judge was not taken in, being too much a man of the South not to know that the police found it more to their advantage to serve the interests of the racketeer than those of justice. But the men were sworn officials and a witness, the Australian, confirmed that the key had fallen from the bartender's pocket. There was no alternative but to free Brigante and arrest Justo. The latter did not protest his innocence, reckoning that for the time being prison was the only place where he was relatively safe. The investigation lasted several weeks and ended in a decision not to prosecute.

Donna Lucrezia spent nearly all day in Chief Attilio's office. Francesco had still not been found. She kept on insisting that the Chief should telephone and re-telephone all his colleagues in the provincial police. She did so little to hide her anxiety that soon the deputy, the police rank and file, and in the end the whole town knew the cause of her frenzy.

Francesco had spent the night in a café in Foggia, drinking and standing other people drinks, thus spending the whole of the five thousand lire he had left. By dawn he was so drunk that the proprietor had made him up a casual bed in the back room of his premises. Towards the end of the afternoon, when he had slept off the effects of the wine, they gave him his bus fare to Porto Manacore.

Donna Lucrezia saw him get off the bus and rushed out into the street. He spotted her coming towards him. Lucrezia's eyes were ablaze with love — he took it to be contempt. He turned on his heels and ran. He doubled back through the side streets and reached the flat through the inner courtyard of the palace. Matteo Brigante was sitting at the dining-room table, writing to his business agents. Francesco took some scores from the shelves in the ante-room, sat down beside his father and began to read, in silence, the music of a *canzonetta*. Father and son did not speak to one another again until next morning, when they discussed matters completely unconnected with the events of the previous day.

As soon as she saw Francesco run, donna Lucrezia returned to the Chief's office. She sat down in the armchair, facing him. 'How could I have loved a coward?' she asked.

The Chief, who was engaged in drawing up a report, went on with his work, without replying. Then, as if he had heard nothing, and as if there had never been any talk of Francesco, he spoke of the death of don Cesare; the old man having refused to see a priest, would he still receive a religious funeral? The Calalunga relatives were arriving; they would soon proceed to the opening of the will; there was a rumour going round that a last-minute codicil favoured one of the girls in the house with the colonnades, a bastard daughter perhaps … The Chief considered himself the shrewdest and most tactful man in the world; he was convinced that he would have Lucrezia sooner and more easily than he had hoped.

Two weeks later, in fact, she agreed to a tête-à-tête in the room in the tower. The emotion unleashed by Francesco, the day he had gone on pressing her hand, not daring to say to her: 'I love you', insisted on being appeased. They saw one another with pleasure, twice a week, for several months. Then she had other lovers, always changing. Still as proud as ever, she scorned discretion. People spoke of her no longer as donna Lucrezia, but la Lucrezia.

Judge Alessandro was informed of his wife's misconduct. He questioned her; she denied nothing. He thought this problem over for months: a man had no right to demand the fidelity of a woman who no longer loved him, but a wife should respect her husband's honour, which constituted the morality, however outmoded, of the land in which they lived; how were these two imperatives to be reconciled? The questions he termed social continued to torment him, too; he committed a series of indiscretions in the minor political trials which came under his jurisdiction, finding the defendants guilty but citing extenuating circumstances to discharge them without sentence, thus setting the representatives of both opposition and government against him. The authorities transferred him. They were sent to a small mountain town, in Calabria.

Through sheer obstinacy, the judge had seen to it that Mario the bricklayer received a passport. In France, Mario could find work only in a mine, where he was killed, the following year, in the course of an explosion.

The agronomist gave up hope of obtaining Marietta now that she was rich, and he asked Giuseppina to keep house for him. She accepted, despairing of snatching the Chief away from the tender Anna, the mad Lucrezia and all the others. A state agronomist did not have the prestige of a Chief of Police, but his salary was almost the same. She surrendered the virginity which she had defended for so long and became a skilful mistress. From living in the South, the Lombard finally came to adopt the morality of the South, and refused to marry a girl who was so expert. In a few years, she would leave him for a landowner who would buy her a little house in Calalunga and include her in his will. The agronomist would die young, riddled with fever and despairing at the failure of all his efforts to improve the breeding of goats on the Manacorean coast.

A few weeks after don Cesare's death, his heirs held a general meeting. The provincial council had rejected the proposal of opening a museum on the site of an ancient city of which there was not a single column left standing, and had taken charge of the collections. They proceeded to exchanges of inheritance. Marietta gave up a large orange and lemon orchard for a few acres of marsh and the house with the colonnades. They were surprised that she should agree to such a poor proposition. They put it down to girlish sentimentality; the rumour was gaining ground that she was don Cesare's daughter (which would explain the size of her inheritance); Julia protested, but they took no notice, knowing that she was on bad terms with her youngest; they were convinced that, although illegitimate, Marietta meant to keep the ancestral home in the family; they admired her for venerating the name, which she did not even bear, to the extent of exchanging a fruit plantation in full yield for a ramshackle old house tucked away on a malarial marsh; they condemned her, too, for being such a fool. She let them talk. She had overheard conversations between don Cesare and some surveyors who, a few months before, had staked out the whole length of the isthmus.

'I've got an idea,' she confided to Pippo.

Julia, Maria and Elvira had each received a small collection of stocks and shares, which would bring them in a moderate income. They entrusted their 'holdings' to a firm of brokers in Foggia who promised to procure them a much higher interest.

In the meantime, they remained in the house with the colonnades, in Marietta's service. After the removal of the antiques, she made them scrub out the whole building, from the attic to the stables, and whitewash everything, inside and out. She summoned a Naples antique dealer and disposed, at a good price, of the eighteenth-century Neapolitan armchair, the Greek vase which the curator of the museum had neglected to take because it was in don Cesare's bedroom, and most of the old furniture. This she replaced with modern furniture of varnished plywood, spending the difference on a Fiat 400 (which she at once learned to drive) and a television set. Of the old furnishings she kept only the canopied bed, in which she slept, receiving Pippo practically every night, without hiding the fact and without anyone thinking of protesting. Indeed, the scale of the property she had inherited, the rumours of her being don Cesare's daughter and her natural assurance had immediately gained her the privileges of a landowner. People would soon be calling her donna Marietta.

Matteo Brigante took the initiative in making peace with Pippo. The boy was too old to go on mixing with the *guaglioni*, even as their chief. Marietta's patronage assured him of the respect of the tradespeople and the lower stratum of leading citizens; people began to call him *signor* Pippo, to refer to him as the *signorino* Pippo. He had a talent for swimming and diving, plenty of breath and a sound understanding of the sea; Brigante, now his friend, trained him methodically, teaching him the modern techniques of underwater swimming, with and without oxygen feed. In the course of one training session, they discovered at the mouth of the lake, at the foot of the rocky hillock, a marble statue of the Venus of Uria. The expert sent by the Foggia museum attributed it to a sculptor of the third century B.C.; it was a good century older than the stone statue in the sanctuary of Santa Ursula of Uria, another Venus, found on the marsh by monks, baptized Ursula, dressed up in the Spanish fashion and hoisted through the town on poles on the saint's day. According to golden legend, only one girl in the pagan city of Uria, Ursula, was found to have conserved her virginity the day God decided to destroy the town as a punishment for its debauchery; He saved Ursula by carrying her to the top of the hill overlooking Manacore harbour. Don Cesare, at the time when he was still poking fun at religion (before he had *lost interest*) liked to scandalize his relatives by all sorts of witticisms at the expense of the Venus-Ursula of the sanctuary, the patron saint, he said, of the old women who refabricated the virginity of deflowered maidens. Despite the high price the State offered her for it, Marietta decided to keep the marble statue, putting it in the big downstairs room of the house with the colonnades, next to the television set; she was convinced that the goddess, of whom she had so often heard her master speak, would bring her luck; just to make sure, she hung a trumpet-shell between her breasts; in fact, she was quite sure she was not losing anything, Matteo Brigante having explained to her that antiques (when it was a question of something really out of the ordinary) had risen steadily in value since the beginning of the century and were continuing to do so. The Venus of Uria thus became an invest-ment as well as a counter-spell.

Two years passed. The foreigners came in ever greater num-bers to the islands, whose cliffs, reefs and grottoes at water level were particularly suited to underwater fishing. Matteo Brigante provided Pippo with a little capital to set himself up there. The boy bought an old house which he scantily furnished and let off in rooms to tourists, a boat in which he took the sportsmen to the underwater caves where the mullet beds lay, and a diving board on which he gave lessons. He would return to Marietta in the off-season.

One afternoon the following summer (the second which Pippo spent in the islands) Matteo Brigante called on Marietta. The two of them were sitting in modern, bright leather arm-chairs, facing the television set. Marietta was approaching her twenty-first birthday. She was a little fuller than in don Cesare's time, her hips broader, her breasts more prominent.

Brigante explained to the girl that land was the poorest money-earner. Colonial oils, with their smaller production costs, were replacing olive oil more and more. The fruit yielded by the orange and lemon trees in Manacore no longer satisfied the requirements of the export trade; in the long run Marietta would not be able to keep pace with the producers in Sicily and on the Tyrrhenian coast, who marketed standard fruit, as in California. But she could still sell her land at a good price, a traditional prejudice, in southern Italy, continuing to favour real estate; she must hasten to profit from it. The capital invested in Marietta's land did not bring her in five per cent. Brigante earned eight or ten per cent from his investments, sometimes more. He was ready to advise the girl.

Marietta burst out laughing.

'Brigante,' she said, 'Brigante! I see what you're getting at ...' She had an idea of her own, which she explained to him.

Work had begun on the two extremities of a coastal road which would cut by half the distance between Porto Albanese and San Severe, along the via Adriatica. It would cut along the isthmus, cross the inlet of the lake over the old bridge (naturally enlarged) opposite the house with the colonnades, follow the edge of the marsh and then slice straight through Marietta's olive plantation. She had heard talk of the project in don Cesare's time; he had been greatly cut up about it, even thinking of retiring to his palace in Calalunga, up in the mountain. The work was progressing rapidly. Marietta had conferred with the Ministry of Transport's civil engineer and the manager of the provincial *Ente Turistico*. The new road would become the main route for foreigners coming south from Germany, Austria and Venice to Brindisi and the Otranto peninsula. The girl's land would rise considerably in value. But she was not planning to sell it. Why not build in the olive plantation a hotel, a restaurant, a service station, villas, a tourist unit — an expression she had heard on television. Beside the sanctuary of Santa Ursula of Uria, overlooking the lake, the isthmus and the whole of Manacore Bay, within easy distance of the embarking point for the islands, the site was admirably chosen.

She laughed again.

'Matteo,' she said, 'I've been thinking of asking you to help find me some capital. And to get you to sink your own capital in my scheme. Let's go into partnership — we'll make a mint of money.'

Brigante quickly saw possibilities in the proposition. On the Tyrrhenian coast, which he had several times visited, the prosperity of Amalfi, Ravello, Positano, Capri had begun in precisely this fashion. Foreigners, especially Germans, were coming to the Adriatic coast in ever greater numbers. The new road would spare them from having to stop off at Foggia, a drab inland town.

Even the house with the colonnades would prove useful, he thought. Madame had not realized her Siponte scheme, the police of the little resort setting too high a price on their tolerance. The Porto Manacore police, who owed so much to Brigante, would be much less demanding. Cynthia was still free, Fulvia too. A brothel, within easy distance of the tourist unit and Porto Manacore, would make a fortune. The marble Venus would lend tone to the main room.

'That may not be a bad idea of yours,' said Brigante.

His wife had just had an operation for cancer of the breast, the third. She would not long survive Marietta's majority. Brigante imagined the girl transported to Manacore, in the flat in the Renaissance wing of the palace of Frederick II of Swabia. The place would be entirely refurnished: Marietta had taste. With such a wife and such an associate — the daughter too, so they said, of don Cesare — Matteo Brigante would clear the barrier; he would be the peer of his former officers; he would run as mayor.

'I'll think it over,' he said to Marietta. 'Your idea is worth looking into. I always thought you were a bright girl.'

These new prospects were some consolation for his disappointment in Francesco, who had just failed his final-year law examination for the third time.

By that time, the Foggia brokers had already frittered away the 'holdings' of Julia, Maria and Elvira. Marietta, after a series of quarrels with her mother and sisters, had sent them packing, together with Tonio. Elvira had found a servant's post, in Calalunga, with a cousin of don Cesare's. Old Julia and her daughter Maria, when an overseer consented to find them work, weeded the orange and lemon orchards, or carted water. Tonio had taken his place among the unemployed, along the walls, in the main square of Porto Manacore. He listened, throughout the day, to the songs which rose from behind the tilted slats of the prison on the ground floor of the court house; he often had occasion to recognize, among others, the voice of Justo, the former bartender in the Sports Café, who was always running into trouble with the new judge, Brigante's grudges being long-lived.

Marietta no longer sang, now that she had a television set.

A Danish historian, on his way through Foggia, discovered don Cesare's collections and the three-thousand page manuscript. He was keenly interested, amazed at the ingenious, and often profound, views of the local scholar and the thoroughness of his documentation. It inspired him to a great work on the ancient city of Uria, a work destined to have world-wide repercussions, among specialists in the history of the Greek colonies, during the Hellenistic age, in southern Italy.

MEMOIRS OF A
BENGAL CIVILIAN

JOHN BEAMES
The lively narrative of a Victorian district-officer

With an introduction by Philip Mason

They are as entertaining as Hickey . . . accounts like
these illuminate the dark corners of history.
Times Literary Supplement

John Beames writes a spendidly virile English and
he is incapable of being dull; also he never hesitates
to speak his mind. It is extraordinary that these
memoirs should have remained so long unpublished
. . . the discovery is a real find.
John Morris, The Listener

A gem of the first water. Beames, in addition to being
a first-class descriptive writer in the plain Defoesque
manner, was that thing most necessary of all in an
autobiographer – an original. His book is of the
highest value.
The Times

This edition is not for sale in the USA

*If you wish to receive details of forthcoming publications,
please send your address to
Eland Books, 53 Eland Road, London SW11 5JX*

Previously published by
ELAND BOOKS

AVISIT TODON OTAVIO
SYBILLE BEDFORD
A Mexican Journey

I am convinced that, once this wonderful book
becomes better known, it will seem incredible that it
could ever have gone out of print.
Bruce Chatwin, Vogue

This book can be recommended as vastly enjoyable.
Here is a book radiant with comedy and colour.
Raymond Mortimer, Sunday Times

Perceptive, lively, aware of the significance of trifles,
and a fine writer. Applied to a beautiful, various, and
still inscrutable country, these talents yield a singu-
larly delightful result.
The Times

This book has that ageless quality which is what
most people mean when they describe a book as
classical. From the moment that the train leaves New
York...it is certain that this journey will be rewarding.
When one finally leaves Mrs Bedford on the point of
departure, it is with the double regret of leaving
Mexico and her company, and one cannot say more
than that.
Elizabeth Jane Howard

Malicious, friendly, entertaining and witty.
Evening Standard

*If you wish to receive details of forthcoming publications,
please send your address to
Eland Books, 53 Eland Road, London SW11 5JX*

VIVA MEXICO!
CHARLES MACOMB FLANDRAU
A traveller's account of life in Mexico

With a new preface by Nicholas Shakespeare

His lightness of touch is deceiving, for one reads *Viva Mexico!* under the impression that one is only being amused, but comes to realise in the end that Mr Flandrau has presented a truer, more graphic and comprehensive picture of the Mexican character than could be obtained from a shelful of more serious and scientific tomes.
New York Times

The best book I have come upon which attempts the alluring but difficult task of introducing the tricks and manners of one country to the people of another.
Alexander Woollcott

The most enchanting, as well as extremely funny book on Mexico... I wish it were reprinted.
Sybille Bedford

His impressions are deep, sympathetic and judicious. In addition, he is a marvellous writer, with something of Mark Twain's high spirits and Henry James's suavity...as witty as he is observant.
Geoffrey Smith, Country Life

If you wish to receive details of forthcoming publications,
please send your address to
Eland Books, 53 Eland Road, London SW11 5JX

Previously published by

ELAND BOOKS

THE
WEATHER
IN
AFRICA

MARTHA GELLHORN

This is a stunningly good book.
Victoria Glendinning, New York Times

She's a marvellous story-teller, and I think anyone
who picks up this book is certainly not going to put
it down again. One just wants to go on reading.
Francis King, Kaleidoscope, BBC Radio 4

An authentic sense of the divorce between Africa
and what Europeans carry in their heads is
powerfully conveyed by a prose that selects its
details with care, yet remains cool in their
expression.
Robert Nye, The Guardian

This is a pungent and witty book.
Jeremy Brooks, Sunday Times

*If you wish to receive details of forthcoming publications,
please send your address to
Eland Books, 53 Eland Road, London SW11 5JX*

TRAVELS WITH MYSELF AND ANOTHER

MARTHA GELLHORN

Must surely be ranked as one of the funniest travel books of our time — second only to *A Short Walk in the Hindu Kush* ... It doesn't matter whether this author is experiencing marrow-freezing misadventures in war-ravaged China, or driving a Landrover through East African game-parks, or conversing with hippies in Israel, or spending a week in a Moscow Intourist Hotel. Martha Gellhorn's reactions are what count and one enjoys equally her blistering scorn of humbug, her hilarious eccentricities, her unsentimental compassion.
Dervla Murphy, Irish Times

Spun with a fine blend of irony and epigram. She is incapable of writing a dull sentence.
The Times

Miss Gellhorn has a novelist's eye, a flair for black comedy and a short fuse...there is not a boring word in her humane and often funny book.
The New York Times

Among the funniest and best written books I have ever read.
Byron Rogers, Evening Standard

If you wish to receive details of forthcoming publications,
please send your address to
Eland Books, 53 Eland Road, London SW11 5JX

FAR AWAY
AND LONG AGO
W. H. HUDSON
A Childhood in Argentina

With a new preface by Nicholas Shakespeare

One cannot tell how this fellow gets his effects; he
writes as the grass grows.
It is as if some very fine and gentle spirit were whispering to him the sentences he puts down on the
paper. A privileged being
Joseph Conrad

Hudson's work is a vision of natural beauty and of
human life as it might be, quickened and sweetened
by the sun and the wind and the rain, and by fellow-
ship with all other forms of life...a very great writer...
the most valuable our age has possessed.
John Galsworthy

And there was no one – no writer – who did not
acknowledge without question that this composed
giant was the greatest living writer of English.
Far Away and Long Ago is the most self-revelatory of all
his books.
Ford Madox Ford

Completely riveting and should be read by everyone.
Auberon Waugh

If you wish to receive details of forthcoming publications,
please send your address to
Eland Books, 53 Eland Road, London SW11 5JX

Previously published by

ELAND BOOKS

THE CHANGING SKY

NORMAN LEWIS

Travels of a Novelist

He really goes in deep like a sharp polished knife. I have never travelled in my armchair so fast, variously and well.
V.S. Pritchett, New Statesman

He has compressed into these always entertaining and sophisticated sketches material that a duller man would have hoarded for half a dozen books.
The Times

A delightful, instructive, serious and funny book. Norman Lewis has the oblique poetry of a Firbank, the eye of a lynx.
Anthony Carson, The Observer

If you wish to receive details of forthcoming publications, please send your address to Eland Books, 53 Eland Road, London SW11 5JX

A DRAGON APPARENT
NORMAN LEWIS
Travels in Cambodia, Laos and Vietnam

A book which should take its place in the permanent literature of the Far East.
Economist

One of the most absorbing travel books I have read for a very long time...the great charm of the work is its literary vividness. Nothing he describes is dull.
Peter Quennell, Daily Mail

One of the best post-war travel books and, in retrospect, the most heartrending.
The Observer

Apart from the *Quiet American,* which is of course a novel, the best book on Vietnam remains *A Dragon Apparent.*
Richard West, Spectator (1978)

One of the most elegant, witty, immensely readable, touching and tragic books I've ever read.
Edward Blishen, Radio 4

*If you wish to receive details of forthcoming publications,
please send your address to
Eland Books, 53 Eland Road, London SW11 5JX*

GOLDEN EARTH

NORMAN LEWIS

Travels in Burma

Mr Lewis can make even a lorry interesting.
Cyril Connolly, Sunday Times

Very funny . . . a really delightful book.
Maurice Collis, Observer

Norman Lewis remains the best travel writer alive.
Auberon Waugh, Business Traveller

The reader may find enormous pleasure here
without knowing the country.
Honor Tracy, New Statesman

The brilliance of the Burmese scene is paralleled by
the brilliance of the prose.
Guy Ramsey, Daily Telegraph

If you wish to receive details of forthcoming publications,
please send your address to
Eland Books, 53 Eland Road, London SW11 5JX

Previously published by

ELAND BOOKS

THE
HONOURED
SOCIETY

NORMAN LEWIS
The Sicilian Mafia Observed

New epilogue by Marcello Cimino

One of the great travel writers of our time.
Eric Newby, Observer

Mr Norman Lewis is one of the finest journalists of his time ... he excels both in finding material and in evaluating it.
The Listener

It is deftly written, and every page is horribly absorbing.
The Times

The Honoured Society is the most penetrating book ever written on the Mafia.
Time Out

*If you wish to receive details of forthcoming publications,
please send your address to
Eland Books, 53 Eland Road, London SW11 5JX*

Previously published by

ELAND BOOKS

A YEAR IN MARRAKESH
PETER MAYNE

A notable book, for the author is exceptional both in his literary talent and his outlook. His easy economical style seizes, with no sense of effort, the essence of people, situations and places... Mr Mayne is that rare thing, a natural writer ... no less exceptional is his humour.
Few Westerners have written about Islam with so little nonsense and such understanding.
Times Literary Supplement

He has contrived in a deceptively simple prose to disseminate in the air of an English November the spicy odours of North Africa; he has turned, for an hour, smog to shimmering sunlight. He has woven a texture of extraordinary charm.
Daily Telegraph

Mr Mayne's book gives us the 'strange elation' that good writing always creates. It is a good book, an interesting book, and one that I warmly recommend.
Harold Nicolson, Observer

If you wish to receive details of forthcoming publications,
please send your address to
Eland Books, 53 Eland Road, London SW11 5JX

Previously published by

ELAND BOOKS

KENYA DIARY (1902−1906)

RICHARD MEINERTZHAGEN

With a new preface by Elspeth Huxley

Those who have only read the tranquil descriptions of Kenya between the two Wars may be surprised by Meinertzhagen's often bloodthirsty diaries. They do not always make pleasant reading, but they offer an unrivalled and startlingly vivid account of life during the early days of the colony.

One of the best and most colourful intelligence officers the army ever had.

Times, Obituary

This book is of great interest and should not be missed

New Statesman

One of the ablest and most successful brains I had met in the army.

Lloyd George, Memoirs

Anybody at all interested in the evolution of Kenya or the workings of 'colonialism' would do well to read this diary.

William Plomer, Listener

If you wish to receive details of forthcoming publications,
please send your address to
Eland Books, 53 Eland Road, London SW11 5JX